for Andy, for Betsy—

for Mateo, a year late!

Martha Polo

Martha Polo

Mateo Lettunich

Rutledge Books, Inc. Danbury, CT

Rutledge Books, Inc.
107 Mill Plain Road, Danbury, CT 06811
1-800-278-8533
www.rutledgebooks.com

Manufactured in the United States of America

Cataloging in Publication Data
Lettunich, Mateo
    Martha Polo

    ISBN: 1-887750-92-4

    1. City and town life -- United States -- Fiction. 2. Domestic
fiction.

813.54   98-65790

for L.A.C.

The Gypsies' Revenge

*I*t all began in the south of France a few summer seasons ago. The dollar was mighty, at the top of one of its peaks, and that was why I happened to be living in Paris, like so many Americans before me; writing a novel, but not noticeably moving forward with my work, like so many before me.

I had accepted an invitation to join my friend Tom Swift for a few days on the beach. That really is his name but he is by no means the Tom Swift of the books, and insists that he has little or no redeeming social value. Maybe that is why people like him. He was my best friend in school and at college.

Tom rang me from Marseille.

"Charlie, I'm on my way to Cap St Sauveur."

Did the name ring a distant bell, or was I thinking of the bottle I had finished off the night before? Clos St Sauveur?

"Come down and spend the week with me. With us. Plenty of room. We'll both be H.G.'s." That had always meant Honored Guests, with or without the irony.

"Take the night train. We'll expect you for lunch tomorrow. The hotel is called Les Sirènes."

"But —"

"You're working too hard."

He knew I wasn't. In fact, I was enjoying a writer's block, that unique way the spirit has of informing the body that all is not well.

"And besides, I want you to meet Roberta."

"Why didn't you say so?" That explained everything.

"I just did. Charlie, the train's pulling out. The first stop after Cassis. Cap St Sauveur."

Click, and I knew I was leaving that night for Marseille.

Tom had been pursuing Roberta Prescott all summer, and Tom had good taste. He might be fickle, but while in pursuit he never lost his 20/20 vision. They had met in Monte Carlo, then again accidentally — so she thought — in La Napoule. If we were to be H.G.'s Tom must have become official. Roberta was from Somewhere-on-the-Hudson, travelling with her Aunt Martha Somebody. "She's the one for you," he said when he phoned from La Napoule in the spring, and he had not meant it the way I took it. "You'll understand when you meet her."

"I need your help. Can I count on you?" were to be Martha Prescott's first words to me the next day at lunch. As she uttered them, and our eyes met, I knew the answer was Yes, no matter what. And sensed that she knew it, too.

In Marseille there was only time for a café au lait before I chugged off in the local headed for Cassis and beyond. The route does not follow the sea, so when I stepped down on the platform at Cap St Sauveur an hour later, where the hills were alive with broom and haze, there was still no hint that we were near the coast. At least twenty of us descended at the station and I saw a resigned look on the face of the sole taxi driver as the others scrambled for the two hotel omnibuses. I gave him my bag, but he was suspicious.

"M'sieur does not wish to take the omni to the hotel?"

"I am not a group," I announced. "I'll ride with you."

He smiled, and we rumbled away while the nineteen struggled with their luggage. As the road wound up the hill a sign proclaimed that we were approaching the Cap, in that uniquely French wording.

Cap St Sauveur (Var)

Son Soleil

Sa Plage

Ses Sirènes

In what other country would a town claim as its own the sun, the sand, and local mermaids? I had been tempted for years to select a particularly unworthy spa and put up a sign of my own:

Malodeur-les-Bains (Ain)

Her Drains

Her Pollution

Her Fevers

A sharp jolt brought me back to reality. Ses Sirènes? The words set me to thinking.

"Her mermaids? Do I remember something in the papers?" I asked my driver.

"Oh, yes, M'sieur. It is now over a year since the mermaids appeared and changed everything."

Then I knew why the name Cap St Sauveur had rung that distant bell. The papers had been full of it: a sleepy village on the coast; and one day out in the bay — mermaids. There they were, cavorting in the water, as the village gaped. Surprise was followed by disbelief, then alarm, and finally ecstasy and publicity. The mermaids never appeared again but the Cap never went back to obscurity either. The site was too beautiful, the bay too blue, and too many people had become aware of it. Soon a proper hotel had been built to accommodate those who came to enjoy its sun, its beach, and its mermaids should they ever reappear to confirm the legend they had created. After all, even the parish priest had seen them before they returned to the deep. His bishop had been unhappy, but what could the good Père LaFrenaye say when reporters questioned him? He could only tell the truth. Yes, he had seen them. No, they were not likely to be canonized (Such a question!). "After all, mermaids are not known for their odor of sanctity." That had been his mistake, a little joke which several papers had quoted, and others had misquoted. "Village Priest Says His Mermaids Are Sexy Not Saintly" had been the headline which caused the bishop to smite his mitre or whatever it is that bishops smite.

At that moment the ancient taxi shuddered over the highest point of the grade and there before us was Cap St Sauveur shimmering at the edge of the water, all in pastels; and alive with people who swarmed everywhere: on the beach, in the water, around the shops in the only street, and at the Parking beyond which only taxis and omnis were allowed.

"They weren't really mermaids, or?" I ventured.

"I saw them, M'sieur." He said it simply and with such dignity that I knew he had indeed seen mermaids.

In five minutes we were at the hotel. I heard my name.

"Charlie. You made it."

Tom took my bag and added, "This is Berte."

I saw in an instant that every descriptive adjective he had used was an understatement. No, she was not a C.B., not an R.B. (Where did we get those mad initials which will not leave us, although we are not tempted into them except by each other, in memory of school days...Classical Beauty, Raving Beauty...how dared we?) But Roberta — Berte in the south of France — was pert, her eyes full of life and mischief. I liked her immediately and unreservedly.

"Aunt Martha is holding a table," she said.

With that Tom dragged us off to the terrace, a tiled and trellised place which would have been serene had it not been for an apoplectic maître d'hôtel who had met his match. Instinctively we paused and listened to the two voices, one almost out of control, the other ominously in control. The maître d' faced us, his eyes wide with outrage, while his opponent sat facing the sea, imperturbable and unruffled under a floppy hat.

"Madame," he began, "you are not even a guest of the hotel."

"Indeed I am not!" was her emphatic reply.

"I say again, all tables are reserved for guests of the hotel — including those arriving on the midday train."

A tremor passed through the floppy hat. "If you cannot fit them in, they can lunch in their rooms. We will be four."

"You will be none, Madame."

"Young man,"— he would never see fifty again — "we are lunching in this establishment only because we have no choice. And you should be grateful to have us. We all know good food and will not allow your kitchen to get away with anything, which is good for them."

"Madame, shall I call the police?"

"Please do. They are friends of mine, and I suspect they all share my opinion of this...hostelry." Her tone carried the implication of lumpy beds full of the enemies of repose, as Baedecker used to call them, which as a matter of fact was not among its faults. Those had to do with rates and service, the former established shamelessly and the latter offered begrudgingly. "However, if the police lunch here with us then you really will be unable to accommodate your paying guests."

"Zut!"

"And 'Zut' again," she replied. "We are, as I said, four and we will start with a loup de mer — a fresh one — grilled on fenouil. Afterwards we will have the gigot —"

"Gigot is not on the luncheon menu."

"Then it is being prepared for the management, and the fragrance is quite ravishing. The gigot, and the tiniest green beans you have ever served, with a bottle of Bandol. And do not hurry us with our coffee."

"Madame, do you expect me to disrupt the entire kitchen for you?"

"If that is required to produce a simple meal, yes. And I want a cheerful luncheon, for which I will pay cheerfully. In return, I promise you we will leave this terrace and never return."

There was an instant of silence, if not repose.

"I always keep my word," she added.

When the maître d' responded, only his eyes, two lasers of hate, betrayed the depth of his feelings.

"I believe Madame's guests have arrived."

Martha Prescott turned to us and observed with a smile, "I believe they have."

"Aunt Martha," said Tom, "this is Charlie."

An extraordinary woman looked deep into my eyes and uttered those prophetic words, "I need your help. Can I count on you?"

It was an excellent lunch. The loup had no doubt swum in local waters that morning before surrendering to flames and fennel, the lamb was pink and redolent of rosemary, the primeurs microscopic, the Bandol noble.

"Charles," Martha sighed as we waited for our coffee. "I wish you had known the Cap before all this —" she indicated the busy, buzzing terrace — "befell it. Avril de Dinde first led us here. It had been her secret place."

Berte saw my furrowed brow. "The duchesse de Dinde. She drops names the way we collect shells on the beach."

"Nonsense. Avril just happens to know everybody."

Tom refilled our glasses as I learned all about Cap St Sauveur and a considerable amount about Martha Prescott.

"Robert and I seldom missed a year at the little auberge here where this terrace now commands the sea. The Fréjus managed it. At that time the entire village consisted of that family and their limitless cousins. They were very poor, but they were content."

As she spoke I observed a radiantly happy woman, of "a certain age" to be sure, but no doubt someone who would never really be old. Her eyes were blue, almost violet and they sparkled. None of the fighting spirit she had shown the maître d' was evident now, simply the joy of retelling a story of happy days. That past spring I had asked Tom to describe Martha Prescott, but he said he couldn't. Now I understood why. There were too many of her, this woman who could be gracious and minuscule, or ten feet tall and imperious if the situation demanded it. Tom had said she could also be quiet and deeply thoughtful, which was the most dangerous Martha.

"When Berte and I came here last year, my first visit in many years, the village was unchanged but the Fréjus Robert and I had known were both old and sad. Their children had not stayed on; they had gone to Marseille or Toulon, or even to Paris, to be part of the big world. Lord, how foolish the young can sometimes be. My dear old André and Nicole longed to retire from the auberge, but they could not afford to. Then, overnight, everything changed."

Was there a pause for effect, or did I imagine it?

"Have you heard about the mermaids?"

I admitted I had, from the taxi driver.

"Marc Antoine. A Fréjus cousin many times removed. He and his wife had the creamery. Now there is a boutique on that corner." Her tone of dismissal suggested high prices and questionable quality. "Cap St Sauveur never looked back after the mermaids, but those elusive creatures would not be pleased today. Just look around you. A Paris syndicate has built this hotel on the site of the auberge — well, some good came of that, for it allowed my Fréjus to buy a house at the end of the village and make it into their retreat. André did not live to enjoy it, but Nicole is still there, as you will presently see, since we are all stopping with her. We were removed — that is the only way to put it — from this hotel."

Tom's voice was tinged with awe as he said, "Aunt Martha was magnificent in the manager's office."

"I was dealing with gangsters and they knew I knew it. Berte and I had arrived at Les Sirènes eager to see the Cap in its new prosperity, and show it to Tom. I knew the minute we walked through the door that only one thing interested the management, and that was money, which was pouring into the town.

"We could have ignored that, but on the day after our arrival the manager summoned us to his office and announced that there had been a double booking, and we would have to leave, thank you very much, good-bye."

Now Martha became Lady Bracknell.

"'Leave the hotel?' I said to the unfortunate man. 'We have just arrived. Here is the confirmation of our reservation.' I gave him the letter, which he read then calmly tore to bits as his secretary looked on approvingly. That was his first mistake, as I do not like being challenged. Oh, he had an explanation. A large group of travel agents was expected, who would assure the success of his entire season when they saw what the Cap had to offer. And there was to be a very important person as well, for the weekend. Brigitte — what's her name?"

"Brigitte What's Her Name indeed," said Tom. "If they get her to come, Cap St Sauveur will be on the map."

"That might be, but not, I thought, at the expense of our confirmed reservation. I told the manager we would not leave. But the next day when we returned from taking tea with Nicole Fréjus, our bags were downstairs. Of course the manager had made the mistake of his life."

Without yet knowing just how, I could see that he had.

"Nicole took us in and we are very comfortable. But obviously something had to be done about the hotel, and it was only a question of deciding exactly how to go about it." She smiled disarmingly, and offered no further explanation of what she meant, but I remembered what Tom had said about the thoughtful Martha.

"Charles, you will share a cool room with Tom. The days will seem short because we have much to do before the weekend. Berte, stop at the draper with Tom and see if my package is ready. I'll go along with Charles. I want to show him La Grotte and our private beach."

She turned to me. "Tom tells me you both swam for Yale."

Martha then asked for her bill, inspected it carefully, and observed, "It is enormous, and worth every sou. Here you are, young man, and please offer my congratulations to the chef."

As we left the terrace Martha stopped before the maître d'.

"Monsieur, we may not be old friends" — it sounded just right in her French — "but I know a superb lunch when I have enjoyed one."

She gave him a hundred franc note, and I believe they experienced an instant of restrained mutual respect.

At this point neither the whats nor the hows of anything were clear to me, but I did not much care. I was in good hands, and willing to help in a good cause, although I didn't realize I was about to play a role in the ordeal of Cap St Sauveur.

During the next three days Martha issued instructions like a confident general, but she called no staff meeting to disclose her grand strategy. As a result I can only report that Tom and I swam in the protected waters of a small cove on the far side of the lighthouse when she wanted us out of the house. There we soon learned at what precise point to dive down in order to come up inside La Grotte, which was dark, dank, and mysterious.

We could only guess at the purpose of other goings on. In one room there was much activity involving wire and wood, stretched canvas, glue and even paint. But Martha firmly closed the door whenever Tom or I came close.

"Don't bother your heads about us," she would say, referring to what seemed chiefly to be the labors of Berte and Nicole. Martha herself was occupied with yards of black cotton material, and the little girl who helped Nicole with the household was often heard talking to herself, as if she were rehearsing lines she was to speak in a play. Tom's guess was that they were preparing a pageant ("But for whom?" I asked) and I thought at one point they were building a boat ("With a black cotton sail?" was Tom's question). Since we could not answer our own questions we simply lay on our private beach, in the mindless way of sun-worshippers, and enjoyed our days.

Then on Friday Martha held a staff meeting with all present: Tom and Berte, and me; Nicole and her grandnephew; and the girl Annie.

"Children, tomorrow is our day. The weather is going to be perfection, and the village will be knee deep in week-enders. Nicole, have you discovered at what time Mlle Brigitte is to arrive at the hotel?"

Nicole turned to her grandnephew.

"Yes, Madame," he said. "Saturday, in time to meet the press and photographers is what the housekeeper said to the maid. My sister heard her."

"Berte, write a telegram for Avril and take it to the post-mistress yourself. You will want to say 'Advise your friend Brigitte So-and-So to cancel her weekend in Cap St Sauveur and to read the Sunday papers instead. Very important. Love. Martha.'"

For a moment, Tom's faith flagged. "Are you sure your duchess knows Brigitte So-and-So?"

Martha almost withered him with her glance. "If Mlle Brigitte is as famous as you say, then Avril is one of her friends."

"Annie," she continued looking to the little girl, "you know your lines?"

"Yes, Madame." Then, her reedy voice raised in simulated excitement, the child started to recite. "M'sieur, M'sieur, the one you should listen to is —"

"Thank you, Annie. Berte will show you whose coattail you are to tug on. Now for our timetable. Tom and Charles, you will go to your little beach in the morning as usual, where you will have your hands full. Come along and let me show you why."

With that Martha led her entire general staff into the room which had been kept closed, and showed us the fruit of their labors. There were ohs and ahs and a round of applause in appreciation of what we all saw.

"Thank you. They are in fact very well made, considering the little time at our disposal. I suggest you go to La Grotte early so you can enjoy experimenting with them. Then precisely at 2:45 in the afternoon we will expect you to spring into action."

The details of that action were then concisely explained, having been well thought out. Now that Tom and I understood the grand design we were lost in admiration of its boldness, the creative imagination it represented, and more than a little apprehensive about the roles we were to play in its execution. However, in the end Martha's confidence was contagious.

"Berte, the telegram. It will be too late now for the hotel to call off the newsmen they have invited because of Mlle Brigitte. And we want all of them here."

Then she added in all innocence and hope, "Nicole, are you planning to give us a rather special little dinner tomorrow evening...to celebrate?"

Dawn on Saturday was particularly beautiful. The red ball of the sun shone through the early morning haze and cast its light on the hilltops to the west, then crept down the slopes toward the village. Tom and I started along the cliff walk towards our beach before the sun could warm our way. We had deposited our burdens in La Grotte, testing them in the cool waters, and retraced our steps before breakfast.

By eight o'clock we were all assembled on the terrace demolishing the warm croissants which Nicole had brought back from the village, along with cheerful news from the hotel via a Fréjus cousin on night duty who had seen a crumpled telegram from Mlle Brigitte expressing her regrets.

"But the manager said it mattered not at all, because the press had arrived, along with the travel agents and the president of the Syndicate from Paris," added Nicole.

"How right he is," purred Martha, a sphinx drinking coffee.

"Look at the beach now!" exclaimed Berte, carried away by the sight of pastoral beauty as a glint of gold from the sun struck the rocks which towered over the sands. It was a beach still in shadow, deserted except for two very young Frejus building sand castles which lazy waves would dissolve before tourists arrived to bake in the midmorning heat.

"The way things used to be," sighed Nicole.

"The way they may be once again," observed Martha. "And now, children, to our posts. We will meet here late this afternoon, at which time there will be a good deal to talk about."

Cap St. Sauveur came slowly to life that day, as had no doubt old Lisbon the November morning in 1755 on which it was destined to be destroyed by the great earthquake. However, by midmorning the beach was crowded. Children splashed in the water while their elders swam out to a float which proclaimed the virtues of Raphael, Vittel, and a French beer (there was of course nothing on the fourth side as it faced out to sea).

The Parking, which had been a field until the year before, was filled and cars were already being turned back to find spaces as far off as the railway station. Three buses from

Marseille had disgorged passengers into the main street and retreated to reserved places in the shade. Assorted articles had already been stolen from two boutiques and the grocer had lost oranges and bananas to quick fingers. The hotel was accepting no further reservations for luncheon or dinner, not even with the inducement of fifty franc notes, and the wisest of the day visitors had long since bought wrapped sandwiches at the tiny Cafe Fréjus.

The travel agents were everywhere, all smiles when they thought of the groups they would soon be sending to Cap St Sauveur and the profits therefrom. The Germans snapped pictures with their Japanese cameras, and the Japanese snapped with their German cameras. In the manager's office the president of the Syndicate studied an architect's plans for enlarging the hotel.

"They will permit sixteen floors?"

"It can be arranged."

"Of course." Then M. le Président turned back to the balance sheets which he found even more beautiful than the drawings.

"Very impressive. The board has voted to build near La Baule this winter, but I think they will reconsider."

Meanwhile the press was gathered in the bar, except for the paparazzi, who had already left on the morning train. There was, after all, no Mlle Brigitte to photo, and a rumor had spread among them that a Swiss industrialist, hitherto above suspicion, had arrived in St. Tropez with a notorious Greek starlet on his arm. The rumor proved false, and it was never determined how it had started, but they were gone. The reporters left behind grumbled into their Ricard. The great

Brigitte was always good copy, but now they were faced with either no despatches or stories which would be ignored. Perhaps even their expense accounts would be questioned.

"Brigitte should not have done this to us," mumbled one old-timer into his glass.

"Don't despair, my friend," said a colleague sardonically. "We can always hope for a first-class natural disaster."

He did not know it, but he was the Cassandra of the bar at Les Sirènes.

During the morning all this news trickled back to us chez Nicole, from well-placed Fréjus on the street, in the bar, even passing through the manager's office with a mop. We were kept well informed until Tom and I returned to La Grotte, where we waited impatiently for my waterproof watch to tell us it was exactly 2:45 p.m.

By that time the sun was high in the sky, the last of the lunches were being served on the terrace as Les Sirènes, and waiters were counting their tips. The shelves at the grocer's were bare, the Cafe Fréjus had closed down, and a watercolor artist was dozing in his folding chair. The beach was black with humanity, its younger representatives full of an inexhaustible energy, the older ones somnolent.

Then a little girl screamed. A Fréjus? Probably, but it was never ascertained who had screamed or who had been the first to point out into the bay where, just below the old lighthouse and near La Grotte, two ominous fins moved serenely through the calm waters.

"Sharks, sharks!" the girl screamed. "The sharks have come back."

Later there was to be much speculation about that first sentence. "Sharks, sharks!" was bad enough but the words which followed announced that the sharks had been there before. Truth from the mouth of a babe? The point was not lost. "The Day the Sharks Came Back to Cap St Sauveur" was the headline in one paper the next morning.

A first frantic reaction came from the beach where the girl's warning had been clearly heard and understood. All who looked saw the sinister fins as they moved slowly and then disappeared from the surface of the water, only to reappear — closer in. People had jumped to their feet, they had buzzed; suddenly they burst into action. Mothers carried their children out of the shallows, swimmers made for the shore when beckoned to, and as the news spread hysteria mounted. Shops emptied as even their owners hurried to stare towards the bay in startled disbelief.

Yes, there they were again; much closer this time. At the hotel there were shouts from the terrace. A table was upset. Countless cameras clicked, mothers screamed again, strong men blanched. After a few moments the excitement penetrated to the bar and as a man the press ran into the midday sun.

"What did she say? The sharks are back?" The man who asked the questions realized that this could be a story bigger than Mlle Brigitte. He turned to a little girl.

"Are you the one? Did you say that?"

"Not I, Monsieur," said the girl who had shouted. "The one you should listen to is old Mère Fréjus. She can tell you about the sharks."

"Who?"

Two of his colleagues heard the name and asked in unison, "Where is she?"

"There is no such person," said the hotel manager who had just emerged from Les Sirènes, his face livid, his future already bleak.

"She always sits by the fountain at the church," said the girl, and then she ran way.

In less than a minute seven representatives of the media were on their way to the church. There, before the fountain sat Mère Fréjus, surely the town's most ancient crone. Her face was almost obscured under a tattered parasol and a torn veil. Half asleep, she leaned forward precariously. The lavender she sold was in her capacious lap, in tiny fragrant sacks. Her ample body was swathed in yards of dusty black cotton.

"Mère Fréjus?"

"Will you buy my lavender?" She came to life and held up one of the sacks.

"Mère Fréjus, what do you know about the sharks?"

"Ah, the sharks of Cap St Sauveur. They will return. God bless and save us. Will you buy my lavender?"

"I can hardly understand her," said one reporter.

"The local accent," suggested another, from the north of France.

"The sharks have returned. Here, take this for your lavender," said a third young man, giving her all the coins in his pocket. "Now, what do you know about the sharks of Cap St Sauveur?"

"Bless you, Monsieur. The sharks? I knew they would return."

"They have been here before? When?"

"Of course. After the curse was laid on the village — "

"Mon Dieu, a curse?"

"In my mother's time — a curse when the gypsies were sent away. They said the sharks would come to replace them and so they did. They always return, even if the village does not like to know it."

"Mermaids and now sharks?"

"Mermaids?" The old woman cackled. "I never believed that story."

"But you were here, surely?"

"Never anywhere else, Monsieur."

The questions tumbled over each other. "It wasn't true?" "It was in all the papers." "Do you mean — " "But only last year — "

Her response was short, but unmistakable in its implication.

"I never saw them."

Just then there were screams from the beach and shots were fired.

"God bless and save us," exclaimed Mère Fréjus again, and crossed herself.

More shots. The press turned and ran. But before they reached the beach the fins had disappeared again, and the gendarmes had put up their guns.

"Monsieur, your lavender, you have forgot your lavender."

These were Mère Fréjus' last recorded words, heard by one reporter who had stumbled and lost his shoe. After that she was seen no more, nor did she leave the lavender behind, thrifty woman that she was.

At the moment no one missed the old crone. The towns-folk could not have missed someone of whose existence they were unaware, and not one of the pressmen went back to the fountain because by that time they had all realized they must compete for the few telephones available in the village. On the beach, while the dread fins did not reappear after the second round of shots, there was no blood on the water to reassure the public. Within an hour the beach was almost deserted, and cars were pulling out of the Parking headed for safer shores. M. le Président of the Syndicate had canceled his reception for the press, and reporters were bargaining for the negatives of some of the pictures which the tourists had taken, the paparazzi having unfortunately left earlier in the day. The manager of Les Sirènes was steely eyed and grim, because M. le Président had just told him, within hearing of an alert Fréjus, that the Syndicate would no doubt build at La Baule after all, and Cap St Sauveur could sink back into the obscuri-ty it had deserved since it expelled the gypsies, an event which no one except that old witch Mère Fréjus cared to remember although a good hotel manager surely had a duty to ferret out such information before he allowed a significant investment to be made with the Syndicate's capital.

"M. le Président, I simply do not believe it."

"You don't believe it?! What do you not believe, idiot? It is what we saw. First mermaids, now sharks. What will it be tomorrow? The Monster of Loch Ness? The Syndicate cannot invest in a town which is cursed."

The first reports beyond Cap St Sauveur were carried on the evening television news in France. They were relatively sober accounts, but nonetheless alarming. It was only when the Sunday papers released their flood of purple prose that the real torrent of publicity began. The improbability of sharks in the sea off the Cap had no restraining effect, for hysteria had set in and the media had a good story on an otherwise dull weekend. One headline ran "Cap St Sauveur, Her Mermaids, Her Beach, Her Man-eating Sharks." Another, "She Snatched Her Bleeding Child from the Jaws of a Monster from the Sea." And still another, "The Gypsies' Revenge — a Plague of Great White Sharks."

Even the BBC carried a reference to "alarm in a small village on the Riviera, until now a favorite bathing place." The commercial networks in the USA reported an invasion of sharks which caused pandemonium in a "once favored resort." Moreover, with distance the story grew more awesome. By the time the news reached Japan it had become "Visiting Japanese Trade Officials Menaced by Man-Eating Sharks." Two American film producers found backers and rushed plans for the shooting of rival properties. A spokesman for Gypsies International called a press conference to remind the world that his people's curses should be taken seriously, and that this was not the only one which had been laid. Isvetzia maintained a dignified silence, confident that none of its happy readers was likely to be exposed to that particular danger in that particular place. But the North Korean press made up for such restraint by announcing "Mediterranean Invaded by Wild Sea Beasts. Hundreds Killed?" In later editions the question mark was omitted.

The sun which set beyond the hills cast Cap St Saveur into

a very special darkness that first evening after the sharks. A full moon was the only thing on the rise over the beleaguered village except for the spirits on the terrace chez Nicole Fréjus.

"Children," said Martha, "you were all magnificent. Annie, your career on the stage is assured if you decide to follow it. Nicole, your grandnephew will one day grow up to succeed Hercule Poirot. And my dear Charles and Tom, I owe you both an apology. I never thought the gendarmes would shoot into the bay."

That was the first we knew about the shots as we had been inside our fins, busy diving and resurfacing. Our disappearance as the shots were fired was simply the completion of our assignment. Back at La Grotte we had discarded our fins, storing them behind a rock until we would have time to return another day and remove them. We had then swum back to our own little beach, per instructions, and lain in the sun so that if anyone were to come by and inquire — as someone did an hour later — we could say,

"Sharks, Messieurs? In the bay? No, they were not on this side, or we would have seen them. Thank you, Messieurs. We will stay out of the water."

As the gendarmes retreated I asked Tom something I'd had on my mind ever since we left the fins behind.

"Tom, did you notice when we dropped the fins, there behind the same rock was something else, half decayed from the salt water, but still recognizable — "

"Part of a mermaid's tail?"

"Yes, that was it."

"No," said Tom solemnly, "I didn't notice a thing."

"A toast," said Martha, and raised her glass. "To Cap St Sauveur. Her bay, her sky, and her future."

As we drank the evening breeze quickened and wafted up from the kitchen a smell of spices and the sea.

"Nicole, what is it?"

"Madame wanted something special. I have made my bouride."

There were shouts of Bravo.

"The catch was good last night. Loup, rouget, rascasse, and we can all enjoy the aioli tonight as tomorrow there will be nobody in the village to offend."

Foul-breathed from the garlic of the sauce, we rested the next day on laurels gathered in a grove of hubris. Still, all those who work together successfully to accomplish a mission can be proud of their achievement, whether they have won a battle, saved a life, or robbed a bank. We felt we had accomplished all three.

The Sunday view from Nicole's terrace was vastly different from what it had been on Saturday. There were people in the village, some even standing on the beach, but they were not there to play and relax. These were the curious who had read or heard about the monsters from the deep. They came armed with cameras and binoculars, but not much patience. They left unrewarded when the sharks did not reappear, a few buying their children the little shark balloons which one enterprising Marseillais had brought on the morning train. The police were present to keep everyone out of the water, had anyone considered venturing into it. Meanwhile M. le Président had returned to Paris and the travel agents were leaving for safer seaports and other spas.

"I could almost shed a crocodile tear for the Syndicate," said Martha benignly. "But I am not a crocodile," she added, managing to resemble a satiated one.

"Aunt Martha, why did you ask me to wire Avril de Dinde to keep Brigitte So-and-So away?" Berte asked.

"Because, my dears, if she is a nice person — and you all seemed to warm at the mention of her name — I saw no reason why her weekend should be spoiled by our little caper. Also, we did not need those photographers here, with their very fine professional cameras."

We all understood which of the reasons was the more important.

"Mlle Brigitte will no doubt enjoy coming to Cap St Sauveur on another more appropriate occasion. Perhaps when Jean Jacques can be her host."

"Who?" we all wanted to know.

"A Fréjus. He lives in Marseille now, but Nicole thinks he might be willing to return and run the hotel, if it became available. He would do it well. But tell me, children, what are your plans?" she continued, turning to Tom and me. "Berte and I want to be back in Monte this week."

"I'll follow you," said Tom.

"B.F.Y.," I exclaimed, forgetting that only Tom would know that meant Bully For You.

"And what is that supposed to mean?" asked the self-same Tom, looking to Berte for approval of his apostasy.

She in turn said to me, "I made Tom promise he would never talk in that awful language by initials again."

"Traitor," I growled.

"O.F.G.S.," Martha exclaimed, and at least I knew instantly what she meant. "Charles, what are your plans?"

"I'm going back to Paris to look for my writer's block," I admitted, "unless I've managed to lose it along the way."

"Nicole," asked Martha, "can you keep us all until Tuesday, when we will ask Marc Antoine to take us to the morning train?"

"It will be a pleasure, Madame Marthe."

On the appointed day Marc Antoine arrived promptly at nine.

Responding to Martha's greeting he said, "I'm glad to have the fare, Madame. I don't know what will happen to the Cap now, but at least the omnis are off the road." He said it with a certain relish.

We drove through a strangely quiet street. Some of the shops were open, their owners standing like spectres in the doorways. We waved to Annie who was carrying a baguette home from the bakery.

"Marc Antoine, stop at the hotel so we can get the Paris papers," said Martha. "There may be an article or two we haven't seen."

As we waited for Tom, who had bounded inside, the manager of the hotel appeared. When he caught sight of Martha he bowed curtly.

"Madame is departing — of course." It was said in the tone with which one would reproach an employee who was leaving on a holiday weekend merely because a plague had broken out.

She replied, in all seriousness, "Of course. They say the bay is far from safe."

"A sad day for Cap St Sauveur." And his penetrating glance told us he would have been glad to hold Martha responsible for all that had happened. "If the Syndicate goes," he added, more a threat than a question, "what will become of the town?"

"I have heard that one of the Fréjus in Marseille would consider returning if the hotel were available — at a reasonable price." Martha was all sweetness and concern when she concluded with, "Perhaps as a sanitarium for the insane?"

As they drove on, Martha said to Berte, "I will ring Nicole tonight and tell her that Jean Jacques should make his offer at once. A very low offer."

A few moments later we were all in the station.

"Won't you come with us as far as Toulon?" Martha asked me. "I know a good restaurant near there where we might lunch — chez Georges Garin."

"I must be strong," I said weakly, "but when you come to Paris I will take you to my own favorite bistrot."

"And I will trust your choice, Charles. I have no intention of letting you disappear.

Nor had she, nor did I, as it turned out.

Then, with sudden candor, Martha sighed and said, "Well, it is all over, and it wasn't nearly as complicated as —" She stopped and we all sensed an ounce of tension in the air. I thought of the mouldering mass I had seen in La Grotte.

Tom asked the question.

"As what, Aunt Martha?"

After the briefest pregnant pause Martha smiled, angelic, and said, "— as it might have been."

The Grand Design

*T*om wired me from Monte Carlo a month or so after I returned to Paris. He was brief and to the point. "B and Aunt M going to Italy tomorrow. Poor Tom not invited. Come on down. Yr despondent T. Swift."

I wired back, "Tough. Sorry. Can't. Yr spondent Ch," and I heard no more until Tom rang me one day in September to say he was in Paris and wanted to take me to lunch and that he had good news. I was still sharing my rooms with The Block, and accepted, happy to be diverted. Also, I was both curious and apprehensive, fearing the good news concerned him and Berte. She had been on my mind all summer long. Tom's cryptic wire had even given me a glimmer of guilty hope. What a friend I was.

"I'll meet you in the Ritz bar at one," he said. That sounded like a celebration. "And then give you a good lunch at Lucas Carton." It *was* a celebration.

Nervous and on edge, I went along to the Ritz, which was

only five minutes and a world removed from my little apartment in St Roch. I entered the hotel from the Place Vendôme and walked that endless corridor to the bar. I was dragging my feet and I knew why. Tom was either married or about to be; the latter, probably, and he was going to ask me to be his best man. Moreover, I would have to agree, even though I would feel like his worst man.

"Charlie, I've got wonderful news," were Tom's words of greeting.

The wan smile I managed hardly concealed my feelings, but Tom was happily oblivious to everything except his announcement:

"Charlie, I'm getting married."

"Congratulations, old man."

"On the last Saturday of October in New York. I want you to be my best man."

"Tom, there is nothing I'd rather be," lied the writer who could speak fiction although he could not write it. "But you'll be in New York, and I'm in Paris."

"I have news for you, Charlie. There are ships, and they cross the ocean regularly. Planes, too. Also, you are a good swimmer. What'll you have?"

"Whisky," I said, "which I seldom drink."

"Let me tell you the whole story. You couldn't use it in a book. Nobody would believe it."

"I believe it," I responded dolefully, and then tried to make it right. "I'm happy for you both. It all started when Martha told you they were going to Italy, and you were not invited."

"Yes!"

"Very shrewd of her. They have a few days sightseeing in Rome while you mope in Monte, then unable to bear it any longer you turn up and declare your intentions."

Tom laughed. "Perfect, except you are a hundred and ten percent wrong."

"Tell me how I have erred," I said testily, settling back with a peanut.

"Martha did drag Berte off to Taormina, to make me show my cards," said Tom, "and she even dug up a friend of her duchess they were going to visit — a Sicilian prince."

"Of course. The competition."

"No, he was one of Martha's old beaux. But she was using the familiar ploy about absence making the heart grow fonder."

It did. I knew.

"She forgot about 'Out of sight, out of mind.'"

I perked up.

"Now you may have noticed, Charlie, that I am not the most constant of God's creatures."

"You are the ficklest man I ever knew," I agreed with indecent relish. "But in something as important as this?"

Then it struck me and everybody in the Ritz bar heard my next question.

"Tom, are you going to marry Berte or not?"

An Englishwoman near us shook her head balefully as if to sympathize with my attempt to force the brute to marry my sister.

"No, Charlie, of course I'm not," boomed Tom in reply, confirming to the tweedy lady that he was indeed a bounder.

"I'm marrying the most beautiful girl in the world. Her

name is Sloane Gifford, and you are going to be my best man."

"Of course I am!"

I positively shouted it, assuring Queen Victoria on my right that I was as depraved as the man who had just declined to make my sister an honest woman.

My joy and relief were boundless, and Tom misinterpreted my motive.

"I knew I could count on you. Now, let's go to lunch and I'll tell you all about Sloane," he continued, raising an index finger for the waiter, who was staring at us in any case.

Suddenly I was ravenous, and realized how thoroughly I was going to savor the next hour, food and conversation.

At Lucas Carton the details were revealed like the hearts of our artichokes as we stripped the leaves from them.

Tom had indeed been alarmed to learn that Martha was carrying Berte off with the season in Monte Carlo in full swing. "They took the morning train and that same night at the Yacht Club I met Sloane."

"You wicked, faithless man," I chortled happily.

"Charlie, it was like fireworks on the Fourth of July, like the dam breaking at Ranchipur."

"I get your drift." How smug I was.

"Sloane Gifford. B.B. for Blazing Beauty. N.Q.A.I. We set the date then and there, in the moonlight."

"I can't tell you how happy I am for you."

And, of course, I couldn't.

That historic luncheon ended with cognac and euphoria. Tom and I agreed to meet in New York in October, and I was not sorry to be called home. I could not sit in front of an unresponsive Smith-Corona forever.

Later the same day I called Tom for an answer to the question I had neglected to ask, so full of his own plans had Tom been, and so happy had I been to hear them.

"Tom, how did you leave it with Berte?"

"Don't worry, Tom Swift did the right thing. I sent an enormous bunch of roses to their suite when they returned to Monte. And a note explaining everything."

Explaining everything. To her Aunt Martha perhaps, but I wondered how Berte had taken it. After all, the summer with Tom must have meant something to her. I was to have my answer sooner than I could have hoped. A few days after Tom sailed for home, a brief letter arrived at my door.

"Charles, dear, we will arrive at the Meurice on Thursday next. We are both eager to try your favorite bistrot. Martha Prescott."

I took them to a late lunch chez Mère Michel, where the food was good and the room quiet. As soon as we were seated and had raised our glasses in a toast to the reunion, Berte said:

"I suppose you know I was left standing at the altar." She said it as happily as anyone has ever uttered those words.

"Not really," I protested.

"No, not really at all," chimed Martha, "but I suspected what might happen and it did. There are always Miss Giffords about, the Lord be praised. Tom seems to have found his in the shortest possible time."

I turned to Berte, wanting to say something appropriate. She did it for me.

"Tom was a sweetheart, but not mine."

I did not contradict her. I just smiled contentedly.

Then Martha changed the subject and struck a raw nerve.

"Charles, how is your novel going?"

I winced. "It isn't."

"Oh, dear," said Martha, "we will have to do something about that when we get home," revealing that she and Berte were also on their way back to the USA.

"Home for us is Sliepskill," said Martha, "and you? Tom said New York City, I believe."

"Number One, Wall Street," I replied, casually.

Berte was surprised, as she was supposed to be. "I didn't know anyone lived on Wall Street."

"Nobody does," I confessed. "My family consists of Petty, Eaton, Petty and Cruickshank. Our relationship is a legal one."

"Are you saying that you are an orphan?"

"P.E.P. and C. have in fact replaced my own totally defunct family."

"But where will you live? Surely not in a hotel."

"I hadn't given it much thought."

"Hm."

Martha was obviously deep in thought, a promising or precarious state of mind for those about whom she cared.

"Berte and I are sailing on the France, Friday week. Are you?"

"I'm booked on the United States."

"Surely there is time to change."

"Well..."

"Then it is settled. Now we can look forward to the voyage.

And you can choose our wines for us. The France has a magnificent cellar."

It was comforting to have the decision made for me.

"In fact, Charles," Martha went on, "to have you accompany us home is Point Number One of my Plan for Charles."

"Don't panic," said Berte, "Cap St Sauveur was an exception. I don't know what Aunt Martha is up to this time."

I was willing to take a chance, not dreaming of the extent to which those five days with the Compagnie Maritime Transatlantique were going to change the direction of my life.

"Are you, dear Charles," beamed Martha, "going to give us some coffee to complement a perfectly splendid lunch?"

Moving out of St Roch proved more complicated than I had expected, and Berte came along one morning to help me pack books and throw papers away. As a reward I took her out to Malmaison in the afternoon.

"Berte, tell me about life in Sliepskill-on-Hudson," I said as we walked through leafy Reuil.

"The sordid truth?" she asked mischievously.

"Your own life will do."

"Well, before I moved to Aunt Martha's I was not happy." She spoke thoughtfully, seriously. "Now everything is different."

I already knew that Berte's parents, or at least her mother, had been what is known as difficult. Tom had told me.

"I've always wanted to work with people, whoever might need me. For mother that meant distributing baskets of fruit at Christmas. Aunt Martha arranged for me to start as a volunteer at our hospital. I loved my work from the first day. But that is not life in Sliepskill. They say the town is full of quiet money, whatever that is. We have two traffic lights in the Lower Town, a volunteer fire department, and lots of churches. Hasn't Aunt Martha told you about it?"

"Of course she has. The nicest town on the river. Forty minutes from Manhattan. And everybody lives on Elm Street."

"Martha Prescott's friends do. In Victorian houses, or Gothic revival. Has Aunt Martha mentioned the Cottage to you?" Berte asked as we crossed the courtyard towards Malmaison.

"Not yet."

But she did, the next evening during dinner at their hotel.

"Charles, Robert and I restored the cottage at the bottom of our garden, as his workroom. It is quite secluded, with a beautiful view of the river. Even I never went down there unless Robert invited me."

Martha's voice, when she spoke of her husband, took on a special glow that reflected the happiness of their years together.

"It might do very well for you, Charles."

"For me?" She had taken me by surprise.

"Yes. You and your books. Do think about it."

I did think; in fact the thought kept me awake several nights. I had always lived in the midst of things, and had convinced myself that I worked better in the madding city which offered all the options and all the temptations. But I was not managing to be very productive in Paris, at the center of the world. Obviously Martha had also come to that conclusion because she brought the matter up when we were next quietly together, in the boat train en route to Le Havre.

"Charles, I may have the answer to your problem of getting on with your novel."

I saw from the way Berte waited for my response that Martha had already discussed it with her.

"Future generations of literary critics will bless you," I said. "Tell me the answer, Aunt Martha."

"I am serious, Charles, and I think you should be, too."

I may not have looked contrite, but I was.

"It is very simple. You feel miserable and no doubt guilty as well as unproductive —"

Thus far her analysis was depressingly accurate.

"Therefore, give up writing altogether and do something else."

The answer was indeed a simple one, and I had toyed with it myself.

"Such a drastic solution had not occurred to me," I said, though no cock crew.

"Are you sure, Charles?" Martha understood her man. "Your manuscript has no doubt vastly improved your command of the language, and helped you learn to express yourself well. There is no disgrace in not having a story that demands to be told."

She was right: no disgrace, but an awful blow to the ego.

"And while you are deciding what you want to do, you can live very comfortably in the Cottage in Sliepskill. If that appeals to you."

Covertly I glanced at Berte, who was covertly glancing at me.

"I hope you'll decide to do it," she said.

I stared out the window. The train was rolling through

Normandy, past fields doted with Camembert cows, and for a moment we were all silent. Suddenly I heard myself say in a loud voice:

"So that was Point Number Two!"

Spontaneously the three of us laughed, and the French couple in our compartment must have thought we were playing some incomprehensible American game. Perhaps we were.

"Of course," Martha readily admitted. "And how sensible it is. The rent will be $75 a month. That way you will feel independent, when you want to be."

I gazed out on the Norman landscape and contemplated the voyage home in good spirits. It was not really the return of the prodigal, although the senior Mr. Petty would interpret it as such and might even ask me to lunch if I told him I was giving up writing. He could recite his set piece on the proper pursuits for a young man of means and congratulate me for renouncing the literary life, which was not on the list.

The crossing was halcyon. None of us minded the North Atlantic roll which overtook the ship for twenty-four hours. Then on the last afternoon I asked Berte and Martha to meet me on deck at the stern of the ship, precisely at four o'clock.

"You're not going to jump overboard, are you?" asked Berte as they arrived.

"Something like it," I said.

Whereupon I took out the all-too-short manuscript of the novel on which I had lavished so many fruitless hours.

"The occasion is a solemn one," I began, "and I want you both to share it with me. Aunt Martha, I have pondered what you said, and I agree with you. If I cannot write, then I should stop trying and not feel guilty about it. Ergo, I am consigning these reluctant pages to Neptune."

With that I loosened my grip on the papers in hand, and watched them flutter down and disappear into the foamy wake of the ship.

Martha was moved and admitted it. "Charles, that took courage, and I am convinced it was a first step in the right direction. Mark my words."

We were to dock early the next morning and I remember nothing about the Captain's dinner, only the conversation Berte and I had up on deck that night.

"Charles," she said, "I'm so glad we didn't have a ship-board romance."

"You wouldn't have wanted that?"

"Oh, no. I'm told they never last."

Gratefully, I kissed her good night.

The next morning, after we had cleared customs, I made a solemn confession. I said, with conviction, "I am glad to be home."

A few minutes later, seated in a Checker cab en route through the Westside streets, we all flew into the air. As we bounced back on the hard seats, we realized we had hit the first of Manhattan's endless supply of year-round potholes. Nothing had changed, and we had been plummeted back into real life.

What transpired in the next months was indeed real life for me, in the best sense. I settled down in the Cottage, and Tom's wedding was one of the few occasions which took me into the city. The rice was hardly settled onto Park Avenue before I was happily headed back to Grand Central and home to Sliepskill — and my typewriter. For I had realized the ultimate wisdom behind Martha's proposal that I give up writing: I had discovered it was simply not possible. I had to write, so I started a new book relieved and released from my block.

"Charles," said Martha when I told her, "do you recall when I asked you to mark my words?" I did. "That was Point Number Three of my Plan. You see, instinctively I believed in you as a writer from the moment we met."

There was still another point to the Grand Design for Charles, I think, and it also came to pass. Berte and I were married the following spring, and started discovering how pleasant it could be living happily ever after. Moreover, I sold my novel when it was finished, once again with Martha's help, although she insisted the book spoke for itself.

"My boy," the publisher said, "you have written about someone close to your heart and that is why I am going to take your book."

He was right, and yes, my first book was devoted to Martha, called Polo in acknowledgment of her adventures and the tales resulting therefrom. Since I am only an incidental character in them, along with Berte and a host of others, the Charles of this narrative herewith retires from the first person singular. From now on this is Martha's story, her whole story, and nothing but her story, so help us all.

It begins a few years back, after her Robert's death, when she had settled in Sliepskill-on-Hudson, where she and her sister Araminta were born, and grew up...

Las Vegas? For a Rest?

Martha Prescott did not look up when her niece entered the kitchen. Her concentration was undivided as she finished a baroque design in chocolate butter cream on her Egyptian cake.

"I'm not a pastry chef...so hold your breath," she said, "or Dr. Cutler is going to have a chocolate pudding for his cake sale."

After a final swirl of the pastry tube Martha stood back to judge her work.

"Yes, it will do." Then she relaxed. "Now I've only got to clean up my mess. Mrs. Brimston does not like to find traces of me in what she calls her kitchen the rest of the week. And why are you so silent, Roberta?"

"Aunt Martha, I told them this morning. Daddy just smiled, but Mother had a fit."

"I expected she would, and I knew your father would just smile because I took Florian aside a few days ago and told him myself."

The phone rang. Without waiting for her sister to identify herself on the wire, Martha took up the receiver and said cheerfully, "Good morning, Minty."

While the voice buzzed on Martha gazed into her kitchen garden. The morning was brisk but sunny, promising one of those rare March days that augur spring. Birds were busy at the feeder, and she wished she had as little on her mind as they had on theirs.

"Minty, hold on for a minute. Roberta is just leaving."

Her niece objected. "But we have so much —"

"— so much to talk about. If I know your mother she is about to march in this direction with a declaration of war. I'd rather you did not witness the battle as I may have to resort to secret weapons."

The words were belligerent but Martha's wink was reassuring.

"Also, I am expecting Mr. Bramble from the bank in New York. He wanted to come in person this time. We will discuss our plans when you come back to take the cake over to Dr. Cutler. It needs an hour to set. And don't worry about me and your mother."

Roberta trusted her aunt's judgment, so she brightened, blew her a kiss and was gone. Martha sat in silence for a moment before she remembered her sister was waiting on the phone.

"Minty, what can I do for you?" She spoke airily, to hide her embarrassment.

Araminta's response was chilly. "I only wanted to tell you that Herbert plans to call you. He needs advice."

"You couldn't help him?"

"He obviously doesn't think so."

"Minty, do I detect a hint of jealousy?"

Martha hoped she did as she had been waiting for more years than she cared to recall for Araminta and Herbert Detweiler to marry.

"Certainly not, Martha. But being human, I am curious."

"Forgive me. I'm on edge because Lucille knows I am taking Roberta to Europe and she is, I gather, spitting mad."

"Lucille has been spitting mad all her life," observed Araminta sagely. "Well, call me when you know what it is that Herbert needs your advice about," she said, her spirits revived.

"I will," sighed Martha, after she had replaced the receiver.

Meanwhile, less than a block away a grim-faced woman started down Elm Street to confront her sister-in-law, consumed with determination and outrage, to say nothing of resentment and rancor. Equally determined, Martha was ready for her.

In the minute before Martha reached her front door to answer the bell, memories flooded through her mind. Lucille Diekenfeld had been a pretty girl, and she could have been popular (popularity is important when you are sixteen), but she never was; too good for the rest of Sliepskill, and quick to let it be known. Then Mr. Diekenfeld lost his money — it was something to do with the Kaiser's war and investments — and Lucille still made no friends when she needed them. Eventually nobody cared. How she met Florian Prescott and married him years later was something else. Robert always said his brother needed a manager, not a wife, and that he had found one.

"Hello, Lucille. Come into the kitchen. I'm just finishing up in there."

Lucille followed her down the hall without a word as Martha was guilty of a Freudian slip. "A cup of coffee to cool you down — I mean to warm you up?"

"I am not here to drink coffee. What is this nonsense about your wanting to drag Roberta off on a wild-goose chase to Europe?"

True to form, in her opening salvo Lucille had managed to be disparaging, insulting and inaccurate, all in a few carefully chosen words.

"It is not nonsense," Martha replied evenly, "and you know very well that I never go off on wild-goose chases. Nor am I dragging anybody anyplace. I have invited Roberta to accompany me to Europe and she has accepted."

"We'll see about that."

"Indeed we will." Martha, having met steel with steel, plunged forward. "Lucille, wild horses couldn't drag out of me what I'd like to say, but —" She paused, then decided to go on. "— but there are no wild horses in sight so I'm going to have my say, and you are going to listen."

The counterattack took Lucille by surprise, but she had one more sortie in her. "Don't forget, I am her mother."

Like a good general, Martha prepared to advance as the enemy faltered.

"No one would ever suspect it from the way your treat her. Sit down."

Lucille sat.

"You and Florian adopted a dear little baby, aged eight months, who has grown into a lovable young woman. You should be bursting with pride instead of taking every opportunity to break her spirit. I know Florian feels differently but he is no match for you, never has been."

Lucille started up out of her chair.

"Don't move. It's high time I took Roberta abroad and showed her some of the world beyond Elm Street. We are going to dip into my past and into Roberta's future, and have a wonderful time doing it. What's more, when we return Roberta can, if she chooses, work at the hospital because I will arrange it for her."

Then, with good will rushing in where anger declined to persist, Martha broke into a smile. "Oh, Lucille, wouldn't it be better if we both relaxed and tried to get along?"

The gesture was in vain. Lucille rose, and stood for an instant, tall and gaunt, before she delivered her final blast.

"At your time of life, Martha, you shouldn't be thinking of going *anywhere*," and she stalked out of the house by the nearest door. In the garden a startled motley of birds scattered in alarm from the feeder and took to the sky.

Well, I got it out of my system, thought Martha. Then she said aloud, "What did she mean 'at my time of life?'"

Before she could seek an answer, simultaneously two bells sounded: the door and the telephone. One signalled Mr. Bramble's arrival, she knew, and she suspected Herbert Detweiler was at the other end of the wire.

"Hold on a minute," she said into the phone, and started for the front door.

"Hello, Mr. Bramble," were her next words, to the neatly groomed little man with portfolio and clipped moustache, whom Robert had always trusted and referred to as dapper. "I will be with you in two minutes."

Back at the phone, Martha said, "Herbert? Well, I thought

it was you. This has been my morning for bells. Minty says you have a question to ask me but I will have to ring you back as I am entertaining another gentleman at the moment."

So, with the object of Herbert's call still not revealed, Martha returned to her guest from the city. "Mr. Bramble," she asked, "are you worried about something?"

"My mind is not entirely at ease." Mr. Bramble then pronounced the words he had rehearsed all the way from Grand Central Station. "Mrs. Prescott, have you lost your confidence in us?"

"Dear Mr. Bramble, not only do I have confidence in the bank, I also have the utmost faith in your personally."

"But," he continued cautiously, "despite urgent reminders in each letter I have sent, concerning transfers to your local account —"

"Oh, dear," said Martha, thinking that Mr. Bramble would have been an excellent school principal, "I have not acknowledged your notes. But that is the bank's fault. I used to read all my mail, but now — to survive — I pick and choose. As far as the bank is concerned, I do not need a calendar in January, nor a packet of seeds in the spring, nor credit cards I have not requested, at any time."

He knew what she meant, and he agreed with her, even if he could not say so.

"In other words —"

"Precisely. I extract what is essential and consign the remainder to oblivion. Here —" She pointed to the petit point wastebasket near her desk.

Mr. Bramble was now a man with one weight removed

from his mind, ("Bramble, have you been neglecting Mrs. Prescott? Is she banking somewhere else these days? And if so, where and why?") and he hoped that Martha would quickly lift the second.

"Then we are still your- er - principal repository?"

"You are indeed, Mr. Bramble. A glass of sherry?"

Not until he was completely satisfied, thought Hector Bramble.

"First let me hand you this confirmation of transfer, and ask that you read the accompanying letter this time, Mrs. Prescott. If you please."

"With pleasure," said Martha, taking the document.

Brave woman, he thought, to handle her own affairs in these troubled times.

Then Martha's face fell.

"Mr. Bramble, you haven't transferred the ten thousand dollars I asked for."

"I will take care of it without delay," he replied, still secure, "just as soon as we receive the funds to - er - reactivate your account. After the one thousand dollars I have transferred to your local account, you have, unlikely as it seems, only eleven hundred dollars on deposit with us at this time."

He laughed heartily, as his superiors had taught him to do when dealing with an affluent client to whom details were oh, so tedious.

Martha looked up from the letter but she did not laugh.

"Eleven hundred dollars is not very much today. During the depression we had very little but at least it bought something."

Mr. Bramble, relaxed now, accepted the Bristol Cream she offered him.

"When do you plan to leave on your trip, Mrs. Prescott?"

"I wonder," mused Martha. He found the reply unorthodox until she added, "That is, as soon as possible. And of course you will receive your — my — funds."

Martha said no more. She allowed the 1:12 train to carry a happy man back to Manhattan. As it gathered speed along the river Martha did not hear the distant whistle. She was deep in thought, staring at the birds around the feeder without really seeing them.

Half an hour later, when Roberta returned, Martha was still at the window.

"Am I too early?"

Martha snapped back to reality. "You are not a minute too soon."

"Did Mr. Bramble think we are extravagant to go abroad?"

"I daresay he would have if he'd known that my balance of just over a thousand dollars in his bank is all that's left."

Roberta jumped to the logical conclusion. "You'll have to transfer some from another account."

"That is exactly what he proposed but the joke is on him. There are no other accounts."

The fact that Martha chuckled as she said the fateful words was somewhat assuring but not completely so.

"Aunt Martha, are we in trouble?"

"No, my dear, not a bit of it, and we are going abroad as planned. Only I shall want to take another, a shorter, trip first. What is the name of that place out west in Nevada?"

"You don't meant Las Vegas —"

"That's it. I'll go to Las Vegas for a few days' rest before we go to Europe. Monte Carlo is going to be our summer headquarters and it is bound to be exciting." Roberta's eyes narrowed. "But now Dr. Cutler is waiting for his cake, so please take it to the rectory at once. Shoo. Get along with you."

Roberta did not move. "Why Las Vegas?"

"Well, I've never been there," Martha answered, as if that explained everything. But she saw and understood Roberta's confusion and doubts, and added "My dear, we will have all summer to talk, and I will have much to tell you. For the moment, trust my judgment. And now scoot — but scoot carefully with that cake." However, she could not resist a tantalizing temptation. "When you get home tell your mother I am leaving for Las Vegas. That will keep her awake all night."

Martha smiled so brightly that Roberta kissed her, and carefully picked up the Egyptian cake. Martha held the kitchen door open for her, and as she left, called out: "Remind Dr. Cutler that my cake is for the sale, not for the raffle. He knows I do not approve of gambling in any form."

That evening at six most of the good citizens of Sliepskill sat before their television sets waiting for the networks of their choice to tell them what to think, and what to buy. Florian Prescott, however, was being denied those pleasures, and, for a retired professor of philosophy, feeling far from philosophical as his own Xantippe carried on. Lucille alternated between cajole and threat, with emphasis on the latter, and she ended with "I told Martha we'd be there at seven."

"Couldn't you and Berta go?" Florian, knowing how peaceful the house would be if she left him with his book.

"Roberta would be no help on an occasion like this. And I hope Martha will appreciate the fact that someone is willing to accept the responsibility of having power of attorney to protect her interests while she is gadding about in foreign places."

It sounded so logical, almost convincing, and Florian knew it was neither. He did not believe in wasting time on lost causes, but Lucille had never been able to grasp that.

"The woman is obviously unbalanced—"

They heard a key turn in the door.

"You are very late, young woman," was her mother's greeting to Roberta.

"I've been helping Dr. Cutler. He thinks his Ladies' Committee is a blessing but it's a burden. They are all generals."

"The man is senile. Exactly like —" But Lucille did not complete the comparison. "We are calling on your aunt in a few minutes," she said instead. "Your father wants to have a word with Martha before she leaves the country."

"Oh," said Roberta gaily, "our trip has been postponed. Aunt Martha is flying out West for a few days first."

"Where in the West?" Lucille was suspicious and Roberta immediately confirmed her suspicions.

"To Las Vegas." The name dropped like a bomb in their midst.

Lucille's glance to her husband told more than words could have done. "Florian, let's get this over with. And don't forget the papers."

He sighed, put aside his book, and rose from his favorite chair.

While they were walking down Elm Street in the starry night, of which they took no notice, upstairs at home Roberta was on the phone.

"I'm glad they are coming," said Martha. "Florian isn't allowed to come my way very often any more. And Roberta, if I seemed a little...well, distraught...this afternoon, just remember that I had been thinking as you came in. And you know how I am when I've been thinking..."

Martha waited for her visitors, resolved not to look upset no matter what Lucille might say. That in itself would annoy Lucille, so the tactic would be doubly satisfying. She had hardly opened the door before her theory was being tested. Florian was silent, caught between a dark cloud and a valiant moonbeam.

"We did not come here to drink tea," was Lucille's icy blast in response to Martha's proposal that she start the kettle. "Florian has brought a paper that he wants you to sign, for your own good."

"How thoughtful of you both."

"As you are determined to go abroad, you should be grateful that Florian, as Robert's only brother, is willing to take the responsibility and help. So just sign and put the idea of this absurd trip to Las Vegas out of your mind —"

"I'm afraid it's too late for that," Martha said sweetly. "My seat on the plane is reserved — for Saturday."

Lucille chose to ignore the announcement. "Here are the papers. You are giving your power of attorney to Florian, not to me."

Martha accepted the papers gingerly and said, as if she

had just received a dozen red roses, "Thank you, Lucille. I'll read them on the plane. And now good night. Florian, wrap your muffler tight. You know what the night air does to your throat."

Outside Lucille's anger knew no bounds. "How dare she toy with me!"

"I thought she did it rather well," was her husband's ill-advised reply.

"If only you did think. I don't know why I worry about you and Roberta. Martha is obviously mad as a hatter and I will get Dr. Benson to certify it. She is not going to Las Vegas or anywhere else."

Florian stared straight ahead.

The next day it was a dejected Roberta who entered her aunt's upstairs sitting room.

"Oh, dear," said Martha, observing the symptoms, "what has your mother been up to now?"

"She's been to see Dr. Benson."

"That may be a step in the right direction. I think Lucille needs psychiatric help."

"She wants him to examine you."

Martha's face lighted up. "Well, I've always wanted to lie on a couch and learn fascinating things about myself. And perhaps I can help Dr. Benson as well. From what people tell me he has problems of his own. You can tell your mother I'll be delighted to see him as soon as I am back."

"No, this is to be in place of Las Vegas."

"I'm sorry, that is not convenient."

"She's made an appointment for Friday."

"Perfect. I will simply fly away on Thursday. Encourage your mother to call the airline and check my reservation for the Saturday flight, which I shall keep. It is in the name of Martha Prescott. I will make one as Mrs. Robert Prescott for Thursday, and cancel the other when I get to the airport. Nothing could be simpler."

Martha was preoccupied with a hundred details, but her eye told her that Roberta was still far from reassured, or even convinced that she should go to Nevada at all.

"Young lady, while I am away for a few days, I will expect you to smile sweetly no matter what your mother says, which will infuriate her. You can always ring me if you need to. I will be at The Golden Fleece. It is a new hotel, and presumably, the last word. You needn't tell Lucille the name of the hotel. And now be off with you so I can lay out my clothes. I'm going to take my beaded Poiret gown. It is rather special and has a story of its own which I will tell you one day."

Early Thursday morning a vintage but highly polished motor car moved slowly down Elm Street to Martha Prescott's door. Mrs. Brimston waited for the driver to come up to the house for the bags. Martha appeared in her travelling costume, and greeted Mr. Barrett with, "Remember, not a word to anybody that you've taken me to the airport this morning."

"You can depend on me, Mrs. Prescott," he replied, believing his every word.

Unbeknownst to Martha, she could not, for later that same afternoon as he was taking Mrs. Brennan's bridge guests to their homes, one of the ladies ventured rather condescendingly, "I suppose you've had a quiet day, Mr. Barrett."

"Not so quiet," he said huffily. "Traffic to the airport is always tricky."

"That must cost a fortune these days. I don't know who can afford it," said another of the ladies.

Mr. Barrett struck back. "Mrs. Prescott didn't seem to mind."

"Oh, Martha!" chirped two of the ladies, with sly glances at the third. Lucille made no comment but she was boiling for she realized that Martha had outwitted her and was on her way to Las Vegas.

What had Dr. Benson called it? Sin City in the Setting Sun...

A Golden Fleecing

*A*loft, incumbent on the dusky air, Martha politely refused a glass of orange juice and asked for champagne. Thus fortified, she was ready for the prolonged luncheon service which she found more elaborate than appetizing. It helped pass the time, but it also provided the occupant of the aisle seat beside her with an opportunity to draw Martha into conversation.

"On your way to Vegas for business or pleasure, chérie?"

"Strictly business," replied Martha.

"Me, too."

He spoke so confidentially and warmly that no one, thought Martha, could take offense at an unexpected 'chérie.' And he had a pleasant voice even if he did not really sound like a businessman. As it would have been less than polite to turn and take a good look, she did not see that he appeared no more businesslike than he sounded, with a mottled silk scarf tucked into his open shirtfront. In fact, a discreet touch of the pencil gave a line to his eyebrows which nature had not foreseen, and there was a distinct hint of artificial color at his cheekbones.

"You had me fooled," he said. "I thought you were going out to invest your savings in the one-armed bandits."

Thus started a long monologue posing as a conversation, which lasted through several courses of plastic food and beyond the ice-cold brie and unripe pear. Martha soon realized he was a lonely person who needed to talk, and she used a technique which reflected years of experience at countless Sliepskill dinners: the Hm...the Yes...the knowing nod...which, unless you were asked a direct question (and you rarely were, by some undefined natural law) left you free to think your own thoughts. If caught you could always fall back on that helpful phrase, 'Now what do you really mean by that?' which invariably led to explanations and revelations. So, while her companion spoke, Martha was in Monte Carlo, in Paris, and even briefly back in Sliepskill, but never aware that a new confidant had revealed his life story to her: the tragedy of a family who never understood him. "My God, they are so square! But you understand. I can tell, just the way you say 'Yes.' And —"

And it was time to fasten their seat belts for landing.

"Chérie, I hope I'll see you in Vegas. Where are you staying?"

"The Golden Fleece."

"I don't believe it. We open there tomorrow night. You can take in the early show. The Fleece is real Vegas Haute. Here — take my card. I'm Jonny De Vine."

Minutes later the plane rolled to a stop and in no time a bearded young driver had swung Martha's bags into his gaily decorated taxi and asked, "Where to, Lady?"

"The Golden Fleece, please."

"No kiddin'. Well, you might as well start at the top."

"And drive slowly," Martha said, not at all pleased with his attitude. "I want to enjoy the scenery."

"There ain't none," he replied, "but I'll be glad to oblige."

Thereupon they sped off down the asphalt strip, hell-bent for civilization, Vegas style, which loomed in the distance. As they approached the edge of town where strings of buildings obscured everything else, the driver, with a touch of irony, asked, "Well, how did you like the countryside?"

"Simply beautiful," Martha said, "in a rather severe way, because nature is not profligate here. But I noticed wild-flowers in the distance, and cattle grazing in the greener spots, which means you have had spring rain. And those glorious mountains which will be casting long shadows when the sun is further along in its path."

"Hey, listen to that, will ya?" exclaimed the driver, not disrespectfully. "You some kinda nature nut?"

As there was no appropriate answer to the question, Martha did not offer one. By now they were in the city proper and she marveled at the excess of neon light (did it blink day and night?) which augmented the dazzling sunlight with a clash of garish colors so different from the muted tones of the desert. She shut her eyes until she heard the driver's voice again, saying, "This is it, lady. The Fleece, a world unto itself, like the sign says."

"As."

"Huh?"

Moments later, having consigned her baggage to a gladiator at the door, Martha entered the inner court of the hotel, designed to recall the atrium of a Roman villa. Beyond a reflecting pool was the Pompeian registration desk.

"Good afternoon, Madam," said the assistant manager on duty, somehow impressed that a well-groomed woman, wearing both hat and gloves, was signing the registration form. Being young and inexperienced he continued with, "We hope your stay with us will be a happy one. You have only to let us know if there is anything we can do to make you more comfortable."

He was to regret his words within the hour.

When Martha reached her room, shepherded by an elderly bell-boy in a Roman tunic which the hotel and his union had told him he must wear, she was relieved to discover that the classical motif had not been carried out upstairs. Here the decorator had settled for Vegas Baroque, and that kind of timeless furniture found only in hotels, doomed never to become antique and a constant reminder that its creators were not inhibited by either cost or taste. The bed was larger than any Martha had ever seen, draped with a purple and gold baldachin. A pottery leopard couchant rested at the foot of a chaise longue which was very longue. Staring malevolently at her from the far side of the room was a pottery monkey. On the gilded bombé commode was an enormous arrangement of artificial flowers. Martha discovered that the vase was screwed to the top of the commode and to remove it the entire piece of furniture would have to go, which was exactly what she had in mind.

Regretting that she had no Roman coin for the bell-boy, she gave him two dollar bills, one for carrying her bag, and the other out of sympathy for the costume he was obliged to wear.

"Will there be anything else, lady?"

"Yes, indeed," said Martha, "I would like the menagerie removed, and also those —" she pointed to the faux flora. "So I can take my hat off and relax."

This was a first for the bell-boy and he was no gladiator. "I'm sorry, lady, but I can't do anything about that."

"You heard the manager. 'If there is anything we can do...' Well, there is."

"I better call the desk," he said. "Here, you talk to him." Martha did.

"We would be glad to move you to another room, Madam, but the hotel is fully booked."

Martha recognized the excuse as one dear to the hearts of hotel managers, and seldom related to the availability of rooms.

"Just send someone to take away these animals, and some of the furniture, so I can breathe. Then I want you to fill my room with fresh flowers." Before he could object, she added the magic words: "I will see that the housekeeping personnel are amply rewarded for their trouble and you may charge the flowers to my account."

To Martha's satisfaction and the amazement of the bell-boy, the manager, caught in his own web, agreed to send someone at once, and in an hour's time the room had been transformed. The worst of the furniture was gone, the animals put in storage, and a great array of fragrant flowers made the room livable if not Martha's choice for ultimate retirement. Only then did she remove her hat and take off her gloves. It was not the Hotel de Paris, but it would do.

Suddenly tired, Martha lay back on the bed, closed her eyes and took a deep breath. An hour later, when she awoke, she was astonished to see herself reflected from the ceiling. Directly above her, discreetly masked by the draperies of the canopy, was a bed-size mirror.

"Now I wonder why in the world —"

In her surprise she had spoken aloud. Then, on reflection, she thought, No, Martha, wonder not...

After she had unpacked and settled as much as any God-fearing woman could settle in an ornate purple and gold Easter egg transformed into a garden, only then did Martha feel a first zephyr of insecurity. It had been so long since Monte and Las Vegas was different, there was no denying that. She had landed in a foreign if not hostile environment. Well, she would go downstairs on the morrow, when the casino opened, and just look. Meanwhile she would order a simple supper and enjoy a good night's rest.

Down in the kitchen regions, the man who had answered her call for room service exclaimed as he reread her order, "Now I've heard it all! Pedro, do you know what's going up to 1222? Not a lobster, not even a steak. Get this, Pedro. A pot of tea, okay, and one order of cream of wheat."

Forty-five minutes later Pedro rattled a service table along the hall to 1222. Once inside he presented the pot of hot water with tea bag attached, and the dish of cereal in its immense silver serving utensil, as if both were standard items of any Lucullan feast.

Martha, now en negligée, inquired, "Do you know at what time the casino opens?"

"In this hotel?" asked Pedro, amazed at the question. "It

opened when the hotel did, and it'll stay open till the place closes down. In Vegas it's day and night, night and day."

Then he managed an un-Gallic "Bon appetite," and was gone. Martha felt slightly better as she poured the weak tea. Tomorrow would be another day, and such an important one. She did not know then that she would always remember it as the longest day of her life.

After a fitful night and an ominous dream (she recalled only that a malevolent Lucille had been a part of it) Martha awoke more dispirited than ever. The momentum of preparing for her flight to the West (in both senses of the word) had buoyed her, but now she had to face the fact that, utterly alone, she was in Las Vegas to revive a part of her life which had long lain dormant. It was an unnerving thought. However, shortly before noon Martha was ready to go downstairs. Once on the ground floor she was astounded to see how many people were already in the gaming rooms. Her first thought was that the Salle Blanche at Monte was so much more beautiful, then she remembered this was no time to escape into the past, and set about her appointed task.

Quietly Martha took her place behind a man seated at a roulette table, his undivided attention devoted to the numbers and the wheel. It was still red and black, odd and even, but for Martha a croupier wore a tuxedo and said "Faites vos jeux, Messieurs," and then "Rien ne va plus," as the wheel spun. All that was missing here. The obsessive silence of these players, and the grim men in shirtsleeves who represented the bank...it all made for a disorienting scene.

'Oh, Robert,' she thought, 'I hope I haven't bitten off more than I can chew.'

Martha steeled herself and concentrated to such a degree that when the man in front of her rose to leave, his last chips having been gathered by the house, she hardly heard him say to her, "Don't mortgage the farm, lady, they'll take everything you've got." He was gone before she could assure him she did not have a farm. She left the table some minutes later telling herself there would no doubt be another class of player in the evening. But upstairs, with the door closed behind her, Martha again felt gnawing doubts.

However, that evening when the maid entered to turn down the bed, she exclaimed involuntarily, "My you *are* all dolled up!"

She found Martha taking a critical look at herself in the full-length mirror of her dressing room, resplendent in a beaded dress of heavy violet silk, sleeveless and low-waisted, to the knee on one side, dipping to midcalf on the other. Martha shimmered in the gown and from the silken band around her head there rose an aigrette, all grace and delicacy.

"Thank you, my dear," said Martha. "Monsieur Poiret told my Mother that good clothes are always in fashion, if you can still get into them, and luckily I can."

"Lord a' mercy, that gennelman was right, yes Ma'am."

"And now if you will kindly hand me my beaded bag, I will go on downstairs."

Temporarily restored in spirit because she looked right even if nothing around her did, Martha sailed out of her room and descended to the lobby where she was oblivious of all those who stopped in their tracks when she appeared.

One man who had caught sight of her as she left the elevator went directly to the receptionist on duty to make inquiries. As she saw none of this she was neither suspicious nor alarmed.

Martha bought five chips, each for a hundred dollars, representing her entire fortune, and found the table she was looking for. Again she stood silently behind one of the players for the obligatory period of watching and concentrating, and in a short time, when a place was free, she slid into it. She hesitated only a moment, and closed her eyes as if to banish doubt and lack of faith — for she felt abandoned and alone — then looked up, saw that the wheel was about to turn, and as she knew exactly where she should place her chips, started to push them forward. At that instant a camera flashed. Martha, startled, gasped with surprise as she caught sight of angry eyes staring at her from across the table — Lucille's. Involuntarily, Martha pushed her chips forward as the wheel spun.

It was all over quickly. Security personnel moved in to find and remove the culprit who had snapped the picture, and when the wheel slowed to a stop, Martha's chips were swept away by the croupier. In the crush and furor Martha rose and fled in full retreat. Calm was swiftly restored around the table so the game could continue as if nothing had happened. But something had happened, something too terrible for Martha to contemplate. She had failed, and she knew it as she disappeared into the elevator and arrived, defeated, in Room 1222. She sank into a chair, unnerved and disconsolate. So ended what was, as it turned out, only the beginning of Martha Prescott's longest day.

She was still sitting in the semi-darkness when she heard an insistent knock at her door. As this was gentle insistence she knew it was not Lucille, but she could not bring herself to move; not, that is, until she heard a familiar voice.

"Aunt Martha, open the door. Please."

"Bless you, child," exclaimed Martha as she admitted her niece.

During the next few minutes it all came pouring out: how Mr. Barrett's indiscretion had led Lucille to bring Roberta, and Dr. Benson as well, to Las Vegas to take Martha home.

"She wants to prove I am incompetent," said Martha, "and I have just done it for her. I am so ashamed. But when I looked up and saw Lucille my mind went blank. And that was the end of my adventure."

Roberta was not ready to admit defeat.

"Aunt Martha, until that moment, and that flashbulb, did you know what you were about?"

"Of course. Oh, I was rather shaky without Robert there behind me, but Prescott's Law is after all one of the foundation stones of mathematics —"

"Prescott's Law?"

"I've always planned to tell you about it one day. But I thought it could wait until we were in Monte. However —"

They settled down on the sofa and at once Martha's voice took on that special quality reserved for moments when she recalled her happy life with Robert.

"It was at the end of the war, shortly after the Potsdam Conference, when few people could travel to Europe. But Robert, who had done some hush-hush work in Washington — they knew he was a mathematical genius — was invited to a monetary conference at Menton. He wouldn't go without me, so I was allowed to accompany him. Among his colleagues we found friends from the prewar years — one of them was that Englishman with the lovely Russian wife, Lydia, who had danced with the Diaghilev ballet when she was younger. She introduced us to some of those romantic Russians who had settled in Monte Carlo after the first great war. But I'm getting ahead of myself. At the conference casual conversation after hours was very light-hearted. On one of those relaxed occasions, Robert's Turkish colleague — Nuri Bey was a favorite of mine — Nuri Bey said jokingly or perhaps not, 'Roberrrrr, my respect for you will turn to admiration when you turn your skill towards practical ends.'

"Robert always liked a challenge, and he asked, 'For example?'

"'Well,' said Nuri, 'for example, apply your principle and give us a way to break the bank at Monte Carlo. *That* would be applied mathematics.'

"There were cheers from everyone and it was obvious where the sympathies of the scientists lay. When we had all returned to our rooms that night Robert said, 'Nuri is right. And it bothers me that I didn't think of it myself.'

"'But neither of us is a gambler,' I reminded him.

"'That is why we,' said Robert, 'are particularly qualified to apply pure mathematics at the casino of the Grande Compagnie des Bains de Mer.'

"Well, no more was said about the matter until the conference was over. Then, on the last day, when the recommendations of the experts had been sent off to their ungrateful (as it turned out) governments, Robert asked me if I'd like to stay on for a few days.

"'Here, or down in Monte Carlo?' I asked, knowing the answer.

"'Lydia mentioned a comfortable pension near the casino,' he said. And that is how we happened to move into Madame Clairmont's pink bedroom. Robert went off each day to the casino — and thought, and calculated, and eventually experimented, all in his mind, of course. The following Thursday he came home with a happy smile and relaxed for the first time. He announced that Prescott's Law had been formulated and tested. He invited me to accompany him to the casino that evening to apply it.

"At nine o'clock we were dressed, and Madame Clairmont said 'O la la' as she waved us out the door with a warning that 'No-body wins at the ca-si-no.' We assured her that we never gambled but two hours later there was no one in Monte who would have believed that statement. Robert had applied the Law and revealed it as a triumph of applied mathematics. 'I wish Nuri Bey was here,' was all he said.

"Being Robert, he did not try to break the bank; neither of us would have approved that. I remember that at midnight, when we gave up our places at the table, an old countess came over and touched Robert for luck. She was ablaze with emeralds which she lost to that same wheel soon afterwards. I was so proud of Robert that night that I almost wept, and I believe the management did, too.

"The next morning we thanked Madame Clairmont for her hospitality, and took a taxi over to the Hotel de Paris which we could now afford. The suite we moved into, all pale

green and gold, was the one they gave us from then on whenever we went back to Monte. That was often, because once we
had begun to apply the Law we found so many good uses for
the money. I became just as adept at it as Robert was, and he
preferred in any case to stay home and read. After the management got to know me they didn't mind at all. The director
himself said, 'Chère Madame Prescott, you encourage others
to play in the hope they will match your truly extraordinary
luck.' I didn't even tell him that luck had nothing to do with
it. We kept our secret and I have never talked about it to anyone until today."

"Aunt Martha, you are a wonder of the Western World,"
said Roberta, hugging her.

"No, my dear, that was Robert, who left this world all too
soon. But Monte means happy memories. Not only of Robert.
Perhaps we will find some of those extraordinary Russian
exiles who were also our friends. They lived for the casino,
bless them, always hoping and believing that they would win
back everything they had lost. 'Butch' Romanoff, for example,
we didn't question him too closely about his name, but he was
a prince of a man and always called me his 'Madame Marthe.'

"So when Mr. Bramble brought his disconcerting news I
didn't really worry once I had thought it out. I knew I could
set things right with an evening here in the casino. And you
see what I have done. My money is gone and your mother will
presently knock on this door, with her doctor —"

"Mother doesn't know you are registered here—not yet.
I've been letting her check all the casinos, since we arrived."

"That does not solve our problem," said Martha, remembering how the croupier had swept her chips away.

"No," said Roberta, "But this does." She pressed six one-hundred-dollar bills into Martha's hand. "Not a word, please. I saved this for our trip and that is exactly what it is going to be used for."

Before Martha could respond there was another knock at the door: precise and authoritative this time, but still not threatening.

"Who is it?" Martha asked.

Another series of knocks was the only reply.

"Open it, Roberta," said her aunt. "We really have no choice even if it is Lucille's Dr. Benson."

Not knowing what awaited them, Roberta opened it wide. There in the doorway was an enormous basket of red roses, with a man behind them — or at least his legs and a voice.

"Madame Marthe, c'est vous? Vraiment?"

The flowers advanced into the room and Martha relaxed into a smile.

"I'd know that voice anywhere. Come out from behind those roses, Butch Romanoff."

A silver-haired gentleman, far from young yet somehow youthful, stepped around the basket and took Martha's outstretched hand in his, kissed it, and said:

"Oui, c'est vrai. When you came out of elevator I knew, but could not believe."

Whereupon they fell into each other's arms and a nimble Roberta caught Martha's aigrette before it floated to the floor.

"Butch," said Martha, "this is my dear Berte," using the French form of her name which she henceforth always preferred. "And you - in Las Vegas?"

"Is natural, no?"

Half an hour later, amid much laughter, explanations were done with and Butch was suddenly serious.

"Madame Marthe, we have work cut out. Night is young, but not so young."

"Oh, Butch, I think I've done enough for one day."

"Dear friend," said their Russian ally, "we descend on all casinos. You will forget Monte; tonight you think Vegas. And with your luck —"

She raised an admonitory finger.

"No lecture. If not luck, what you call it, and with it we create legend. Tomorrow we rest. Then is time to see others. Anatoly, Fédor —"

Martha was amazed. "Anatoly is here, too?"

"Is general manager. He brought us."

"And Fédor," she said to Berte, "was the best chef on the Riviera."

"Is good," said Butch, "tomorrow we are all together for brunchfest. Now we work. Are we ready?"

"Oh, yes, Butch. My spirits are soaring. I am not only ready, I am eager."

"I knew," said Butch to Berte.

Martha put the six hundred-dollar bills in her beaded bag, restored the aigrette on her headband, locked her arms around both her loved ones, and exclaimed, "If we are going to create a legend, we'd better get started."

That night was launched the Vegas legend of the Lady with the Feather in her Hair. According to the story, she appeared briefly at one casino after another, played a while, collected her winnings, and moved on. It was not true that she broke the bank, though later this became part of some of the tales. No, she seemed content with a bag full of money at each stop. And the feather in her hair never once wavered, nor did she cease smiling gently, just smiling, placing her bets, and raking in the chips.

A legend once born soon moves beyond control, so the line dividing fact from fiction eventually became blurred and even those who were not present found themselves adding details they remembered. It was certainly not true that her hair was bright red, nor that she wore dead white makeup with kohl around her eyes, nor that there was nothing in her beaded bag except thousand-dollar bills and a tiny pearl-handled revolver with notches in it. It was not even true that her fingers were encrusted with jewels or that her red-tinted nails were long and dangerously sharp. Nevertheless such details, added as embellishments, became traditional in Vegas until the last one to recognize Martha Prescott would have been Martha herself.

Even the casino managements were not above adding a few details of their own. It did their images good to have the world talking about the Feathered Lady who left with a shopping bag full of money. Had she come from outer space, and where did she disappear to, a rich woman? It was a picture calculated to encourage more visitors to try their own luck and leave some if not all their worldly goods behind. In every sense a golden fleecing.

The night of the legend, and Martha's longest day, finally ended after four the next morning, when she and her companions staggered back to the hotel exhausted but triumphant.

"My dears," said Martha, "I wouldn't want to do it again soon, but I loved every minute. Butch, our breakfast will have to be a very late one."

"At one o'clock in afternoon. Your suite."

"I just have a room."

"Will be suite. We take sitting room 1224."

"Berte, ask your mother and Dr. Benson to join us. I look forward to seeing them both, even if my motives are not noble."

"Now I see you to door, Madame Marthe. Then, all, we sleep."

"First," said Martha, "you will see me to the safe-deposit box of this hotel. We must —"

"Deposit the loot," volunteered Berte.

"—our dividends. In a safe place."

They were crossing the lobby when, like a sudden shower, a bevy of chattering young creatures in costume surrounded them. The sequined extravagance of their costumes identified them as part of the show which The Fleece boasted was the best in town.

"What an adorable getup!" exclaimed one, catching sight of Martha in her beaded gown.

Before Martha could say "Thank you" for the compliment, the most magnificently coifed of them all, resplendent in sparkling rhinestones, cried out, "Chérie, it's you!" and took both of Martha's hands. "We flew to Vegas together, and you promised to come to our opening. Where were you?"

"Working," she said, "but come and have brunch with us tomorrow—that is, today. If you're free."

"We'd adore it. I'll bring The Kids."

They all squealed and having ascertained time and place, were suddenly gone. The quiet was deafening.

Then, as Butch arranged the safe-deposit box, Martha said to Berte, "Tomorrow we will have to buy another suitcase. Otherwise we will never get back to Sliepskill with our loot—to use your word."

Martha slept soundly, the victor's rest. It was the insistent ringing of the telephone which finally aroused her.

"Aunt Martha, mother wants to speak to you."

It was hardly the conversation she would have chosen to begin her day, but Martha managed a cheerful "Good morning, Berte, come early and help put me together. Now let me have your mother."

Martha stole a glance up at the ceiling mirror and discovered that she had dropped off to sleep complete with headband and a now mortally crumpled aigrette

A familiar voice brought her back to Saturday morning.

"Martha, do I understand you are willing to see me, and Dr. Benson?" Lucille's tones were Alpine: lofty and icy.

"Why of course, and how nice that we should all be in Las Vegas together," she replied, impressed by her own duplicity. "At one o'clock."

An hour later, when Roberta had buttoned her up the back, Martha suggested they go in to the salon through the connecting door and wait for their guests. They entered a room now dominated by a large buffet table, where a man in a white chef's hat was inspecting the dishes.

"Fédor!" Martha exclaimed.

He beamed and kissed her hand. "Tell me if I have

remembered food you like."

It was only then that Martha and Berte noticed the full splendor of the table. There was a pearly mountain of caviar, and vast plateaux of smoked salmon, smetana, and all the other garnishes.

"And my blinis. Also quail eggs because this Vegas does not have plovers. For those very hungry, a coulibiac."

At that moment Butch Romanoff arrived with more roses, and announced, 'Manager General!" Anatoly, his face one enormous smile, stepped into the room, followed by a corps of waiters bearing wine coolers.

Anatoly spread wide his arms to greet an old friend.

"Berte, meet Anatoly, who took care of all his Russian compatriots in Monte. And me as well."

Roberta moved forward and extended her hand, which to her delight was not shaken but kissed.

Then Anatoly snapped his fingers and corks popped.

"Lanson Brut," he said, "which you and Monsieur Robert preferred."

At that precise moment, as if they had been waiting outside for the sound of the corks, Jonny De Vine and The Kids burst into the room.

"Hello, hello, you wonderful woman."

Martha realized he meant her, and she noted also that he had chosen to appear in mufti, if that was what it could be called: white flannels with a raspberry and cream striped jacket over a ruffled shirt.

"We didn't know if you needed more boys or girls, so the Kids decided on half and half," he added. They rivalled the buffet table for variety and color.

"Look at that foooood!" exclaimed a flapper with bee-stung lips. Everybody did, but there was a moment of hesitation as they stole glances at Anatoly. He was, after all, their general, too. Anatoly solved the problem instantly, saying, "It awaits your pleasure."

From then on good spirits and hilarity reigned and Martha momentarily forgot that two more guests were expected. She had just accepted a little mound of beluga on toast when she saw them in the doorway. Their presence was felt, and the room fell silent, except for a squeaky voice (which one of The Kids was it?) asking, "Hey, who are the No-no's in the door?"

"Dear Lucille," said Martha, "we have been waiting for you. Dr. Benson, I presume?" These words, à la Stanley to Dr. Livingstone, were addressed to an overweight, balding young man who stood beside Lucille, bewildered by what he saw.

There was another awkward silence, but Jonny De Vine ended it once and for all by raising his glass to Lucille and crying out, "Matron, don't send us back to our cells just yet!"

The laughter which followed started the gaiety off once again, and even Dr. Benson, ill-advisedly, smiled. Lucille, however, came right to the point.

"Martha, how do you intend to pay for all this?"

Anatoly stepped up to Lucille with the answer.

"Allow me to introduce myself, Madame. As the General manager of this hotel, I am your host. This little repast for her friends is the least we could offer as an *hommage à Madame Marthe*, who has honored The Golden Fleece by choosing to stop with us. Now, please — try some of the specialties of his kitchen which Fédor has prepared in Madame's honor. You will not be disappointed."

So the party resumed, with Lucille suspiciously accepting a blini with smetana and caviar. Before she realized she was eating fish eggs she had found out how delicious they could be.

Dr. Benson, seated on a sofa, precariously balancing a glass of Lanson Brut, was a center of attention for two of The Kids, one in basic black with pearls, the other in peach polyester. They had found their beau ideal and wanted him to know it, somewhat too effusively for a doctor unused to such attentions in Sliepskill. Lucille looked up from her blini and did not like what she saw. She cut across the room and rasped out to Dr. Benson's admirers, "Brazen creatures!" not realizing that they were brazen male creatures.

"You're just jealous," replied basic black.

Their pudgy hero was after all the youngest man in the room, and the polyester peach contented himself with running his fingers through the doctor's thinning hair. And, as flattery and Lanson Brut had taken their toll, Lucille got no support from the man whose fare she had paid to Las Vegas. In fact, he smiled happily as she turned away in disgust.

"A quail's egg, Madam?"

She stared at Fedor as if he had insulted her, and he retreated with the basket.

Lucille looked for Martha, determined to suggest that it was time to end the unseemly revelry, and saw her just disappearing into the bedroom with Butch Romanoff. For ignoble motives of her own Lucille decided to wait a few minutes before following them.

"Butch," said Martha sitting on the edge of her bed and motioning him into an armchair, "I want a quiet word with you because there may not be time later."

"But you will stay — week, month —"

"No, Berte and I have to go home tomorrow. However..." and she hesitated.

"Lecture, for own good?" he asked, grinning.

But Martha remained serious. "Butch, put your pride in your pocket just this once, and do me a great favor."

"For you, anything, but I am suspecting when I hear putting pride in pocket."

"Butch, let me help you, if only to please myself."

"Chère amie," he said. "Butch is happy man. I think you see. I save money now, in bank, like Americans. And for holiday, where do I go?"

"To Monte, of course."

"Where else? Two weeks, sometimes three. Depends on — my luck. Then I fly back to Vegas. Is happy life, admit it, at my Golden Fleece with Anatoly and Fedor."

Martha wiped away a tear. "I could do no better for you," she admitted.

"Madame Marthe, you understand. Is why I love you. We will not lose us."

"Never again."

He pressed her hand to his cheek, just as the door flew open.

"Lucille!" Martha exclaimed. "You have caught us in what they call flagrante!" And two of them laughed...

Back in the sitting room the buffet table was showing signs of wear and Anatoly spoke up: "Ladies and gentlemen — thank you all —"

Jonny and his Kids knew when a hint was a command and they kissed Martha good-bye, followed by the Russians. Lucille took Berte with her, saying pointedly at the door, "Martha, I will leave you with Dr. Benson."

Martha had a final word for Berte. "My dear, your mother will not want me to travel alone tomorrow in my condition, and she will be glad to save the fare, so I have taken a ticket for you."

Then Martha closed the door and turned to face Dr. Benson. He was still on the sofa, his look blank, his eyes glazed.

"Dear Dr. Benson, we are alone at last."

He stirred, started to rise, then fell back into the depths of the sofa, awash in Lanson Brut.

"Don't move," she said. "Why don't you stretch out and I will sit here, near you."

He relaxed into the pillows as Martha sat down in anticipation of her first session with a psychiatrist.

Finally, he said slowly, "We all need help sometimes."

"Indeed we do." So far so good.

A long silence followed before Dr. Benson took her by surprise with his words. "It is a terrible thing, Mrs. Prescott, to be unloved."

Was that how Lucille had described her?

"My mother," he went on, "is a carbohydrate tragedy. By the time I was ten she weighed 230 pounds and I was well on my way to join her. She is also a chocaholic. One of my first memories is waking up in the middle of the night when Mother came home from the movies and stuffed chocolate kisses into my mouth."

With an effort Martha held her peace.

"She made a chocolate cake that my father called The Coronary. It was delicious. And a pudding he named Cardiac Arrest. They were both delicious. By the time I was fifteen, I was ashamed to go to gym class. Do you know what they called me? My name is Wilber —"

"It is a nice, old-fashioned name."

"I was Big Wilma. When we moved to another town Dad dropped out of our lives. Mother compensated with more desserts, and me. I gained. She gained. We gained. The Korean War brought me back to 180 but after, in college, I started back up again. 190. Then 200, 220. My hair started to fall out. I was Baldy Benson at 25. Is it any wonder I can't get a girl to go out with me twice? I've tried all the diets. They work for a week, then it's my compulsion and my mother. She cooks for me now. She hasn't been out of the house in years." His final question was a cry from the heart. "Am I going to go on this way, alone, forever?"

Martha realized that an answer to the agonized question was required.

"Dear Dr. Benson, the situation is hopeless, but not serious."

He smiled weakly.

"And you start with a great advantage — you recognize your problem. With some encouragement you will find your way out of the dark tunnel. And if you will allow me, I'll be glad to help, and see that you lose weight and enjoy it."

What am I saying, thought Martha, but she knew she could do it. She might have to give the task to Mrs. Brimston, but why not.

"I believe you," he murmured. "I don't know why, but I do."

Her smile was almost beatific, and for better or worse, Wilbur Benson was now at peace, his breathing deep and regular.

"I think we both deserve a nap," said Martha tactfully. "I will wake you in an hour's time."

Dr. Benson did not answer. He had already drifted off. As Martha lay down, in her bedroom, she wondered what Lucille was paying Dr. Benson for his services, and what she should charge for hers.

Two hours later when Martha again opened her eyes she was aware that she was at the very least a deficient hostess. Dr. Benson might well have already departed in silence. Cautiously she opened the door. Wilbur Benson, MD., was sitting upright on the sofa, stretching his arms. Their eyes met and each broke into a happy smile.

"I had a wonderful dream," he said, "if it was a dream."

"It was a reality. I'll arrange for you to take all your meals under the supervision of my Mrs. Brimston when I go abroad. She will love the challenge. But your mother is going to dislike me, I'm afraid."

"I hope so," he said. "You know what I mean."

A knock at the door took them by surprise. They both hoped it was not Lucille. Martha opened the door and admitted a waiter from room service.

"Compliments of the chef, lady, he told me to tell you it was a light supper just in case."

"I'm hungry," said Dr. Benson, "but that is no way to begin a diet."

"Don't call it that. The word sounds so punitive." Then she lifted the covers off the dishes. "Pilmeni!" she exclaimed. "I'll show you how to eat them with hot mustard and smetana. And a Stroganoff — with dill, the way I like it."

The waiter hesitated in the door. "Say, ain't you the lady what ordered mush the other night?"

"Yes, and it was delicious."

"You sure got the other end of the stick this time."

He left and Martha led Dr. Benson to the table.

"You pour the wine," she said, "then everything in moderation — but everything."

Early the next morning Berte came to collect Martha. "Dr. Benson sent you these," she said. "For your album, he said."

Berte handed her two polaroid pictures. In the first Martha saw her startled self, full of alarm and misgiving, as snapped by Lucille at the roulette table.

"The evidence," she admitted.

"The other one is better," Berte said.

Martha held it up. The photo had immortalized a row of slot machines, and poised to insert a quarter into the second one-armed bandit from the left was - seen in profile - a furtive Lucille Prescott.

"She doesn't know he took it."

"Berte, a Christian woman would destroy that print, but I am going to keep it, just as Dr. Benson proposes, for my album."

She took a last look around the room.

"I'll never forget The Golden Fleece. Do you suppose we can get away now with just a quiet farewell to Butch and the others?"

It was not to be. When they emerged at the lobby level, they found Lucille and Dr. Benson staring incredulously at the reception committee awaiting Martha.

Anatoly stepped forward. "Chère Madame, you break our hearts —"

Martha was truly moved. "Anatoly, you will never lose me again. The visit was perfection even if I did not have time to visit the Hoover Dam, which I believe is nearby."

"If we had known," said Butch, "we would have brought it to you."

Martha enveloped him in an embrace, then kissed Anatoly and turned to Fédor.

"Madame Marthe," he said, "Piroschki for your journey to save you from airplane food."

"Bless you," said Martha as his sous-chef started down the hall toward the hotel limousine with a hamper.

As the procession moved to the entrance, with Lucille and Dr. Benson walking behind, the entire population of the lobby paused to watch and wonder.

"She's got to be mighty rich," a woman whispered to her husband.

"Then why can't she afford a cheerful maid," he answered, pointing to Lucille.

At the door and in the limousine with Berte, Martha waved farewell as they drove off, while Anatoly signaled to the doorman who blew his whistle and summoned a cab into which Dr. Benson followed a defeated Lucille.

In the air, with the vision of Las Vegas fast fading as they climbed to cruising altitude, Martha turned to Berte at her side.

"Did you remember to call Mr. Bramble?"

"Oh, yes, and I have the impression he's meeting the plane in an armored car."

"There is one thing on my conscience," admitted Martha. "In the rush of getting away to Las Vegas I never did return Herbert's phone call. He was upset about something, and I'm afraid it has to do with him and Minty."

Herbert and Araminta. That was a saga in itself, and the complications arising therefrom were soon to plummet Martha into what she remembered as her Double Disaster.

The Farm's the Thing

*H*erbert van Riyk Detweiler was the first of his family to be born in Sliepskill-on-Hudson, as it was then called. Previous generations on his mother's side had all entered the world at the van Riyk manor house further up the river, and the Detweilers had lived in New York City since a Hessian ancestor settled there during the post-Revolutionary period of forgive, forget and forge ahead. After his birth Herbert's mother never returned to the city, determined not to resume what had become a life of conjugal discontent. The arrangement suited his father, who seldom came to Sliepskill except for occasional Sunday lunches which coincided with the signing of legal documents.

As a schoolboy, Herbert grew to dread those Sundays, sitting with silent or battling parents who fed on roast beef and resentments. Nature carried off the boy's robust father when Herbert was eleven, but quixotically granted him his delicate mother until he was past forty. The consensus was that Mr. Detweiler, found with his eyes open in the reading room of his club, was well out of it. His companion of many years, a Miss Delaney, did not appear at the funeral. Soon after his death, as women do, Mrs. Detweiler began to speak well of her late husband, who had amassed a sizable fortune from the combination of his own resources and her considerable inheritance. "Detweiler," she admitted, "had a good head on his shoulders."

Unlike his son, she might have added. Herbert grew up in a hothouse atmosphere, a shy boy and later a reticent young man. It was almost inevitable that he should have found in Araminta van Horne his blessed damosel from the day he first saw her at Miss Wickett's dancing class when they were both thirteen.

Araminta, known to an affectionate family as Minty, was also shy although she grew up in a household full of love and bustle. Perhaps because her parents expected too much of her, delicate Minty retreated early into a private world she shared with no one, not even the sister she adored, Martha, to whom everything came so easily.

Minty was blessed with limitless enthusiasm when she was not cursed with it, for discretion was not native to her. Their father had once said in exasperation, "Don't talk to me about enthusiasm. I'll settle for common sense and the girl doesn't have any!" He spoke with reference to Minty's ill-fated Picnics for Pickaninnies Fund, designed to give certain deprived children a summer's day in the sun. Even then, however, the title Minty had chosen (Don't you think it's a catchy name, Papa?" "Yes, like a cold.") aroused the ire of the very families who were to be helped. "Minty," said her mother gently, "you must realize that people no longer like being given baskets of fruit at Christmas!" No," bellowed her father, "they want to buy their own and throw it at you." Minty did not understand. There had been no question of baskets of fruit, and it was July, not December.

Long before Martha met and married Robert Prescott, everyone had assumed that Herbert and Minty would eventually marry. The adverb faded with the passing years, and they never had. It was only Martha who realized better than the principals themselves that they were still meant for one another. Moreover, Martha was ready to help with a push in the right direction whenever it might be appropriate.

Half an hour after Martha was back in Elm Street, light years removed from Las Vegas, she was on the phone to Herbert.

"It's me," she said, preferring usage to grammar, "guilty of gross neglect, but I hope you will suspend sentence and invite me to lunch."

"Come tomorrow. I'll ask Mrs. Halston to make us something special."

Her conscience assuaged, Martha was ready to concentrate on the trip abroad, and on maneuvering Mrs. Brimston into providing some very special meals for Dr. Benson during her absence. She was counting on the animosity which had smoldered for years between her Mrs. Brimston and Herbert's Mrs. Halston to solve that problem. Both were dragon ladies and never did the twain peaceably meet. That same evening Martha opened the subject, choosing her words with great care.

"Mrs. Brimston, I have promised that nice Dr. Benson to supervise his diet until he finds his natural weight, which is considerably less than what he now carries about. I had thought you might enjoy having him to meals here while I am abroad. However, I suppose I might mention the matter to Mr. Detweiler..."

Mrs. Brimston did not hesitate. "If you want Dr. Benson to have a properly prepared diet he is not going to find it in Mr. Detweiler's kitchen. I'm sure we can manage."

That night Martha slept deeply and well, not yet aware of the Himalayan challenge that Herbert Detweiler was going to put before her on the following day.

Herbert was at his ease, as he always was with Martha, but she was still curious when they had finished their floating islands.

"And now," said Martha over coffee, "tell me what it is, Herbert."

"How shall I put it?"

While he searched for the right words Martha remembered what her father had once said about Herbert's inability to make a simple, direct statement. "The boy's as bad as Henry James, except that he doesn't produce those endless novels."

Martha took Herbert by the horns. "I hope it is good news."

"It's about your sister."

The words were significant. If Herbert had something good to say, it was "about Minty." If he was worried and sympathetic, it was "about Araminta." But if he referred to her as "your sister" he was annoyed.

Overcoming his Jamesian tendencies, he went on with neither hem nor haw.

"You might say it is Elmira Crisp's fault," he began, referring to Sliepskill's maiden librarian who shared a dominant trait with Minty — no common sense. "Elmira dragged Minty and me into the city last month to the Sunday matinee of what she called a Very Off Off Broadway play."

"Minty has always loved the theatre," said Martha weakly, thinking of the Lunts.

"Elmira's nephew wrote the play, and I assure you it was not only, forgive the word, pornographic, but excruciatingly dull as well. Minty, I regret to say, came back enthusiastic, and you know what that means."

Martha did know. Minty had returned from the city with a cause.

"Araminta intends to have the Historical Society present the young man's latest play. The author has told her it would be a sensation in Sliepskill and I daresay he is right. Unfortunately, the Society owns the only suitable auditorium in town and, in view of her annual contribution, they are likely to accept the suggestion."

"I'll think of something," said Martha, knowing that she must, but wondering what it would be. She rose to go.

"Before you leave, I would appreciate your advice on another matter, Martha."

"Of course," she said,, deciding that the luncheon had been good but perhaps not worth the price.

A moment later Herbert handed Martha a manuscript letter written in a bold hand and addressed To The Editor of the Times.

"Cyrus van Riyk was my great-grandfather," he explained. "I found this letter and the papers attached to it while going through a desk which was sent to Sliepskill when Mother sold the Fifth Avenue house. Nobody had ever bothered to unlock the drawer. The letter was written by great-grandfather on September 10, 1865, but never mailed. He died a week later, after choking on a fish bone. He was, I believe, very fond of fish."

Martha read what Mr. van Riyk had written:

Dear Sir,

The Greensward Plan as envisioned by my friend Frederick Law Olmsted has had my support from its beginnings since it is intended to create in our city an oasis in which gentlemen and their ladies may breathe salubrious air and admire Nature's prodigality.

I am alarmed, however, at the city's plan for this central park. If it is to be thrown open to 'all the people,' with the attendant misuses which can be anticipated, I for one will certainly not complete the deed of gift of my land, and assist an ill-advised administration to create an amusement ground for footpads, ne'er-do-wells, and the motley crowds which plague our city. I am, Sir, yours etc...

Martha smiled. "Mr. van Riyk should see Central Park today."

"Quite so. No doubt he would find his predictions more than fulfilled. However, I feel the matter should be set right."

"Set right?"

"The unsigned deed of transfer is still attached to the letter." He handed it to Martha.

"But his land stretches from 71st Street north to 73rd," she exclaimed.

"Indeed. Those acres are still part of the van Riyk farm as the land was never transferred."

"But the city —"

"The city was a bureaucracy even then. Somehow the matter was overlooked."

For the first time since she had sat down after luncheon to talk, Martha was animated and happy.

"Herbert," she said, "bless dear Cyrus van Riyk," although she did not add, for dying at exactly at the right time.

"I want to take appropriate action."

"You must, Herbert, and I will help you."

"I knew you would, Martha."

"This is an important cause, and we will support you wholeheartedly."

"We?"

"Minty and I."

"Hm. I thought perhaps a letter to the mayor."

Martha, elated, had already left Herbert far behind. "May I borrow your file, and that map of Central Park?"

"Of course. The van Riyk property includes the Bethesda Fountain, and extends almost to the statue of Horace Greeley. It also includes a monument to city employees who fell in war, a monument, I might add, now in a disgraceful state of disrepair."

"Capital!"

"Eh?"

"And," she continued, aglow with delight, "does your land cut right across the East Drive?"

"Oh, yes."

"Perfect." Martha was exultant. "First I will stop at the library and have a word with Elmira Crisp. I think I can count on her help as far as her nephew's play is concerned."

"The Historical Society won't cancel their meeting. They take themselves very seriously."

"We don't want them to cancel, Herbert. Can you think of a better forum for our cause? After all, the Society is devoted to historic preservation."

Alarm spread over Herbert Detweiler's face; panic was not far behind.

"Dear Herbert," Martha reassured him, "we must pick up the gauntlet thrown down by your great-grandfather, and save Central Park from the ravages of 'all the people.' And it will divert Minty into something really important."

"Ah, yes, perhaps it will."

On the steps she paused. "I trust you haven't mentioned this to anyone else."

He stopped short and Martha had a terrible premonition.

"Not Alexandra Faucitt!" She waited to hear any other name.

"As a matter of fact, Alexandra called to ask me to dine next week while I was studying these papers and the subject did come up."

"I doubt if she grasped their significance," said Martha, allowing herself an observation she wanted to believe.

Ten years before when Alexandra Faucitt settled in Sliepskill she had been the object of much conjecture, as it was not immediately apparent why this Anglo-American widow had bought a large house and gone about establishing herself in a community where she had no previous ties.

The only child of a wealthy American mother and a well-born English army officer, Alexandra India Kimberley — named for the Queen and for the subcontinent — was born in Ootacamund and spent her childhood in the rarefied atmosphere of the Raj, summers in Ooty, winters in Madras. At the proper time her by-then-widowed mother chose Switzerland chez Mlle Brueggli-LeFabre where Alexandra might share classes with a Braganza princess who, in the end did not appear. Two Egyptian princesses — the one giggly, the other perennially serious — were acceptable substitutes. Eventually, mother and daughter settled in London where their money was helpful in establishing them even if the Kimberley connections were not.

India (there were too many Alexandras about) was soon swept off her feet by an attractive but indigent Northcountryman, Algie Faucitt, known to his friends as Tap. Her sensible mother forbade the match so they eloped to Paris and were sublimely happy for a fortnight, until India discovered that her mother had been right about Faucitt's motive in marrying her. She returned to Kensington in tears and a solicitor was engaged. The matter was resolved when Tap Faucitt, who drank to excess, was instantly killed in a motor accident involving a large lorry and his new Aston Martin sports car. The ladies were relieved only to have to pay for the funeral and the car.

The mother went home at the threat of war, but her daughter lived happily in London until the blitz drove her into volunteer Red Cross work near one of the American air bases in the Home Counties. There an heroic lieutenant colonel from Texas beguiled her and promised marriage at the war's end when he had arranged his divorce. In 1945 he went back to Texas and almost at once rediscovered the pleasures of home on the range. The rest was silence.

Alexandra (again — the India was dropped with independence) sought consolation on a trip to Egypt to visit her school friends in a large but unsanitary palace. Later, not happy in postwar England and now bereft of her mother, who had perished of natural causes (and an erroneous diagnosis by her doctors), Alexandra was ready for new challenges, and she chose America where she would be at least partially an exotic flower. It was only after she had rejected Princeton, Connecticut and the entire Delaware Valley that she came upon the house in Sliepskill, sent for her Daimler and her butler, and moved in. At mid-life, she was a vigorous and still attractive woman whose insecurities were few, if distinct, and outmatched by her securities, which were gilt-edged. She made a place for herself in the small community she had chosen as her seat with little difficulty as she had engaged an excellent cook. The majority of eligible Sliepskillians saw Alexandra frequently, and the few whose interests were wider — including Martha Prescott — accepted and returned an occasional invitation. If Martha was reticent, and she was, her feelings were no doubt fortified by the latent realization that Alexandra Kimberley-Faucitt (as she now styled herself) was a potential rival to Minty for the attentions of Herbert Detweiler, the town's perennially eligible bachelor.

This, then, was the only other living soul to whom Herbert had confided that he was the owner of some eighteen acres of Central Park.

Martha's first stop was at the library.

"Elmira," she said, "I've heard about your nephew and his plays."

"Oh, yes," exclaimed Elmira, immensely pleased.

"Are you certain you are not contemplating something which might actually hinder his career?"

"Oh, no," said Elmira, less brightly.

"If he is as talented as you and Minty know him to be, then his plays surely belong in New York, for all to see. You remember the Drama Society's King Lear here last year..."

"It's true," confessed Elmira, who had chosen the play and the actors, "Octavia Glover just wasn't Lear, even with her deep voice."

"Well, if a modest contribution to a new production of your nephew's latest play in the city would be welcome, I'll gladly send a cheque — and I believe Minty will want to."

"Oh, yes," said Elmira, reviving.

"The Historical Society, devoted as they may be, are not really equipped to advance the cause of the drama."

"Oh, no, I mean oh, yes," Elmira burst out, in gratitude or relief, she was not sure which.

Her mission accomplished, Martha turned to go.

"Lucifer Crisp!" Elmira called out after her.

"I beg your pardon?"

It's his nome de plume. He was christened Franklin Delano Crisp but for the cheque —"

"I'll make it out to Lucifer," said Martha. "And send it in care of you."

By evening Martha had won over the officers of the Historical Society without having given them much information, a feat in itself. And after a few well-placed calls to the city she had been assured that The Times as well as the tabloids would be represented at the meeting of the Society. Shortly before midnight, Martha reread the statement she had put together for Minty to present on Herbert's behalf at the meeting. Cadenzas were appropriate at the opera but improvisation had no place before the Historical Society. Martha felt that even Herbert's great-grandfather would have approved her carefully chosen words and stage directions, to wit:

"Cyrus van Riyk, whose great-grandson is Herbert van Riyk Detweiler (*here a gracious gesture to Herbert seated at your left*) was a friend of Frederick Law Olmsted and he supported Olmsted's proposal for a central park in New York City. He offered to contribute eighteen acres of the van Riyk farm for the park, land which faced Fifth Avenue between 71st and 73rd streets. However, apprehensive of the use that politicians of the day planned to make of this site, and perhaps in anticipation of what might happen to the park in a hundred years, Cyrus van Riyk reconsidered (*pause here*) and did not make his gift. Therefore (*pause here*) Herbert van Riyk is today the owner of eighteen acres of what we know as Central Park (*pause for this to sink in*). What action should he now take? Should he simply sign the land over to the city? Or should Mr. Detweiler, as a concerned citizen, keep his land until the city and its citizens demonstrate that they are worthy of it? Mr. Detweiler has chosen the Historical Society of Sliepskill as a forum through which to solve his dilemma. He invites you to advise him. Only then will he announce his decision.

Yes, that would do nicely. Minty's words might not have the impact of those which Martin Luther nailed to the door of the church in Wittenberg, but they were not intended to be incendiary. They were simply to invite reflection and lead to reform.

As Martha had anticipated, Herbert authorized the statement and was pleased to know that Araminta would present it for him. That left only Minty to be dealt with.

"Of course I will, Martha it is an important cause."

"Commit the text to memory, Minty, so you can speak directly into the hearts of everyone, including the press. Do you think you can manage that in forty-eight hours?"

"Oh, yes."

In truth, Minty could, in that length of time, manage a great deal more.

Berte looked in on her aunt later that morning with a list of questions and one nagging doubt.

"Aunt Martha, I thought—"

"Take very little. It will be such fun buying things there. We are leaving on Thursday week. I want to be here for the meeting of the Historical Society this Friday. And I gather Minty has accepted an invitation for herself and me to dine with Alexandra Faucitt on the following Wednesday, so we'll be off the next morning." She guessed that Herbert would by then have every reason to be mightily pleased with Minty, which would annoy Alexandra and send Martha to Europe at her ease.

"Aunt Martha —"

This time she was not interrupted but she stopped of her own accord.

"What is it, my dear?" Martha spoke gently, anticipating a cloud on the horizon.

"Are you sure you want me hanging about your neck like a millstone all summer?"

Martha was relieved. "Oh, my dear, if you only knew how much I look forward to having you draped around my neck like a string of pearls. You and I are going to spend the next little time of our lives together and I only hope you will enjoy it as much as I intend to. Now, off with you, before we both break into tears. I must get to the phone. Mr. Bramble is waiting for instructions on the transfer of some of our money to Monte."

At that exact moment Minty was also on the telephone. Her voice aquiver with enthusiasm, she said, "Lucifer, now listen to me —"

And he did.

Meanwhile up at the Dower House, Alexandra Kimberley-Faucitt had chosen a menu for her most important dinner of the season. The guests of honor were to be a Latin American couple. Dona Inez was an old acquaintance from London (Alexandra remembered her as dark-eyed and fragile), now married to a South American industrialist of great wealth. Her brother-in-law, described as a distinguished diplomat without portfolio, would be with them. That was why she had asked Colonel Pomfrey, who had once been attached to an American embassy somewhere down there; at last his reminiscences might be appropriate. Along with Dr. Cutler and his wife (she was almost totally deaf but not demanding about it) they would be ten at table. She would remember to seat Araminta between Dr. Cutler and the Colonel, and perhaps let Martha have the ambassador. Herbert would be on her own left, as far away from Araminta as possible.

Only Herbert spend a tranquil Thursday, reading a late-nineteenth-century assessment of Olmsted's Greensward Plan. Towards evening Martha rang to ask if he planned to call for Minty in the morning.

"Nothing I'd rather have done," was his honest reply, "but Alexandra has asked me to escort her to the meeting. She is coming around for me in the Daimler."

"I suppose you can't disappoint her," murmured Martha, wishing he would decide to. Then she added, "I'm so proud of Minty. She has taken your cause to her heart."

As indeed Minty had. Was it mere coincidence that three falling stars were seen in the clear and moonless sky over Sliepskill that night, and that a two-headed calf was born in Mr. Patchin's barn just before dawn on the fatal Friday?

Bon Appétit!

*T*he half dozen newspapermen who found themselves on the 8:47 out of Grand Central that Friday morning were sullen and skeptical.

"The Sliepskill Historical Society!" snorted the man from the News. "Rip van Winkle presiding?"

"The order came from the front office," said his colleague on The Times, resigned.

"George Washington Slept There," said the Post. "Maybe they found out who with."

The others dozed, except the man from the Journal who had lost the toss and was delegated to waken them all when the train slid to its brief stop in the Sliepskill station. He had also been to Sliepskill once before, and remembered Gogarty's Tavern, across from the station, open every day from 8 a.m.

The ladies of the Historical Society met in the hall which Agnes Barstow had given them when her passion for amateur theatricals dimmed. Some Sliepskillians, notably those not nominated to the Society, considered the setting an appropriate one for the Society's meetings. On this Friday morning all the available chairs were filled except those down front and roped off — to the left marked PRESS, and on the center aisle, right, reserved for Herbert Detweiler and Party. His arrival just before ten caused heads to turn. Alexandra, whose Achilles' heel was her folie de grandeur, swept down the aisle on Herbert's arm, nodding regally as they proceeded to their seats in Row A. Martha, who had left Minty at the stage door with an encouraging squeeze of the hand, took a seat in the second row, behind the press seats, from which she could survey the scene. Herbert sat down and concentrated on the basket of early forsythia on stage, hoping the meeting would begin promptly so he could get back to his books. Alexandra gazed about, her lorgnon aloft. She was now aware of the reason for the meeting and wondered that Herbert had chosen Araminta van Horne as his spokeswoman when she, if pressed, might have spoken for him. Then she caught sight of Martha, and understood at once the how and the why. She nodded and smiled. Martha did the same.

A low buzz, as in a contented hive, filled the hall until promptly at three minutes past the hour, and despite the fact that the seats marked PRESS were still unfilled, Mae Plunkett appeared from stage right and crossed to the lectern. The ripple of polite applause died as she looked up and over her glasses.

"Good morning, ladies —" She got no further because the press arrived, noisily, having commandeered two taxis in front of Gogarty's Tavern minutes before.

A sea of fruit, flowers and feathers came alive as the well-hatted ladies turned to stare. The gentlemen of the press, somewhat taken aback at the sight of all these American Gothic faces crowned with American Rococo headgear, slithered down the aisle to the seats pointed out to them. Fruit, flowers and feathers resumed their original positions, and Mrs. Plunkett went on, somewhat frostily. "As this is an extraordinary meeting of the Society, Gladys Peake will not present her paper on Hammered Dulcimers of the Hudson Valley."

At this announcement there were stirrings among the pressmen. Could this be for real? Was it in fact heartland America speaking, the man from the Journal wondered, himself a refugee from Council Bluffs.

Mrs. Plunkett concluded with, "I will therefore turn the meeting over to Araminta van Horne, who will tell us all exactly why we are here," and retreated to the only chair on stage.

The sole photographer among the press knew that all self-respecting members of his profession (and he did not consider the description contradictory) would instinctively have avoided this excursion into the sticks. He hated himself for being there and muttered an obscenity at this point, covering it with a cough. Martha noticed that none of the reporters had made the effort to take out a pad or pencil.

After a long moment Mrs. Plunkett cleared her throat and looked off right. She was about to rise again when a cloud of green and mottled chiffon, wisps of which trailed and flew in all directions, wafted onto the stage. It headed for the lectern to a gasp of astonishment from the members of the Society, and then applause, which was taken up by almost everyone present, including the press. Only Martha contained herself, for now she knew what Minty had been wearing under her long cloth coat. Her wraithlike sister was a moving, swirling vision of Mother Nature as The Greensward Girl, which could only have been conjured up in conspiracy with Nellie Bloch, Sliepskill's sole surviving seamstress. That worthy widow must have taken a costume worn by Minty at some long forgotten pageant and responded to a request to "Do it à la Botticelli-environmental." On those terms Nellie had succeeded.

Already nervous, and flustered by this response, Minty reached for the gavel and with a mighty blow sought to restore order. Instead she drove that blunt instrument through the lectern where it remained impaled, tomahawk-like. Her excess energy was greeted with more applause and a "Bravo" from the photographer, who snapped a shot of the startled, wild-eyed Minty which was later captioned "Mother Nature Out of Control" and brought a good price from a city editor. For, as the bulb flashed, Minty was suddenly panic struck. Martha knew the look and tried to attract Minty's attention. Fortunately their eyes met. Martha mouthed the words "READ THE STATEMENT" and to her relief Minty took up her sheaf of papers. Ignoring the buried gavel, Minty raised an admonitory hand. The room fell silent and expectant. Herbert closed his eyes. Alexandra smirked. Martha prayed. And Minty read, but in a monotone which told Martha that her sister was still in a state of shock.

"Cyrus van Riyk whose great-grandson is Herbert van Riyk here a gracious gesture to Herbert seated at your left was a friend of Frederick Law Olmsted," she droned.

Dear God, she was reading the stage directions too. Martha could only hope the message would overcome the medium.

"— and he supported Omsted's proposal for a central park in New York City. He offered to contribute eighteen acres of the van Riyk farm for the park, land which faced Fifth Avenue between 71st and 73rd Streets however —"

Minty paused, as her words were starting to take effect despite the presentation, then she went on, omitting much of the detail but capturing the explosive essence.

"In anticipation of what would happen to the park in a hundred years, Cyrus van Riyk reconsidered pause here and did not make his gift and today Herbert another gesture finds himself the owner of eighteen acres of Central Park pause for this to sink in —"

Minty took a deep breath then responded to the man from The Times, who shouted, "You mean somebody actually owns eighteen acres of Central Park — today?"

"Yes," exclaimed Minty, speaking now ex tempore and from her heart, "that is exactly what I mean. Eighteen acres which have been allowed to wither and become a dumping ground for an ungrateful and destructive citizenry."

There was a smattering of applause from the ladies. More important, pads and pencils had appeared in the front row. At last the press realized why they were in Sliepskill.

Martha, with her lizard bag shielding her face to disguise the source of her words, spoke out distinctly and urgently, "Miss van Horne, READ your text."

Minty had now regained control of herself and she did so skipping, however, directly to the seven most important words: "What action should Mr. Detweiler now take?"

"You tell us!" shouted the press. "Is he going to take possession?"

The question might have been ironic, but everybody wanted to know the answer. Minty did not disappoint them. She threw her papers high in the air and cried out, "Yes, of course, what other choice does he have?"

More questions followed, obscured by the buzzings and murmurings of the ladies, whose sea of hats had once again come alive. Minty raised her voice and plunged ahead to the increasing alarm of Herbert Detweiler and the consternation of Martha who heard unequivocal and unauthorized statements and saw them being taken down by frantic pens and pencils as the camera flashed.

"New York does not deserve its park, and henceforth you —" These words were aimed directly at the press who suddenly became for Minty the entire undeserving citizenry of the megalopolis. "— you will have to pay for the privilege of entering at least eighteen acres of it. There will be a fence, and a gate. Admission will be charged —" Minty was improving on the notes she had prepared, which read, "Admission might even be charged."

Becoming lyrical as she went on, she cried, "And once inside this magic acreage you will find a park as it was dreamed of by Olmsted and Cyrus van Riyk, a green place of quiet beauty, safe paths, calm walks, placid waterways, of statues not vandalized, trees not wounded unto death, green lawns and meadows untrampled. Paradise Regained!"

The pressmen were now on their feet. The fruit, flowers and feathers behind them were a maelstrom of motion, the ladies alive with amazement, conjecture and disbelief. Mrs. Plunkett could not restore order because her gavel was too firmly embedded and Minty, now thoroughly enjoying herself, was not to be stopped.

"A rally is planned," she announced, "on Monday at twelve noon." Martha bit her lip in chagrin.

"We will march peacefully from Fifth Avenue at 72nd Street to the Bethesda Terrace and there meet our friends who will have marched from the West Side. At the head of our column will be Herbert van Riyk Detweiler himself."

Herbert blanched and did not hesitate when Alexandra said, "Quick. The car is outside. Now, before they realize who you are."

They fled none too soon, because at this point Minty made the delayed gracious gesture. But Herbert was safely up the aisle and the press unable to follow through the forest of ladies who sought to offer him their congratulations. He escaped, but Minty did not, nor was she in any mood to be saved.

"Join us," she cried, "and bring green boughs. Birnam Wood will march to Bethesda Terrace in the name of Ecology!"

The meeting was never properly adjourned because suddenly all the lights in the hall went out. It was pitch black for only a few instants but when the light was restored Minty was nowhere to be seen. Martha Prescott was also missing.

As Mrs. Plunkett struggled with her immobilized gavel, the press ran for their waiting taxis. One reporter reached over and scooped up a sheet of paper that Minty had discarded, hoping it might clarify a few points. Were these nuts really planning to burn wood at the Bethesda Terrace, and what wood? Bernie's? Who was he?

Twenty minutes later the newsmen were on the train en route back to Manhattan, and the primary diversion of their journey was provided by the sheet of paper caught on the run, which contained a list of "Steps We Might Consider:"

No radios.

No motor traffic.

No pets except on leash.

No food vendors.

No bicyclists.

No children except with their nannies.

No carriages.

No pigeon feeding.

No drinking.

Then, written at the bottom of the page were the positive thoughts: only the trees, the greensward, the water, the paths, the peace, the quiet.

The man who read it aloud said, "This text could be dynamite." He then carefully creased the paper, tore off the top, then the bottom, and held up the remaining fragment. "Now it is dynamite."

Gone was Steps We Might Consider. All that remained were the prohibitions and the curtailments of individual liberty, the stuff real news is made of.

They all instantly understood.

Martha's first words to her sister, back in Elm Street with the door safely locked behind them, were: "Minty do you realize, even remotely, what you have let Herbert in for?"

"Oh, yes," exclaimed her unrepentant sibling. "Herbert will never again have such a chance to present his point of view."

Martha fervently hoped not.

"It will be a peaceful march of concerned citizens holding aloft green branches that symbolize renewal. Herbert will understand. You can convince him."

"No," said Martha firmly, "this is your doing and you are going to convince him, if anybody can. We had better go over at once, before his phone starts to ring."

"I knew we could count on you, Martha."

"We?"

"We concerned citizens of God's green world," she replied, sensing that this was no time to introduce the name of Lucifer Crisp.

"He's lying down," said Mrs. Halston when they arrived.

I am sure he is, thought Martha, with cold packs on his head. But Herbert had heard the bell and he appeared at the top of the stairs.

"Minty insisted that we come right over," said Martha.

Moments later in the library, Martha was eloquent in defense of Minty's motives, which she assured Herbert were golden. As for the reporters, well, the press were not paid to report good news, it was controversy they thrived on and they had sniffed it here. But if it all contributed to the cause of conservation...

"What do you have to say, Araminta?"

Herbert had not called her Minty, but at least he had not asked Martha, "What does your sister have to say?"

Minty then plunged in, carried aloft by the passion of her convictions.

"Oh, Herbert, you must give the rally your blessing and

lead it. Have you gone into the city and seen your part of the park?" He had. "Then you know why I wept when I went there and saw those scarred and wounded trees. And the monument on your knoll which is a rotting flagpole flying no banner, mounted on a pedestal defaced by graffiti." Minty's eyes glistened with tears. "We must stem the tide of wanton destruction. Today the park is only beautiful when snow covers its ugliness. Herbert, on Monday we must all walk behind you, and then stand in silent prayer before we disperse —"

"Why not on Sunday when there would be less traffic?"

He did not reject the idea outright. Herbert was trying.

"Because we want people to stop. To stop and think."

Then she was silent, quite overcome. After a moment Herbert spoke again.

"Alexandra is of the same opinion," he said. "She has offered to drive me into the city in the Daimler."

Martha's relief at Herbert's tacit approval was somewhat reduced by the introduction of Alexandra Kimberley-Faucitt's name. It would have been replaced by alarm had she guessed that in Lower Manhattan Lucifer Crisp had called a meeting of his most trusted cohorts to get it all together for Monday noon in the park. To please that old canary up the Hudson where his aunt lived. This time she was really singing. Like there was an extra handful of hemp in her birdseed.

Meanwhile, at the Dower House, sipping a glass of amontillado before luncheon, Alexandra permitted herself a tiny smile as she recalled the old adage: give her enough rope...

The rains came on Saturday, the kind which fill reservoirs, and persisted through the weekend. Monday dawned drizzly and dank, and Martha was filled with foreboding before they even left Sliepskill. The weekend headlines had been as ominous as they were slanted. "Man Seeks to Hold C.P. for Ransom." "Says He Owns the Park." "Poltroon or Buffoon?" Even the Times carried a misleading article which confused the issue. "Elitist Says Park Not For Public" was its caption. Elitist meant, Martha knew, that Herbert lived on Elm Street and did not send Mrs. Halston to market with food stamps. Had they deliberately misunderstood that it was he who wanted to save the park for the people?

Only Herbert, who had declined to answer his telephone all weekend, remained serene, confident that the rally would clarify everything. Minty, he understood, had produced a large banner and found two local schoolboys willing to carry it at the head of the procession. "Save The Park For The People" it proclaimed. That should make it crystal clear where he stood.

But the ambiguity of the press accounts and the perfidy of network television coverage made it easy for confusion to spread. One network had broadcast an interview taped in Spanish Harlem, wherein its intrepid reporter began by asking passersby: "How do you feel about an Anglo who threatens to keep you out of Central Park unless you pay him?" As a result on Monday the roadway from Fifth Avenue to the Bethesda Terrace was lined with an unruly crowd negatively disposed towards the very people who espoused the cause of the park; nor were matters helped by the weather which had thinned the ranks of the Sliepskill contingent. Moreover, Alexandra insisted that she and Herbert, as well as Martha and Minty, who had accompanied them, should remain inside the car.

"Conway will drive us at the head of the procession, behind the banner," she said.

The impression was hardly that of the champions of a green park for the people. It seemed to imply for the right people, which had in fact been old Cyrus van Riyk's original idea. There were catcalls as the car rolled slowly toward the Terrace, the two boys in front of it struggling to keep the banner aloft in a rising wind. Several vegetables, and an egg which trailed its golden yolk down the window of the Daimler to the chagrin of the chauffeur, were cast at the symbol of a privileged way of life abhorrent to those who could not afford it.

Minty was only restrained from marching because she knew Herbert would not join her. Martha hoped for a natural catastrophe, say 6.9 on the Richter Scale. Alexandra simply smiled.

Just before the procession reached the Terrace things took a turn for the worse. Many of those lining the road had fallen in behind the few faithful Sliepskillians, shouting outrageous epithets to the delight of the television cameramen. The horns of taxis and other cars trapped in the park blared loud and insistent; the wail of police sirens was added to the cacophony. Then, suddenly, the friends of the good green earth saw their peaceful rally transformed into a melee reminiscent of the French Revolution, with themselves in the roles of beleaguered aristos.

The Daimler was within fifty feet of its destination, where a group recruited from Sliepskill's Garden Club waved green boughs in greeting, when there appeared, approaching from the West Side according to the master plan which Minty had not mentioned to Martha, Lucifer Crisp and his company of hangers-on. They walked and swayed in various stages of dress and undress, some happy, some belligerent, many of them stoned. Not having found green boughs in the Village they had settled for barren branches torn from dormant trees in the park. Brandishing the results of their vandalism, they had become a Paris mob of the 1790s. The banner which preceded them, to proclaim a text identical with the one Minty had provided, had somehow come out "Save The Park From These People."

The stage was set. A meeting of what was to have been two phalanxes of the same army quickly became a confrontation of opposing forces. Skirmishes broke out with war whoops, and in the heat of battle no one stopped to think what he was doing to whom. Fists hit out, rocks flew, and sticks were brandished. Both banners hit the mud. New York's Finest, assigned to the emergency, did what they could but it was impossible to expect anybody to be selective. Relentless, the television cameras ground away for the six o'clock news. Herbert simply closed his eyes. Alexandra had the presence of mind to call out to Conway, who had snapped all four doors into lock. "Home, Conway. Home."

He accelerated, scattering Lucifer's troops, and was soon clear of the crowd, left behind in pitched battle. The police moved in and sorted out the legs and arms where they could. As is often the case when emotion replaces reason, many of those swinging had hit and bloodied their own allies.

As the Daimler sped towards Sliepskill, Alexandra broke the silence with a single pejorative comment. "I knew something like this would happen."

Indeed, thought Martha, then why did you encourage it? But she knew the answer.

Minty wept. Herbert stared straight ahead, grim.

Tuesday morning, just as Martha finished reading a report of the rally which compared Herman (sic) Detweiler to a nineteenth-century robber baron, Minty rang.

"Martha, I can't possibly go to Alexandra's dinner tomorrow."

Martha's reaction was immediate and unequivocal. "We cannot give Alexandra that satisfaction. I will call for you just before eight."

"Oh, dear."

"Minty, you had the courage of your convictions yesterday; have the courage of mine tomorrow."

More important, Martha knew that if a reconciliation had not been achieved between Minty and Herbert before she boarded the plane for Paris on Friday, the rift might be permanent. This could not be tolerated between two people who were meant for each other, especially with Alexandra waiting to leap into the breach.

"By the way, Minty," she continued, "I understand from Herbert that all those taken into custody yesterday were released with the exception of Lucifer Crisp, who insisted on spending the night in jail. Herbert has spoken with the mayor and has sent him the deed of gift. His Honor was good enough to say that perhaps the city had been taught a lesson."

"You see!" Minty's spirits rose at once.

"However, I suggest that you not bring the subject up tomorrow evening. Just be your gentle, charming self."

Minty had every intention of following Martha's wise advice. It was not her fault that she failed and launched the second of that week's disasters.

The elegance of her table was as important to Alexandra Kimberley-Faucitt as the quality of what was served. Her dinners were black tie, because one had to maintain standards, and what a pity it was that Dr. Cutler did not have gaiters. Moreover, she permitted no dawdling over drinks, and had dinner announced thirty minutes after the arrival of her guests. On this occasion she had taken the precaution of sending Conway into the city to collect her South American guests of honor, remembering that Latins did not necessarily consider it polite to arrive on, or even near, an appointed time.

Wednesday evening Alexandra, in black velvet and her pearls, came down at ten before eight to distribute the place cards. She noted with satisfaction that Araminta van Horne would hardly be able to communicate with Herbert, who was safely on her own left.

Shortly after eight the entire party was assembled in the drawing room and conversation, abetted by alcohol, flourished on all topics except the one on everybody's mind (the South Americans excepted as they had not read the Times). Alexandra would not have recognized Dona Inez. Her once fragile friend had broadened into an ample matron whose dark eyes followed her husband ceaselessly around the room. Alexandra understood why from the moment he kissed, and squeezed, her own hand. But she also noted happily that Herbert was exceedingly reserved in greeting Minty, and she determined to invite him to the Dower House more often.

Then a sudden primal instinct told her that this was not going to be just another dinner party. The idea flashed into her mind during the brief silence which followed a loud remark by Dr. Cutler in response to his wife's "What did he say?" The he who said was Colonel Pomfrey, commenting that, because of world conditions, the position of missionaries in Asia and Africa had become precarious and "downright dangerous to those good souls." Trying to be succinct, Dr. Cutler had boomed to his wife, "The Colonel is defending the missionary position, my dear."

As the company resumed polite chatter, and Minty joined the Cutlers to listen to one of Colonel Pomfrey's oft-repeated stories, Martha found herself deep in a conversation of which she understood very little. Not only was the diplomatic English of the ambassador-sans-portfolio heavily accented, but she was keeping a keen eye on Herbert who had not responded when Minty sought his attention. Then the Colonel came over and said to Martha's companion, "I understand, Sir, that conditions in your country are unsettled."

"Dear man," replied the diplomat, "soon we will enjoy a revolution."

"Bad as that, eh? I remember when I was down that way —"

Mercifully he was cut off before he could tell that one again, as the ambassador preferred talking to listening.

"Of course we oppress our people," he said, "but the present regime...they make them work, the worst kind of oppression."

"Oh? Hm." The Colonel, not sure how he felt about that analysis, chose to move back to the Cutlers.

"So, dear lady," continued the ambassador to Martha, "I

will soon be a man without country, and without visible means to support. I must discover a rich wife. I am told America is full with them."

Did she detect a questioning glint in his eye?

"Our hostess, for example," he continued.

Yes, he was fishing.

At that moment Martha saw Herbert turn away as Minty joined him and Dr. Cutler, and she was mightily tempted to point out Minty to the ambassador as a woman infinitely richer than Alexandra. It would not be entirely untrue, as Alexandra's income could never match the riches of Minty's enthusiasm. And if a distinguished diplomat were to pay her court for an evening, might that not rekindle Herbert's flagging interest? Martha succumbed to the temptation and whispered the incendiary words into the ambassadorial ear. His eyes lighted up and he saw quite another Minty, infinitely more appealing to him than the woman he had hardly noticed when they were introduced.

Martha moved on, having caught desperation in the eye of the industrialist brother, abandoned to Mrs. Cutler's monologue on spring bulbs. Before she had exchanged more than a few pleasantries with Senor Munoz y Martin, Dona Inez joined them, her eyes narrowed and focused on her husband as if to say, "I am here, I am watching."

Martha was glad to retreat because she recalled from the chart in the hall that she was to be seated next to the ambassador at dinner and what a pity, when it might have been Minty, who would then be sitting directly opposite Herbert. To switch the cards one would need no more than a few seconds, undisturbed, in the dining room...

Precisely at eight-thirty, as the company sat down to dinner, Alexandra's alert eye caught Minty being helped into her seat at the ambassador's right.

"Araminta, my dear, I believe that is Martha's place," she said in a honeyed tone.

"Oh, no," exclaimed the innocent of the two sisters, "it reads quite clearly Miss van Horne," and she waved the card to show that she was right.

"But of course," said the ambassador, "and I am charmed," which he was.

Martha returned Alexandra's piercing glance by lowering her eyes and then complimenting Dr. Cutler on the Church Fair to which she had contributed her Egyptian cake less than a fortnight, but a lifetime, ago.

"What did you say, Mr. Ambassador?" Minty asked, honestly not understanding what her ardent dinner partner had just murmured, softly and seductively into her ear.

"My dear, you must call me Luis, and I have only said you are a ravishing female, quite beyond resistance."

Minty dipped a spoon into her soup with a blush.

Don Luis, emboldened by the whisky he had consumed before dinner, the sherry in the soup, and having caught sight of the Montrachet which was being poured to accompany the oysters en croute, pressed his suit. Araminta protested a lavish compliment in tones loud enough to be heard around the table.

"Your Excellency!"

A tiny silence fell upon the company as Minty continued lamely, "Is the winter in your country severe?

He recovered with aplomb. "We have no winter, dear

lady, only eternal spring," he said as the others turned back to their partners in relief. Then Don Luis added, sotto voce, "It beats eternal in our hearts, like hope."

Minty felt distinctly uneasy. If only Dr. Cutler would rescue her, but he was deep in conversation with Martha. And his wife, on the ambassador's left, was still rambling on to Senor Munoz y Martin about her preference for late-blooming perennials. Minty was as isolated with the ambassador at a table of ten as if they were alone in a cave together.

Don Luis was a man of action when the situation required it. As general conversation engulfed the remainder of the company he leaned towards Minty's ear as if to bite it, and in a fervent whisper declared himself irrevocably.

"My dear, I am smit by your attraction. I find you nonresistant." Then before she could even correct his usage, he leapt. "I would like nothing more than to mount you."

As it dawned on Minty what he meant, her eyes opened wide in alarm. Still her reaction might have been nothing more than horrific disbelief had not her fiery admirer, ablaze now with the heat of his ardor, chosen to make clear his meaning by taking her hand in his, safely concealed under the damask cloth, and pressing it firmly between his legs.

Her reaction was instinctive and immediate. She screamed and rose precipitately from her place just as Dr. Cutler on her right was helping himself to the oysters en croute. The serving dish flew into the air and Minty started to collapse - until she realized that the arms she was falling into were the willing ones of Don Luis, at which she screamed again and tried to free herself. Herbert was up and around the table in time to catch her as she fainted dead away.

"Into the library, Herbert," exclaimed Martha, thinking only that Minty should be quickly removed before she revived and screamed again, for whatever reason.

Herbert got her through the door and Alexandra was left to reassemble her dinner party with the oysters intended for half her guests on the floor. Senor Munoz y Martin, knowing his brother, concentrated on avoiding his wife's eyes, which were glaring in his direction.

In the next room Herbert had just put his hand on Minty's brow to see if she was feverish when she opened her eyes and became conscious of another manly hand, at which she became completely hysterical. That brought the entire company to the door, led by Don Luis who winked at Herbert as if to say, "I could have warned you, mon vieux."

"Minty, stop it!" Martha said sharply, and she shook her.

Minty was suddenly silent. Then she said in a voice hardly audible, "Martha, take me home."

"I'll bring my car around," said Colonel Pomfrey.

So it was that only seven sat down to enjoy what remained of the dinner. By the time the Colonel returned, the South Americans had remembered an early morning appointment the next day and Dona Inez, her eyes blazing, was not speaking to her brother-in-law. Herbert excused himself with a headache and there were only the Cutlers to be driven around the corner. Within minutes after everyone had said good night Alexandra went upstairs fuming and took a sleeping pill.

The next morning Martha woke with the comforting thought that this was to be her last day in Sliepskill for months to come. Roberta stopped in early.

"Berte, will you arrange flowers to be sent to Alexandra Faucitt in my name and Minty's. They had better be the most expensive ones available."

"Was it a special dinner?"

"Very."

Later, when she had finished packing, Martha called Florian to say good-bye, choosing a time when she could leave greetings for Lucille who would be out playing bridge. She did not take dinner that evening with Dr. Benson, who was enjoying steamed vegetables at her table, but she slipped in to ask a favor.

"Dr. Benson," she said, "I have been thinking about that cake your mother used to make. The Coronary? If you will write out the recipe I would like to add it to my book alongside my Egyptian cake."

He gave her his promise and felt a surge of carefree complacency because the thought of that caloric masterpiece no longer tempted him in the least.

Martha also went to see Minty, who was not yet herself.

"I want to tell you why it happened, Martha, but I simply can't." Then she did, at which Martha concealed a smile that Minty would not have understood.

"And now you are deserting me," Minty added, as if she were the last intact Sabine woman.

"Minty, you are surrounded by friends. And you have Herbert."

"Do I?" Minty asked plaintively.

Martha did not say so, but she thought Minty did. She had gone round to say au revoir to Herbert that afternoon, not planning to mention the rally or the dinner. He had raised both subjects himself.

"Martha, I realize Minty intended to help with the park, and last night —"

"Last night?"

"I had the impression that the ambassador was forcing his attentions on Minty. I was seated directly across the table, as you may recall." She did recall. "Alexandra should have known better than to seat them together."

Martha's response was not completely candid.

"Yes," she said, "it was thoughtless."

Early Friday morning Mr. Barrett was again en route to the airport. Martha turned to Berte as they left the sleeping town behind them. "You don't know what it means to me to get away and back into the real world after all these Sliepskill years," she said. "I can hardly wait."

"Nor can I," answered her niece, starry eyes. "Oh!" she exclaimed, remembering, "Dr. Benson asked me to give you this."

She handed Martha an envelope on which was written: The Coronary.

"Dear me, I didn't mean I wanted to take the recipe abroad. We aren't likely to be baking this summer."

"One never knows," replied Roberta gaily, coming closer to the truth than she realized.

Noblesse Obliged

*T*hey sat on their balcony after breakfast at peace with the world. Berte was lost in the sight of the serene blue sea. Martha was happy simply to be in Monte Carlo again. A crisp knock announced the post, and Berte returned to Martha with two letters.

"The answer to yours," she announced.

"Shall we see first what Avril has to say?" replied her aunt, "if I can decipher it without a Rosetta stone." She opened an envelope postmarked Le Barre en Ouche, scanned the letter with narrowed eyes, then smiled and said, "Listen to this: 'Dear One, when you hear from the Principe he will express his regret that he cannot receive you at the Castellino. He wrote me the same thing in January. How can we find out what is wrong? By the way, we are in for a sticky summer here. New neighbors at the Chateau. Appalling. Love and so forth.'"

Martha put the letter aside. "And now the Principe. I'm sure she is wrong."

Berte, who had already met Avril de Dinde briefly in

Paris, wondered if Mme la duchesse might not have correctly predicted the contents of the second letter. She had recognized her at once as a truly remarkable woman, perceptive, demanding, yet infinitely kind, in fact a match for Martha, which explained why they were friends.

Martha looked up from the second letter, puzzled. "That is exactly what he says. He cannot invite us to the Castellino at this time. The letter is full of affection and no information." Then she perked up. "Well, mysteries exist to be solved, especially when they concern old friends. We will leave for Sicily as soon as we can get ourselves together. Would you enjoy that?"

"Yes, but —"

"No 'buts.' We will write the Principe and tell him we are arriving in Taormina on, say, the seventeenth, and that we will stop with the Signora Clementina at the Hotel Timeo. Since he will certainly not permit us to stay in the town he will call the Signora and cancel our reservation, and take us out to the Castellino. You will like the Principe, Berte."

Berte wondered if he would like his old friend for pointedly ignoring his clearly stated regrets.

"And we have been lazy enough for one summer," said Martha.

"Lazy? We arrived here one week ago!"

"Shall we put pen to paper?"

They took the night train from Monte Carlo to Rome and directly on the Naples where they paused for a day at the Excelsior. Martha wrote letters home while Berte went out to Herculaneum.

"I'll not go with you," had been Martha's decision,

"because I don't traipse and I do not intend to trudge. You will have a fascinating glimpse into another world, but do not buy anything. No matter what it is supposed to be, it won't be."

Perhaps for that reason Berte returned at the end of a long day with two Roman coins which her guide, he assured her, had found in the ruins and which, according to Martha, lacked only the imprint of the factory in Naples.

"How much did you pay him?"

"It was a bargain." Berte declined to say any more, except that she was starved.

Merrily they went along to dine.

Their flight to Catania the next day was brief, and shortly thereafter they were seated in a hired car en route to Taormina. Etna simmered on their left, and what had once been called the African Sea shimmered on their right. The driver was inordinately proud of his country and long before they started the steep ascent up to Taormina he had surfeited them with the story of Sicily — named for the Sikeli, who had sent the Sikani packing, then had come the Greeks, the Saracens, the Normans, the Spanish, the Austrians, the French —

"And yet, Signora, Signorina, we are still Siciliani, and always will be."

"Amen," breathed Martha, inaudible to the front seat, as they caught sight of the venerable Hotel Timeo defiantly clinging to the hillside below the ruins of the Greek theatre.

"And now you will see," said Martha to Berte. "The Principe will be waiting with his driver to take us to the Castellino."

They were shown into the garden where tea was laid and

presently Signora Clementina joined them to greet her old friend La Signora Marta.

"Alas," she said, "the Principe has rearranged. He expects you to go with him to the Castellino."

But he's not here, thought Berte.

"Drink your tea and he will appear, surely," said the Signora as if in answer.

When no Principe had arrived by five, Martha was uneasy. Then from behind them they heard a soft, breathless voice.

"Signora —"

Martha turned and broke into a smile of relief.

"Marco!" she exclaimed, and told Berte, "He is the best driver in Sicily."

Marco bowed, then spoke almost in a whisper.

"Signora, do not tell the Principe I have kept you to wait. Let it be thought, per favore, that the driver from Catania was late.

"If you wish it, Marco," she said because she trusted him.

"Grazie, Signora." Then he adopted a more official tone. "The Principe waits you at the Castellino. We go?"

They went, speeding along the narrow roads towards Monte Venere. Finally, after Mola, Martha pointed out the Castellino on the slopes of Monte Zirotto. It crowned a verdant rise, gleaming in the late afternoon sun, its crenelated tower softened by vines which reached for the sky; thick walls and deep windows gave a promise of cool depths within. For Berte, as they drove into the courtyard, it was as if she were entering a fairy-tale world.

The great oak doors swung open and a kindly, aristocratic

eminence advanced with open arms to greet Martha and to kiss the hand of her niece.

"We kept you waiting. I am sorry and ashamed." It was too late for Martha to interpolate the agreed upon excuse as the Principe turned a stern gaze on the hapless Marco. "Signora Clementina telephoned."

Marco hesitated an instant then uttered the single word "Rocco," almost as if he were afraid to say the name. An angry shadow passed over the Principe's face before he turned back to his guests.

They met for drinks in the paved court which had once been a place of contemplation for the religious community in residence with the Principe's family. A fountain on the open side splashed water over steps leading down to formal gardens.

The Principe made no mention of his letter but almost as soon as they were seated he said, "An old friend of yours has asked permission to say Hello."

Then, emerging from the shadows bearing a platter of prosciutto wrapped around figs, the Principe's cook and household oracle appeared.

"Silvia!" exclaimed Martha and presented her to Berte.

La Zingara, for she was in fact part gypsy and not from the Principe's village, bowed deeply and smiled broadly. Martha made a mental note to seek her out at an appropriate moment, for a few well-chosen words — and questions.

When they were alone again, Martha said, "But I have not seen Michele."

"Michele is no longer with me," the Principe answered, waiting a moment before adding, "he is not well."

"Michele," Martha explained to Berte, "is the most nearly perfect of all major domos. I cannot imagine the Castellino without him."

Nor can I, the Principe's eyes told her.

"Now there is Rocco. You will see him tomorrow."

Although he spoke in a pointedly off hand manner, Martha sensed that Michele's replacement would prove to be a far cry from his predecessor. The very name Rocco sounded hard on the Principe's tongue.

Then after the sky behind Etna had faded in the lingering sunset they went in to supper, which was served by Marco. Martha was pleased with the Principe's particular attentions to Berte but she was taken by surprise when he turned the conversation abruptly from flora to the future.

"Berte," he said solemnly, "I want you to remember this visit with pleasure as it may be the first and last time I can welcome you here. I am leaving the Castellino to live in Rome."

Martha was astonished. He had never liked Rome.

"Or perhaps even Milano; at least both are closer to your headquarters in Monte."

She knew he detested Milano. He was after all a Sicilian.

He smiled wickedly. "Berte, observe the face of your aunt. See the consternation there. Yet she shows admirable restraint — she asks no questions. But noblesse must be obliged and I will not tease. Dear friends, the Castellino is to be sold."

To Berte the announcement was disappointing; to Martha it was unbelievable.

"I was not able to meet you this afternoon because a gentleman from Torino, with his wife, was appointed to come.

They did not appear but they will take lunch with us tomorrow. We are negotiating. You ask yourself why, chère Marthe. Believe me, it is necessary."

Martha knew the Principe was a proud man. If the fate of so many great landowners had now befallen him — declining revenues and increasing costs — he would not wish to dwell on it, even with her. Moreover, she realized that a diversionary tactic was called for or she would break into tears.

"We intend to enjoy every minute of our visit, and I think you should now tell Berte about St. Silentius."

He laughed. "With great pleasure. He is the only saint in our family."

After midnight Berte stood in her window, too stimulated to sleep and gazing onto a countryside drenched in the white light of a three-quarter moon. She was tempted to waken her aunt and exclaim that if the Principe were looking for a Principessa she would say Yes without hesitation. It was the story of St. Silentius which had won her over completely and hopelessly.

They had taken their coffee in the garden, and there the Principe told his tale.

"Silentius and his twin, Hilarius, were younger sons, many generations ago, both aptly named. Hilarius was a lively child, the favorite of everyone, which is perhaps why God took him to Himself at an early age. Silentius became melancholy as well as silent after his brother's death. He was also clumsy and prone to every accident which might befall him. If anyone tripped and fell into a well, or toppled off a window ledge, it was Silentius, who suffered silently. One day the

Church claimed him, and he became Fra Silentius in our own cloister, beloved by all — or almost all. A few made fun of him, but many brought their children to be blessed by him, at which they invariably stopped crying and were — people said — cured of their ailments. As a skilled gardener he was asked to bless new plantings, and it was said that the fruits which had his benediction were the sweetest of all. That compensated for the candlesticks dented when he dropped them, and even for the chipped baptismal font.

"Silentius' end came quickly and all too predictably. It was his turn to cut bread in the refectory. He took a sharp knife and started to cut the slices towards himself as simple people still do. He lost control and ran himself through. It was a sad evening, although one of his more cynical brothers in God was heard to mutter, in the degenerate vernacular of the time, 'Sara n' cen',' which might be freely translated as 'There goes our supper.'

"That should have been the end of Silentius but it was the hilarious beginning."

Martha, her eyes closed, listened contentedly to a story she knew well. Berte, with eyes wide open, did not know whether to laugh or cry.

"A legend grew up about the holy Fra Silentius, and became intertwined with a second story, that of the Saracens who once plagued our coast. No matter that the time of the Saracen danger was long past when Silentius lived, it was alive in the memory of the people. Today, mothers still threaten unruly children with 'The Saraceni will take you.'

"Saraceni - sara n' cen'. Do you see how two tales met and became one? It was probably our own villagers who first spoke of the day when Silentius had saved the Castellino from the Saraceni. They told the story to their children, and in the end it sounded like this:

"Silentius, while at prayer, caught sight of the Saracens approaching to attack. He ran to sound the alarm, but the Saraceni saw him, too, and one of them overtook him and fell upon Silentius with his sword. What happened next is not clear, even for a legend, but later the body of that Saracen was also found, some say struck down by God, others say dead by his own weapon which Silentius turned upon him before he expired. For Silentius' shout had been so loud and so uncharacteristic that the startled community had time to prepare an ambush and to cut down the marauders to a man. The final tableau is the most loving of all: The Saracens dying, the holy Silentius mortally wounded beside them, his serenity such that the infidels were converted and all died in the odor of sanctity.

"Centuries later the Church sponsored the cause of the Holy Silentius as saint and martyr, but the real miracle is that Silentius' memory inspires the faithful to this day. He is the guardian of our house. So it is a happy story."

"And there is a footnote which completes the tale," Martha said.

"Your aunt means the painting. In the 17th century the head of my family was host to an extraordinary man. I speak of Caravaggio. Scandal forced him to leave Rome, and then Malta, after which he fled to Sicily. While on his way to Messina he stopped at the Castellino, heard the story of St. Silentius, and stayed to paint the masterpiece which has remained the least known of Caravaggio's major works because we have never shown it publicly."

Martha waited, but the Principe did not offer to take Berte into the chapel where the painting hung in a place of honor.

"Rinaldo," she said, using his given name for the first time since their arrival, "may Berte not see St. Silentius?"

"Alas, no," he said. "the painting is no longer at the Castellino."

"It is being restored?" she asked, meaning one thing.

"It will be restored," answered the Principe, meaning something else.

With their breakfast trays came a message that the Principe would be busy that morning with the Torinesi. He hoped they would enjoy the gardens or the library, and would expect them for drinks before luncheon. Berte decided in favor of the gardens, and Martha, with an ulterior motive, planned to seek out her friend Silvia in the kitchen.

At the entrance to the maze she had seen from her window, Berte stopped to read an inscription carved on a stone marker: Lasciate ogni *dolore* voi ch'entrate. Leaving sorrow behind was indeed better than Dante's admonition to abandon hope! She entered a path leading between the high green walls, not realizing that in the center of the maze she would find a clue — to deepen the mystery — if not to solve it.

After only a few wrong turns, Berte found herself in a clearing at the heart of the maze.

"Marco!" she exclaimed. "You are a gardener, too?" For there he was, pruning shears in hand, sitting dejectedly on the stone bench, obviously not having left his *dolore* behind.

"Signorina, I am not a gardener, not a waiter; I am the

Principe's chauffeur. But I am punished because I kept you waiting yesterday. It was not my fault. Rocco told me to drive him to his village. When Rocco commands, we obey. Others who did not are no longer here. Such as the gardener." Then Marco regretted his frank words. "Signorina, I have said nothing. We have not met ourselves."

He disappeared into the green of the maze and left her alone at the heart of the puzzle.

Martha found Silvia rolling out fresh pasta and after the obligatory exchange of compliments she observed pointedly, "I am sorry to hear Michele became ill and had to leave the Castellino."

Silvia's answer was explosive. "Signora Marta, Michele is not sick. He has disappeared. I have spoken with his mother in the village. She will say nothing. Some say he is dead, but I know he is not." She was, after all, La Zingara. "He was frightened and he is gone. Then Rocco came."

"Rocco?"

"Yes, Signora, and it is true, the Principe will leave the Castellino."

"Tell me about Rocco."

Silvia's eyes flashed, but before she could respond one of the kitchen maids entered from the herb garden. She, too, was a new face to Martha, a new face in a household where there had never been any change. Instantly Silvia's tone changed and she spoke formally.

"The Signora flatters me. The seasoning of the fish last evening was made from fresh salvia and chopped rosemary. The same which Rosa here, who is the cousin of our Rocco and from his village, has just brought from the garden. Show the Signora, Rosa."

Martha understood.

"Thank you," she said. "I will remember the combination."

"Thank you, Signora," Silvia replied with the hint of a smile as she returned to her rolling pin and Martha left the kitchen.

Martha and Berte went down to the terrace shortly after one thirty, where the Principe introduced the Crespi-Dolcis. Irreverent but concealing it (she hoped) Berte had only one thought as she said "Hello." She wondered if the Italians had an equivalent of Jack Sprat and his wife. For the Dottore was tall and very thin, while his wife, who obviously ate no lean, was short and infinitely wider. Martha, for her part, saw only two pairs of hard eyes: penetrating, curious. She was more interested in a man who stood in the background waiting to know what they would drink.

Rocco was swarthy, deferential, and attentive. Above all, as she was to discover, he betrayed nothing of what he thought or felt. The perfect servant? That depended on the character of the man, of which she knew nothing — as yet.

"Punt e Mes?" asked the Principe, "or a glass of wine?"

Martha's mind was made up as soon as Signora Crespi-Dolci commented, "The wines of the south do not of course compare with those from the Piemonte."

"Sicilian wines are said to be too fragile to travel, but we can enjoy them here. Berte, I suggest you join me in a glass of wine. The soil, courtesy of Etna, gives it a very special flavor."

The Dottore grinned mirthlessly. "Madame is a good advocate for our host's property, but it is not necessary. We are already well disposed towards it."

Where his wife had been impertinent he was impolite and Martha took up the gauntlet.

"I am surprised to hear you say so. It is so unlike anything in the Piemonte. Do you agree with your husband, Signora?"

"Not always," replied that plump lady in a tone which established whose mind would change if she did not agree. "But this time I do."

The Principe saw his party falling apart before it had begun and glanced to Rocco who immediately announced luncheon.

At table Silvia's pasta had its euphoric effect and by the time they were back on the terrace for coffee they were all more relaxed. Martha managed a private word apart with the Principe.

"You cannot allow them to have the Castellino."

"They are the only ones who have bid for it."

"Hm."

After a few minutes of polite generalities the Principe and the Dottore excused themselves and retired to the library to discuss terms.

"Signora," said Martha in what she hoped was a beguiling manner, "you must see the view from the end of the Belvedere path." Reading the Signora's mind she added, "It is not far, and all perfectly level."

"Bene," was the unenthusiastic reply.

"Berte, may I borrow your floppy hat for the sun?" was Martha's next unlikely utterance.

"Of course, I'll fetch it."

"No, you keep the Signora company."

Martha left them and returned in a few minutes holding the hat, which she had found only inches from what she had really gone to borrow. Berte dutifully took her leave and as she turned to look back she saw that Martha was leading the Signora down the garden path.

Beyond the Belvedere the ladies sat on a stone bench to admire the panoramic view.

"Madame," said the Signora, "I think you want to say something, yes?"

"As a matter of fact I do."

Would this ridiculous American woman now warn her that there were not enough bathrooms in the Castellino? That the kitchen was primitive? Did she think they cared?

"I only want to tell you how fortunate you are to acquire the Castellino."

The unexpected platitude brought forth a defensive reply.

"The Principe is fortunate to sell when no one is buying in Sicily. Now Elba —"

"Ah, but there is no comparison. This is the classical world. I hear stories of Roman settlements in these hills, as yet undiscovered."

"The Principe has not mentioned them to us."

"He insists they are only legendary, but ruins are my passion —" Martha hoped her words, highly inaccurate, had the ring of truth. "— so if I could be sure there had been temples here, I would not hesitate to buy the Castellino myself."

"You cannot. The Professore —"

The Signora stopped abruptly, but she had betrayed a

more than casual interest in the Castellino. At once she regretted her lapse.

"I mean, the negotiations are almost complete."

"Ah, then I am sure your husband has heard the talk of an undiscovered Roman town hereabouts."

Before the Signora could assure Martha that her husband knew nothing she did not know, Martha suddenly rose from the bench.

"But what is that?"

She walked a few paces, dug her fingers into the soil and held up a small object.

"A Roman coin! How extraordinary."

"May I see it?"

Martha handed the coin to Signora Crespi-Dolci who examined it suspiciously. The script was in Latin, and on one side was the worn but clear outline of a profile.

Martha did not conceal her excitement.

"We must find out which emperor this is so we can date it. My dear, do you realize it was not more than this which led to the discovery of Pompeii, of Troy? Blessings on you, dear Signora, for having helped me to find it, so to speak."

"Everybody finds coins. It is probably worth very little."

"In itself, perhaps, but how significant that it was here — most likely turned up by a gardener's rake. Yes, surely this promontory would have been the logical site for a temple."

The Signora was now annoyed. If this wretched woman went to the Principe with her accursed coin it might complicate the sale and raise the price.

"A coin is not a city."

"No, it is more, it is the promise of something still to be

found." And then, her mind made up, Martha announced, "I will do it. I will make an offer to the Principe myself."

"But no —"

"But yes, and why not? I can call in an archeological team and we will start a dig. Oh, Signora, the possibilities! But only if I can match your husband's offer. That I must of course be prepared to do."

"The Principe is obligated to accept the best offer." The impertinent woman probably had no idea of the value of the property.

"I can offer him a million," Martha said. "In dollars, that is."

"But that is an enormous sum." The Signora was indignant.

"Not if the property is worth it to me."

"It is a ridiculous price. My husband would not consider offering so much."

"I am delighted to hear it."

"But, Madame, there is no market for property in Sicily —"

"There is now," beamed Martha.

Without another word Signora Crespi-Dolci rose and returned to the house, Martha following in her wake. In silence they reached the cloister just as the Principe and the Dottore returned from the library.

"Temo, I must speak with you," his wife announced and took her husband aside.

"Martha, what plots do you hatch under that hat?" the Principe asked. "Before lunch you were a tiger and now you are the cat who has swallowed the mouse."

"Rinaldo, how much did he offer?"

"Two hundred million lire."

"In dollars that is nothing —"

"He knows I must accept. There is no other offer."

"I told his wife I am offering a million in dollars."

"You are mad. You do not want the Castellino."

"But I do. I am going to dig in the garden for the Roman city."

"What Roman city?"

Martha ignored the question. "Unless of course the Signora insists that her husband pay what is necessary to meet my offer. Rinaldo, if you lose the Castellino you are going to receive a fair price for it."

"Marta, Marta," he could but marvel.

"Principe," said the Dottore as he returned to them with a poisonous glance towards Martha, "I must have another word with you."

"By all means," answered his host, pointing the way back to the library.

"And I will go with you," announced the Signora, who was not going to leave anything to chance. "Come, Temistocle."

Left behind Martha suddenly sensed the presence of another person. She turned and saw Rocco standing in the shadow of the cloister. Instinctively she knew he had been listening while she spoke with the Principe. Why else would his eyes be afire with undisguised hatred — for an enemy who stood in the way? Then Rocco stepped forward, bowed, and disappeared into the house.

Later that afternoon the Crespi-Dolcis departed, having met Martha's offer for the Castellino.

"I have accepted it," said the Principe with a wan smile, "along with a cheque for one hundred million lire, which obliges them — and me — to complete the transaction. Our attorneys will now prepare the papers. Tonight we will celebrate with a gala dinner. I have instructed Silvia to be inventive."

Martha was quick to perceive that while his words were festive, his mood was not. As if reading her mind he added, "Believe me, chère Marthe, there is cause to celebrate. This had to be."

At that moment Rocco entered bearing a letter on a salver. "For the Signora."

Martha accepted the envelope and glanced at the postmark. "Ah, from St. Cloud —"

Martha saw Rocco, who had been about to leave to room, hesitate and busy himself at the refectory table, facing away from them but attentive. She did not want to disappoint him.

"—and you know what that means," she added.

Neither Berte nor the Principe had any idea what it meant but before they could ask Martha glanced towards Rocco.

"Thank you, Rocco," said the Principe in dismissal.

Rocco left the room but Martha knew full well he was at the other side of the door, and to accommodate him, she spoke rather more distinctly than usual.

"It is no doubt from the Pavillon Interpol."

Then she motioned Berte and the Principe into the garden where they would not be further overheard.

"It is a joke between Avril and me," she confessed, delighted to have discomfited Rocco and left him with a mystery.

"Avril's uncle, Hyacinthe, has a house in St. Cloud which she calls the Pavillon Interpol because it is near the Interpol headquarters and also close to Robert de Montesquieu's Pavillon Rose. Hyacinthe and Montesquieu were old rivals in society. Does that make sense?"

"Only if you know Avril," observed the Principe as Martha put the letter into her bag, unopened. "And now we must discuss our plans for the week. We can do anything you wish except we will not dig in my garden for Roman cities."

"Could we visit some of the villages?" Berte asked.

"My village, of course," their host assured her, "but not the others just now. There have been...troubles of late."

Martha reverted to that observation when she and Berte were upstairs. "Each time Rinaldo tell us something my mystery deepens. Now it is trouble in the villages."

"Yes, that is why I asked if we could visit them."

"Whatever do you mean?"

"After lunch I saw Marco again. This time he was frantic; he told me an old vendetta had flared up in the village of his fianceé, and it is the family of Rocco who had revived this quarrel."

Rocco. Was Rocco the key to everything?

Berte was about to disappear into her own room when she reminded her aunt about the letter from St. Cloud.

"I think I know what Avril wants to tell me," Martha said, delving into her bag. "She told me in Paris she might need my help with her mother-in-law. D.D. is sometimes quite impossible."

"D.D. for Dowager Duchess?"

"No, D.D. For Dagmar the Dreadnought and she deserves

the title. At the moment she is feuding with the people who bought the Chateau from the family. I gather they are threatening to subdivide the park. Avril wants to bring them together to discuss the matter before it gets out of hand. She hoped her uncle, who is D.D.'s brother, would help her, but he can also be impossible —"

Martha opened the letter and quickly read the two sheets, writ large in Avril's notorious hand.

"She is still trying to get Hyacinthe to be reasonable, and meanwhile both sides have agreed to meet at the Chateau next weekend. If she needs me she will wire. I hope she doesn't...because we would have to go." Her last words were spoken almost absently, as if her thoughts were elsewhere — which indeed they were. "Berte, I am going to do something wicked."

Martha tore off the corner of one of the blue sheets of paper and put a match to the remainder as Berte watched, fascinated. In no time the grate was filled with cinders. With another match she carefully singed the torn fragment, then folded a plain white sheet and put it into the blue envelope, leaving the singed blue in the grate among the cinders.

"Rocco will not be able to resist looking for the letter while we are at dinner. He will find a blank white sheet and see cinders of the blue, so he will know that we expected him. His curiosity will be doubled." Then — rather pleased with herself — she added, "What shall I wear tonight?"

That evening the Principe said little more about the sale except to volunteer that he would first go to his cousins at the

Palazzo in Naples, and that he would take Silvia and Marco with him.

"They know my habits," he said. "But now let us think about tomorrow. Martha, you shall choose."

"A picnic at the limonaia?"

"Perfect. And we will walk to the end of the valley, then back to the grove for our fête champêtre."

At that moment Silvia entered bearing on a silver platter a gossamer masterpiece of meringue, cream, hazel nuts and chocolate. Martha thought of Dr. Benson and was glad he was not along to see them discard dietary caution so enthusiastically.

"Rocco," said the Principe after the dolce di Cavour had met its fate, "Take a glass of champagne to Silvia with our compliments."

It was late when the ladies retired as the Principe kept them amused with more tales of his family. But once upstairs they went quickly to the dressing table where Martha had left the blue envelope. It was gone.

"There," said Berte, pointing to the grate.

It lay crumpled into a ball, the white sheet with it, atop the cold cinders.

"He is not a fool," said Martha, "and he was confident enough, or angry enough, not to care that we would know he had been here. I wonder what Signor Rocco will do next?"

They found out in the morning when they went down to join the Principe for their outing. Instead of meeting a smiling host they heard voices raised in anger, coming from the library. A moment later the Principe appeared, not betraying that his had been one of the voices. Not, that is, until Rocco entered. Rocco did not bow; he simply waited.

"Yes?" The Principe's question was a challenge.

Rocco's response told Martha and Berte what the argument in the library had been about.

"Does the Principe wish to ask the Signora at what time she will require Marco to take her and the Signorina to the airport — tomorrow?"

At another time such insolence would have resulted in instant dismissal. Now there was a tense moment before the Principe spoke. "Rocco means to be helpful," he said in icy tones. "Please forgive him."

In the car as they started towards Monte Zirotto, the Principe said only, "Rocco is not Michele."

The ladies said nothing.

Their spirits rose as they drove through the hills, past gnarled olive trees and up through stands of native pine and down again until they entered a sheltered valley between two verdant hills.

"As your aunt knows," explained the Principe, "this blessed place is protected from winter frost, so long ago we planted it with lemons, oranges and almonds. At the end of the valley you will see hills to your right, Etna straight ahead, and far below on the left, the blue sea."

He turned to Marco who was waiting for instructions.

"We will have our luncheon here in an hour's time. Hand me the field glasses. We may spot some birds in the valley."

Berte noticed a fervent request in Marco's eyes, one he did not dare to voice.

"I think Marco wants to ask you something," she said.

"Of course he does," said that kind man, "and I have been avoiding his eyes." But it was a tone of voice which encouraged Marco to respond.

"Principe," pleaded Marco, "it is only fifteen minutes to the village and fifteen minutes back —"

"And you could spend fifteen minutes with Elena. Go, but be back in good time."

"Grazie, Principe." Marco gave the Principe the glasses and his eyes darted to Berte, full of gratitude.

"Lucky Marco, to have you on his side. Elena is Marco's fiancée, and her village is one of those where there is trouble."

"I don't understand," said Berte, who thought she did, but wanted to know more.

"It is very sad. Vendetta was once a kind of rustic justice here, when the feudal system declined. Now, alas, it is more basely motivated, but that is down in the valleys and we are in the heights, so let us not dwell on the failures of the human spirit."

Then he led them into a dell such as that in which Daphnis met Chloe, where dryads, naiads, and Pan would have been at home. The sunlight was hot, but filtered and benign; no leaf stirred. Effortlessly they surrendered, all three, to the beauty and the tranquillity. When at last they reached the crest and looked down on the vistas the Principe had promised them, Martha took the glasses and trained them first on Etna, from which a wisp of smoke curled into the sky, then down into the valley below.

The Principe broke their silence. "If the villagers appreciated the countryside perhaps nature would change them by its example. But the men sit in the wine shops and the women go no further than the church."

"Not true," said Martha, looking through the powerful glasses. "I see a family group like ourselves in the valley, also out for a picnic. An older woman, in black, naturally, and two young men carrying the blanket. And of course they cannot agree where they should stop to eat. Look for yourself, Rinaldo."

He was eager to do so as he knew the scene she described was not possible. Villagers did not have picnics at the side of the road. She handed him the glasses and instantly he saw something quite different from what Martha had interpreted so idyllically. There were indeed three figures, an angry old woman and two exasperated young men. The latter, over her protests, had now started to turn over the earth with shovels, but she continued to badger them. Then she pointed to a ravine off the road and they stopped digging, took up the heavy blanket, and heaved its contents into the ravine. Compulsively the Principe put the glasses aside, but he had seen what he did not want to see. From the blanket, a limp body had rolled into the grass and out of sight.

"My turn!" exclaimed an impatient Berte.

"No!" He spoke so sharply that she let her arm drop. The Principe saw that Martha had taken out her long scarf and was waiving it vigorously. He tried to stop her.

"Marta —"

He hoped they had not seen her, but in the next moment a single shot rang out and echoed up the mountainside.

"Follow me," he commanded. "Quickly."

The urgency in his voice was unmistakable, and they retreated into the valley.

"I'm sorry," said Martha, "I only wanted to salute them."

"It was not a picnic, Marthe." Then he gave a logical explanation he knew to be untrue. "Poachers, I believe, who do not like to be observed. That is why they fired a warning shot into the air." He did not add that he had heard the zing and snapping of a twig near them on the crest. The single shot had been dangerously close to its intended mark.

Martha and Berte chattered on the way back to the spring near which lunch was laid out, wanting to reassure the Principe that they were not alarmed. He, meanwhile, pondered the problem now his to solve: what to do with his guests who, while they had not actually seen a crime committed, had been seen by the criminals. It could easily be ascertained who had been on the crest that day, the more so because Marco had driven in the car to the village from which the three conspirators came. For the Principe had recognized the old woman. She was the matriarch of her family, the mother of Rocco.

They arrived at the pool where Marco awaited them and the Principe saw immediately that all was not well. As soon as the ladies were settled on pillows he remembered to take his field glasses to the car. "So I will not forget them, as is my habit."

Marco followed and said in an agonized voice, "Principe, it has happened. The brother of Elena has disappeared. I have little hope that he will return."

The Principe rejoined the others and pretended to enjoy what Silvia had prepared for them but he knew now he had no choice: he must ask his guests to leave the Castellino as quickly as possible. Martha had seen too much even if she did not realize it.

Their luncheon consumed, the party took leave of the enchanted valley and drove back to the Castellino, now a strangely silent group. Martha and Berte were content with the memory of a perfect pastoral day. Marco's brow was furrowed with worry. The Principe considered the impossible alternatives: he could not ask his guests to leave without an explanation, and yet to say anything would lead inevitably to more than he was willing to discuss. Not knowing exactly what he would tell her, the Principle, as they alighted in the courtyard, said, "Marthe, I must speak with you. In the library before you go upstairs."

Then, as the doors were opened for them, suddenly everything changed. Rocco approached Martha with a message on the salver.

"A telegram for the Signora."

His eyes challenged hers and she felt the malevolence of his glance. She knew that Rocco had already read the message.

She handed the wire to the Principe, who read:

NEED YOU ST CLOUD COMPLICATIONS MEET MAURICE FRIDAY 1052 ST LAZARE. A.

"What does it mean?" he asked.

"That we must, after all, drive to Catania tomorrow morning and fly to Paris."

The Principe was both sad and immensely relieved.

"As it is necessary, Rocco will make the arrangements." Then when Rocco had left them he added, "What does this really mean, and who is Maurice?"

Martha told him about Avril de Dinde's problem with her mother-in-law, and that she had promised to help if needed. "D.D. behaves better when someone outside the family is present. I believe that is a common phenomenon. As for Maurice, *he* is simply a misspelling for Meurice. Avril knows I always stop at the Meurice."

They had moved toward the stairs and Martha said to Berte, "I will join you in a moment, my dear."

"Secrets, secrets," said Berte jauntily, touching on something all too true.

Martha led the way to the library. As the Principe closed the door behind them he was still unsure what he would say now that the telegram had solved his problem. Then, suddenly, he knew.

"Chère amie, Berte is a charming girl with whom I have fallen in love. I would like your permission to give her a present in parting. It is the gown which Mariano Fortuny made for my mother. His famous plissé à la grec. As you know, they do not go out of fashion and until now there has been no one whom it would suit. Do I have your permission?"

"Dear Rinaldo, she will be touched, as am I."

Gratefully, and relieved, he kissed her hand.

After fond farewells in the morning, which included the kitchen, they sped down the road in the Principe's car towards Taormina and on to Catania. Rocco had not appeared nor did the Principe mention his name. During the drive when Berte asked Marco only said, "He was called to his village, Signorina."

Then Martha remembered to reach into her bag.

"Berte, I have your coin."

"I thought perhaps Rocco —"

"No, I borrowed it, and I confess it proved more valuable than I had originally thought."

"But you are still worried about the Principe."

"Yes, because I don't like a mystery which has a beginning, a middle point, and no end."

The mystery was to be solved sooner than she could imagine, and it was their precipitate departure from the Castellino which was to provide the key.

Sur Risle or Surreal?

*L*ong before their plane landed at Paris-Orly Martha's spirits improved and she kept her promise to tell Berte how Avril de Dinde had started out as Junie May Bigelow of Colorado and ended up in the Almanach de Gotha.

"Her mother," Martha said, "was determined that Junie May should marry a title, for which the Bigelow Copper Company would provide the means. Junie May was nineteen when she met Maurice LeFermier at Enghien, a dashing young man who had just become the third duc de Dinde and had also inherited all his father's debts.

"The first duke had been a self-made man, granted his title by Napoleon III, whose wars he financed. Avril assures me he was a man of spirit — that's how he happened to style himself M. le duc de Dinde, after the humble bird on which his fortune was based, and to challenge the snobs of the Jockey Club who called him 'the turkey' behind his back. He even proposed "Sauve qui peut" as a motto for his escutcheon, which might be translated as Never Lose Sight of Number One. The emperor laughed and changed it to "Sauve qui *on* peut" — Save Whom You Can, which is of course a much more noble sentiment."

"I like the grandfather duke already," said Berte.

"So did many people, I gather, but not the survivors of the ancien régime, who were never eager to welcome anyone so recently risen to the upper crust. So the first duchess received no invitations to tea in the Faubourg St. Germain, but that was solved a generation later when the second Maurice married Dagmar von Glatz und Glienicke. She provided the quarterings, he the gold francs, and all went well until the second duke died in the 1930s after losing everything at the gaming tables. But once again a good marriage solved the problem because the dowager duchess did not hesitate when a romance blossomed between her son and a vivacious young American, especially after she had made inquiries about Bigelow Copper. Fortunately it was a happy marriage until he died, all too young. And that is the saga of the Bigelows, the LeFermier de Dindes and the von Whats-their-names, except for the unlikely way that Avril and I first met — long before either of us married.

"I was in Paris for the first time and went with Mother to Monsieur Poiret's salon for her fitting. While the seamstress was pinning and hemming her, behind the curtains, another girl came along and sat next to me. We soon discovered we were both Americans and each glad to have a new friend. She said her mother was being fitted into the most glamorous gown ever, so I peeked, and discovered that Mrs. Bigelow was being sewn into the same beaded gown as

Mother's. We giggled and hatched a plot — with a whoosh we pulled back the divider, surprising the vendeuse and two furious mothers who both felt betrayed. Monsieur was called and he asked each lady to accept her gown with his compliments and then to choose another to be fitted exclusively for herself. They both refused and dragged us off to our hotels before Junie May and I could exchange addresses. The next day Monsieur Poiret sent Mother her gown but she never wore it. However, I have, as you know — in Las Vegas, and on another occasion, also, to a ball when Robert and I were in Paris together after the war. I made a brilliant entrance and found myself being introduced to the same gown — which Avril was wearing. It was a happy reunion and we've been best friends ever since.

"I like stories with happy endings," Berte observed, "even if I don't understand how a Junie May became an Avril."

"Avril explained that," said Martha. "'Can you imagine anyone being presented to Junie May, duchesse de Dinde?' she asked me. 'Of course not. I subtracted a month a so now I am Avril.'"

An hour before Martha and Berte arrived at the Meurice Avril de Dinde, in the company of her erratic Uncle Hyacinthe, had already left Paris for Normandy, which was explained in the letter she had deposited at the hotel for them, confirming that she expected Martha to depart as scheduled on the 10:52 from St. Lazare on Friday morning.

"She says she dare not leave D.D. and Hyacinthe alone together as they would be capable of plotting almost anything," Martha said, looking up from the letter. "I am to descend at

Conches-en-Ouche where Albert will collect me. They have told the Durant-Perrichons — what a strange name — to expect me at the Chateau for luncheon on Sunday. Oh dear, it seems the Durant-et ceteras are really threatening to subdivide the forest."

"You keep all the good invitations for yourself," said Berte.

"Wicked girl. Wouldn't you like to come along?"

"I think I'd rather hear about it — afterwards."

When the 10:52 glided off from St. Lazare Friday morning Martha had the compartment to herself until a woman addressed her in English from the corridor.

"May I join you?" It was a purely rhetorical question as she was already halfway through the door. "I do need to talk with someone," she continued, pulling the door shut.

Martha looked up and saw tweeds, a sensible pair of shoes, wool stockings, and a well-worn portmanteau, all undeniably British. Surely a governess on holiday.

"I have just made a terrible mistake."

"You have taken the wrong train?"

"Much worse. I am convinced I have accepted the wrong position. You won't have guessed it, of course, but I am a governess. Mabel Parfit. Not the Hampshire Parfitts. They have the two t's."

The woman was so perturbed and so sincere that Martha was unable to resent the intrusion into her own privacy.

"I spent my summers as a girl on Guernsey so I am bilingual and I do love children. It was quite natural, when we got over the shock of father's will, that I should become a governess. I've had some delightful charges and some — well, some others. Oh, I could tell you tales."

Please, please don't, Martha begged silently.

"And as it was really impossible to stay any longer with Cousin Claire, I left Leamington and registered with an agency in Paris. In no time they found me this."

"This?"

"It sounded quite suitable. One little boy and he has had some English already. His father is an avocat, and they live in the country, quite elaborately, I believe."

"It sounds ideal."

"Precisely, and that is why I took it. Then yesterday whilst I was at the agency I happened to fall into conversation — you know how that is —" (Martha was finding out) — "with a governess who had come to report why she had left her last position. Her experience must have been terrifying. I know she was truthful. She had lived twenty years in Bath."

Here, Martha noted, was rare logic.

"Quite by accident it came out that she had just left the address for which I am bound today. Now I don't even want to get off the train. But I don't see how I can go back to Cousin Claire."

Then Mabel Parfit waited for words of wisdom and advice from a perfect stranger, as women do.

"I can only give you my immediate reaction, dear Miss Parfit, and that is to stay on this train all the way to Cherbourg, then take the first channel steamer back to England. Buy a large box of good French chocolates for your cousin. Tell her you simply did not realize how nice it was in Leamington, even if it wasn't, and how glad you are to be back, even if you aren't."

"I wouldn't be derelict not to keep my appointment?"

"The agency was derelict in sending you there."

With that Martha turned to the scenery outside and was rewarded by the silence she had hoped for as Miss Parfit struggled with her conscience. It was not a long battle as presently the governess said, "Cousin Claire likes chocolates."

Martha smiled encouragement and turned back to her Figaro, which she read until Conches-en-Ouche was announced.

"I think you have made the right decision," Martha said as she prepared to disembark.

"Yes," was Miss Parfit's thoughtful reply, "I shall go home to Claire and take her half a pound of Lapsang Oolong from Fortnum's instead of the chocolates. We both like Lapsang."

Martha was one of the few who set foot in Conches that morning and the others quickly disappeared, leaving her alone on the platform. There was no sign of an Albert. Had D.D. or Hyacinthe forbidden Avril to send him for the guest who might spoil their mischief at the Sunday luncheon? No, there was the Rolls, swerving around a corner; a surprisingly new one, but badly in need of a wash and a polish. And if Albert was not as old as she had anticipated, at least he was cranky.

"What a nuisance, hauling everybody from the station," was his greeting. Then, after he had placed her bags inside, he indicated the door beside the driver's seat.

"Hop in."

She hopped.

As they disappeared down the road towards the river

Risle, another car, an ancient Delahaye, driven by a man at least twice the age of the highly polished cabriolet, pulled up to the station. Albert, at the wheel, was surprised to find no one waiting. He was only a few minutes late.

Meanwhile the Rolls sped through the countryside, scattering errant hens. Martha inclined her head slightly towards the chauffeur. "Tell me, Albert —"

"Tell me, who? My name is Georges. And yours is Mabel. What is that for a name?"

Martha opened her eyes wide in momentary panic. It was the wrong car, and she was en route to the fate for which Mabel Parfit had been destined.

"We've never had a Mabel at the Chateau."

"Chateau?"

"De la Barre sur Risle. Didn't the agency tell you anything?"

To Martha the entire situation was becoming surreal. "All I remember is the name of the family," she said, guessing. "Durant-Perri-something."

"That's them. What a kettle of fish!"

At least, Martha thought, they were driving in the right direction. Better to say nothing and simply to telephone the manoir from the Chateau. Meanwhile she might learn something about the new occupants from a point of view less critical than that of their noble neighbors.

"Tell me about them, Georges."

"One worse than the other. Jules will tell you."

"The child?"

"The butler. The boy is Jean-Claude. Jules runs everything and if you listen to him you'll have no problems."

Martha dwelt silently on this prospect until they reached the gatehouse, where iron grills were already open for them and Georges called out to the young woman who stood by, "Lock the gates, Annie, and if Jean-Claude tries to leave with my Rolls, shoot him."

They drove a short distance through woods and then up a long allée at the end of which Martha saw a box-bordered lawn, and beyond it a graveled court leading to the noble seventeenth-century facade of the Chateau. Moments later she was deposited outside the kitchen wing where a drudge opened the door and shouted with a half-turn of her head, "Jules!"

He appeared and gave Martha a penetrating look. Tall, dark and thin lipped, Jules was not a man Martha would have chosen to preside over her house. He turned and led the way into the kitchen where a red-faced woman was wiping her hands on a soiled apron.

"This is Marie. She is our chef de cuisine and my wife." Then he turned to the woman who had opened the door. "Jeanne, who helps us both. Georges' wife."

Martha also saw that Marie was Georges' twin sister. It was a family operation. She caught, too, a disarming whiff of garlic and herbs and saw a great pot from which steam was rising, beside it a high mound of moules. To one side in a roasting pan was a tired piece of veal for the staff. Instantly she decided, if possible, to lunch with the family; the savory smell from the pot was irresistible. As soon as she had stated her preference she saw that she had offended Jules, not a good beginning for the new governess. But since she planned to eat and run she was not worried.

"Your first mistake," Jules muttered.

"Exactly who are the family?" Martha asked.

"Madame Mère is in charge," interrupted Marie. "She's a terror."

Jules continued the catalogue. "She has the money. Then there is her son, the cher maître, who practices law in Evreux, and his son Jean-Claude. You'll have to deal with him. If you last."

"He has no mother," said Jeanne. "They say she died."

"I think the boy poisoned her. He's mean enough." This from Georges, who had just entered with Martha's bag.

"Not his own mother!" exclaimed Jeanne.

"Didn't he drop a pot from the ledge on Mlle Georgette?" Georges demanded.

Jules had the final word. "Unfortunately, he missed. She is the cher maître's girlfriend. Never been inside a chateau before, front door or back. As a matter of fact, none of them have."

Suddenly a wiry boy of twelve burst in and stood defiantly before Martha, challenging her with a provocative stance. He dug both hands into his trousers pockets, quickly withdrew them and put his clenched fists behind his back.

"Right or left?"

Martha responded to his game with what she hoped was a winning smile, and said, "Right."

"Put out your hand."

She did so and he placed a dead frog in her palm. Marie screamed.

"A little frog!" exclaimed Martha. "Keep him and we will dissect him during our biology lesson." She returned the frog.

The boy's disappointment evaporated when she went on. "And I want to know what was in your other hand to welcome me." She extended her own left palm.

Triumphant, Jean-Claude produced a very small live snake. A second scream from Marie as even Jules and Georges drew back.

"A garden snake! They do so much good. Run along now and put him back where he can catch his lunch of insects."

Defeated and baffled the boy took the wriggly creature and ran out of the room.

"At least it wasn't a worm," Martha said to the others. "I don't like worms."

A few moments later Jules opened the door to the library and announced Martha — alias Mabel Parfit — to the assembled family. Even the boiserie was friendlier than the stares which pierced her. Madame Mère's was black and distrustful, the cher maître's resigned, Mlle Georgette's uncertain and hostile. None of them said a word, so Martha did.

"Isn't it a lovely day!"

This observation only intensified the silent appraisals.

"And such a beautiful house."

Jules, at the door, broke the silence with "Luncheon is served."

At table a desultory conversation sputtered fitfully and expired before the food was served. As Jean-Claude did not appear there were no more small creatures, dead or alive, to spoil Martha's anticipation of the moules and other good things to follow.

Then Jules served Madame Mère and Martha saw the

platter of warmed-over veal, with boiled potatoes. When he reached her Martha caught the wicked gleam in his eyes. They both knew she might heave been dipping a piece of crusty bread into the marinière of the moules destined for the staff. There was no question where the seat of power lay in the Chateau de la Barre sur Risle.

Only after an uninspired pudding had been offered and rejected by Martha did the subject of the weekend arise.

"We will need your help on Sunday," said the avocat.

"To keep Jean-Claude out of the way," added his mother. "Those snobs from the manoir are coming to lunch."

Avril would be well advised to send regrets, Martha thought. D.D. liked her food and if this was an example of the fare they might expect the meeting was doomed.

"I don't see why we had to invite them," complained Mlle Georgette, wiping a broad streak of unbecoming lipstick on the linen serviette in her hand.

"To let them find out they can't always have their own way," said Madame Durand-Perrichon. "Who do they think they are?"

"They know who they are," her son said. "And so do we."

"I think I'll go back to Evreux in the morning," said Mlle Georgette.

"An excellent idea," muttered Madame Mère.

"You will stay here where you belong," announced the master of the house wearily.

In those three reactions Martha had it all: Mademoiselle's panic, Madame Mère's scorn, and Monsieur's resignation. Was it any wonder, in this circle, that her charge was growing up out of control? Her charge!

She did not intend to play the role any longer than it would take to find a telephone.

As they left the room M. Durant-Perrichon repeated his first statement. "We will need your help to get through Sunday. You can start the boy's lessons on Monday." Then he added, "He is not a bad sort." At last she had heard someone say something which implied understanding and compassion.

"Don't you suppose," Martha volunteered, "the best solution is to plan a really good menu?" She was thinking of herself as well as the others. "They say food soothes —"

"The savage breast? Not with the staff we have."

She knew what he meant, but she also remembered the moules. Could the kitchen be won over? The luncheon was important — after all it was the reason Avril had sent for her in the first place.

Martha announced she was taking a walk in the park. It would give her time to think. As she started off she noticed a walled potager and looked in to inspect it. Yes, the kitchen garden was a treasure house of young vegetables and herbs, few of which, she guessed, ever reached the table of the Durant-Perrichons.

A derisive voice rang out. "How did you like your lunch with the family?"

It was Georges, passing an open window.

"You won't last. Jules will see to that."

Martha neither answered nor glanced in his direction. This time Jules was not up against someone as easily defeated as the Mabel Parfits of the world.

Once in the woods Martha noted an abundance of succulent

mushrooms in the leafy shade. More than enough for a good soup on Sunday. Suddenly she felt a sharp sting; involuntarily her hand sought the back of her neck. A bee? Then another. No, not a bee. She turned quickly and caught sight of a movement from behind a thicket.

"Jean-Claude," she said sternly, "come out and give me your peashooter. We are not in the jungle and you are not a cannibal seeking his dinner." Silence. "If you do not move this instant I will pull you out, roots and all."

Jean-Claude emerged, somehow impressed. Defiance, already tempered with curiosity, was being replaced by respect for her authority. Who was this strange woman who felt sorry for little snakes? Would she be on his side, too?"

"You can keep the peashooter, but put it away and use it only when we both decide somebody deserves it."

Jean-Claude liked conspiracy, which this implied.

"That old Georgette?"

"No, because she is your father's friend. Perhaps Georges at one point."

"Oh, yes!"

"But I will tell you when. Jean-Claude, who keeps the potager in such good condition?"

"Annie's father. He's all right. So is she. They were here before."

"Is there a phone at the gatehouse?"

"Oh course."

"Then let's go along there and ask Annie if I can use it."

Contentedly Jean-Claude found himself walking down the path with the governess who had come to make him learn boring things about uninteresting subjects. He even pointed out has favorite places along the way including the cool bower where he was wont on hot days to hide from a governess.

"The last one was a real English pill. You're not."

I'll tell you a secret, Jean-Claude. But don't mention it just yet. I am an American."

"Do you know any gangsters?"

"Oh, yes. Jules and Georges."

They laughed together.

At the gatehouse Martha found Annie obliging and she rang Avril while Jean-Claude waited outside.

"Chère Marthe, I thought we had lost you."

Martha told her what had happened since the arrival of the 10:52 from St. Lazare that morning. "And Sunday is going to be a disaster unless I can save it. But it is worth my staying on here as Miss Parfit, to find out. Give me overnight to decide."

"How right I was to send for you," said Avril.

That night when she had retired to a lumpy bed Martha knew there was only one possible answer if Sunday was to be salvaged. All of them — Jules and Marie, Georges and Jeanne — had to go. She had seen that clearly, before evening, after she had endured insolence and even a threat from the arrogant Jules. "Remember, I am in charge here. If anyone leaves, Madame, it will be you."

Martha was up early, still occupied with strategy and hairpins when Jean-Claude knocked on her door to say good morning. She asked him to go down to the kitchen and bring her café au lait upstairs. He returned with hot water and a tea bag.

"Jules says the English drink tea in the morning." Then, because he liked this extraordinary governess who had said good night to him and stopped to talk at his bedside before he drifted off to sleep, he added, "I brought you a croissant. Marie makes good croissants. Just for them."

Jean-Claude knew when he had a public, as children often do.

"Bless you," said Martha. "Now please take this note to your father. I have asked to see him in the library at nine-thirty."

"You aren't leaving —"

"Gracious, no. Do you think I can be frightened away simply because my life is in danger?"

But she smiled as she said it and he understood. He took the letter and ran.

When Martha knocked at the library door and entered she found not only Monsieur but also his mother, his mistress and his son, all expectant and worried.

Madame Mère was the first to speak. "Jean-Claude tells us you are leaving."

The boys eyes sparkled in anticipation.

"His little joke. Jean-Claude knows I would not desert him. Your son, Monsieur, has a good character even though he conceals it at times."

"You are the first governess to say so."

"The first one to notice, perhaps?"

"You have a complaint?" That from Madame Mère.

"I certainly do."

"I knew it, she wants more money," Georgette burst forth. "And she only arrived yesterday. Oh, the English."

Madame Mère, who was more perceptive, said, "The servants are impossible. But replacements would be as bad or worse. We have been through that, too."

"Listen to me. Please," said Martha firmly. "Tomorrow at one-thirty you are expecting two duchesses, among others, to lunch."

"What are they going to think?"

"The worst, Mlle Georgette, and they will be right." Martha saw that the avocat was about to object. "Hear me out," she said. "The luncheon is important because you want the former owners of the Chateau to know that the present owners are worthy of their surroundings —"

"As if we cared," Georgette was again on the defensive.

"Of course you care. Everybody has pride of family. Moreover, you wish to live contentedly beside your neighbors, in mutual if distant respect."

Jean-Claude clapped his hands enthusiastically.

His father cut him off with a warning glance. "And how do you propose, Madame, that we get through tomorrow without being made fools of in our own house?"

"As things stand it isn't remotely possible, especially as the dowager duchess, I am told, is known to appreciate a good table."

"To the point, Madame!" His mother stamped on the carpet with her stick.

"Monsieur, you must call Jules in and remind him that he and his family are employed, and no doubt well paid, to make you and your guests comfortable —"

"Impossible. They will threaten to leave, without notice. They've done it before."

"Let us hope they do. Otherwise you must discharge them."

Jean-Claude applauded again.

"And when they leave?" asked the cher maître.

Martha crossed her Rubicon. "Jean-Claude's lessons do not begin until Monday. I will take full responsibility for the luncheon tomorrow."

At this all three spoke up while Jean-Claude whistled and cheered. Martha stopped them with a raised hand.

"Trust me. You have nothing to lose. And we have very little time. Please summon Jules now."

"They will certainly not leave today."

"I think they will if you offer an extra month's wages on condition that they are gone, let us be generous, before noon."

While opinions and objections filled the air and Jean-Claude jumped up and down with excitement, Martha sat quietly. Finally, Madame Mère commanded silence with her stick.

"Madame is right. Armand, ring for Jules."

Martha was pleased, but sensitive to the niceties. "Perhaps Monsieur would prefer to see Jules alone?"

"By no means," said his mother. "He will need our support. And yours as well."

Before his father could stop him Jean-Claude tugged at the bellpull as if he were ringing in a revolution, which indeed he was. For a fleeting moment Martha half expected they might all burst into the 'Ça ira.'

After what seemed an eternity to the cher maître Jules stood before him insolent, waiting. There was a pause as the avocat, a specialist in briefs and not used to court appearances, struggled to organize his attack.

Jules took the initiative. "Monsieur, we are very busy this morning."

"Jules, we have guests tomorrow —"

"I am aware of it, Monsieur. It is Marie's free Sunday. I cannot promise much, but there will be something."

Martha saw that the cher maître was simply not up to his task.

"Jules," she said, "something is not enough. There must be an excellent lunch."

Jules turned to her, said nothing, then back to the master of the house. "Will there be anything else, Monsieur?"

"Yes," thundered Madame Mère. "Much more and Monsieur has asked Madame to speak for him. Madame — speak."

It was all over in a few minutes. Sure of his ground Jules made his threat — they would all leave. This time the challenge was met. Monsieur proposed the terms for immediate departure and greed won out. Haughtily, but shaken nevertheless, Jules assured him they would, all four, drive to the station in time to take the noon train.

"Let me drive them, let me!" pleaded Jean-Claude, expressing the great desire of his young life, officially to be entrusted with the Rolls.

"No," said his father, then he added to Jules, "you can ring for a taxi. And I will have your cheques ready in half an hour."

"Two taxis." To humiliate him Jules addressed the words to Martha.

Monsieur answered. "Two taxis if you need them."

As Jules turned and left the room everyone relaxed and smiled; the first real smiles Martha had seen at the Chateau, aside from her own and Jean-Claude's, and she told them so.

Shortly after eleven two taxis motored up the drive and were presently filled with the unholy four and all their luggage, which included a number of hastily tied cartons. The family watched discreetly from their windows, all except Jean-Claude to whom Martha had whispered, "Don't forget the peashooter." As Georges helped a driver secure the bags on the roof of one taxi Martha saw him flinch and put his hand to the back of his neck — more than once. He cursed, but helplessly.

As soon as the heavily laden taxis had disappeared among the trees everyone descended to the kitchen regions to see in what condition the rooms had been left. There was hardly a sign that anyone had ever worked there, or ever slept in any of the staff rooms. Madame Mère was the first to remark that they had taken the linens off their beds. Monsieur said nothing, glad to have them out of the house. Martha opened the pantry doors and saw that there was little food on the shelves. That explained the cartons. But in the refrigerator she found two plump chickens, no doubt left behind because they were uncooked.

"Thank goodness," she said to the somewhat dispirited family. "At least we can have a good meal. Jean-Claude, run to the potager and bring me a large bunch of tarragon. As soon as I have put the chickens in the oven you and I will go back and choose some vegetables and salad greens. Mlle Georgette, perhaps you will be good enough to set the table."

"I'll try."

"I will help you," said Madame Mère to everyone's astonishment. The old woman was actually enjoying herself, possibly for the first time since they had moved into the Chateau.

Monsieur was the realist.

"A good lunch today is all very well, Madame. But what about tomorrow?"

"Will you give me carte blanche?" Martha asked.

"Yes," cried his mother, in the doorway.

"Yes," confirmed Monsieur. "Tomorrow must go well. It is, after all, a question of our future in the neighborhood."

"Then don't worry," said Martha, who planned to ring Fauchon and have everything except the soup of mushrooms sent down from Paris. "We will have an abundance of Dom Perignon. Good champagne always helps."

Amazing, thought Madame Mère. The agency gave no hint of a governess like this one.

As soon as she was alone Martha sat down at the phone. First she rang the Meurice to tell Berte what had happened since her departure for a quiet weekend in the country. There was no answer in their suite. Berte was out enjoying Paris, so she left a brief message, then rang Fauchon. A sympathetic voice on the other end of the wire agreed to the four dishes she proposed to accompany ten bottles of Dom Perignon, and a selection of desserts. Everything was to be delivered to the Chateau, at no matter what cost, by twelve noon the next day.

Martha's last call was to Avril. "I think I can promise you a rather good lunch."

Sunday began as a warm and summery day, and all went according to plan. Martha's mushrooms were sautéed gently into a fragrant soup. A white jacket was produced for Jean-Claude, who was to be their butler. The delivery from

Fauchon arrived as appointed. While helping Annie to unpack the food for Martha's inspection the driver asked if they were expecting the President of the Republic, or perhaps a football star.

Jean-Claude was in the pantry practicing with soup plates, as that was to be his only solo number. The remainder of the meal would be available at the buffet, where everyone could make his or her own selection, à l'américaine.

"What shall we call you, Jean-Claude?" asked Martha. "Your butler's name, I mean."

"Jean-Luc?" he asked.

"No," said Georgette, "that's a film star, not a butler. Guillaume. It sounds responsible."

"I agree," said his father, "and it is a very responsible job."

"Guillaume," repeated Jean-Claude happily. "Yes. Thank you." He addressed his thanks to Mlle Georgette, who, he had begun to think, was perhaps human after all.

At 1:25 the family assembled in the drawing room, except Jean-Claude — alias Guillaume — who waited near the phone for the call from the gatehouse which was to warn them that the car had started up the drive. At that point, it was agreed, Martha would disappear. How and when she would manage her transformation from English governess at the Chateau to American guest at the manoir she did not know; there had been no time to worry about it.

But 1:30 came and went. Had Albert lost his way? A different thought sped through Madame Mère's mind. Had these upper-crusty ones accepted her son's invitation only to insult him by not appearing? Angered by the thought, Madame Mère brought her stick down on the parquet with a resounding clap.

Caught off guard, Mlle Georgette pulled at her necklace and the strand broke, scattering pearls over the floor.

"Now look what you've done," exclaimed Monsieur.

"On purpose, do you think?" responded Georgette in kind.

"Don't just stand there," shouted Madame Mère. "All of you. On the floor — gather them up. Do you want them to think we have pearls to throw about? If they come."

In answer they were suddenly all on their knees, in all directions, even Martha. Madame Mère directed the operation, pointing with her stick. "There. There. No — there!!" It was as if they were playing some mad, compulsive game controlled by an old woman who was keeping score with a gold-headed cane.

At that moment, from the terrace window, the two duchesses and Hyacinthe, le comte de Silésie, looked into the room in silent wonder. Astounded at what she saw, D.D. rapped imperiously on the window. Those inside looked up and, in total shock, stopped dead.

"They are completely mad," exclaimed Hyacinthe.

"Are these the people we have floated down the river to lunch with," Dagmar asked, "in constant danger of drowning before we arrived?" For they had come to the Chateau by water in the old swan boat which Hyacinthe had conspired with Albert to launch from the boathouse where it had been stored for thirty years. Had the landing party looked back to the river as they crossed the lawn they would have seen that Albert, having lost an oar as he tried to tie up at the shore, had started to float with the current, down the river Risle and out of sight.

Monsieur Durant-Perrichon recovered sufficiently to open one floor-length window and to kiss the dowager duchess' hand as she stepped into the room.

"May I present my mother, Mme Durant-Perrichon —"

Hyacinthe, to whom the words had not been addressed, exclaimed, "Percheron? Excellent workhorses."

Mon Dieu, thought Avril, is he going to do his deaf act?

"And this is —"

Before Monsieur could bring forward Georgette at whom Hyacinthe was now staring in disbelief — she did look like a Christmas tree with her hennaed hair, green dress, and a handful of pearls which now again fell to the floor in abundance — before Monsieur could present her, Dagmar caught sight of Martha, who had had no time to escape.

"My dear, you have turned up after all!"

The confusion which reigned for the next few minutes was actually helpful, as it gave the Durant-Perrichons no time to dwell on the fact that Mabel Parfit was in fact Martha Prescott. The scene only became tense when Dagmar and her brother both engaged Martha in conversation and turned their backs on the family who all stood to one side, increasingly resentful. Avril took it in and dragged Hyacinthe towards Madame Mère, despite his hoarse whisper of "No, no!" Then she joined Monsieur. As she commented on the weather she heard Madame Mère observe to the count that the party had been brave to risk the river, "known to be treacherous."

"Ah, that we are," he confirmed.

"Treacherous?" asked Mlle Georgette.

He scowled. "Brave. One of my forefathers lost an eye to

a flying champagne cork — without a murmur, and of course he proceeded to propose the health of his guest, the king."

Georgette giggled nervously.

As if in warning there was a distinct pop! in the distance, which signaled that Annie had started to open the Dom Perignon. Before Hyacinthe could faint, Guillaume entered and announced solemnly, "Madame est servie."

They passed into the dining room and Hyacinthe trained his lorgnon on Guillaume who was rather small for his age.

"Extraordinary!" he murmured to Madame Mère on his arm. "A dwarf! Just as at the Spanish court."

Guillaume served the soup perfectly, without thumbs. But at first the conversation either languished or took an unfortunate turn.

As an opening sally Dagmar said to Monsieur, "Frankly, I think it is quite disgraceful, what you intend to do with the woods."

It was not a diplomatic way to introduce a controversial topic, and she would have received a sharp answer had she not exclaimed, after a first spoonful of the soup, "Delicious! You must send the recipe around to the manoir. And some of the mushrooms as well."

Madame Mère heard the first remark, and she also headed into dangerous waters. "Will you not agree," she said to Hyacinthe, glancing to the dowager duchess, "that one has to put up with entirely too much foolish pretense these days?"

"Indeed, chère Madame," he replied evenly. "Especially among the nouveaux riches and their maisons fondées-the-day-before-yesterday. I assure you they are the ones who will bring the revolution down on our heads. And I shall be the first to go."

From the other side of the table Avril observed, ill-advisedly, "And furious if anyone goes before you."

"How could I expect you to understand?" hissed Hyacinthe, to wound.

He turned abruptly to Georgette on his right. "Mademoiselle, have you no conversation? Nothing at all worth saying?"

Desperately Martha signaled to Guillaume to offer the champagne, seeing it as the only way to save the luncheon before open warfare broke out. Then she told the table how she had arrived at the Chateau as Mabel Parfit, intending to stay only until she could get to the telephone. She said it had been an experience she would not have missed, which her hosts took as a compliment.

That carried them to the buffet, where even Dagmar and Hyacinthe found much to tempt them, as did the Durant-Perrichons, who had never suspected that such delicacies could emerge from their kitchen. Simultaneously and miraculously the mood of the room changed. Hyacinthe heard, while demolishing a stuffed quail, that Madame Mère's needlework was, by her own account, admired far and wide. He promised to call again so they could compare stitches and techniques; after all, his own petit point was considered exceptional. By the time Dagmar had refused a second slice of the marjolane from among the desserts the moment for a discussion of more serious matters had arrived.

"Madame la duchesse should know," said Monsieur Durant-Perrichon, "that I would never consider destroying the beautiful forest which lies between our two properties."

"I am prepared to believe you, Monsieur," was D.D.'s reply. "No one who sets a table such as this could have intended to do what was rumored. Will you invite me again soon?"

It was over coffee in the library that the dowager duchess made a confession.

"I will admit that I was not happy when you acquired the Chateau from my nephew, who, I feel, had no right to sell it. There are other ways to settle debts of honor." Here she put a finger to her forehead, clearly implying that a pistol would have solved her nephew's problems without requiring her to move to the manoir. "Also, I found the haggling distasteful."

"The haggling, Madame?"

"What else can one call it?" she asked, taking another chocolate truffle. "You see, I know the value of the property."

"So did I," he replied. "That is why I accepted the price set by your nephew."

"Did you really, Monsieur?" She was skeptical. "With your final offer of 3.6 million new francs rather than the 5 million which were anticipated? I remember it well because at 3.6 million he was not able to repay what he still owes me."

"Madame," said the avocat, now in his element, "would it interest you to see the contract your nephew signed, for the sum of 5.2 million?"

Astonished as she was, Dagmar realized instantly that M. Durant-Perrichon no doubt spoke the truth. After all, she knew her nephew.

"The villain. It is the price I pay for trusting him."

"Not necessarily, Madame." His lawyer's mind could see

the possibility of a happier solution. "The final payment has not yet been made. It is due on the first of October of this year. The sum of 1.7 million."

"Cher maître," said the duchess, her eyes gleaming bright, "the next time I find it necessary to sue a relative or a friend, I hope you will represent me. Meanwhile I will visit my nephew on the last day of September, with a copy of the contract. The sum you mention will liquidate his debt to me and even leave him a few hundred thousand for his horses. I hope he will realize how lucky he is."

She rose, content, and ready to return to the manoir.

"Where is Albert? I told him to have the car here at three. It is almost four."

Albert was, in fact, just driving up to the cour d'honneur. None of them knew that, as they ate their lunch, he had argued with the police in the next town downstream, where the swan boat had come to rest. It had done only slight damage to the low bridge before it sank out of sight and he was lifted to safety. Albert had found a ride back to the manoir just in time to arrive at the Chateau an hour late.

Amid the farewells, Martha heard Avril assuring Mlle Georgette that if she would come to Paris, Avril would send her to her own hairdresser for a complete renovation and help her with some essential shopping as well.

Dagmar, no longer a dreadnought (at least for the day) leaned towards M. Durant-Perrichon and said from the depths of her soul, "Never lose your chef. You have a national treasure." As for the unpredictable comte de Silésie, he kissed the hand of Madame Mère.

It had been agreed that Martha would follow them to the

manoir before evening, as she wanted to have a few words with the family before she gave up her post. Avril, through Annie, would find them a local staff, not one imported from Paris to make them miserable. And the transformation of Mlle Georgette would no doubt ease the tensions between her and Madame Mère, who now also had a companion in needle-work whose visits she could look forward to as long as she fed him well. Above all, there was Jean-Claude. In him, after all, rested the hopes of the house of Durant-Perrichon de la Barre en Ouche. All this she told them and Madame Mère spoke for the entire family when she said, "Madame Prescott, we are in your debt."

Martha turned to the cher maître and asked if he would grant her a favor.

"Anything," he replied.

"Then ride with me to the manoir and permit Jean-Claude to drive us."

"He is a child; it is against the law."

"Think what it will mean to him."

"Jean-Claude," said his father, "would you like to drive our guest to the manoir? After all, Georges is no more."

With these words a new relationship was forged between father and son. Minutes later a proud and happy Jean-Claude brought the Rolls around. With his father and Madame Marthe in the back seat, while Madame Mère and Mlle Georgette looked on, he saluted smartly, and off they went.

Martha took the Monday afternoon train back to Paris. Avril accompanied her as far as St. Cloud where she was com-missioned to choose a few of the better examples of

Hyacinthe's dexterity with the needle at the Pavillion Interpol and despatch them to the country for his next meeting with Madame Mère. Martha and Avril agreed to dine together that evening at a time and place to be set when Martha had spoken with Berte and knew that young woman's plans. For once again, when Martha had rung the hotel from the manoir, Berte had been out on the town. Martha had left a message to say she would be back late Monday afternoon "to tell all."

Martha arrived at the Meurice full of anticipation and was taken aback to find, under the door of their suite, the message she had phoned through that morning, unopened. More alarming, there on the table lay the message from Saturday. She rang the concierge and in answer to her question Sergio said, "But Mademoiselle left for the weekend on Friday, shortly after Madame. I remember, she was collected before lunch."

Collected by whom? Without leaving word? Martha went into her niece's room. Open on the writing table was a letter she had begun to her father. There was no sign of disorder; the pen had been returned to its tray. Something, someone, had interrupted her, but not startled her. Suddenly quiet, the emptiness of the rooms was ominous.

Martha's first instinct was to speak again with Sergio, and then, if he could tell her nothing more, to notify the police. When the phone rang, giving her a start, she took it up instantly and involuntarily exclaimed, "Roberta?"

"It is Sergio, Madame. The gentleman is on his way up. He explained that you were expecting him." And thinking to reassure her he added, "It is the gentleman who collected Mlle Roberta for the weekend."

A Cake in Time

*F*or a moment after Sergio's announcement Martha's worry was replaced with annoyance. Had Berte then really gone off for the weekend without leaving word? But no, that was utterly unlike her. And who was this, coming now instead of Berte?

A light but insistent knock on the door ended her speculations. Martha opened the door wide. A man entered quickly and shut the door behind him. Astonished, she saw that it was Rocco.

"Signora," he said, his face impassive, "the Principe sends a message. Go with Rocco, he says, if you want to see the Signorina."

Anger and doubt were mingled in her reply. "The Principe would not send such a message. But to be sure, I will ring him."

She moved towards the phone.

"No. The Signora will ring nobody if she wants to see the Signorina again. The message is from the Professore."

"Professore? The Crespi-Dolci woman at the Castellino had referred to her husband as the Professore.

"I think the Signora is fond of the Signorina."

She resisted an almost overwhelming urge to hit him.

"You will come. At once."

"Give me a few minutes —"

"No minutes, Signora. We take your bag which you have not unpacked. And you are wearing black which is appropriate for a widow." She had no time to ask what that meant.

At the door Rocco paused: "We will leave the hotel with a smiling face and speak to no one."

Martha's mind raced, but to no logical conclusion. She said no more because no words could express the mixture of revulsion and fear with which she was filled. Her one concern now was for the safety of her niece.

A silent pair, they entered the lift. Downstairs, Rocco took Martha's arm firmly as they crossed the reception rooms. Just before they reached the Rivoli entrance, Martha heard her name.

"Madame Prescott?"

She turned to see Sergio approaching.

"The telephone for you, Madame. It is Madame la duchesse-"

"Tell her —" She felt pain as Rocco's fingers dug into her arm. "Tell the duchess that I cannot dine with her this evening. I am going to the opera." Rocco relaxed his grip.

Outside a black limousine drew up as they appeared and when they pulled away Martha found herself sitting between Rocco and a thin, dour-faced woman. The windows were heavily shaded with dark glass, still Rocco said to the woman: "The veil," which was then draped over Martha's head. Long and black, it was lined and barely translucent, so she could see nothing through it. She understood the remark about a widow's weeds.

"Signora," said Rocco, "you will speak to no one until we are in the plane. If you make troubles, we have a needle which will cause you not to care."

Martha was certain the woman had the needle ready and she planned to give her no opportunity to use it.

"Rocco," she said, hoping for a shred of information, "you spoke of the Professore Crespi-Dolci —"

He interrupted her with a short, cynical laugh. "No, Signora, I spoke of the Professore, not the Dottore Crespi-Dolci who is only a little man from the north. We will talk no more."

Left alone with her thoughts as the car sped through the streets and onto the highway — Martha guessed they had entered the périphérique because they no longer stopped for cross streets — she tried to assemble all she knew. It was very little. Rocco had come for Roberta on Friday, and said something which convinced her to accompany him without question; perhaps...Signorina, if you wish to see your aunt again you will come. They were going to a plane. Had Roberta been taken to the same plane? And flown where? The Professore was, moreover, not the Dottore Crespi-Dolci, whom Rocco obviously despised. Then Martha remembered that Signora Crespi-Dolci had been alarmed when Martha proposed that she might buy the Castellino, and said, "But the Professore —" before she caught herself. She had not, then, meant her husband and Martha should have realized it because the Signora was certainly not afraid of him. The Professore was someone whose displeasure she did fear. But what possible interest could he have in her, or in Berte? For the answer Martha could only wait until she faced this Professore, whom she assumed she was being taken to meet. And why — but it was all whats and whys.

After what Martha judged was half an hour the chauffeur turned the car sharply to the left and they came to a halt.

"We go," said Rocco. She heard the car door being opened. "In silence."

Supported on both sides, as befitted a grieving widow, Martha was guided to a gangway and up into the cabin of a plane. There were no formalities, so it was a private plane, which meant they were at Le Bourget. Martha was placed in a seat, the belt buckled around her. No one spoke above the sound of the engine. The cabin door was closed (it changed the sound of the motor in her ear) and almost at once the plane taxied off.

"Rocco," said Martha in some exasperation, "can't I remove these draperies now? They have served their purpose."

There was no answer. She decided to take a chance, needle or not and with a quick movement she threw off the heavy veil to find herself alone in the cabin of a small jet aircraft. The only decoration was a series of color reproductions, renaissance portraits of the saints or the Holy Family. How inappropriate, she thought. The oval windows were blacked out and Martha was not tempted to move about as the plane rose into the sky.

An hour later Martha felt in her ears that they were losing altitude. Rocco had not asked for her passport so she assumed they were still in France. However, when they had landed and the cabin door was opened, a man entered and addressed her in Italian.

"The veil, Signora."

Resigned, she put it over her head again and wished she had thought to remove the lining during the flight.

"Do not speak."

"I know," she replied, shortly.

They descended the gangway and at the bottom the man was joined by another so that she was guided away from the plane just as she had entered it. In the distance Martha heard a voice on the public address system announcing the departure of a flight in Italian. They had, then, crossed an international border and landed without any formalities. The Professore was either very important or had the best connections, or both. That would not keep her from giving him a piece of her mind as soon as she met him.

Martha sat silently but impatiently as they sped along what seemed to be a flat, country road. The air was heavy, as if they were not far from the sea. Finally the car stopped and she was helped none to gently over a doorstep and down what must have been a long passage, through a door, and into a chair. Presently she realized she was again alone and lifted the veil to see a small room, simply furnished with bed, table and chair. There was a single door; she tried it, knowing it would be locked. The one window was shuttered. Her suitcase had been left beside the bed. The table had a drawer in it, which she opened. It was empty.

"Buona sera, Signora."

Startled, she turned around. There stood an old woman with a tray of food. Behind her was the man who had told Martha to replace the veil, now guarding the door.

"The Professore," Martha said, "I want to see the Professore at once."

The woman hesitated, looked to the man, who shook his head impatiently. She deposited the tray on the table.

"Eat and drink, Signora," she said in no unkindly tone, and in an accent typical of the Veneto.

Martha took a chance. "Then let me see the Signorina. I have come to see her. She is my niece."

"Eat and drink, Signora."

The woman left and the door was quickly shut behind her. In addition to the lock, a bar clanged into place. Martha was not hungry but she knew she might need her strength, so she sat down at the table to simple country fare and a carafe of red wine. Martha took up the fork, then stopped. The food could be poisoned. No, that was an hysterical reaction. She had not been flown to the north of Italy to be poisoned on arrival. She tasted and found the food delicious. The polenta, as well as the woman's accent and the heavy air, all gave Martha a good idea that she was not far from Venice, probably in a villa of the Veneto, for this was not the house of a contadino. The carved door and quality of the shutters on the window told her it was a residence of some importance.

The food demanded drink. Martha poured herself a glass of the wine and drank. Almost at once a great torpor overcame her and she realized there had been something more than wine in the carafe. In alarm she started to her feet, but she could not fight against the numbness which increasingly possessed her. She sank to the bed, realizing only vaguely that the fork, still in her hand, was slipping to the floor. And remembered no more.

When Martha opened her eyes the old woman was sitting beside her on the bed, patting her hand reassuringly. Martha was conscious of an intense headache. She put her hand to her forehead.

"Signora, drink."

She handed her a glass. Martha sat up and looked about. They were alone; the door was shut. Her bag had been unpacked. All at once Martha's anger at being not only kidnapped but drugged as well overtook her. It showed on her face even before she could find words to express it. The woman saw, and tried to calm her.

"Drink, Signora. You will feel better. The Professore wants to see you. It is tomorrow afternoon." Her disjointed sentences told the prisoner all she wanted to know.

Martha took the glass and drank.

"I am Lina," said the woman as if the statement would inspire confidence. Strangely, it did.

An hour later Martha, refreshed and prepared for battle, walked with a steady step down the long corridor to another wing of the house. Lina, who went before her, opened double doors which gave onto a large room.

"La sala, Signora."

The elegant hall was sumptuously furnished in a style predating the villa, which was eighteenth century. The room was bathed in the bright sunlight of the south — the first natural light Martha had seen in twenty-four hours. Lina stopped before another double door, knocked timidly and waited. Only when she heard a "Si," did she turn to Martha, open the door, and motion her to enter.

Martha stepped forward alone and entered a room dark in contrast to the sun in the sala. The door closed behind her. Suddenly a light shone full in her face. Out of the darkness a voice sounded.

"Ah, yes, Signora Pres-cott."

Indignation overcame Martha and she cried out, "Who are you? Where are you? Kindly turn off that light. And where is my niece? You must release us at once."

Silence. Then the light was deflected and she saw that it came from a desk lamp which had been turned towards her face. Now it gleamed down on a polished surface, and reflected equally on Martha and a man seated behind the desk in a high-backed armchair.

"You are in no position to demand, Signora."

The voice was unruffled, the man wholly at his ease.

As Martha's eyes adjusted to the light of the room, a library, she peered at the thin elderly man who faced her. He was fastidiously dressed in an old-fashioned way, complete with waistcoat, watch chain and stiff collar. His hair was tinted that jet black which never looks natural, his moustache waxed. His face was lined, and his mouth turned down. As she looked at him Martha knew at once that he was a sick man, with his sallow skin and eyes partially closed as if the life had already started to go out of them. He rose, hesitating as a man will when he is unsteady and wants to be sure of his step before he takes it.

"Thus far you have not been helpful," he said.

He indicated two chairs which faced each other. She sat in one, he in the other.

"I want to see my niece at once."

He ignored her words and completed his own thought. "Not helpful at all. Last night —"

"I was drugged."

"Last night they questioned you. You told them nothing."

"Has it occurred to you that I may have nothing to tell?"

She spoke in exasperation as to a petulant child. He raised his voice in annoyance to answer her.

"No, Signora, that has not occurred to me, nor is it likely to."

Then he winced, put his hand into his waistcoat pocket and took a small tablet into his mouth.

"I am a prisoner of my doctors just as you are my prisoner. It is a beautiful prison, this, if you have a sense of history."

He raised his arm to draw her attention to the room, which was that of a scholar, filled with leather-bound volumes and precious objects. Whatever his physical condition, the Professore had enough pomp for any circumstance.

"Why am I here? How did you even know of my existence?"

"I did not know about a Mrs. Prescott until she arrived at the Castellino, contrary to the regrets which the Principe had sent her. From that moment I had no choice but to become interested."

"Rocco kept you well informed, I am sure."

"That was his duty." Then he opened his eyes wide as if to mesmerize her. "The affairs of Interpol are always of interest to me."

"Interpol!" she exclaimed, half to herself. So that was it. "Rocco kept you very well mis-informed. Pavillon Interpol is what we call the residence of the comte de Silésie in St. Cloud — as a joke. The comte is interested only in petit point."

"Signora, you must not take me for a fool."

Then Martha learned how dangerous circumstantial evidence could be, as in terse sentences he repeated facts which made it clear to him that Martha Prescott had arrived in Sicily on assignment as an agent of the organization he obviously considered a threat to his well-being.

"You were asked not to come, you came. You arranged to arrive while the Crespi-Dolcis were there to negotiate for the Castellino. Perhaps you even know that I also come from a village near Taormina where your Principe's family has looked down on my people for many centuries. But his family was important in a world which no longer exists. We are the ones who count today."

Here was passionate feeling.

"Now you understand why I can only have the Castellino if your Principe does not know who is going to own it."

The malevolence of the man sparkled like diamonds in his eyes.

"You chose to threaten me. Why? And because of you that fool Crespi-Dolci agreed to pay much more than I want the Principe to have. Then, Signora, a letter arrived from St. Cloud. That gave me the first clue."

Martha remembered that they had moved into the garden as she explained about the letter and joke of Hyacinthe's address. She had done it to tantalize Rocco. Instead she had convinced one spy that he was dealing with another.

"You burned the letter, of course. Rocco understood why. Then the telegram. You were called back? Why? To report what? On your last day at the Castellino you went to the grove where you could talk with the Principe and no living creature could overhear you. What you said there I do now know. Not yet."

She could imagine how he would react if she told him they had simply enjoyed the scenery, so she said nothing.

"Nor do I know what you reported to Maurice. You pretend not to understand?"

He handed Martha a sheet of paper on which was transcribed NEED YOU ST CLOUD COMPLICATIONS MEET MAURICE FRIDAY 1052 ST LAZARE A. "What are these complications? How do they concern me? These are my questions."

He had built his case against her and an explanation of Maurice for Meurice was not going to tear it down. Martha simply expressed her feelings.

"It is remarkable how far from the truth a man can stray with nothing to guide him but a guilty conscience."

He pounded his fist on the arm of the chair.

"I am not spoken to like that — by anyone."

"Perhaps it is time you were. I have no connection with Interpol except to wish them well in their attempts to run down criminals. You have convinced me that they no doubt have good reason to be interested in you, but —" Here she raised her voice so he would not interrupt — "I do not want to know the unsavory details. Moreover, I do not believe you could force the Principe to sell the Castellino for any price unless he wanted to sell it for reasons of his own."

He waited a moment, then said, "Perhaps you and your niece are not the only hostages, Signora Prescott." The Professore rose, once again with care, and moved to the book-lined wall behind Martha. In a space between the shelves hung a large painting backed by velvet draperies which enhanced the frame simply and elegantly.

"Is it not very fine?" he asked.

She saw that the painting was indeed a masterpiece. It was Caravaggio's Death of St. Silentius.

The Professore waited for her reaction, the cold gleam of the acquisition in his eye.

"You are a thief."

He spoke calmly in return, as if she had murmured her congratulations: "Of my two Caravaggios it is my favorite. The other is also very good. A nativity."

He crossed the room and turned light on a second painting. Martha followed and stood before it in silence.

"You have seen it in Palermo? The Church of St. Lorenzo. I had to cut it down to fit this space. I keep only three of my paintings here, the others are in the Galleria. I am certain you know the third one also."

With that he lighted a third painting and Martha gasped. Before her was one of the great Piero della Francesca madonnas, perhaps the greatest. It was a painting which she had Robert had once driven half a day to admire.

"You know it from a wayside chapel in the Tuscan hills."

"Yes. This is a remarkable copy."

He raised his voice. "There are no copies in my collection." Then he continued quietly again: "A very fine copy now hangs in that same chapel, and if you ask the sacristan he will pull back the curtain and proudly allow you to see it. Of course he does not know of the substitution, nor does anyone else. I do not show my collection."

"And yet you have shown these paintings to me. Is that

not dangerous?"

"Not for me," he replied. "You must understand," he continued, passing lightly over the threat, "that the art of confiscation has progressed since the day in 1911 when an Italian patriot cut the Mona Lisa from her frame in the Louvre and returned her to Italy, temporarily alas."

Faced with that extraordinary statement, as well as the two great Caravaggios and an incomparable Piero della Francesca, Martha stared at the man, perplexed.

The Professore took out his watch. "It is time. The doctors require that I rest in the afternoon." He returned to his desk. "Signora Prescott, you have an appreciative eye as well as a bad memory. If you will take supper with me tonight I will show you my Galleria. The collection is not large, but the quality is high."

Martha accepted, not only to see the paintings but also because she wanted to know as much as possible about this man who obviously had a criminal mind and yet could give himself completely to the admiration of great works of art devoted to the most inspiring religious subjects.

The Professore pressed a button on his desk.

Martha sought to take advantage of the moment. "May I expect that my niece will be allowed to join us this evening?"

"Do you really think I would detain my two important guests in the same villa, where they might meet?"

"Do you really believe my niece is an agent of Interpol?"

"Signora, she is important to me only because she is important to you. She is far away from here, and for now, she is safe."

Another threat. The benign influence of the masterpieces

receded as he moved away from them. There was a knock at the door and Lina appeared.

"Take the Signora to her room. She will return for supper."

"Si, Don Carlo."

Martha followed the old woman back through the sala and down the long corridor, bereft now of any hope that she would see Berte that day, and not aware that the evening was going to end on a note of qualified exhilaration. For without her host realizing it she would discover where Roberta was being held. The qualification would come from her realization of the mortal danger which threatened them both.

Lina had pressed a gown for her and Martha agreed to wear it to please that kindly woman. They talked as she dressed, and Martha was careful not to ask any questions which might alarm Lina or put her on her guard. It was Lina herself who volunteered information. Yes, Don Carlo was a sick man. Lina touched her heart and her stomach. He was difficult because he suffered. But beyond that she had nothing to say about her employer.

Promptly at nine o'clock Lina took Martha to the sala where she waited to face her adversary, curious but lacking any compassionate feeling for him. He joined her almost at once and led the way into an adjacent room.

"We dine very simply," he said, as a young man wearing white cotton gloves served them, "and my meal will be even more Spartan than yours. Contrast the fragrance of your broth, Signora, with my so-called healthy soup of two humble vegetables, the zucchini and green beans."

Martha looked up in surprise at his words, but she asked casually, "And what magic are they supposed to perform?"

"Magic, yes. It seems that these two lowly vegetables have in them all the minerals we need to nourish us."

"May I taste your medical soup?"

"Of course. Guido."

Martha hoped her excitement did not show, because as the green soup was set before her and she tasted it, she recognized her own cure-all for stomach ills, a soup she had often made from an old recipe of her mother's ("Drink it often, it contains everything you need and nothing to harm you."). This was unmistakably her brew.

Nothing had ever tasted better, because it meant to Martha that Roberta was in the villa, had recognized the Professore's digestive problem — perhaps at a meal shared in this same room — and had suggested a remedy she knew from her aunt.

"An old family recipe?"

"No, it was proposed by an acquaintance." He responded as casually as she had asked.

"An acquaintance who forgot a very important point," Martha said. "I have read of this soup and I remember that it is essential it be served cold."

"Cold green soup? It is bad enough hot. But I will tell Lina to serve it cold tomorrow."

Martha smiled almost demurely and took the perfectly prepared costaletta milanese which Guido now offered her. Hot versus cold. Berte and she had always disagreed on this point and now if Berte heard from Lina that the soup was to be served cold because somebody had told Don Carlo so, she might guess Martha was in the villa.

"A delicious cutlet," she exclaimed in genuine appreciation. "I wish you could join me."

He pushed his soup plate away. "You make it impossible for me to eat my vegetables," he said, tempted by the sight and aroma of the golden cutlet. "Guido!" he commanded.

So they both enjoyed the same menu and Martha took a certain satisfaction in anticipating that Don Carlo would probably have to reach into his waistcoat pocket for a pill before the evening was over.

The Professore looked up from a second serving of the zuppa inglese which had been intended for Martha and which they had shared.

"You find it difficult to believe that a copy of the Piero della Francesca could remain undetected in the chapel at Monterchi. It could not be done with a painting from the Uffizi, perhaps, but if you are willing to pay, a good copy can be made of anything. And, under the right circumstances, by which I mean a private collection or a wayside chapel, it can be substituted.

"Come, you will see my Tintoretto, the Virgin and Child. It was in a collection in Milano from which I also have a Correggio. The owners are satisfied that the police recovered their Tintoretto and they only mourn the Correggio."

He led her through the library into a spacious gallery. Paintings filled most of the available space in the style of the Pitti. Once again this extraordinary man changed from tyrant to proud possessor, as he came into the presence of the masterpieces.

"Here is one Correggio, and there is the other, contributed by the Malaspina in Pavia."

A few steps further on Martha stopped before a painting that was unmistakably a Fra Angelico.

"Ah, yes," said Don Carlo, "a national treasure. It will interest you to know that it comes from the palazzo of your Principe's cousins in Napoli. They have a very fine copy which was 'restored' to them."

"It reminds me of a Fra Angelico in the Vatican Museum," said Martha. Then she added, almost as a taunt, "Surely you have something from that collection?"

The question annoyed him. "I have nothing from the Vatican. Not yet."

He moved on. "You will appreciate this Mantegna." It was a triptych of Christ the King twice adored by St. James. "From the church of the Eremitani in Padova, which was sadly damaged in your war." His use of 'your' set him aside from Martha and the rest of delinquent humanity. "I understand the police have sought it all over Europe."

"And how close to home it is," she said.

"Very close," he confirmed.

Then Don Carlo noticed a ladder near the far wall. A frown crossed his face until he recalled why it was there. "Guido is cleaning this side." But his reassurance was quickly replaced by alarm. "He has removed the Sodoma."

They saw a blank space on the wall where the velvet was unfaded as suddenly the Professore stumbled. By instinctively putting out a hand to the ladder he steadied himself, but when he glanced down to the floor his eyes turned to stone. He had narrowly missed stepping on a painting. Immediately he crossed to the bellpull and waited there until Lina answered his call.

"Bring Guido."

She disappeared and he returned to Martha who had now stopped before the Martyrdom of Santa Lucia.

"I hope you will not force me to play the Roman to your Lucia," he said darkly.

Martha looked again at the picture, which showed the fate of that Christian lady whom the Romans had dispatched after removing certain unmentionable parts of her body. The saint was portrayed as tradition decreed: holding on a plate what the Romans had nipped off, and clothed in no more than a look of beatific resignation.

"— but I have the means to do so."

Without comment Martha moved on until she came upon a painting which depicted another favorite Renaissance subject. She said evenly, "And I on the other hand would very much like to play Judith to your Holofernes, but I do not have the means, alas."

The last word piqued him, as she intended it should, but before he could reply Guido entered. Lina hovered in the background, sensing trouble.

"Come here."

The tone of voice was ominous and Guido knew it. Don Carlo pointed to the ladder and turned the cold fire of his eyes on Guido.

"You removed the Sodoma from the wall."

"To clean the velvet, Don Carlo."

"And left the painting on the floor — face down in its frame." Then he thundered, "Why? So I would put my foot through the canvas?"

There was no answer to the questions, and the young

man knew better than to offer one. He bowed his head.

"Idiot!"

Then, as Guido looked up to ask forgiveness for his negligence, Don Carlo hit him hard across the mouth with the back of his hand. Guido did not flinch but neither did he offer an apology.

"Signor —" It was Lina who spoke, but she was not allowed to plead.

"Be quiet," said Don Carlo without looking in her direction. "Give me the painting," he said to the hapless Guido from whose lip blood trickled.

Guido picked up the Sodoma and put it in Don Carlo's hands.

"Now get out. Both of you."

They left and Don Carlo muttered, "Do you wonder that my heart needs medicines when you see the stupidity with which I am surrounded?"

When he had re-hung the painting and closed the gallery doors behind them Don Carlo reached into his waistcoat pocket for one of the pills. He had not recovered from his burst of spleen, and she was not surprised when he said to her, abruptly, "Signora Prescott, I am not a man of unlimited patience. We will meet again tomorrow morning and I advise you to be ready to tell me what I need to know. Otherwise..."

"Otherwise?"

"If you do not speak, Rocco will bring the Principe to us."

This was a trump card and he played it as such.

"The Principe will not come. Not with Rocco."

"I think he will." His voice took on the unpleasant edge of a man who knew he was completely in control. "When he knows his friend the Signora Prescott is a guest at the Villa Dolorosa he will come."

Martha realized that Rinaldo would be trapped as she had been, as Roberta had been, and then they would all be hostages — three who knew too much about Don Carlo.

"Lina," said the Don as they entered the sala where she waited, "The Signora will come to me in the morning. At ten o'clock."

That night she faced a grim reality: Don Carlo could only keep the paintings if the secret of his collection was his alone. Unimportant were the simple people who served him, who probably did not realize either the significance or the sources of the pictures. But for Martha, Berte, and now perhaps the Principe, to be brought to the Villa Dolorosa could only mean they were not meant to leave it. Martha weighed her options and by morning she had devised a plan which a committee would have rejected as visionary, but under the circumstances the faintest glimmer of light was as bright as a ray from the sun. So she plotted.

The first step depended on the goodness of Lina, who would not have imagined that it lay within her power to help. When Lina brought Martha her cafè latte shortly before nine, she stayed to straighten the room. The door was securely bolted behind her as Martha had hoped it would be.

"Dear Lina," said Martha in her best, deliberate Italian, as soon as they were safely alone, "listen to me."

Lina continued her work but Martha knew she was listening intently.

"I am here against my will, you know that, as is my niece who told you how to prepare the green soup." She had decided to introduce this information matter-of-factly. Lina betrayed no surprise. "We were brought here in error, but I cannot convince the Professore that he has made a mistake. In two days' time we will be in great danger." At that Lina stopped her work, and waited to hear more. "Rocco will come," she concluded, and relied on Lina's sense of people to confirm her point. There was a flicker in Lina's eye. "My niece and I must be gone before he arrives."

That was the background, now came the test. "This message will save us," She held out a small piece of paper.

The old woman spoke in a whisper. "I cannot, Signora."

"You are afraid. I understand. But no harm will come to you. This telegram must be sent today. I can only give you these French francs to pay for it."

"Signora, we are all afraid. Guido is my grandson; he is afraid."

"Guido, you, and I will all leave together, with my niece and anyone else you tell me should go with us."

Martha said nothing more but she smiled, desperately hoping it was the reassuring, melting smile it had to be. She extended her hand, in which were the message and one hundred francs she had found in her bag. She waited. Then with a swift movement Lina took the note, but not the money. Martha understood and breathed, "Bless you." Lina put a finger to her lips, went about her work, finished it quickly and knocked to be let out of the room.

Martha sat for some minutes drinking her coffee. She had made no copy of the message but she knew that the words, to Avril's cable address in Paris, were her only real hope. PARIDINDE 75016 SEND HELP VILLA DOLOROSO

VENETO RINALDO NOT TO COME HERE WITH ROCCO. Her initial was unnecessary because Avril would have discovered that she and Berte were missing from the hotel. And the post office from which the wire was despatched would identify the location in the Veneto.

This part of the plan depended on Lina. Martha, meanwhile, could concentrate on part two, which required the unwitting cooperation of Don Carlo himself.

Precisely at ten Martha entered the library.

"Good morning," she said pleasantly, in a voice which belied her feelings.

Don Carlo looked up and waited for her to be seated. Then he spoke, as deliberately as she had spoken to Lina an hour before. "You have something to tell me, Signora?"

"Yes. But not what you expect —"

He waited.

"It is about the green soup."

He brought his palm down hard on the desk, a symbolic slap in reaction to her impertinence.

"I cannot oblige you with a confession," she continued, "because I do not know enough to lie convincingly."

"Very well," he broke in impatiently, "Rocco will be here tomorrow night and your Principe will be with him."

As if he had confirmed a visit of mutual friends, Martha went on lightly.

"And meanwhile, Don Carlo? Shall we not exist as pleasantly as possible?" She hoped her casual tone was disarming. At least it was not what he had any reason to expect. "You eat your green soup and you starve. But doctors say we may eat whatever we choose as long as we do so in moderation. That is better for us than the shock of a rigorous diet. You have an excellent cook; allow Lina to prepare her specialties. They will be a revelation to me and do you no harm — in moderation. In fact," she concluded with an insincere smile, "your temper might improve along with your digestion."

At least he did not come down hard on the desk with his other palm.

"Signora," he said instead, "since your arrival I have listened not for what you have told me, but for what you have left unsaid. When I casually mention the name of this villa you seem to take no notice, but of course you log the information in your mind. Now you pretend we are here to enjoy ourselves —"

For an awful moment Martha thought Lina had taken the message intended for Avril direct to her employer who would presently crumple it into a ball before her eyes. But he continued: "You are well trained. My respect for Interpol grows. They will no doubt miss you." His final words were spoken with unmistakable emphasis. Did he expect her to fall on her knees and beg for mercy? "Meanwhile, as you say, why should we not follow the doctors' advice? At luncheon we will eat a pasta carbonara, for which Lina is famous. And after that — but we shall see."

"All in moderation," said Martha, thinking of the sauce of pancetta, butter, egg yolks and cheese.

Martha counted on Don Carlo not to know the meaning of moderation and she was not disappointed. Lina's pasta, and the courses which followed, were all superbly to her purpose, for the Professore simply could not resist the temptations of the table. With any luck, according to her plan, he could soon take to his sick bed and that would temporarily divert his attention from 'business,' which was herself. Also, it would give Avril time to arrange their rescue from the aptly named Villa Dolorosa. As she watched Don Carlo consume an enormous portion of dolce Martha even saw the grim humor of the situation: she was a Scheherazade relying not on tales but on food, her thousand and one nights limited to forty-eight critical hours of sumptuous, rich repasts.

Expansively, after a meal of vast proportions and immoderate consumption, the Professore dismissed his guest with a hint of geniality.

"Until this evening, Signora."

Almost happily she allowed Lina to lead her back to her room, knowing that another rich dinner, which fitted her grand strategy perfectly, would be served at nine o'clock.

Alone, Martha blessed Dr. Benson, at home in Sliepskill and presumably still shedding extra pounds, for having pressed the recipe of his mother's chocolate cake into Berte's hand before they left for the airport. She had found it while searching her bag for a scrap of paper on which to write out the message to Avril, and it had given her the idea of the gustatory gamble. The Coronary, Dr. Benson called it. That was perhaps too much to hope for, but the confection would surely contribute to the Professore's crise de foie on which she was counting.

At teatime Lina brought her a tray. Martha translated the recipe and asked that the cake be made for luncheon the next day. So intent was she in her explanations that Martha failed to notice Lina's nervous agitation, until with a covert movement Lina thrust a piece of paper into Martha' hand.

"I cannot, Signora," she said with tears in her eyes. "Guido cannot." Quickly she wiped her eyes on her apron, knocked on the locked door, and was gone.

In Martha's hand was the scrap of paper on which she had written her message to Avril.

By evening Martha had sufficiently recovered from the shock of failure to assure Lina with an elegiac smile, "It is not your fault. I understand." But she went to dinner in low spirits. The return of her note, and with it the collapse of her hope that Avril would arrange their rescue, left Martha and Berte wholly at the mercy of a man who, as far as she could determine, was unaware of that word.

Don Carlo, for his part, approached the food with his usual gusto and to excess. Loathe to leave the table he lingered over a plate of marrons glaces. He spoke at length about the stupidity of the Padovani who, by relying on God to protect their painting, had provided him with his Mantegna. How the affair had almost cost the Maresciallo of police in Padova his job, because the people who did not want to pay to have their treasures properly guarded were the first to blame the police when the masterpiece they did not deserve was removed from their careless custody.

"Do you not agree, Signora?"

Too dispirited to disagree, Martha merely nodded, which could be interpreted any way her captor chose, and took the first opportunity to rise from the table.

"You are intelligent, Signora," said Don Carlo, "I will

hope you have something to tell me in the morning."

"Good night, Professore."

Martha turned to Lina, who once again led her down the long corridor to her room. Inside, with the door still open and guard waiting outside, Lina went to the bed and fluffed the pillows. She stood between the guard and the bed and as she said "Buona notte, Signora," she made sure that Martha saw a scrap of paper she had placed under the pillow.

As soon as the bar outside had slipped into place, Martha reached for the folded sheet. The brief message was in Roberta's hand, and Martha did not know whether to laugh with happiness and relief at the sign that Berte was indeed in the villa, or to weep at her own helplessness to free them both. The message showed that Berte's spirit was not bowed. She had written I'M ALL RIGHT. BORED STIFF. HOT GREEN SOUP INDEED. HELP! and then had drawn a happy face.

Before she slept that night Martha had devised an answer which she inscribed on the same piece of paper, certain that Lina would deliver it to Berte in the morning. She rejected all the things she wanted to say in favor of a laconic. BLESS YOU MY DARLING BE PATIENT. At least it was a sign of life and hope. At the same time she resolved to speak frankly to the Professore at lunch and ask him to allow Berte to join them. It could do no harm. It would simply be a gesture of decency.

During the night it rained and there was thunder. When Lina brought breakfast she and Martha exchanged perfunctory Good Mornings for the benefit of the guard. Martha put the note for Berte in Lina's hand whence it quickly disappeared in the deep pocket of her voluminous skirt.

Before she left, Lina opened the shutters. The window

faced the green of a walled garden, now sparkling with rain-drops and sunshine. It had become, from the first time Lina had let the light of day into her room, Martha's only contact with the outside world. She stood in the window, no longer depressed as she gazed through the grill at the sky, brilliantly blue after the downpour. She even looked forward to midday and hoped she would find Don Carlo in a benign mood, willing to grant the favor she intended to ask of him.

It was almost two o'clock before Lina came to take her in to luncheon. Lina said nothing but rolled her eyes and as soon as Martha had joined the Professore she understood. There was still thunder in the air. At best she would be able to ask if Berte could join them that evening. Guido entered with the pasta. Lina had again accomplished a miracle, a great platter of gnocchi à la parisienne. But despite that offering and those which followed, including an incredibly rich eel in the Venetian style, luncheon remained difficult. Martha decided to take the initiative.

"Professore," she said, "the storm is over, the sun is out."

For a moment he regarded her balefully, then spat out the words which explained his anger. "The storm is not over, and you have brought it on yourself by choosing not to speak the truth."

"I have repeatedly told you —" she began, but she got no further.

"You have told me lies. I have spoken with Rocco. He is in Paris to keep a watch on the Principe. Do you know where your Principe spent the morning? In St. Cloud at the head-quarters of Interpol."

Avril had summoned Rinaldo to Paris, that was clear. But

did either of them know enough to give Interpol any helpful information as to her whereabouts? Did the Principe after all have some connection with that organization?

"He has interfered and he will regret it."

At that moment Lina entered with the dolce de cioccolata she had created from Martha's recipe. It was unacknowledged and unhonored, but the Professore helped himself to a large slice.

Then he gave her one of his penetrating looks. "Signora, this is your last chance to tell me what you know. Otherwise, Rocco will bring the Principe to the villa tonight. He awaits my instructions. And before you answer, think of this — your niece is also my guest — in another place. You have it in your power to secure her release and return to Paris, a journey I can no longer offer you or the Principe if you choose to have him come here. She can be set free, or she will not be heard of again. It is up to you."

Martha responded to his threat with vehemence. "You are a despicable, wretched man, so consumed by your megalomania that you do not recognize the truth when you hear it — because it does not fit your suspicions. I cannot tell you anything and I think you know it!"

"Foolish woman!"

"Let me be the only one on your conscience. Leave the Principe in Paris, and release Roberta now from this house —"

"I have told you the Signorina is not in the villa."

"You are a liar as well as a bully, and you will be destroyed, because the police will search you out for the punishment you deserve. Your pictures cannot save you — these paintings you steal from the helpless because you are afraid to attempt the Uffizi or the Vatican!"

He pounded on the table, and cried, "Lina!" She entered quickly, nervously.

"Take the Signora to her room. She is mad. Una donna pazza. I will not see you again, Signora, until you face me in the presence of the Principe."

"If Rocco manages to lure him away."

"He has already done so. The car left for the airport half an hour ago. The Principe could not resist coming to the rescue of his friend — and colleague."

"In other words, Don Carlo," and Martha spoke with biting sarcasm, "when you said the Principe would be abducted unless I told you the lies you want to hear, he was already on his way here. Oh, you are a man of honor, indeed!"

"Take her away."

Lina hesitated just long enough for Martha to express her feelings in a final epithet. "Odious creature," she exclaimed and left the room.

Furious, he slumped back in his chair. Then, impulsively, he took up his knife and gashed deep into the dolce where Lina had left it, and slid another immense slice onto his plate.

An hour later Lina was still in her kitchen, a vast space with vaulted ceiling which had remained largely unchanged since the eighteenth century. As she dealt with the pots and pans her grandson sat morosely at the long table finishing a piece of the chocolate confection she had served Don Carlo. Across from him, similarly employed, was Tonio, the old gardener. Lina put her hand on Guido's shoulder.

"Be happy, mi caro," she said, "soon Don Carlo will go away to Milano or Palermo, then we will be alone again."

But he took no comfort in the future, being concerned with the painful present and a lip still sore.

"Someday," he said, expressing his dark thoughts, "I am going to take off my white gloves and throw them in his face."

"No, Guido," she exclaimed in alarm. "He will turn you over to Rocco and the others."

"I'll just walk out. Disappear."

Tonio looked up from his plate. "They will find you."

But Guido was too full of his resentments to recognize the realities.

"Nonnina," he said to his grandmother, "why does he keep the American Signora here? And the Signorina? How do they harm him?"

"These are things we do not understand," Lina answered. "The reason lies in his heart."

The boy laughed. "Don Carlo has no heart. You know what would happen if you went to him and said that Tonio had fallen into the canal and was drowning? He would say, 'The more fool he,' and tell you to find someone else for the garden. The same with me, and even you. He cares only for himself."

"He loves his pictures."

"No, he loves having them because they make him important in his own eyes. Remember what happened last year when the small painting on wood arrived. He opened the case and found it cracked. Of course, because it was very old. He turned on the man who brought it, but did he repair the painting? No, he was angry that it dared to break so he burned it. I saw it go up in the flames. You are too kind, Nonnina. Others are not like you."

A bell rang. It jangled in the corner of the room where it was one of several on the board. It jangled again.

"He never rings at this time of day. He sleeps."

"Don't go," said Guido.

Again the bell.

"You forget, Guido, we depend on Don Carlo."

She left the room, wiping her hands on her apron. The two men sat in silence over their coffee, unaware that the ringing of the bell signaled an end to their life at the Villa Dolorosa.

Lina knocked lightly and waited. When she heard no "Si?" she opened the library door cautiously and looked inside. Don Carlo was at his desk, but his head was thrown back. She crossed towards him, stopped before the desk and gasped. He was ashen pale, beads of perspiration on his brow. His mouth was open, his breathing spasmodic.

"Dio!"

He put his hands on the desk to brace himself, moved his head, and saw her through glazed eyes. He spoke with a rasp.

"My medicine. Quick."

She saw the bottle of pills on his desk.

"Here, Don Carlo —"

"Not that, you fool." His eyes flared in anger, he rose unsteadily to his feet and lunged around the end of the desk, knocking the bottle out of her hand. The little green capsules spread in all directions across the floor.

"Lazy fools, all of you." He could hardly manage the words but his voice rose to a shout. "The other bottle! My room!"

He lunged again and this time hit out at her, striking Lina

across the chest as he fell. Nevertheless she helped him into the wing-backed chair near the painting of St. Silentius, where he breathed heavily, his pallor livid.

All energy spent, he muttered, "I will get rid of you all. My medicine!"

She hurried from the room, his voice following her, alternately in the tones of an outraged child and a panicky old man. Lina's eyes filled with tears of pain and resentment. In Don Carlo's quarters she found the other bottle, a liquid, and filled a glass with water before hurrying back to the library.

"Liiiina!"

Crossing the sala she heard him call her name again, followed by a string of recriminations. As he cursed her for not caring, suddenly she did not care. She stopped, ready to return to her kitchen because he deserved no more. Then her better self took possession and she entered the library He saw her and spat out an insult. Silently, she held the water glass as he grasped the bottle. He was not able to unscrew the cap.

"Open it —"

She put the glass down and opened the bottle, which he again snatched from her. It slipped from his fingers and fell, the dark liquid streaming across a small rug. She quickly picked it up just as Don Carlo reached down to retrieve it. His sudden movement and the shift of weight pushed the top-heavy chair over and knocked it against the painting behind them. For an instant the chair was balanced precariously, but Don Carlo's arm fell heavily on the armrest, causing it to topple over as the painting broke from the wall, loosened by the shock of contact. Don Carlo half turned and saw St. Silentius coming down hard. A corner of the frame struck him a glancing blow on the head. Just as suddenly, Don Carlo slumped and lay partially under the painting which was now leaning against the overturned chair.

"Don Carlo?"

But his unseeing open eyes told Lina that Don Carlo was dead.

Martha heard the key in her door being turned. It was not the guard but someone who was having trouble. Finally the door opened and a distraught Lina cried out, "Signora — Don Carlo —"

"He is ill?" She dared to be hopeful.

"Morto. Come quickly. We will go to the Signorina and then we must leave the villa at once."

"The guard?"

"He has gone with the driver to the airport to bring Rocco."

Martha followed Lina down the corridor with no chance to ask any of the other questions which crowded into her mind. She forgot them as Lina unlocked another door and Martha saw Berte jump up from her bed.

"Oh, my darling," she exclaimed and took her niece into her arms.

Lina allowed them no time for explanations.

"Signora," she pleaded, "come. We will find Guido and Tonio. We must all be gone before the others come back."

First, at Martha's insistence, they went to the library where Don Carlo still lay on the floor. Lina closed his eyes and crossed herself. Then Martha led them back into the sala, conscious of the fact that Rocco was arriving with another prisoner — the

Principe. The safety of all of them was important but it would not do for Rocco and the guards to return to an empty villa and find Don Carlo expired, with the Principe in their power.

"Lina," she asked, "where are we, exactly?"

"On the Brenta, Signora. Between Stra and Mira Taglio. But now we must go to Fusina and take the motoscafo across the lagoon to Venice. There we will be safe."

"When will Rocco be here?"

"They usually arrive before dark."

That would give them several hours. "Go if you wish, Lina, but I cannot leave the Principe with Rocco, who is bringing him here. I am going to summon the police. We are not far from Padova?"

"Half an hour, Signora."

"The airport is much further. Will you stay and help me?"

With misgivings because it was against her better judgment, Lina said, "Si."

"Then go to Guido and tell him what happened. Watch the gates and if the car returns early, warn me."

Lina scurried off.

"Berte —"

"How can I help?"

"Stay here, outside the library door and if anyone but Lina or Guido appears, go inside at once and bolt the door behind you. I am going to get through to the police in Padova." Then she added lovingly, "Be patient. We will have a lifetime to discuss everything."

"I'm ready to break down and cry now, but I'll wait," said Berte with a tiny grin as Martha disappeared into the library.

"Hello? Operator?" said Martha a few seconds later, in the midst of discovering that what she had heard about Italian telephone service was all too true. "Hello, get me the Maresciallo of police in Padova. Quickly. This is an emergency."

Seconds passed like decades until finally she heard a "Pronto?" on the other end of the wire.

"The Maresciallo, please. Let me speak with the Maresciallo."

"Who are you, Signora? The Maresciallo is a very busy man."

Pitted against bureaucracy, Martha quickly lost patience. "Connect me with him at once. I am calling from the Villa Dolorosa."

The name of the villa had its effect on the voice at the other end of the wire. "The Signora is calling on behalf of the Professore Carlo Mongiuffi?"

"Yes," she said, adding to herself, 'so to speak.' At last she had heard Don Carlo's full name.

"One moment, Signora."

Another eternity of seconds, then the same voice again. "I am putting you through," followed by static and a different voice.

"I am the Maresciallo, Signora."

"You must come to the Villa Dolorosa at once, with a detachment of police, armed."

"Pardon?"

She tried to explain but it was not easy to sound convincing rather than deranged about a sudden death and a great collection of stolen art. The Maresciallo tactfully suggested it was an ambulance he would send if the greatly respected Don Carlo was indeed dead. Then Martha remembered what Don Carlo had told her about the Mantegna in his collection.

"Maresciallo," she said firmly, "you have been searching all through Europe for the Mantegna stolen from Padova. It is here, in the Galleria of the Villa Dolorosa. But within the hour there will be desperate men here to keep you from finding it. Do nothing and you will be the laughingstock of Italy by tomorrow, and possibly an ex-Maresciallo. Or come here as quickly as possible with armed police and you will return with your painting and be the hero of Padova. Take your choice."

Despite the seeming lunacy of her words there was something imperative in the woman's voice and the Maresciallo sensed, as a good Maresciallo should, that this was a time for action.

"I will come."

"We are in no immediate danger," said Martha as she and Berte joined Lina, her grandson and Tonio, who waited nervously in the kitchen. "The police are on their way from Padova, and will take charge. If by any chance Rocco and the others return before they arrive we must barricade ourselves in the library. We will let them break down the door, if they can — but that will give us extra time. If they succeed, then we will talk and talk and talk until the police arrive. But I think the Maresciallo will be here first. He wants his Mantegna. Lina, when Rocco arrives, tell him the Professore wants to see the Principe at once in the library, alone. He will not disobey the

Professore's orders. Take them both to the library door, go inside with the Principe, where we will all be waiting, and immediately bolt the door behind you. That will be a signal for the police to emerge and take Rocco prisoner, along with the guard and the chauffeur. Only then, dear Lina, will we all be safe.

"Dio," said Lina, crossing herself a second time within the hour.

"Guido," continued Martha, "watch with Tonio for the Maresciallo and bring him here to me at once. Tell him to leave the police cars completely out of sight so the others will suspect nothing when they drive in. And show him where the police can hide themselves in the sala until the Principe and Lina are safely in the library with us. Now I must make one more call while we wait, to put Avril's mind at rest. I hope I get a better connection to Paris than the one to Padova."

"Dio," said Berte.

The next day four friends sat contentedly together on the terrace of the Gritti in Venice. Martha, Berte and the Principe had arrived the night before from Fusina, accompanied by Lina, Guido and Tonio who had gone to cousins near Santa Maria del Pianto. Avril de Dinde had flown in that morning from Paris.

"I have the most to explain," said the Principe. "It is all so clear when I look back, and it was so clouded while it was happening. As soon as Avril phoned me to say you had both disappeared, I flew to Paris —"

"I knew something was very wrong, Marthe, when you left a message that you were going to the opera. There was no performance that night."

"There seldom is on Monday," said Martha. "I took that chance."

"When I arrived in Paris," continued the Principe, "I went to Interpol, which I should have done the day Silentius disappeared. I told them about the kidnapping of my patron saint and that Rocco had appeared soon after, when Michele left me—no doubt when his life was threatened. And that I kept Rocco because he promised to get Silentius back through the 'family' to which he belonged. And that there were conditions—I must not report the theft, and I must sell the Castellino to a Dr. Crespi-Dolci.

"As soon as I mentioned Crespi-Dolci Interpol informed me he was the attorney of Carlo Mongiuffi. Then I knew with whom I was dealing, for Mongiuffi comes from a village near us, on the Monte Pernice. He was known for his sinister connections but I did not realize he coveted my property. He was clever enough to know he could only acquire it anonymously, and if he restored Silentius."

"He would never have returned St. Silentius," said Martha. "The Professore's sin was the pride of possession."

"Among other sins, yes. Even Interpol knew very well where his money came from, without the evidence to close in on him. But they were unaware of the collection. Now at least his lieutenants, including Rocco, will have a long time to sit and think, and the vendetta which Rocco's relatives revived with the support of their patron will subside. I think my Michele will return as suddenly as he disappeared."

"Well," said Berte, "it's a plot that Agatha Christie couldn't get away with."

"Of course, my dear," responded Avril, "because it is

true. And what did your Silvia always say, Rinaldo?"

"That I would leave the Castellino — which I have done — but that I would return. She was right, as always. And I will go back with Silentius."

"Rinaldo," added Martha, "I hope you will not forget that it was St. Silentius who delivered the coup de grace which shocked Don Carlo into the next world."

"Shall we simply say he was clumsy and fell — at the right moment?" the Principe asked.

A waiter approached them and gave Martha a basket over which a white napkin was draped. "For the Signora, from Lina, she said."

"Ah yes, Lina promised me a basket of fruit from her cousin's tree." She lifted the napkin and showed them a nest of ripe black cherries bursting with sugar. "I shall have them for lunch, and allow each of you a taste."

"But chère Marthe," objected her Rinaldo, "I am giving you luncheon today at Harry's —"

"Dear friend," she said, interrupting him, "I plan to eat nothing but a few of these cherries until Berte and I are safely back in Monte Carlo." She put the basket to one side. "And I beg you not to speak to me of rich food," she added, choosing not to explain why.

Houseparty at Shivverly

*S*ummer descended on the coast with a vengeance that year and hordes of motor cars turned the Côte d'Azur into an anthill of ceaseless motion except in such quiet enclaves as the Hotel de Paris, where Martha and her niece settled on their return from Venice.

"Aunt Martha," said Berte, looking up from her book, "did you know that an earthquake struck Monte Carlo in 1887? The churches crumbled but the casino was spared. Was that significant?"

"Highly significant," replied Martha, looking up from her book, "as the churches were no doubt supported by faith and the casino by steel beams. Why aren't you on the tennis court this morning?"

"You promised not to nag."

"I only want you to meet some young people, and buy some clothes. It would give me such pleasure."

"Surprise. I have an appointment with the tennis pro at eleven-thirty."

They were interrupted by the ringing of the phone, insistently, the way old-fashioned operators had of telling you they thought the call was important.

"Martha?" the voice was unmistakably Minty's.

"My darling, are you all right?" Martha knew her sister was not one to sit down and telephone across the world unless there was something to report. "And Herbert?"

"Oh yes. We've been planning a trip to England."

"I'm delighted to hear it."

"Alexandra and I," answered Minty, as if it were the most natural assumption in the world, which it was not.

"Oh," said Martha. Although she wanted to see Minty she resolved not to encourage the travelers to come to Monte Carlo. The principality was not spacious enough comfortably to accommodate Alexandra Kimberley-Faucitt and herself.

"It was to be a week in London, then a week in the country with Sir Willoughby Backwatter, who is one of Alexandra's old beaux. And now suddenly Alexandra can't go. She insists that I mustn't give up the trip."

"You can come to us in Monte."

"Martha, I've counted so on England." Then Minty's sentences tumbled out in an eloquent plea. "Alexandra has written Sir Willoughby to expect us — you and me, and Roberta as well. The house party has been put together in our honor."

No doubt, thought Martha. Alexandra prefers to have Minty in England with a Sir Willoughby, leaving her good self to offer the solace of the season to Herbert in Sliepskill.

As if clairvoyant Minty added, "Herbert is going away, too, to that mountain top in New Hampshire where the Detweilers always go."

At least he knew enough to escape from Alexandra's net before it could be spread.

"We'd love to meet you in London," exclaimed Martha impulsively.

"Oh, to be in England now that August's here," said Berte.

A few days later it was all arranged. Martha proposed that she and Berte fly to London the afternoon before Minty was due to arrive. Then came the surprise.

"I've just started my tennis lessons. I'm beginning to enjoy the Club, and I..." Berte stopped, but Martha understood.

"You have plans of your own! I should have thought of that. You can stay right here and in two weeks' time we'll both have tales to tell."

Grateful, Berte hugged her aunt.

"Incidentally, I rang Avril and asked her about Sir Willoughby Backwater. He is, it seems, the sixth baronet, and his mother was Lady Irene Kimbolton, known as one of the most trying women of her generation. That is not in Debrett but Avril had it on good authority."

Martha landed at Heathrow to find England in the throes of an August heat wave. By Hudson Valley standards it was not very hot, but the humidity did invite swelter. Relief was forecast, and that was ominous; the temperature, she knew, might well drop to a blowy, midsummer 50 degrees.

All speculation about the weather was banished when Minty joined her sister at Claridge's the next day. They lunched in the Causerie ("Whitebait! The first thing Father always asked for in London.") where Martha heard all the

Sliepskill news and Minty learned about the trip to Italy, with significant omissions.

"Alexandra says Sir Willoughby is very special."

"Let us hope," said Martha somewhat tersely, "that he has inherited the estates and not his mother's eccentricities."

"Shivverly is on the Ouse," Minty added, her mind far away in Huntingdon.

"I beg your pardon?"

"The river. One day we must drive over to Little Gidding. It's only an inch away on the map. T.S. Eliot, the Four Quartets. And meanwhile," Minty concluded, with the enthusiasm of a child standing before an entire shelf of cookie jars, "I have a long list for London."

During the days which followed they managed three plays, a concert, the museums and a heart-to-heart talk during which Martha cautioned Minty not to trust Alexandra insofar as Herbert was concerned. Finally, on a cool dull morning they were ready to leave for the country. Minty had rung Sir Willoughby to say they were motoring down, and would arrive for tea. After an initial "What's that? Who?" he had at length understood with an "Oh, Alex's friends. Jolly good. We'll expect you, old girl." Martha told her to take the 'old girl' as a compliment. "It is an affectionate form," she said, not adding that it was often reserved for a favorite mare.

Downstairs, Martha stopped to leave their country address with the hall porter.

"You would like your post forwarded, Madam?"

"No, but should we decide we must get away earlier —"

"He is expecting us to stay the week," protested Minty.

"And we intend to," answered Martha, "however, it is always best to have an arrangement."

"Certainly, Madam," said the hall porter. "A telegram, requiring you to return to London without delay?"

"Exactly. But only if I ring you."

"Thank you, Madam."

The drizzle began before they reached open country, and as they turned off the Great North Road it became a downpour. Deep in Huntingdon their driver stopped on a straight unpaved stretch to consult his map. Suddenly there was a clatter of hoofs as a horse and rider cleared the hedgerow at the turning behind them and galloped up the rainswept road. The spectral mount overtook them, spattered the car with mud and then, ahead where the road turned left, disappeared with a magnificent leap over the hedgerow. In frustration as the thick liquid ran down his windshield and window, their driver sounded his horn helplessly.

"Bleeding country squire, thinks he owns the road," escaped from the chauffeur's lips despite himself.

"Was the rider wounded?" asked Minty.

"No," said Martha, "that is a manner of speaking. Do you know where we are, driver?"

"Yes'm," answered that far from gruntled man. "We should be coming to a crossroads within the mile, turn to the right, then up the drive."

"'You can't miss it' is what Sir Willoughby said," added Minty, unaware that the cliché meant 'You can easily miss it.'

Moments later, however, they came to the elm-lined drive and through the rain caught sight of Shivverly. The rambling house sat proudly at the top of a slight rise, a Tudor pile with Victorian additions. The car crunched across a gravelled court to the porte cochère and the great doors were opened by a wraithlike figure who helped the driver with their bags.

"Sir Willoughby's not about," said the old man, "but 'e's expected momentarily. 'ad to drive Missus Bullen to St. Neots."

Martha was certain the last words were accompanied by a distinct leer.

Without further explanation he led them inside and up the principal staircase, along an endless corridor which served as the picture gallery — chiefly consisting of those second-rate canvasses of first-rate painters which so often end in country houses.

The butler, for so they supposed him to be, paused briefly before a door to their left. "The bath," he said. Further along he inclined his head silently to the right, towards a door on which were writ the reassuring letters O.O.

"The W.C.," whispered Martha to a puzzled Minty.

When they finally arrived at their destination Martha found herself in a large square room dominated by a four-poster bed. Just as Minty was doing next door, she went to the window and gazed down on the lawn which sloped to a field. In the distance flowed the Ouse, snaking through flatlands that alternated between open fields and clumps of woodland, the remnants of an earlier, forested England. The vista was impressive, if melancholy.

"Tea is laid in the 'all," had been the butler's final words on leaving them. Martha removed her hat, opened her bag, then knocked at Minty's door.

"You won't believe what the W.C. is called," Minty marvelled. "The Roaring Zambesi. And it does."

"Vintage Victorian," said Martha. "They built things to roar forever in those days. Shall we go down and see who else has arrived?"

"Oh, yes. I hope there will be somebody with literary interests."

Martha did not offer an opinion, but she considered the possibility remote.

At the foot of the stairs the ladies hesitated, not knowing which way to turn. An impressive door with ancestors framed above it turned out to be the correct choice. They entered a baronial hall at the far end of which was a high Tudor fireplace. Before it tea was set on a low table at which two other guests sat in fervent conversation. The woman would have been called handsome once, but had lost interest. She wore a sleeveless frock, draped loosely over a bony figure. Her shoes were long and narrow. As she nodded in agreement with her companion the ash from a cigarette between her lips spilled onto her less than ample bosom. Was there after all a poetess in their midst?

An oath which blew the cigarette out of the woman's mouth dimmed that hope. "They're all alike these days," she affirmed vehemently, as she retrieved the burning stub and crushed it into a saucer.

The man had once been hale and hearty, but was now red faced and gouty. He had probably worn a uniform most of his life, at some distant outpost, and would have known exactly how to deal with the natives. They learned later that he was Brigadier Cumberley-Bligh, retired, and she was Mrs. Gwillam.

At first no notice was taken of the ladies' arrival as the litany of complaints continued, but at last the malcontents looked up to see who had intruded upon their colloquy.

Minty smiled.

Martha said, "I am Martha Prescott and this is my sister —"

"Perfectly filthy!" exclaimed the man as he sprang up. "The weather—"

"Yes, isn't it," answered Martha, then she added with irony aforethought, "and it doesn't seem to be improving."

"Milk?" asked the woman, holding up the jug.

Before they could take their teacups in hand Sir Willoughby burst into the room, an extremely tall man, booted, extravagantly moustached, no longer young, every inch a countryman.

"Bloody awful day," he boomed. "Welcome to Shivverly." These words were directed to Martha and Minty, which told them the others were familiars. He went directly to Martha.

"You are Araminta van Horne. Alex has told me all about you." He turned to Minty. "And you're her sister Maisie. Been around a bit, even if you don't look it. Alex again. Has the Brigadier tried to sign you up for the Kimbolton Irregulars? Ha, ha. That's a joke. Are you going to give us some tea, Nell? Ring for Phillips, that's a good girl. I want an egg. Beastly drive to St. Neots, then the blasted doctor kept us waiting. In his surgery picking his nose, I'll wager. No, by Jove, Mrs. Bullen hasn't got the plague or anything, is going to have a baby, that's what she is. Damned inconvenient when you think that old Bullen has been dead for a year now. She wasn't telling me whose it is. Not Phillips, ha, ha. But she's a good cook so we'll have to bear with her—Oh! Ha, ha. Jolly good, wot?"

Phillips answered the summons and was almost knocked off his unsteady feet by two plummeting Norfolk Lurchers which dashed past him to join their master. It was immediately clear where the sixth baronet's affections lay.

"Down, Lady. Lick 'em later, Hector. Down, damn you."

So began an unequal struggle which was never successfully concluded during the ladies' stay at Shivverly. The dogs were seldom out of sight unless Sir Willoughby was, and they remained a constant threat to hose as well as an affront to the nose of everyone in their vicinity.

"And more sandwiches, Phillips," called Sir Willoughby to the retreating figure as he tottered away. Then he turned to Minty and spoke with earnest solicitude.

"Eat a hearty tea. It's a long drive back to London. Too bad you can't stay the night. However, another time."

Almost to Martha's regret, Minty exclaimed, "But we've come for the week."

"Jolly good, of course you have. My little joke. Ha, ha. Best way to find out how long guests intend to stop." Then he turned to Nell Gwillam. "Any sign of her ladyship?"

Another of his jeux d'esprit? At the expense of his mother's ghost?

"We've been spared," was Nell's acerbic reply.

They were not spared for long. Before Sir Willoughby's egg had been boiled Lady Irene made a dramatic entrance, very much alive. Martha reckoned she must be well into her 80s. Sir Willoughby was there to prove it.

Lady Irene brought the wet weather with her. Still wearing her riding habit, she used her crop to beat some of the water from her costume. Her sharply angled face, dominated by two piercing black eyes, was unembellished by makeup although adorned by drops of rain and a smudge or two.

"Great day," she cried. "Gladiator took the hedges like a prince. Had a close call. Damned trippers in a great black charabanc. Hogging the road, almost ran us down. Infernal driver had the nerve to sound his horn. But we got away and back into the field with one of Gladiator's great leaps. I wish he had trampled them."

He almost did, Martha recalled.

"Hullo," said her ladyship, "new faces?"

"Alexandra's friends from America."

Lady Irene took a good look at them. "Willoughby, did you tell your guests that they *are* the house party?"

"Never mind, old dears, we'll have a jolly time just as it is," responded Sir Willoughby unconvincingly.

"Not quite as it is," said his mother. "I've asked Harborough to motor over for luncheon tomorrow."

"You haven't!" exclaimed Nell.

"Well, the old boy's one of the family," said the baronet to show how broadminded he could be. "Even if he is a bit of a bore."

"Crashing, I'd say," said the unrelenting Nell.

"Not a bad sort for a chap who collects butterflies," added the Brigadier.

"Thank you, Phillips," exclaimed Lady Irene, as he tottered in, "I'll have those sandwiches with my whisky and lemon. And a jug of hot water. Upstairs." Then she turned to the hapless Nell. "Harborough may not be as brilliant as some, but at least he is well-born."

With riding crop aloft Lady Irene swept out as she had

swept in, leaving behind a puddle of muddy water and an outraged Nell Gwillam. The dogs, who had cowered beneath the sofa, emerged, the Brigadier relaxed, and Sir Willoughby turned to his American guests.

"You'll find mother's bite is worse than her bark," he said. "Ha, ha."

After tea Martha and Minty withdrew to prepare themselves for the next ordeal: dinner at eight-thirty.

"Alexandra Faucitt knew what she was doing," said Martha.

Minty was more charitable. "She hasn't seen Sir Willoughby in years."

"I can understand why not." With that Martha tugged on the bellpull and hoped it made a suitable noise somewhere in the house. "We must see to our creature comforts. I do not think they have been anticipated."

"What do you suppose Sir Willoughby has planned for tonight," mused Minty. "Charades, do you think?"

"Perish the thought. Nothing could be more dangerous, given this group."

There was a timid knock at the door and a pert young maid appeared, breathless.

"Yes'm?"

"What is your name, my dear?"

"Rose, milady."

"Rose, I hope we can count on you."

"Oh, yes'm," answered Rose, not sure what American ladies might require.

"Please draw me a bath."

"At once, Mum. Hot or cold?"

"Steaming," said Martha, taken aback at the question.

The drains at Shivverly were lethargic and the ladies had just managed to bathe and dress when the gong in the hall warned them that it was time to join the others. Sir Willoughby, in a wing collar and a brocade waistcoat, was quite if not quietly elegant. The Brigadier wore his mess jacket and epaulets. Nell Gwillam had added a string of pearls. Only Lady Irene was missing, but when she did appear, just as Phillips banged the gong again, it was obvious that she had already enjoyed a drink or two upstairs. Her eyes were slightly glazed and she listed to port as she stood in the doorway costumed in red and black with ruffles.

Sir Willoughby got them quickly to the table where he carved with a flourish. As for the food, Martha could only assume that impending motherhood had dulled Mrs. Bullen's other creative impulses. But the regulars ate huge quantities, and the regrettable result was that her dinner restored Lady Irene's sobriety so that by the time they returned to the hall for coffee she had resumed her attacks on Nell, and included the Brigadier for good measure.

"Gracious lady," he started to reply, not without irony, "if I may be permitted to say it —"

"Better not, old chap," said his friend and host. "You know how grateful we are for your company."

"And for your complaints," added his mother, gathering steam. "Nell doesn't complain but that's the only thing she doesn't do."

Nell turned to Sir Willoughby. "If you don't muzzle your

mother, I shall go upstairs."

"Upstairs, yes, but not home to old Fred Gwillam. Well, that's understandable, too."

Minty watched the two women spar as if from the stands at Wimbledon. Martha closed her eyes.

"Will," said Nell, "let us have one of your stories. Your American guests haven't heard any of them." She also knew that Lady Irene had heard them all and detested them. "He is a great storyteller."

"He has no idea how to tell a tale," muttered his mother.

Sir Willoughby was pleased to be asked and Lady Irene resigned herself to the inevitable. Whereupon he began a narrative which, it soon became apparent, had neither beginning nor middle point, and seemingly no end. Martha assumed that several tales had somehow become intertwined. Minty, concentrating desperately, tried to make some sense of what she heard. Nell and the Brigadier, experienced listeners, dozed, and the Lurchers crept under the sofa. Meanwhile, Sir Willoughby meandered on and on.

"The woman, the woman!" exclaimed Lady Irene. "Don't lose sight of Lady Pam, if that is the story you are telling."

"Yes, to be sure, well, Lady Pamela's knowledge of Mother Nature's children, including the beasts which graze in our lower field, was limited, to put it mildly. So she said, 'Tell me, dear Will, how do you know which are the bulls and which are the cows?' Now you'll admit there's a great variety of possible answers to that one."

"And what did you say?" asked Nell, who had heard his answer a score of times.

Sir Willoughby was hardly able to keep his incipient

laughter under control. "All I said was, 'Dear lady,' and I pointed to the left, 'that is a bull,' then I pointed to the right, and said, 'and those are the udders.'"

His hoots and the modest smiles of Martha and the Brigadier were not echoed by Lady Irene, who sat stony faced.

"I don't think I understand," murmured Minty.

"Minty," said Martha, jumping into the breach and committing her principal error of the evening, "why don't you tell us your Mont St. Michel story?"

"By all means, Miss van Horne," said Nell, revenging herself on Sir Willoughby who, she knew, liked to think of himself as the only spinner of tales at Shivverly.

"If you must," mumbled the baronet, out of sorts.

Minty began to tell a story from their childhood, one their father had always asked for when there were guests he disliked. Shy in real life, Minty easily lost herself in narration and carried her audience with her. This time was no exception and her listeners, including their reluctant host, were soon under her spell.

"It was many years ago, the summer Martha and I were in Normandy so Madame could give us French conversation. An excursion was arranged to Mont St. Michel. The car was parked at the shore and we crossed the sandbar in a pony cart, as you could in those days when the tide was out."

"Dangerous, that tide," said Sir Willoughby, "and famous. Called the bore."

"La grande marée, and dangerous indeed," said Minty sweetly as to an impatient child.

"We saw the church and ate our omelets before Madame hurried us back to the mainland where we discovered that the chauffeur couldn't start the car. So we went down the beach looking for shells, and sooner than we realized we were out on the sandbar. By the time Madame had noticed, we were well on our way back to Mont St. Michel. She called to us but we paid her no heed. And there was no danger, or so we thought, because there was no sign of the tide — not at first. Then the sand between our toes became noticeably wetter and started to leave little puddles where we stepped."

Minty paused, as she always did at this point. She saw that the company were on the alert and one step ahead of her, as they were supposed to be.

"Madame ran onto the sandbar to fetch us and we ran faster in the opposite direction, to tease her. By now we were more than halfway across the bar and suddenly we became aware of people on the Mont St. Michel side beckoning us back to the shore. All at once we were frightened."

"Run for your lives," murmured the Brigadier.

"We couldn't make our legs do our bidding. We could only feel the water which had started to swirl around our feet. Madame caught up with us, but it was too late. The great tide, the marée, was bearing down upon us from the open sea. Madame clasped us to her and prayed. We screamed, but our voices were lost in the roar of the water as the current swept us up."

Sir Willoughby could not contain himself. "What happened, dear lady? How did you escape your fate?"

This question was the raison d'être of the story and why it was their father's favorite for special occasions. Minty answered quite calmly and with unexpected nonchalance, "Oh, we didn't. We were drowned. All three of us."

At first there was dead silence in the room. Then Lady Irene cried, "Bravo! A capital story."

Nell giggled nervously. The Brigadier wiped his brow, not sure how he felt. But Sir Willoughby paled. He had been taken in, and he resented it. He rose, stared for a baleful moment at Minty, then strode to the door, muttering, "Confound the woman," and stomped out, followed by the faithful hounds.

Martha realized that through her own error in proposing it, and Minty's skill in telling it, the story had lost them their observers' status at Shivverly. They had both become players in the game, which could now lead to a skirmish, or even to a decisive battle before the week was up.

The next day dawned clear and dry. Rose brought them early morning tea and announced that breakfast would be "laid out at nine." The ladies discovered that meant a battery of covered dishes on the sideboard as well as racks of toast and pots of marmalade on the table.

The Brigadier had arrived before them. "Splendid day, wot?"

Nell Gwillam entered with a warning. "Willoughby is in a foul mood this morning, but don't take it personally, Miss van Horne. He's upset about Mrs. Bullen's condition. Lady Irene has asked if he was responsible."

"Good God," exclaimed the Brigadier, genuinely shocked, and with a fork-load of kedgeree suspended in midair.

"She doesn't know that Ann Bullen and Peters had been carrying on a long time before old Bullen died, or so Willoughby tells me. Peters is the chauffeur. Not the marrying kind."

Lady Irene was the next to appear, dressed and ready to challenge the hedgerows again. She sat down just as the master of the house entered, with dogs. His sullen "Morning" was addressed more to the sideboard than to the company. Nell knew exactly the wrong thing to say, and said it.

"What have you planned for today?"

"You can go to the devil."

"Temper," said his mother with unnatural sweetness. Then to Martha she added, "His father was impossible, too."

Minty proposed an answer of her own to Nell's question. "I was hoping we might drive over to the Giddings one day."

"Who?" asked Sir Willoughby. If he had not heard of them they were not worth visiting.

"Not who, old boy, but where," said the Brigadier who knew his ordinance map. "As a matter of fact, about ten miles up the North Road."

"Yes," said Minty, glad of an ally. "Where Nicholas Ferrar settled."

"Ferrar? Roundhead, I suppose. Just about everybody around here is, present company excluded."

"No, Sir Willoughby, he was a Cavalier. King Charles visited him." Minty knew her facts.

"King Charles? Good grief woman, are you talking neighbors or history?"

Martha interceded. "My sister is interested in Little Gidding because of T.S. Eliot."

Only the Brigadier reacted. "The poetry chap?"

"Poetry is one of Minty's specialties," Martha added.

"Well, we can't hold that against her," said Sir Willoughby, moved to pity. "Probably exposed to it an early age and was too young to know any better. But I'm afraid there's no motorcar to send anybody careening about the countryside, not today. Anyhow your friends the Ferrars might not be at home. Can't just drop in."

"There aren't any Ferrars at the Giddings any more," said Minty, ready to explain that Robert Ferrar's experiment in Christianity had withered on the vine after his death in 1637.

"Moved away, eh? Well, that's settled. You'll have to amuse yourselves until lunch. Then Harborough will keep you in stitches. Ha, ha. Biggest bore in the county."

"He is my nephew and he does not lose his temper," observed Lady Irene.

"Never had one to lose."

"Nor does he employ a cook who is about to give birth to a bastard baby."

"She didn't do it alone," Sir Willoughby shot back. "Had some help, you know."

"Indeed she did," said Lady Irene, "and I'd like to horse-whip the man. Whoever he happens to be."

"Another rasher of bacon, Miss van Horne?" asked the Brigadier rather too pointedly.

She declined, and they finished their meal in oppressive silence. Lady Irene was the first to rise. She said nothing until she was safely in the doorway, and then addressed her son.

"You will have to give her notice. The sooner the better."

She disappeared to avoid hearing his reply.

"I've no intention of doing any such thing," he shouted after her. Then to the others, "The woman makes the best kedgeree I ever ate."

It was true. Breakfast was Mrs. Bullen's good meal and Sir

Willoughby was not going to allow a moral lapse to interfere with its regular preparation.

"Well, I for one shall seek out the library and choose a book," announced Minty.

"No books in the library. Young fool from London bought the lot years ago. Keep my guns in there now." With that proud boast, Sir Willoughby left them.

"I'll find you a book," said Nell. "There's a Barbara Cartland in the loo —"

"Lu-minous the day," interjected the Brigadier, stressing the first syllable to take the curse off her reference. Will anyone walk in the garden with me?"

"I will," said Martha.

He was pleased. "It's all terra cognita to me, you know."

"I shall set up my easel and do a landscape," announced Minty.

Only Nell Gwillam was left behind to wonder if Willoughby was in fact responsible for Mrs. Bullen's expectancy. She was not a jealous woman, still Nell did not like to think that perhaps Sir Willoughby had — in the classical phrase — deceived her with the cook.

During their walk Martha found the Brigadier filled with redeeming social values. Between the rose garden (neglected) and the topiary hedge (badly trimmed) she discovered that he had first met Sir Willoughby when they were both out in India ("The finest jewel in the old Queen's crown") and yes, as his means were limited, he had retired to Huntingdon where he was comfortable in the shadow of the big house.

"Nell and I are the only two regulars left. Lady Irene is the problem, bless her. Did actually disappear once, after one of Will's towering rages — you haven't experienced one and I trust you never shall — but she was soon back with flying colors. Nell doesn't have an easy time of it with Will. They've been...um...friends for years. Old Fred Gwillam doesn't seem to mind. Lives in Northampton and she looks in on him from time to time. I think he rather likes being left in peace."

Then, embarrassed, he changed the subject.

"Look at those yews. When Bullen was alive to trim them you could tell which was the hen and which the squirrel. However, you get a good view of the river and the lower fields from here. Huntingdon is austere country, but it has its own kind of beauty, you know."

She did know and Martha was content to gaze onto a scene which Constable would have been happy to paint.

The clock in the tower had struck twelve before Martha could compare notes with Minty, who had also had a conversation, with Nell Gwillam.

"She said she was glad we were here."

"I think she's lonely, Minty. Sir Willoughby has enough to handle with his mother, the dogs — and himself. And now we are going to meet the head of the family, Lord Harborough. I can't help wondering what he will be like."

"Blithering idiot," said Sir Willoughby at 1:20, "where is he? At Shivverly we wait for no man. He'll get no soup."

A few minutes later, as the soup plates were being removed, Henry Kimbolton, Earl of Harborough, joined them at the table, with a soft-spoken apology. He had understood Lady Irene to say 1:45.

"So I did. At Buckden Court we never lunched before 1:45."

Martha caught the narrowed eye with which Sir Willoughby favored his mother and knew what he was thinking: then you'd better go back to Buckden Court.

Lord Harborough was quiet and inoffensive, which was refreshing. He might collect butterflies but he was not what Martha would have called a lepidopterous man.

"Do you go to Sawtry?" asked Minty shyly.

"I do indeed, Miss van Horne, but how do you know about Sawtry?"

"What's there to know about Sawtry?" demanded their host.

Minty smiled across the table. "I believe it is famous for its butterflies."

"Most unlikely," muttered the baronet.

"But true," said Harborough. "I was in Sawtry only last week."

"Then you passed near the Giddings."

"Omigod," muttered Sir Willoughby.

"Of course. I often stop in the chapel at Little Gidding."

"Well, I'll be damned," said their host, helping himself to the fish.

"I'm sure you will be," observed Lady Irene, "if you don't watch your tongue."

Her sally killed conversation for the moment, after which they subsided into trivia except for Sir Willoughby, who concentrated on his food and treats for the dogs under the table.

As they rose Harborough exclaimed to Minty, "You mean to say that Willoughby hasn't told you about the conservatory?

It is the glory of Shivverly. Added under the supervision of Capability Brown who was in the neighborhood to landscape Buckden Court.

"Great blooming jungle, costs a fortune to heat."

"I'll show it to you, Miss van Horne, if Backwatter will permit me to."

"Don't be long about it, I'm going to run some film in the library for our guests."

Those ghastly films again, thought Nell.

"India and all that, you'll see your friend Alex, Mrs. Prescott. Damned attractive filly she was, even then."

Martha remained discreetly silent but Lady Irene was frank. "I never thought so," she said, and Martha felt a soup-con of sympathy for Lady Irene, her first.

Sir Willoughby showed them into the gun-lined library, while Lord Harborough led Minty off to the conservatory. Then began an excruciating ordeal as life during the Raj flickered past them, endlessly.

"Our villa in Outy...the Durbar at Lucknow...there's Alex twirling her parasol. Shivverly now, spliced in somehow. The servants' ball when we had a full staff. That attractive young thing on the right grew up to be our Mrs. Bullen."

The sight of an earlier, innocent Ann Bullen reminded Lady Irene that she had a duty to perform. She rose and left the room unobserved.

"The Governor and his Lady...Ah, yes, the cobra we killed on the verandah."

Before she dozed off Martha marveled that there seemed to be no Indians in Sir Willoughby's India.

"Alexandra again with her mother in the station at Outy..."

A distinct snore rent the air. Nell nudged the Brigadier and he jerked to attention.

"I hope I'm not boring anyone." There was an edge to Sir Willoughby's voice.

"Splendid pictures, always a pleasure," said the Brigadier a little too brightly, before he slumped over again.

When the lights finally went on, Sir Willoughby discovered that he had put his entire audience to sleep. Without hesitation he picked up a large crystal vase full of dried flowers and dashed it to the floor with an explosion, shattered glass and broken blossoms. Three pairs of eyes opened wide.

"Sorry to disturb your rest," he snarled, just as Harborough and Minty entered the room. "And what have you two been up to in the conservatory all afternoon?" he demanded.

"Clerihews," said Minty.

"Clerihews, be damned," exclaimed the baronet, "we've got every plant in the book, but I never heard of a clerihew."

Minty and Harborough laughed.

"Afterwards we walked along the river," answered his cousin. "Did everybody enjoy the film?"

"Ask them. They're all begging me to run it again."

"Will you stay for tea, Lord Harborough?" Nell asked.

"Harborough never stops to tea," said his ungenial host.

"As a matter of fact I cannot, but I hope you will bring the ladies over to Buckden Court for luncheon one day."

"Not bloody likely."

Upstairs Martha asked her sister, "What in the world is a clerihew?"

Minty was delighted. "I'm so happy to know something you don't know. It's a kind of nonsense verse. Lord Harborough has a wicked one about Sir Willoughby. Do you think we can go over to Buckden Court one day?"

"We will not receive any encouragement from our host. Meanwhile, we have to get through dinner tonight. We disgraced ourselves in the library this afternoon and Sir Willoughby is not likely to let us forget it."

The evening started reasonably well, but the storm broke when they returned to the Hall for coffee and were responding to Sir Willoughby's rhetorical question, heavily laced with irony, "And what will it be this evening?" Russian roulette?"

It was the Brigadier who asked the fatal question, "Miss van Horne, do you have a suggestion?"

"Well," said Minty knowing she must not mention charades, "there is always Truth or Consequences."

Martha paled. Compared to it, charades would have been child's play.

"And pray, what is that?" asked Lady Irene.

"You ask someone a question. If the person declines to answer truthfully then he or she must face the consequences."

"I like it. What are the consequences?"

"A forfeit. That is, to do whatever the questioner requires."

"I think I'll go upstairs and read." Nell Gwillam started out of her chair.

"Sit down," said Sir Willoughby.

"You mean," continued Lady Irene, "if I were to ask Mrs. Gwillam 'What is your real age?' and she declined to reveal it, then I could require her to get down with the Lurchers on all fours and bark at Willoughby's feet?"

Nell's coffee cup clattered to the floor, and she burst into tears.

"Don't bawl," commanded her lord and master. "I can't stand weeping women."

"It was a purely hypothetical question," said his mother, appealing to the Brigadier for support.

"And quite unnecessary, if I may say so, Lady Irene," replied, that gentleman staunchly.

"Quiet, all of you," cried Sir Willoughby, "we obviously can't play the game. Not in this company."

Martha sighed in relief, transient as it turned out. For while they abandoned Truth or Consequences, a few truths did come to light that evening with disastrous consequences. It began when Phillips entered and coughed discreetly.

"What is it?"

"Mrs. Bullen, Sir. She asks for a word."

"Not tonight."

Phillips hesitated, then bent low and whispered into the baronet's ear.

"She what?" he exploded.

"She's given notice!" exclaimed Lady Irene.

Sir Willoughby's suspicions were immediately aroused. "Why do you think so? Are you responsible?"

Lady Irene adopted a high moral tone. "No, only the girl herself is responsible."

"Rot. She'd never give notice on her own. Where would she go? You put the idea into her head, didn't you?"

"I knew my duty," replied, the mother-martyr.

"Damned interfering woman." Sir Willoughby turned scarlet and seemed about to burst. "This time you've gone too far."

"Or did you go too far with Mrs. Bullen?" Lady Irene's angry words cut like a steel blade.

"Blast you!" shouted her son.

The Brigadier roused himself. "See here, old boy, don't say anything you regret."

"Keep out of this. Or have you been sowing your wild oats in my kitchen? I'd written you off as an impotent old bugger." It was a relief to spread his anger in other directions.

The Brigadier sat back deeply wounded.

"Peters is not going to marry her," said Nell. "She told me this afternoon."

"So you've been into it, too. Meddling women!"

"Sir Willoughby," said Minty, "it may be my fault."

They all turned to her. Martha held her breath.

"Lord Harborough and I came across Mrs. Bullen down at the river. She was very distressed and I — well, I told her the best thing would be to get away and start a new life somewhere, with her baby."

"What was Alex thinking when she sent you here? And by what right did you tell the girl anything?"

"Willoughby," said his mother, "someone had to take the initiative. Phillips, you may tell Mrs. Bullen that her notice is accepted."

"You'll tell Mrs. Bullen nothing, Phillips. But tell her ladyship to move back to Buckden Court if she wants to run a house. Harborough won't stand up to her. I'm fed up."

Seething, Lady Irene rose, slapped Sir Willoughby hard and left the room.

Pleased at the thought of life without Lady Irene, Nell Gwillam rallied to the baronet's defense. "You did right, Will. She deserves to go."

"Oh, shut up. You're no better, just lazier. Old Fred knew what he was doing when he shipped you off to Shivverly. Happy man today."

Nell bolted out of her chair, slapped him on the other cheek and ran out of the room.

"My dear fellow —" began the Brigadier.

"I'm not your dear fellow and I'm sick at the sight of you."

Without another word the Brigadier bowed to Martha and Minty and departed.

Martha knew she had no words which could help, Minty had turned to stone, so it was Phillips who ventured to speak up, and regret it.

"You will see Mrs. Bullen, Sir?"

Sir Willoughby erupted with a great blast of steam. "No," he thundered, "I will not see Mrs. Bullen. Now get out of here!" With that he raised his arm and Phillips swayed perilously out of sight. Sir Willoughby glared at his two American guests, uttered a rasping "Faughhhhhh," and kicked at Hector and Lady who lay at his feet. The dogs whined and slunk under the sofa as the outraged baronet threw open the doors to the terrace and disappeared into the black night.

Minty turned to Martha. "What are we going to do?"

"We are going to ring the hall porter at Claridge's. At once."

There was lightning and thunder during the night, a

heavy shower and hailstones, all of which were appropriate to the gloom which settled over Shivverly. Only Martha and Minty slept soundly; the others tossed and churned. They were also the first down to breakfast, where Martha found the telegram at her place.

"Good morning, dear ladies," said the Brigadier solemnly as he joined them.

Then Nell Gwillam entered, looking as if she had slept fitfully in a narrow bed to which she was unaccustomed, as indeed she had done.

"Good morning," she managed. "I'm afraid I shall have to leave you. Fred is not well and I must look after him. He is my husband, after all. Peters will drop me off."

"Quite right, Nell," said the Brigadier. "I was about to tell our friends that my housekeeper phoned this morning in a state about our thatch. Last night's storm did some damage and I shall have to see to it. I'll ride along with you, if I may."

Lady Irene made her entrance in a hound's tooth travelling costume. She went directly to the sideboard where she picked among the dishes.

"I rang my sister in Kent. Peters is driving me to the Huntingdon station. I'll take the 9:41 to Kings Cross and a taxi to Waterloo."

Quietly Martha put the telegram in her pocket.

Presently Sir Willoughby took his place at the head of the table. Dispensing with any form of greeting he addressed Martha and Minty. "Bad news, I'm afraid. Have to go up to London. Nasty business at my Club. May have to expel old Colonel What's-His-Name. Went berserk and pushed the porter through a window into Pall Mall." Pleased with his own inventive powers he concluded triumphantly, "The bow window."

"Just the sort of situation you are well qualified to handle," observed Lady Irene. The fires still smoldered.

He ignored her and said to the ladies, "You are welcome to stay on at Shivverly. But Peters will be driving me into Bedford to catch the 11:22."

Peters, thought Martha, is going to have a busy morning.

"Thank you," said Minty, remembering the telegram, "but —"

The toe of Martha's shoe met Minty's shin under the table. "Thank you, Sir Willoughby," said Martha, "but in that case we will accept Lord Harborough's invitation to lunch and ask him to drive us to the station after tea. I believe he was eager to take us to Little Gidding as well."

"Capital. The poetry people wasn't it? Ferrar. Don't know them."

Harborough sent his car to fetch them at noon. They rewarded Rose for taking care of them and sent an envelope to the kitchen for Mrs. Bullen, who would need it. Martha handed a small folio to Phillips and asked him to see that it reached the Brigadier. "A watercolor with the compliments of Miss van Horne," she explained.

At the door, as if to reassure them, Phillips announced, "Come back to Shivverly next year, ladies, and you'll find everything like it was. Aye, that you surely will."

An appalling prospect thought Martha, as she and Araminta settled back in the Bentley.

"Minty," she asked as the house receded from view, "what

was Lord Harborough's curlicue about Sir Willoughby?"

"Clerihew."

"Whatever. We might want to remember it for Alexandra."

"He composed it when Sir Willoughby returned from India, and said he has never seen fit to revise it. Now, let me see...oh yes:

"Sir Willoughby Backwatter

Is home from the slaughter.

In such a rage

Is Shivverly's sage!"

Martha's reaction was immediate and honest.

"Henceforth," she said, "I shall always think of Sir Willoughby as the Sage of Shivverly. What a pity he never took Alexandra to be his Sagesse."

Jean Tristan

A day at Buckden Court did much to obliterate the memories of Shivverly, and when Martha proposed that her sister join her in Monte Carlo the invitation was quickly accepted.

"But I have to be home next week. Elmira Crisp is retiring and I am giving the tea."

A reason more urgent than the library's release from the limp but clinging grasp of Miss Crisp required Minty's presence in Sliepskill. On their return to Claridge's the ladies had found a postcard from Herbert Detweiler. The message was routine, but the postscript was alarming. "Sunny and pleasant up here," he had written, and then the words which revealed everything: "P.S. It's Alexandra's first visit to New Hampshire." Minty would have three nights in Monte, and then she must reestablish her rights on the east bank of the Hudson.

A carefree and animated Berte collected them at the airport and that evening at dinner heard the saga of their foreshortened visit to the sceptr'd isle. Berte laughed with them, but seemed preoccupied, and made her excuses as soon as she could — to join friends. And the next morning she was off early, for the day.

"Shall we all have lunch at the Club?" asked Martha.

"Tomorrow, perhaps?" suggested Berte. "My lesson is at one o'clock today."

That evening Berte did not dine with them. At eight-thirty she waved a kiss in their direction and went out wearing a summery dress that Martha had begged her in vain to buy only a fortnight before.

"Berte has blossomed," exclaimed Minty. "She isn't the same girl at all."

"Indeed she's not," replied, Martha, delighted at the transformation. She did not add that the change had taken place quite suddenly, and that she had her own idea of what might have caused it.

The next day there was no more mention of lunch, but that night Berte joined them for a gala dinner along with a surprise quest — Butch Romanoff.

"Minty and I ran into Butch this afternoon," said Martha, "Yes, en route to the casino."

"Is last visit," he had said. "No more Monte for Butch."

"Can I believe that?" asked Martha.

"Da. Heart tells me. But now, champagne to honor Madame Araminta. Butch hopes, Madame not going home to Sliepskillskoi because she has lost her everything at Casino..."

Minty had beamed, entranced by the suggestion that she might have visited the gaming tables across the square.

"Berte," said her aunt the next morning, after they had put Minty on her plane and were at last alone, "now, tell me everything!"

"Well, I took your advice and bought some clothes, and the world looked brighter. I am also enjoying my tennis and I've made some friends at the Club. That's all."

All the trivia and none of the essence, Martha suspected.

"Am I right to think your friends include a young man?" Martha asked, as kindly as she knew how.

Berte blushed. "There is a boy, as well as some others. His name is Jean Tristan, and we...get along very well."

"I'm delighted. I hope you'll allow me to meet him."

"Of course. One day soon."

But in the days which followed Berte proposed no meeting. Finally, after they had spent a carefree afternoon at the boutiques in Beaulieu, where Berte allowed Martha to buy her an elegant scarf of red, blue and white squares, Martha again took the initiative.

"Berte, let me give you lunch at the Club tomorrow. Ask your friend to join us."

"I'll ask him."

It was no surprise to Martha when Berte told her that evening that Jean Tristan was not free for lunch the next day. As a result Martha felt she had to meet the young man as soon as possible, a protective reaction based on more than mere curiosity.

Luncheon was not as relaxed as each might have wished.

"Aunt Martha, I know you are disappointed that Jean Tristan couldn't come today, but there is a reason. He worked at the Club until ten days ago, then they were terribly unfair to him and he left. Now we usually eat at a little place around the corner, Le Beau."

"My dear, all three of us could have lunched around the corner if I'd known."

"He wouldn't have wanted that."

"And we can all lunch any day you choose at the hotel."

They heard raised voices and Martha turned to see the maître d' in argument with someone he did not intend to allow onto the terrace. The someone pushed his way through and started towards them, the maître d' in angry pursuit. As he drew closer Martha saw an attractive, dark-haired young man in white duck pants and striped sport shirt. Suddenly he was smiling down at them.

"Berte," he said in a pleasant but questioning voice, "aren't you going to introduce me to your aunt?"

"You are Jean Tristan!" exclaimed Martha as the defeated maître d' faded from sight.

"Jean Tristan de Valois," said the boy with a winning smile.

"Sit down and have some lunch with us," said Martha.

"Thanks, I've had a sandwich," However, he sat down in the chair between them.

"I'm sorry you weren't free to join us today."

"Oh?" Then he understood and his eyes flashed for an instant.

"Another time," continued Martha, who had seen the momentary fire. "Will you dine with us at the hotel? Tomorrow evening?"

"Of course. If Berte agrees."

She knew it was a taunt but she said, "I think that would be wonderful."

"It's settled then. At eight-thirty. We will meet you in the lounge and we won't be dressing."

"Aunt Martha only means —"

"I understand." He cut her off sharply, but grinned when he said to Martha, "I don't have a little black tie and a wing collar anyhow." Then, when he turned to Berte it was with a perfunctory question, "See you tonight?" He stood up.

"Yes," she said in a tiny voice, and he was gone.

"I like him, Berte," said Martha. "He has a mischievous smile."

"I'm glad you do." Then she added, very seriously, "So do I."

All at once the absurdity of that statement struck them both and they laughed together for the first time in days.

Nevertheless, that evening Berte left the hotel with an uneasy heart, afraid that Jean Tristan would still be angry with her. A few minutes later she saw him sitting at one of the curbside tables at Le Beau with two of his friends. All three were eating wedges of pizza and drinking beer.

"You didn't want me to meet her," Jean Tristan said, hardly looking up.

"Of course I did. But not at the Club —"

"Because Dino fired me? I should have punched the old windbag. Zap!"

Fist into palm, he demonstrated what he meant. The boys laughed. Jean Tristan was still resentful. "Are you invited to this dinner?" He pointed to the remains of the pizza before him.

"I hope so," she said, trying to win him with her smile. "I'm starved."

Jean Tristan jumped up.

"Good, then it's all yours. We've got a date in Menton."

He went to the curb, the others close behind him, where their motorbikes were parked. The friends jumped on one, and Jean Tristan on his. They raced their motors, ignoring the protests from other tables.

"See you tomorrow night at the Hotel de Paris," shouted Jean Tristan as they sped away towards the Moyenne Corniche.

Berte fought back her tears. Louis, the Patron, brought the addition, but he only said, "I'll keep this till the next time they come. It's not for you to pay, Mademoiselle."

She sat for a few minutes, then as casually as she could manage, started home. At the cinema down the street, impulsively, she bought a ticket and disappeared into the comforting darkness. She neither knew nor cared what the film was. She closed her eyes as soon as she sat down, and then she sobbed, unnoticed by the few others in the theater who were all absorbed in the celluloid drama they had paid to watch on the screen. She sat there until the lights came on, wiped her eyes, and returned to the hotel shortly after eleven.

"I've asked Butch to dinner, too," said Martha the next day. "I thought your young man would be pleased to know I have my beaux as well. And I've ordered a table on the terrace."

"Perfect."

Berte had recovered from the disastrous evening as only a

girl in love could; she was now happy because she would see Jean Tristan soon. She hoped he would be in one of those sunny moods which delighted her: witty, alert, and even — as Martha had noticed — mischievous.

Martha and Berte went downstairs early, and were presently joined by Butch.

"Berte's friend Jean Tristan de Valois will be our fourth," said Martha.

"Is quite a name, young lady," said Butch.

"The family is poor now, but he is proud and can tell you all about his connections, back to the thirteenth century."

"I will like because of today connections," Butch replied gallantly.

"Berte," said Martha, "will you tell the desk that we are behind this potted palm so they can point the way to Jean Tristan?"

Berte delivered the message, then glanced out the door into the Place. At the foot of the steps a motorbike had just pulled up. A man, clad from head to toe in black leather, buckles and boots to match, jumped off the seat and flung his keys to the doorman, who was obviously reluctant to take them until they had exchanged a few words, after which he saluted smartly. The driver removed his helmet and Berte saw that it was Jean Tristan.

"Hello, Berte!" he cried, bounding up the steps. "Am I late?"

"Where did you get that outfit?"

"Why? Will your aunt be shocked?"

Maybe not, thought Berte, but I am.

When they crossed the hall heads turned, as he had hoped

they would. Jean Tristan admitted, "Your aunt is a real VIP. Until I mentioned her name the doorman wasn't going to let me land."

She smiled despite herself. "Land. That's the right word."

At that moment Martha caught sight of them and instinctively put her hand on Butch Romanoff's arm and murmured "Steady."

"Good evening, Madame," said Jean Tristan formally, his helmet balanced under his left arm. "Monsieur." He offered his right hand to Butch.

"We are delighted to see you, Jean Tristan. This is our friend Butch Romanoff. And now shall we go upstairs?"

"Upstairs?" asked Berte, remembering that the reservation was for the Terrace, and knowing that spoons would clatter no matter where they appeared.

"No, no, my dear," Martha said, inventing a story to fit the occasion, "I have ordered dinner to be served in our own salon, where we can be quiet, and alone."

It was Jean Tristan's first disappointment of the evening but there was nothing he could say, so he simply smiled.

"I must only ring and tell them we are ready." And, Martha might have added, instruct Albert to send up a menu of his choice, for four, along with a magnum of Lanson Brut.

The first minutes upstairs did much to dispel the doubts Martha had begun to entertain concerning Jean Tristan. Despite the leather and the buckles he was charming and likable. So much so that Martha asked him if he wanted to remove what was obviously a very warm jacket for a summer's night.

"I can't," he admitted, "I'm not wearing a proper shirt underneath it. I bought the outfit today. Do you think it caused a ripple downstairs?"

"Oh, yes," answered Berte, knowing also that it must have cost a fortune, which he did not have.

"Good," he said, "these types should know what the rest of the world is all about." Martha felt there was more emotion than logic in his statement, but she withheld comment.

"Man of principle," said Butch. "Takes courage."

"I'm not afraid."

Nor was he, as Berte had come to realize in the past weeks. On the bright side, he had a forthright way of saying what he thought, but there was a shadowed side, too, a rebellious reaction which pushed him beyond reason. He would rise to almost any challenge, and then bravado overcame good sense. Inevitably, it happened that evening when Butch Romanoff brought up his own obsession with gambling.

"Madame Marthe," he said, "I am glad not to see you at Casino. Is depressing. People I would not let through door."

"Why not?" asked Jean Tristan in a tone which alerted Berte to an incipient danger.

"Not ladies, not gentlemen."

"If I was not a Monagasque I would play every night until I broke the bank," said the boy fervently. "The casino should be for everybody, not just —"

"Not just?"

He accepted the question as a challenge, " — the filthy rich."

Butch's mistake was to take it lightly. "Ah, young are so radical. Is amusing, but they outgrow." Then he tried to change the subject by whetting Martha's curiosity. "Chère amie, come with me one day, just to look..."

But Martha gave the response he had expected. "No, Butch, you know how I feel about gambling."

Butch smiled broadly and winked to Berte. This was a private joke amongst the three of them and they forgot for an instant that Jean Tristan would not understand the wink. He glowered and the resentment inside him burst out.

"Radical, young, amusing!" He spat the words. "But don't forget, we are going to inherit the world, because you can't hang on forever. I will be rich one day —"

"I hope will make you happy," said Butch, still genial. "Is no guarantee, but I wish you big bank account."

"My money won't work for the bankers, they rob the poor. Why not rob the rich who can afford it! Most of them are nobody. Do you know who we are, the Valois?"

"Frankly," said Butch, annoyed at this outburst of petulance, "I thought you died out."

"You have heard of Louis IX? I am named for his son Jean Tristan. Louis IX loved a good woman of the people and their son founded our branch of the Valois. We are proud even if we are poor, and that will change."

Once again, in the heat of emotion, logic had been banished and Martha, to divert Jean Tristan, spoke up.

"I would like to meet your mother."

"My parents are dead, Madame. I am alone."

His 'I am alone' was a manifesto which reflected his insecurities as well as his strength.

Butch attempted to restore the pleasure of the occasion. "My apology," he said to Martha, "no place for serious talk.

All here to enjoy. Who knows when we meet again?"

But the mood of the evening had changed. The conversation, in which Jean Tristan now took little part, was perfunctory. When they rose Martha asked Jean Tristan to follow her out onto the balcony to enjoy their view of the harbor.

"I know Roberta is very fond of you," she said when they were alone.

"Are you afraid of that?"

"Heavens, no, but for me she is the dearest person in the world, so I look forward to knowing you better."

"Come for a ride with me tomorrow. On my bike."

The idea was so novel that she did not immediately say no.

"It's safe."

"I'm sure it is, or you wouldn't have asked me."

"My mother has ridden with me." Then he quickly added, "In the past. And Berte is an expert."

Martha felt if she accepted it should be with enthusiasm. "I'll do it — as long as you guarantee to take no pictures. A short ride, around the Place. And let it be our secret. Berte might not approve."

He was pleased. "I'll show you how to hang on. It's easy."

"And I will expect you at three. Shall we have coffee with the others?"

The evening ended early and Berte went downstairs to see Jean Tristan off on his motorbike. In the corridor he said, "I don't like your Russian friend. He doesn't respect me."

"Butch is an old friend of Aunt Martha's."

"I like her."

As they descended the steps outside, the doorman gave

him his keys and pointed to the bike parked across the way, for which he was rewarded with a ten franc note — or so he thought at first.

"M'sieur," said the man, because he was honest, "this is one hundred francs."

"So it is," replied Jean Tristan. "Thank you."

The man offered a second salute, perhaps to youth and foolishness, as Jean Tristan mounted the bike.

Berte could not resist saying, "You shouldn't have."

"Why not? He did me a favor, so I did him one. He respects me. Le Beau? One o'clock for lunch tomorrow?"

"Yes."

"Not for dinner. I'll be away for a couple of days."

She wanted to ask where, but she had learned that he considered most questions an invasion of his privacy. At least this time he added, "I have to help a friend in Cannes. He's moving."

"I'll miss you," she admitted, "and remember, you promised I could take you to dinner on Saturday. You choose the restaurant."

"We'll see. My pals will want to celebrate my birthday, too."

"Jean Tristan, it was to be just the two of us."

"We'll see."

He was now sitting on the bike, helmet in hand. Suddenly he leaned forward and kissed her. It was quick and he did not linger. His head once safely inside the helmet, he grinned and sped away.

Upstairs, Butch was taking his leave of Martha. "Chère amie," he said, "watch out for boy."

"I know," answered Martha, "but Roberta has fallen in

love so I want to help him. He is very young. They both are."

"Good-bye, Marthe." He kissed her hand.

"Good night, rather. We will see you again."

"I hope," he said, "but is five minutes before midnight, chère amie." Impulsively he kissed her on one cheek, then the other, and left.

His remark struck Martha as unlike Butch. She only understood it a month later when a letter arrived from The Golden Fleece in Las Vegas. Anatoly wrote to tell her that Butch Romanoff had returned there the day after the dinner with Martha, and had died shortly after. It was his heart, and he had known. Martha realized what Butch had meant by "Heart tells me..." She lingered over Anatoly's final words, "Believe me, Madame Marthe, our friend loved every day of his life, and his friends. We must be happy for him..."

It was true. Nevertheless, Martha had wiped away an incipient tear.

Punctually at three the next afternoon Martha stepped out of the hotel, pausing only an instant to be certain that Jean Tristan was waiting for her. He waved.

"Good afternoon," she said in greeting. "Once around the Place, Jean Tristan, then we'll have a cup of tea together." She was relieved to see no signs of leather or buckles; he was wearing his white trousers and a knitted shirt.

He grinned and jumped onto the seat.

"Now hop on behind me and hold tight, with both hands. Relax when you feel balanced."

To the astonishment of the doorman, Martha hopped. She put her arms around Jean Tristan, he put his foot down to start the motor, and a moment later they were off and away. Somewhat to her surprise Martha discovered that she was comfortably seated, and with her arms entwined around the driver did feel secure.

"Okay?"

"Okay."

"Side saddle next time," he shouted.

"I'm happy this way," she cried just before she became unhappy. For Jean Tristan had turned to the right and into the town.

"No, Jean—"

"Yes, Aunt Martha," he shouted back. "To the Corniche to see the view."

They sped through the streets and Martha feared her hat would not hold, even though it was securely pinned down. They turned up to the Moyenne Corniche, and then up again towards La Turbie. Fortunately it was the sleepy time of the afternoon and there was little traffic. Only mad dogs and Jean Tristan. Still, Martha was far from pleased that the decision had been made for her, and contrary to her better judgment.

At the Grande Corniche they turned left and started west, in the cliff-side lane; at least she was spared a view over the precipice.

Then, almost before she realized what was happening, they were racing a small van, the driver of which sounded his horn impatiently to pass them. Jean Tristan did not move to the right and the van driver had to wait for an open stretch. At the first opportunity he overtook them, but not without shouting an insult which Jean Tristan returned in kind. From that instant the boy thought no more of the passenger perched behind him. He concentrated on gaining speed and passing the van.

"Jean — let him go."

But he had been challenged and he had no intention of overlooking it.

The van driver, who could see them in his rear view mirror, put out his arm and gratuitously offered an insult which further enraged Jean Tristan. They were hurtling along dangerously close to each other when they came to another straight stretch and Jean Tristan saw his chance. He accelerated and swung into the left lane to pass. Martha held her breath. It was a foolish chance to take, yet she knew enough not to cry out and distract him from the road. The van driver saw what Jean Tristan had in mind and pressed his own foot to the floor, gaining speed. This intensified Jean Tristan's anger and he shouted another imprecation. Nothing could have stopped him now.

The bike kept apace with the van without gaining on it when suddenly a sports car driving east rounded the corner ahead. Instantly Jean Tristan and Martha both saw there were only seconds in which to avoid a head-on collision. It was too late for Jean Tristan to fall behind the van again. He cut sharply to the left and off the road on the wrong side, into a paved lookout stop. To miss him the sports car braked and skidded across the median line, where he grazed the van. Even though the van driver had also braked, the momentum and the graze turned his van around, and both cars came to a spinning halt in the middle of the road. Jean Tristan shouted, "Hold on!" and accelerated again, crossing back to the right side of the road as they sped around the corner and away from the accident.

"Jean Tristan — go back."

He gave no sign that he had heard her. Instead, at the first opportunity he turned down a steep side road, so fast around hairpin curves that Martha hung on for her life. By now she wanted only to get away from this dangerous young man who, despite a certain charm which he could display when he wished to, was irresponsible and completely lacked a sense of the difference between right and wrong. It was only after they had descended into the town again that he came to a stop at a red traffic light.

Martha saw her chance. She withdrew her arms, moved quickly, and was off the bike — free.

"Jean, you caused an accident and you did not stop —"

"He had no right," he snapped back.

"You had no right. You endangered our lives and you did not stop to find out what you may have done to the others."

"Those types can take care of themselves. I'm not a child to be afraid of them."

"That is exactly what you are, Jean — a wanton child. Until you grow up I do not want to see you again."

She now fell into the category of challengers, and he rewarded her with sarcasm.

"I suppose you don't want Berte to see me either?"

Before she could reply the light turned green and he shouted, "That's up to Berte and me, isn't it? And my name is Jean Tristan." He roared across the intersection without looking back.

Martha returned to the hotel shaken but determined to

speak seriously with Berte, for whom she felt responsible. Berte surprised her when she came back from tennis by speaking seriously with Martha.

"What happened between you and Jean Tristan this afternoon?"

"Was he upset?"

"No, but he said you were. In fact he said you owed him an apology. But he laughed when he said it."

"Indeed." Martha was as close to being grim as she had ever been. "Let me tell you what happened."

She did, in vivid terms, and Berte responded in a tiny voice. "Oh, Aunt Martha, I'm so sorry." She was taken aback, yet not astounded, for she knew Jean Tristan all too well.

Martha asked her not to see Jean Tristan again, adding in a moment of weakness when she perceived the pain in Berte's eyes, "— for a while."

However, Berte's only thought was of Saturday and Jean Tristan's birthday.

For the first time, Martha and her niece concealed their true feelings from each other, by silence on the one topic on both their minds. But during the days which followed they found it impossible to live with this dishonesty, and each chose the same moment to admit it. So they talked calmly and openly about Jean Tristan — his problems, the good side of his character, the other side, and about the reality that Berte was in love for the first time.

"I don't think he wants to change," Martha said finally. "That is why I ask you not to see him."

"Today is his birthday. Tonight at nine o'clock we are

supposed to meet at Le Beau, and then have dinner together. I have bought him a watch. I have to go, even if —"

She broke off, but Martha said nothing to help her.

"— even if you don't understand why."

"I understand all too well, Berte, and I am terribly unhappy about it. If you go, and I think you will, I won't rest easily until I know you are back. That is a melodramatic way of putting it, but I am speaking from my heart, too."

Then Martha relented, and said, "Bless you. Don't be late."

Berte was not late in returning to the hotel that night. A few minutes after ten Martha heard her niece's key in the foyer door. She turned off her reading lamp, not wanting Berte to know she was awake. Berte was relieved to see no light from under the door to Martha's room because she could not tell her aunt why she had come back so early, certainly not the whole story, although she now realized that she should indeed not see Jean Tristan again. And yet, haunted by conflicting emotions, miserable and hurt, she lay in her bed thinking back on the disastrous evening until she heard the bell of St. Nikolas across the port strike two. Shortly thereafter she fell into a fitful sleep.

Later than usual, and alone, Martha sat at breakfast the next morning hesitating to wake Berte. She had seen, from the balcony which connected all three rooms of their suite, that her niece was still asleep. Before she could decide what to do there was a short ring on the phone.

"Inspector Gaglione of the police would like to see Madame," said the concierge. "He asks if he may come up."

Then he added a reassurance. "We know him."

"Certainly," Martha replied. Immediately she knew what had brought him. The driver of the van had made note of Jean Tristan's license number and it had been traced. They had already been to Jean Tristan and Lord knows what he had told the police. Was she the accessory to a crime?

But as soon as the Inspector entered Martha discovered she was wrong.

"Madame," he asked after apologies which she assured him were unnecessary, "Do you know one Jean Mazzili?"

"No, I do not recognize the name."

He gave her two photographs mounted on a single sheet — one full face, the other in profile, the kind she imagined the police kept along with fingerprints.

"Yes, I know this young man as Jean Tristan de Valois."

"Jean Mazzili," the Inspector repeated. "Father, Gaston Mazzili, Monagasque, present whereabouts unknown. Mother, born Francine Dupont, in Crèpy-en-Valois, currently employed by the Société des Bains de Mer as a cleaning woman."

"How very sad."

"Please?"

"The young man is a friend of my niece. Now I understand how he came to call himself de Valois. I only meant to say how sad I feel for someone who so desperately wants to be what he is not. Is Jean Tristan, or Jean, in trouble?"

"He was, Madame. Do you know when your niece Mademoiselle Roberta Prescott last saw him?"

"Yesterday evening. It was — perhaps — his birthday."

"They met at a cafe, Le Beausoleil?"

"Berte calls it Le Beau."

"That is the one. It has an unsavory reputation because of the people who frequent it."

"They were to meet there before going to dinner. Berte left here just before nine."

"Do you know at what time she returned?"

"Yes, because I was surprised and pleased. She was back shortly after ten. So they did not dine, for some reason."

"No. May I ask, Madame, if you recognize this scarf?" He took from his briefcase the red, blue and white scarf which Berte had chosen in Beaulieu.

"It belongs to my niece. She was wearing it when she went out last evening. She must have lost it. But we can ask her, Inspector."

"First, Madame —"

His words stopped her although she had risen.

"Let me explain that the scarf was found tied to Jean Mazzili's motorbike, which had been abandoned in the Exotique. The Garden, that is."

"Inspector, tell me what has happened."

"I will, Madame, and that is why the time of your niece's return last night is important — for her. I believe what you have said, that she was here minutes after ten. And there can always be a logical explanation for the scarf. But I have to make certain your niece was not wearing it late last evening."

"Inspector, before I call Berte, please tell me where Jean Tristan is now."

"Jean Mazzili is nowhere, Madame. One hour ago his mother identified his body."

Martha sank back into her chair. Then the Inspector told

her the story, and being a logical man he started at the beginning. "Jean Mazzili has been in our books since he was seventeen. It is the typical case of a boy with whom his parents could do nothing. He kept bad company and was once let off with a warning. But the men who go to Le Beau boast of what they do, and that is perhaps the worst example for a young man who has nothing, wants everything, and has also lost his job. He was dismissed from the Tennis Club a few weeks ago because they were convinced he had stolen money, although they could not prove it. Lately there has been a series of robberies on the Côte, not an unusual occurrence, I am sorry to say, but this time there seemed to be a pattern. Invariably the houses were empty when entered. An habitué of Le Beau gives us tips from time to time, and the trail led us to two of the boys often seen with Jean Mazzili. They, too, have honest parents, their fathers are gardeners. The sons were using information innocently revealed by their parents about their employers' comings and goings. In Menton, even as far away as Cannes, and last night — up in Eze Village."

"You are certain, Inspector, that Jean was one of them?"

"Unfortunately, he has proven it with his life. Last night your niece must have found Mazzili at Le Beau with those friends. As it was Saturday the bar was very full and the patron remembers only that when they left on their motorbikes Mazzili led the way with a girl on the rear seat. She was trailing, he said, a scarf in the air. This scarf, I believe. She was not your niece as they did not leave the bar until after eleven."

"There was a girl with him?"

"Oh, yes. Many girls were attracted to Mazzili. They went to Eze Village where they expected to find the villa of M. de

Vilmordin empty and unguarded. But Monsieur had not left as he planned. He heard someone break a window and he had a gun. He caught Mazzili with his hands full of jewelry. He tells us that Mazzili threw everything at him, but he side-stepped it, and as Mazzili started to run, he shot — twice at random or so he thought. One of those bullets stopped Jean Mazzili. It is the chance a thief must take. He died instantly. Vilmordin heard a motorbike start and speed off down the road. Whoever she was, the girl was more interested in her escape than in waiting to see if Mazzili needed her to make his own getaway. We will find her in time, and also the other two. A second villa in Eze was also entered last night, some minutes earlier. They also took jewelry. It is a very sad story, and I am glad your niece is clearly not a part of it. But you understand, Madame, we had to be certain."

"Inspector, this is going to be a shock to Berte, and difficult as it may be, I want to be the one to tell her."

"I understand. Georges is rounding up the night shift who were on the lift and at the desk last evening. If they remember Mlle Prescott returning around ten, as I expect them to, it will not be necessary for me to see her at all."

When the Inspector had taken his leave Martha remained seated, her eyes closed. Suddenly aware that she was no longer alone, she looked up and saw Berte in the open door to the balcony. At once, Martha knew that Berte had heard the Inspector's story. She extended her arms and in the next instant Berte was at her feet, her face buried in Martha's lap to blot out reality with bitter tears. It was a long time before Berte raised her head.

"When I saw Jean Tristan at the café —"

"Not now."

"I want to tell you. He was with his two friends, the ones I don't like, although he had promised we would be alone for his birthday. But from the beginning everything went wrong. His first words, when I wished him a happy birthday, were 'Oh, so she let you come.' He was in one of those cynical moods so impossible to deal with. I gave him his present. I knew how much he wanted a watch. He opened the box and asked the others, 'What do you think? Is it as good as this one?' On his wrist was a Cartier watch I had never seen before. 'Now I have two,' is all he said.

"The café was crowded, it was impossible to talk. I reminded him we were going to dinner. No, he said, his plans had changed. They were going up to Eze Village first and I could go with him on the bike. Afterwards, maybe we would have dinner. We argued and in the end I stood up and said I was leaving whether he came with me or not. You know how he is — was — about challenges. He just said, 'What's keeping you?' Then he pulled the scarf off my shoulder and said, 'Leave us a souvenir.'

"I was hurt and angry. I don't remember what I said but they were all laughing and I came back here, grateful that you were asleep. I knew then that it would be impossible for me to go on with Jean Tristan, even though — no, I am not going to break down — even though I loved him."

Berte rose and went to the window.

"Now I feel empty. I don't care about anything and I wonder if I ever will!"

"All Ashore What's Going Ashore"

*S*ome days later the local train from Toulon deposited Martha and Berte at a tiny station marked Cap St Sauveur. Martha had known that Berte would recover from the nightmare which had engulfed her, but in anticipation of a difficult time, she had telephoned to old friends up the coast, to ask if she and Berte could spend a few days at the inn there.

"How did you find it the first time?" Berte asked, more to be polite than with any real interest in the answer, as her heart was not in the trip, nor in anything.

"Avril called this her secret place and said it could be ours, too. Robert and I came here often in the old days. Look — there they are!"

An ancient Citroen rumbled into the station and Martha saw two smiling faces, her Fréjus. Older, yes, but the same André and Nicole. A few minutes later the car was puffing back up the road with the baggage on top and when it reached the summit, Berte had her first glimpse of Cap St Sauveur and its sparkling bay.

Once settled in the little Auberge they joined their hosts for an aperitif. It was then that Martha first fully realized André was far from his robust self.

"It is true, Madame," he confessed, "and I am no longer the optimist I once was. Cap St Sauveur is as beautiful as ever, and yet it remains undiscovered. Is it any wonder that our young people leave for the cities? They cannot afford to stay here."

"I am still an optimist," said Martha sunnily, "so give Berte and me a few days to relax and then we will see if we can't do something to help Cap St Sauveur to be discovered."

"Madame," he said, "we dare you to solve our future for us, and meanwhile Nicole is going to grill a platter of rougets fresh from the sea for your...dégustation, do you say?"

"We don't say, but we do dégust."

"And before, les palourdes, the way you like them."

Just as she had felt many years before, Martha was completely at home and she fervently hoped the Cap would restore the sparkle to Berte's eyes.

The next afternoon they walked along the beach and dug their toes into the sand, shoes in hand. They strolled to the end of the village and over to a second, hidden beach and a grotto. Berte was a silent companion, appreciative of the sun, air and sand, but incapable as yet of any enthusiasm.

"Berte, let's sit down here." They sat down in the deep, cool shadow, where they could gaze at the sparkling sea, and Martha played her trump card.

"I want you to hear the story of Robert and me, from the

day we met. I've never told it to anyone. It says a great deal about me, about Robert, perhaps about people in general."

Roberta said nothing, but she was listening.

"I have to start before the beginning," Martha said. "In the '30's everyone's life had changed with the closing of the banks and fear about the future. Father thought he left us well provided for, and mother, bless her, never believed otherwise. But our means dwindled with the stock market and mother's generosity to those 'less fortunate than ourselves' did not help. Minty tried, poor dear girl, but we lost more than we could afford on her projects. Her homemade 'bitter marmalade for bitter times' did not strike the right note."

Berte almost smiled.

Mother went ahead writing the cheques, but I was the one the bank called with bad news. So I devised a plan — yes, even then! I announced I was going abroad for the summer, unlikely as it sounded. I reminded mother how many friends we had in Europe and said they would all be happy to see me, and added that my absence would cut down on household expenses. Mother accepted the logic of that, and my summer away from home was such a success with our bank account that I did the same thing for three years in a row."

Martha noted with satisfaction that Berte now wanted to interrupt her with a question but she gave her no time.

"By the third year some of our friends, including Lucille and her mother, old Mrs. Diekenfeld, began to be suspicious — just as you are now. I don't think they knew exactly what they suspected, but they found it strange that Martha van Horne could go abroad and enjoy herself in such difficult times. Of course I never left the country. I slaved those entire summers until I thought I would drop. But I was able to send money home to the bank and maintain the genteel facade so important to mother in Sliepskill, where the van Horne girls did not work except for charities. You see, I just rode the train into New York on a day when one of my favorite liners was sailing — I was partial to the Cunarders — and once in the city I crossed to Pennsylvania Station and took the train down to Virginia and a summer job at the Blueridge Springs Hotel. Father had been a director of the company and that is probably why they hired me. I was in the kitchen, and goodness knows they needed expert help there. I didn't earn much by today's standards, but it helped in the days when a dollar was a dollar."

"But when they didn't get letters from abroad —"

"They got postcards, no letters. I had friends in England and in Switzerland, and I regularly sent cards over — to be mailed back home. They understood and plotted with me.

"Then as I was about to leave for my third summer Lucille announced that she and Minty would see me off at the boat. In those days parties on board were great fun. I said I was delighted, but I took no chances. I went into the city the night before, on some excuse, and in the morning I checked my bags at Pennsylvania Station. I boarded ship as a visitor before they did, to get an idea where the best parties were. When Lucille and Minty arrived I had everything arranged. They met me in the first-class lounge and I still remember the disappointment on your mother's face when I said I was in Stateroom 32 on A Deck, where, I added, my traveling companion was already receiving some of her friends. 'You remember the Donovans,' I lied baldly. You see, I had asked the cabin steward outside

32-A whose stateroom it was when I saw the party getting under way there. 'Miss Dorothy Donovan,' he said. And do you know that dear Minty managed quite honestly to remember the Donovans — an entire family we had never heard of.

"The party was in full swing when we arrived, there wouldn't have been room for another sardine. I went up to the first young man we saw and gaily introduced Minty and Lucille. They were launched and in the crush I managed to avoid Dorothy Donovan. But I was immensely relieved at the first call of 'All Visitors Ashore,' and I quickly took my guests to the gangway. They promised to wave from the dock, but they never found me in the crowd, for a good reason. I had picked up some writing paper in the library — for notes during the voyage - and slipped down to the tourist class gangway and was on my way to Pennsylvania Station. It was by far the most exciting sailing I've ever attended."

She squeezed Berte's hand, exhilarated by the memories which her story had revived for her.

"As you have gathered my summers during those years were based on deception, and so was my first meeting with Robert.

"I had very little free time at the hotel, except after lunch when the guests took their naps and the kitchen staff collapsed. I had discovered a secret place at the end of the garden. There I spent enchanted hours in the dappled sunlight, reading, writing those postcards, and forgetting the kitchen. I was annoyed one day to arrive and find someone else in possession of my bench.

"'Hello,' he said, then he smiled and surprised me with "I thought I was the only one who came here.'

"'I come every day at this time,' I replied, rather huffily I am sure.

"'And I am usually later, so today I am the intruder.' He stood up and I saw that he was not only handsome, but tall.

"'What are you reading?' I asked.

"'Weierstrasse's Gesammelte Abhandlungen,' he said. I still remember that tongue-twister. 'I'm a mathematician. I guess I'd have to be to get through Weierstrasse, or even to pronounce it.'

"That broke the ice, in fact it melted instantly and forever. Guardedly, hesitantly, we began to learn something about each other.

"'This is our first time at the Springs,' he said.

"'It's my third season,' I answered, glad to be able to tell the truth.

"'We are in The Cottage,' he said.

"I couldn't say I was in the attic, so I just said I was in the main building.

"Then he told me he had been teaching at Ohio Wesleyan, but that he'd applied to Columbia, and said he had to get back to The Cottage, and asked if I would be there the next day. I was longing to say Yes, but I always had to work straight through on Thursdays — my baking day — so I said No, but I would be on Friday.

"'Good. Then so will I,' he said.

"He left and I read no more that day. He was so good looking and he had such a quiet, quick sense of humor. I almost burst into tears when I realized I didn't even know his name, nor he mine. I inquired at the front desk, as there was only one Cottage, our deluxe accommodation, 'Oh, sure,' they told me, 'that's the Rittenhouses. Columbus, Ohio. Mr. and Mrs. and their son. Even brought a couple of servants with them. Rich, rich, rich. Were they complaining? I hear the son's kinda uppity.'

"Rittenhouse sounded so reliable, and the son was definitely not uppity. I didn't know how I could wait until Friday.

"'My name is Robert,' he said when we met the second time. 'I should have told you the other day.'

"I told him mine was Martha and after that we met every day except Thursday, when I always made some excuse. I had discovered from Housekeeping that both the elder Rittenhouses were unwell, which was no doubt why the danger of an invitation to meet them was averted. We talked about a thousand things, the way young people do — or did —"

"Do," said Berte.

"Nothing we said was really important. We talked about Halley's Comet, or hominy grits, or math, or Bertrand Russell, or FDR, but all the time I'm sure we were both listening between the words and getting more interested in each other.

"Then a terrible thing happened. One Thursday when I 'd almost finished decorating a cake, the catering manager walked through the revolving door — with Robert. Our eyes met, but neither of us spoke. I think we were both too shocked. They kept right on through the kitchen and out the other door but I was humiliated and utterly crushed. I hadn't been honest with him and now I might never have a chance to explain. After a miserable night and morning I went to the garden on Friday not sure he would even appear. At three-thirty I was still waiting, then all at once he was there, out of breath. And he said to me exactly what I had planned to say to him.

"'Don't say a word until you've forgiven me. I wasn't honest. Mr. Rittenhouse needed somebody to take care of him for the summer and I needed the money to help my brother Florian through college. I am Mr. Rittenhouse's valet.'

"Well, after a few minutes of explanations we were laughing in relief and happiness. Robert kissed me and we both knew that something had begun between us that was going to be more than a summer romance.

"Robert went to Columbia that autumn and I made two important discoveries. First, he was much more than just 'in math.' He was one of the outstanding young men in his field and any university would have wanted him. More important, I realized that Robert and I were never, ever going to run out of things to talk about. Fortunately he came to the same conclusion, so we married in the spring. It was the most wonderful thing that ever happened to me."

Martha stopped, and Berte's eyes glistened.

"It's a beautiful story."

"Robert and I had too few years together. Now I have my memories. Berte, remember only the joy of your happy times with Jean Tristan, who touched your heart —"

"Yes, but I didn't touch his."

"That doesn't make it any easier."

"It is beginning to."

"Believe me, your heart will be ready to receive someone else, at the right time."

"Is yours, Aunt Martha?"

"Of course it is, in theory. But you are so young, my dear. Time is still on your side."

Then she abruptly changed the subject. "Now look at that moon, coming up so early. If a painter put it on canvas you'd say he had gone too far."

To her delight Martha noted a difference in Berte during the next days. She perked up, she was on the way to becoming her cheerful self again. Martha was grateful to have her back.

One morning on the beach, as Berte picked up a shell, she said, "Aunt Martha, I'm going to be all right, but would you mind after we go back to Monte Carlo if I go on home to Sliepskill? I'd like to work this winter at the hospital, and you said you could help me arrange it."

"I'll miss you, my dear, but of course I'll help, and I'll ask two favors in return. First, that you consider living in my house, since I won't be there. And second, that you'll promise to come back to Europe next summer again, to be with me."

"Both invitations accepted with pleasure!"

"But before we leave Cap St Sauveur," Martha added, "we have to fulfill our promise to Andre and I've been thinking. When Robert first saw this bay he said these were waters in which mermaids would be happy to cavort. I think he was right."

"Mermaids?"

"Yes — mermaids. Shall we go back and tell André and Nicole what we are going to do for Cap St Sauveur?"

The Sliepskill Broadsider

*S*hortly after Martha and Berte had successfully carried out the mermaid maneuver at Cap St Sauveur
they returned to Monte Carlo and Berte flew home to
work for a season at the Sliepskill Hospital. She fulfilled her
promise to rejoin Martha the following year, when time had
done its work and the memory of Jean Tristan was no longer
painful. That was the summer when Tom Swift and I met
them both, and learned to swim like sharks.

Yes, I promised to retire from the first person many chap-
ters ago. This book, after all, belongs to Martha. I am breaking
my word, but only briefly, because two events took place
which had primarily to do with me. One salvaged Lucille
Prescott's reputation in Sliepskill, and the other concerned my
novel, which was finished and needed a publisher to recognize its virtues.

By this time Berte and I were living in Manhattan with a
lively newborn son, in an apartment facing Gramercy Park,
the only private green space in the city where our Robert

could be aired while his mother sat on a bench and checked my manuscript for typos. We had removed ourselves from Sliepskill principally because of Lucille. Perhaps she could only see me as Martha's invention, for all my other admirable qualities eluded her and she remained relentlessly hostile. We were happy on our own and still had wonderful weekends with Martha, who was back in Sliepskill that year. Then one golden Saturday when the few remaining leaves were rapidly falling, Martha welcomed us to Elm Street with alarming news.

"Children," she began, "Sliepskill is on collision course. There is a madman, or madwoman, loose in our midst."

"Elmira Crisp has gone off her rocker at last," was Berte's flippant reaction. It drew a stern response.

"As a matter of fact," Martha said somewhat loftily, "poor Elmira was the first victim."

"Victim of what?" I honestly hoped there was not a Sliepskill strangler on the loose.

"Two weeks ago Elmira saw three women standing in front of her house laughing. A few moments later old Mr. Bailey came along, stared, then hobbled off as fast as his lame leg would allow. As soon as they had all moved along Elmira went outside to investigate and there, nailed to the trunk of her birch tree, was a broadside. Here it is."

She held up the offending sheet and we read:
ELMIRA CRISP LIVES HERE
75 AND STILL A VIRGIN HA HA

"She removed it at once but when four people on Elm Street have seen a broadside it might as well have been published in The Echo. By noon the whole town was buzzing, and so was Elmira's phone, mostly with expressions of sympathy that her age should have been so crudely revealed. I might add that the same mixture of truth and bad taste has been typical of all the broadsides since."

"There were more?"

"It has become a plague. Not even Dr. Cutler has been spared. He was, I believe, number three."

"The same text?" This time it was my turn to be flippant.

"Charles, this is no laughing matter. The second broadside was tied around the gatepost at the Dower House. The message was quite on the mark. It read, I believe:

MRS. FAUCITT'S A DRAIN

ALSO POMPOUS AND PUSHY."

By now Berte and I were biting our tongues despite Martha's insistence that we take the crisis seriously.

"Since then there have been half a dozen more. The town can hardly wait to parade up and down Elm Street of a morning to read the latest, posted on a gate or a tree, or even one day on a front door."

"Have you had one?"

"Not yet, I am sorry to say."

"What does that mean?"

"You will understand presently."

"You didn't tell us what was said about Dr. Cutler," Berte reminded her.

"It was the shortest of all, and the most harmful:

DR. CUTLER

LIKES LITTLE GIRLS."

"Uhf," was my sincerely concerned reaction.

"He destroyed the poster but some Christian was kind enough to shout the text into Violet Cutler's deaf ear. The most she will say is that 'Robin loves all little children, just as Our Saviour did.' But only this morning we experienced the worst so far and some of those who were amused in the beginning are starting to examine their own glass houses. The latest broadside was devoted to Horace Craig."

"I never liked Mr. Craig," Berte admitted.

"Few people do. He is undoubtedly Sliepskill's gruffest attorney. When his turn came the broadside was not even on his own door. It was on the Thompsons' across the street:

HERE LIES HORACE CRAIG —
EVERY FRIDAY NIGHT

"Unfortunately it was still up when Fred Thompson returned from the city on the morning train. He spends Friday in Manhattan and usually sleeps over. He tore it down, but people are talking about a vigilante committee to protect our citizens from—"

"Each other?"

"Calumny, I was about to say."

"Or big chunks of the truth," said Berte.

"Which can be equally destructive when carelessly scattered about," answered her aunt. "And let me add, before you ask, that Horace Craig has left town and the Thompsons are not answering their phone."

"Why are you sorry you haven't been favored so far?" I asked Martha.

"Because people are starting to indulge in speculation, and that has led to an unfortunate rumor. They are saying that the villain is Lucille."

"Not possible!" Berte knew her mother was difficult but she also knew she was sane, and Sliepskill's self-appointed town crier obviously wasn't.

"It is pointed out that Lucille has not had a message nailed to the tree on her lawn, nor have I, so they are saying that her family is exempt. I'm about ready to nail one on my own flowering cherry. Of course Lucille's personality does not help, and no champion has risen to defend her. That is why I am counting on you, Charles."

"Aunt Martha, what do you want him to do?"

"The whispering will only stop when the broadsides stop —"

"Agreed. How do I fit in?"

"You have an inquiring mind, Charles, and a keen eye. If you'll stay here a few days I will play Miss Marple to your Holmes."

"Of course he will," said Berte even before I could. "Does Mother know what they are saying?"

"She wouldn't tell me if she did."

But before Berte returned to Gramercy Park on Sunday we discovered that Lucille did know what was being said. Berte had stopped in to see her parents and found Florian upset.

"No doubt your aunt has told you. People are claiming your mother is responsible for the so-called Sliepskill broadsides. Only the other evening an anonymous voice on the phone warned me that Lucille had better realize the war is over and desist. The war referred to was Kaiser Wilhelm's. There was a great deal of hysteria then about German Americans, and old Mrs. Diekenfeld, I gather, wrote an unsigned letter to the mayor at that time pointing out certain lapses concerning his family, Irish Catholics, who were all in the highly profitable junk business. It was traced to her and caused hard feelings. Mrs. Diekenfeld was no more popular in some circles than your mother is now. It is all most unfortunate."

When Martha and I sat down to discuss strategy Martha admitted she had as yet devised no plan.

"Can't the police help?"

"Hopeless," she replied. "They looked for fingerprints but they only found their own. The Lower Town — and I use the term in a strictly altitudinal sense — has not really been concerned, perhaps because there have been no broadsides posted down on Main Street."

All that changed on Monday morning when placards were found pasted on shop windows at River and Main. One graced the Elite Meat Market where Mr. Pannaloni catered to those who preferred their roasts and chops cut to order. His prices reflected the quality and the care he took, but now he was accused of something that many had long suspected:

MR. PANNALONI
GIVES SHORT MEASURE

A second accusation was attached to a sliding grill with which the proprietor of the town's only cleaning establishment protected his premises. It proclaimed that:

MR. ROTHMEIER
LEAVES SPOTS

"Now that the town has been drawn in," Martha said, "there is no telling where this will end. Did you have any thoughts in the night?"

"A good number," I said, "and I have concluded that we are dealing with a woman."

"Male chauvinist that you are!" exclaimed Martha. "But I happen to agree. For a number of reasons."

"Including an interest in things a woman is often concerned about? Such as short weight and spots and other women's ages and faults?"

"Exactly. We are dealing with a canny and well-informed woman, one with a nasty streak just below the surface. And I am beginning to have an idea of who it might be, Charles. I'll share my thinking with you."

She did, and I listened in respectful silence.

"In some ways it is unthinkable," Martha concluded, "but an aberration can lie dormant for years, then suddenly erupt. However, if I am right, what are we to do? Her good qualities far outweigh the things which annoy me from time to time, or so I tell myself."

I was silent because I had no idea what the next step should be.

"We must find a way to bring her crusade to a halt. If the established pattern tells us anything we have a day or two before we need expect another provocation."

Martha was wrong and greeted me with a worried look the next morning.

"She has struck again! In the worst possible way. With a pronouncement on Herbert Detweiler's doorstep—"

"She wouldn't—"

"She has, and with a text very much to the point:
HERBERT DETWEILER
MARRY A.v.HORNE NOW

"Charles, we must act today. I'll ask everybody to come here tonight. At eight o'clock."

"Will she accept?"

"She won't be able to resist. How many shall we be? Lucille and Florian, of course. Herbert. I don't think I'll ask him to collect Minty under the circumstances. Elmira Crisp, as the first to receive a noxious notice. And I thought Dr. Benson. Psychiatry is his field so he should find the evening of professional interest. He might even pick up a new patient before the night is over." That was a fascinating prospect, I thought, in view of the identity of the prime suspect. "And of course the Cutlers. How many is that?"

"Haven't you forgotten someone?"

I did not for a moment imagine that Martha had forgotten anyone, but there was a name missing. She did not deign to break her train of thought with my query.

"And now, Charles, let me give you my ideas for tonight, especially as everything depends on you."

"On me?"

"Oh, yes, I couldn't get away with it, but I think you can. This is what I propose —"

They all arrived promptly. It was like the final scene of countless thrillers except that there were no police waiting, hidden, to lead the culprit off to justice.

"Do come," Martha had said to everyone. "It has to do with the broadsides. Eight o'clock." She had not given anyone a chance to ask questions before she rang off.

It was not a stormy night, there was no thunder, no wind, but neither was there much general conversation exchanged among the group which gathered at 36 Elm Street. Elmira Crisp, known to be uncontrollably talkative, was silent and merely waved when the Cutlers came in. Lucille was surprised to see me; she left it to Florian to greet me. Minty found it difficult even to glance in Herbert's direction, and he pretended to read. In contrast, a slender, lithe Dr. Benson chatted with Martha and smiled across the room to Lucille who had not spoken to him since receiving his bill after the trip to Las Vegas.

Then Mrs. Brimstone opened the double doors for the last guest, the one who had not received an invitation.

"Good evening, Alexandra," said Martha fulsomely.

"Dear Martha," was the response as that galleon sailed into the room. "I never got your message, but I knew you expected me."

"Of course I did."

Then Martha turned to her guests and clapped her hands together for silence.

"You all know Charles," she began. "I believe he wants to tell us who has been posting the Sliepskill broadsides."

Her announcement, unexpected by me at least in that challenging form, made my impossible task all the more difficult. There was an instant of silence, then a murmur ran through the room, as well it might. Nervously, I stood up as Martha crossed the room and sat down with Dr. Benson at the bridge table, where she could observe the entire company.

At once I understood why pipe smokers had pipes, why men wore beards: anything for something to hide behind. I could not imagine how I was going to get my next words out; nevertheless, I heard myself speak.

"I have not had much experience solving mysteries —"

"Then why are we here? I am sure we all had other things to do."

The question was typical and of course it came from Lucille. Florian cast his eyes down, but Martha spoke up in my defense.

"Charles only consented to put his mind to this when I told him that certain voices were encouraging the rumor that you, Lucille, are the author of the broadsides."

Another ripple ran through the room.

"What did Martha say?" Mrs. Cutler asked in a loud voice.

"That Lucille did it," answered Elmira Crisp for all ears to hear.

The chorus of No's was led by Dr. Cutler.

"I mean, they are saying —"

Mrs. Cutler nodded to indicate that she understood and they all turned back to me with relief.

"However," I continued, and waited a moment for the suspense to build, "I have come to the conclusion that we are dealing with a feminine mind, a woman who has taken it upon herself to express some uncomfortable and inadmissible —"

"Lies," boomed Alexandra Kimberley-Faucitt. "And a feminine mind could belong either to a woman or a man, wouldn't you say so, Dr. Benson?"

"Yes, I would."

Again there were murmurs as this observation opened up new vistas. Lucille darted a sharp look in the direction of Herbert Detweiler. I realized that I had to keep them in control so I raised my voice and began with a loud "In any event —

we cannot condone what has been done, even if it represents the actions of someone more misguided than criminal."

Then I told them that I saw the Sliepskill broadsides as the work of an unfortunate woman afflicted with an illness from which complete recovery was possible. I was especially eloquent on the need for everyone to understand that the perpetrator of these cruel hoaxes had only succumbed to a temporary aberration, that she needed understanding more than punishment — and above all, forgiveness.

"Charles," exclaimed Minty with the delight of discovery, "I do believe you are on her side."

"Regrettably." Alexandra again and her tone proclaimed a moral judgment — on me.

"I am not on her side, nor can any of us afford to be, even if our anonymous poetess is only setting the record straight —in some instances, and strictly from her own point of view, of course. But this sensitive and perceptive woman must have realized by now that she can do incalculable harm to the community as well as to her role in it, if she continues this unwelcome campaign to spread the truth — as she interprets it. Far better that she should stand up now, confess her error, and let all of you, her friends, forgive her."

With that I rested the case for the prosecution. Or was it the defense? The room was very still. At this point, according to our plan, I was to turn to the suspect and ask her if she had anything to say. We had been certain she would break into tears, make her confession, and accept the forgiveness of her peers — but a glance around the room showed me little evidence of incipient mercy.

"Charles," asked Martha as if spontaneously, "tell us who it is."

But I had caught a look of anguish in those guilty eyes, and knew in a flash that even though we were right in our suspicions, I could not proceed. To reveal her name would destroy her life in Sliepskill, just what we hoped to avoid, and where else did she have a life?

"Well, Charles?" asked Martha, not knowing why I had stopped.

So much for a grand strategy when the heart has rejected it. I knew what I had to do, and I did it.

"Under special circumstances, and perhaps stress," I began, "I believe that any of us might have been the Sliepskill Broadsider." There were some rumblings at this, and some flashing eyes. "Luckily, we all happen not to have been, except for the one person who now has to live with what she has done. She will post no more broadsides, of that I am convinced, and therefore to name her tonight would serve no purpose."

I had addressed these last words directly to Martha, who instinctively understood. Alexandra Kimberley-Faucitt was not so understanding. With one hand on her pearls, she said imperiously, "Do you mean to say you have boasted of your insight and now you do not intend to reveal the name of the criminal?"

She had her nerve, I thought. Much of the information which appeared on the broadsides might well have first been launched at her own table.

"— if indeed you know it," she concluded icily.

"I do know her name," I responded quickly, "and she

realizes I know. That, I assure you, is sufficient."

I caught another glimpse of the guilty eyes as they closed in blessed relief.

"And you must all realize," I said, "That Lucille Prescott was not, could never have been, the offender."

"No, Charles, of course not," said Herbert Detweiler. "Lucille has none of the qualities you so convincingly ascribe to the guilty party."

Herbert did not realize the irony of his statement, even though it effectively closed the door on suspicions cast towards Lucille. I had, after all, ascribed both gentility and sensitivity, albeit misguided, to the Broadsider, qualities Lucille certainly did not possess.

Now they all had something to say, including the isolated and confused Mrs. Cutler, whose somewhat strident voice could be heard above the others, exclaiming, "Then it was Lucille after all!" at which once again the No's flooded the room.

"A final word of caution," I said, bringing them once again to order. "Some of your friends may know that you came here tonight and why." I knew full well that all Elm Street was holding its breath and keeping telephone wires clear. Even the Lower Town was eager to know the results of this seance, news of which had no doubt spread faster than a brush fire in October. "I strongly recommend you to say that the problem has been solved, and very little more. If anyone is insistent, simply state it was a stranger in your midst."

"Yes," said Elmira Crisp, "that is a good idea."

"I concur," said Dr. Cutler, with the authority of the pulpit, "it is the Christian thing to do."

"Nonsense," said Alexandra, "it is highly unsatisfactory, but I do not see that we have much choice. And we will soon know if Charles' theory is correct. Possibly tomorrow morning."

That was a chance I was prepared to take.

"Herbert," said Alexandra as she rose, "Bowles is outside with the car. Can I give you a ride up the hill?"

"Thank you, Alexandra, but I shall see Araminta home."

"Dr. Cutler? There is room for you and Mrs. Cutler."

"Many thanks, m'lady," replied the Church, slipping into a salutation which, while inaccurate, gave great pleasure whenever he used it.

They were all on their feet now. Before she and Florian left, Lucille came over to me and said quite civilly, "Thank you." Not "Thank you, dear boy," or even "Thank you, Charles," but it was a breakthrough and she was less hostile towards me from then on.

As the others left the room Dr. Benson lingered, no doubt looking forward to a chat about the psychological overtones of the evening.

"Good work," he said. Then casting little lustre on his professional acumen he added, "Who'd ever have guessed it was Mrs. Cutler, after all?"

"Not I," was my reply as Martha gently steered him into the hall and left me alone with the last of the guests, Elmira Crisp.

"Thank you for a lovely evening," she said, as if she had come to dinner and enjoyed the small talk.

"And if you had written the broadsides," she added coquettishly, "what would you do now?"

I pretended to be considering an answer which I had

ready. "Perhaps only what I suspect the writer of them is even now planning to do, Miss Crisp."

"And pray what is that?"

"I think she may post one more notice before putting away her scissors and paste forever. Just to demonstrate that the Broadsider was an out-of-towner. Say, down at the railway station where it can be found after the 5:58 pulls out tomorrow morning. A simple 'Farewell, Sliepskill.'"

Martha rejoined us at that moment.

"Elmira," she teased, "what are you and Charles plotting now?"

Miss Crisp laughed giddily. "I'm just going. No, don't show me out. I know my way."

She scurried off, and Martha waited for me to say something.

"It was those imploring eyes," I said, "I'll never forget them."

The next morning word reached Elm Street from the Lower Town that Sliepskill's Broadsider had struck again. Her message was found on the wall outside the railway waiting room.

"Just two words?" I asked Martha.

"No, the message was more eloquent than you anticipated. She wrote:

FAREWELL SLIEPSKILL

YOU DON'T DESERVE ME."

She had added a personal touch. I was delighted.

"And," Martha concluded, "Mr. Pemberton at the station saw a woman boarding the 5:58 carrying a small valise."

Martha caught my questioning look. "No, I have just spoken with Elmira. She is at home and she rang to thank me for the evening."

The following spring Elmira Crisp sailed off on a cruise to the Caribbean courtesy of Martha. When she returned Martha arranged with the library board that Elmira should come in afternoons and work in the Historical Sliepskill Section, which had always been her favorite. Thereafter she sat at a small desk in the corner of the reading room, directly under a framed sign in gros point which read, "A Busy Bee Is A Happy Bee."

We never learned who the woman with the valise on the 5:58 had been, she who provided the official solution to our mystery by creating one of her own.

"Charles, I shall always be in your debt," said Martha that same afternoon as I left for Gramercy Park where a devoted wife, child and completed manuscript all awaited me. "I hope I can return the favor."

"You can pray that my agent will find me a publisher," I quipped. "And something else," I added. "Tell me what put you on the right track about the Broadsider."

"Elementary, my dear Charles. When I thought it over I realized that all the broadsides were frighteningly accurate except the first one. You see, Elmira is eighty if she's a day."

Martha took to heart what I said about needing a publisher. No believer in wasting time, she rang me early the next week and asked a question.

"Charles, do you ever go to literary parties?"

"When my agent tells me I have to. If you come to town next Wednesday, I'll take you to a big bash in Murray Hill," I offered. "Berte refuses to go. She calls them jungle warfare."

"Who will be there?"

"Everybody, as the saying goes."

"Wednesday, the 30th? I'll stay the night and give you both lunch on Thursday. Thank you for the invitation, Charles."

"Now tell me," said Martha the following week, after a bucolic hour with Berte and our Robert in Gramercy Park, "exactly who is the everybody I'm going to meet this afternoon?"

"Authors, agents, publishers, editors — and civilians, including some who were not invited. But you don't meet them, you just keep talking and moving."

"That doesn't sound very civilized."

"It's not. If Darwin had attended a New York literary party he wouldn't have had to sail on The Beagle."

"Don't let him frighten you," said Berte.

"He hasn't, but he has whetted my curiosity."

We arrived at 7 in response to an invitation which read 5 to 8 for a party which probably went on until after midnight. The house was a nineteenth-century brownstone and we paused under an arch leading from the hall into the double drawing rooms. At any given time one room was packed with humanity and the other almost empty, the usual party phenomenon.

"You will notice small groups and large clumps," I pontificated. "The clumps are gathered around publishers and the groups are waiting to edge in. Over there — that's your host in the turtleneck and blazer. He made his money in soft porn but now he's respectable. Everybody likes him because he gives good parties and gets good press. That enormous clump — those are the aggressive ones trying to register with Alexander Pogor. I believe 'Pogor' is the Russian word for button. He is tough as nails, but his house has a great list. Are you ready to dive in? I'll run interference for you."

"You seek out your friends and let me muddle along at my own pace, Charles. Later we can compare notes." With that she crossed the room and was absorbed into the crowd.

It was half an hour before we coincided again and broke into smiles over the absurdities we had seen and heard. Before either of us could say a word a tall, gaunt woman wearing enormous purple-tinted glasses pushed her way up to us.

"Have you both met Stacy Greenspan? Come here, Stace."

An angular young man in Navy surplus dungarees and a windbreaker moved in our direction just as a gaily over-garbed creature from another part of the forest pounced on Martha and cried, "But I know you!"

I saw uncertainty, or was it incredulity, in Martha's eyes.

"Not —?"

"Sure thing. Jonny De Vine. Joanna now."

The gaunt female slid her glasses up into her hair to get a better look. "I hear you got a whopping advance on your book," she said, not without envy.

"Well, of course. Sex change is in," Joanna explained to Martha. "I had a divine surgeon. He said it wasn't even major nowadays. But Oh, the difference to me!"

"Wordsworth!" exclaimed Martha.

"No, Dr. Birnbaum."

Not thinking it appropriate to explain about the Lake Poet, Martha was at a loss for words, and simply smiled in the direction of Stacy Greenspan.

"I gotta take a leak," he muttered, and disappeared.

"Poor dear," said his horn-rimmed sponsor, "he's so shy. He probably just wanted to make a phone call and was too embarrassed to say so. You should read his poems. Earthy, like worms."

With that she left us for greener pastures and as Joanna had already been pulled into another group jealous of her contract, Martha and I were alone again.

"Are you ready for fresh air?" I asked.

"Not quite. As I'll probably never experience anything like this again I intend to make the most of it." Then she exclaimed, "Oh, look. Father had one of those —"

My eyes followed hers to an elephant's foot wastebasket and when I looked up she was gone. Then my agent dragged me away and I lost track of Martha until she finally rescued me from six other authors in search of a publisher.

"Where have you been?" I demanded.

"I slipped into the library to catch my breath."

Then Martha told me in such vivid detail what had happened in the library that I still feel I was there with her...

The room, she said, was dark except for a fire in the grate. Martha sank into a comfortable leather chair facing the flame and did not notice a man sitting in the shadows.

"Please do not jump out of your skin —" he began.

She almost did.

"But what does a gentleman do when a lady sits down, obviously hasn't seen him, and is bound to get a shock when she does?" He was bemused but also concerned.

"He tries to warn her, discreetly," Martha replied. "I am grateful."

She saw now that this was a small, wiry man of a certain age, who held a brandy snifter in the palm of one hand.

He smiled. "And what is a sensible woman like you doing at a party like this?"

"I came with an ulterior motive."

"I daresay you are not the only one. Are you here to sell a book?"

"Nobody can do that. A book has to sell itself."

"Dear lady, I wish other people realized that. How are you connected with the book trade?"

"I'm not, except that books are important to me. My father said books didn't talk back, and were always available whenever you needed them."

"A perceptive man."

"It was just that he refused to suffer fools gladly, especially pompous ones. He took great pleasure in deflating what he called the literary balloons."

"What would your father have said to a gathering like this one?"

"He would never have come. Our only literary connection was the James family."

"That's pretty high on the hog."

"Father couldn't stand Henry or William. He once introduced Henry James to a friend with a casual 'You know Hank James. Bill's brother.'"

Martha's companion broke into hearty laughter. "Tell me, what exactly was your ulterior motive in coming here today?"

"Someone in whom I believe has written a novel I have reason to think is first rate. So I came along with Charles rather naively thinking I could help him meet a publisher for it."

The door flew open, and a man lurched inside, creating a corridor of light across the room. Then he thought better of it and shut the door again, but not before the intolerable buzz and hum of the multitude had penetrated their peaceful retreat.

She went on. "I hadn't been out there very long before I realized that no one could meet anyone and talk seriously in that tower of Babel." Then she smiled. "I may have failed in my mission but these few minutes have been the nicest part of it."

"For me as well. Hank and Bill James, eh? I will be glad to read your young man's book."

"You mustn't say that just to be kind."

"I have never been accused of saying anything just to be kind."

"Well, I am sure Charles would let you have a copy if you really want to read it."

With a tiny gold pencil he scribbled a few words on the back of his card and gave it to Martha. "I have written 'I want to read this.' If your author sends me his manuscript, tell him to enclose this card. I will know where it comes from."

"Thank you," said Martha, putting the card into her bag.

"That's the least I can do for an honest woman with an unrequited ulterior motive."

They rose together, and Martha's friend added, "You slip out first and I will follow after a decent interval. We don't want to start rumors racing through the world of letters."

When Martha finished telling me about her fireside conversation I was not particularly keen about sending a manuscript to a chance acquaintance encountered in the library. Copies were expensive and had a way of getting lost. Then she produced the card. I looked at it in astonishment.

"Do you realize you have just been alone with Alexander Pogor, and that there are fifty people in this room who would mortgage their grandmothers for what you managed by chance?" Then I noticed the sparkle in Martha's eye. "You knew who it was all the time."

"Charles, you pointed out Mr. Pogor when we arrived and told me he was important. Later I saw him slip into the library. But I don't see how you can call him hard as nails. You will send him the novel, won't you?"

I did, along with his card, and he asked me to lunch a week later. We met several times subsequently and in the end we signed a contract. When I told Martha she said, "I knew your book would speak for itself." Perhaps, but only because Martha had once again planned a grand strategy for me.

As promised, Martha stayed in town and gave Berte and me a good lunch on Thursday. We were seated at Table Number One in a restaurant where a reservation in my name would have procured us a corner in Outer Siberia. In Martha's case the maître d' thanked her for coming. Moreover, the elderly owner kissed her hand and reminded her that he had sailed from the Caucasus in 1917 with a fellow officer known to Martha as Butch Romanoff.

When we returned to Gramercy Park the phone was ringing insistently.

"That'll be for Mrs. Prescott," said Robert's sitter. "They've been calling all afternoon."

I took up the receiver and heard a unique accent. I handed the phone to Martha. "Your favorite duchess," I said.

"Avril!"

"Marthe, I must see you at once. It is urgent."

"Are you in Paris, or —"

"Ma chère, I am in your Sliepskill."

"I'll be on the 6:13 from Grand Central."

"And I will meet your train. A bientôt."

"A bientôt."

Fenton in Extremis

"**W**hat a wonderful surprise," was the first thing Martha said when she stepped down from the train. "I hope you have come for the long visit you've always promised me."

Avril de Dinde, betweeded and bejeweled with a dazzle of bracelets, had opened her arms in joyous greeting and a hug, but her words were sober.

"Alas, on Sunday we celebrate D.D.'s birthday and I must be in Normandy. Officially she is 90, so she must be close to 100."

As soon as they were seated in the car Martha said, "Now tell me —"

But Avril inclined her head towards Mr. Barrett up front in a silent "pas devant les domestiques" gesture, so they chattered, happy in each other's company until they reached Elm Street, where no leaf stirred on any of the well-kept lawns.

A few minutes later, in the library, before a crackling fire, Avril was ready to talk seriously.

"Did I ever speak to you about John Julian Fenton?"

"Has he anything to do with Fenton Industries?" Martha asked.

"Will Fenton — his friends call him that — *is* Fenton Industries, at least he was. When we both lived in Paris I saw a great deal of him and if I hadn't been married to Maurice I would have pursued Will. He was, always has been, an exceedingly attractive man.

"Will inherited a modest fortune and turned it into a great one, but he never allowed his business to consume him. He always had time for books and music, and people and ideas. Then he met and married the most beautiful woman in Paris.

"I had never liked Yolande, so Will and I drifted apart. My life was in France, even after Maurice died, and they lived everywhere. London, Sintra, South America. They had a house in Palm Beach, one in Marrakech. Once in a while Will would ring me, and we'd spend an evening together, usually when Yolande was in some other part of the globe. He adored her and that was her one saving grace in my eyes.

"Then six months ago I read she had been killed in a plane crash. Their plane was flying her to Marrakech when it was caught in one of those treacherous storms which sweep down from the Atlas. I wired Will, and tried to phone, but could not find him. Finally, I thought of calling the chalet in St. Moritz, the one house he did not share with Yolande. There I reached Will's valet. Niko considers me his special friend because he met his wife, Tita, while she worked for me. Niko said, Yes, Mr. Fenton was there but he had instructions not to report any calls to him. That alarmed me, but Niko assured me he would be in touch if there was something I could do. I heard from him a week ago."

"Dinner is served," announced Mrs. Brimston most inopportunely.

While they were at table Martha gave Avril a vivid account of the autumnal affair of the beastly broadsides, sighed with her over the problem of Lucille, and admitted her growing conviction that Minty and Herbert might never marry after all. As soon as Mrs. Brimston had left them back in the library with coffee and the ginger jar, Avril continued her story as if she had never been interrupted.

"Niko rang me from a public telephone in St. Moritz. He didn't dare call from the chalet. He said Will was not getting over his depression. He and Tita felt he was not trying. He called me because they had no one else to turn to.

"I told Niko I could be in St. Moritz the next day. I knew if I appeared at the door Will would not turn me away, so I left for Switzerland on the night train. That was last Friday. The chalet is off the Pontresina road, and quite remote. I arrived in a taxi. Niko pretended to be surprised and led me to the room where Will spent most of his time. I found him there, staring out the window. He managed a wan smile, but chère Marthe, I had to fight back a crise de larmes when I saw the change in the man. Will is big, an imposing figure. I found him diminished to a shadow. His eyes were dull and apathetic. He was obviously struggling with quiet desperation, the worst kind. I knew something had to be done — at once — or Will would be lost to the world forever. I also realized I'd only succeed in helping if I seemed to be concerned about Niko and Tita, the two human beings he had allowed near him since Yolande's death.

"'Will,' I said, 'surely by now Niko and Tita both need a rest —'

"He interrupted me. 'Did they tell you that?'

"'There was no need to,' I told him, and it was true.

"Of course he said he couldn't do without them. I replied that problems existed to be solved, and he looked me directly in the eyes for the first time. He had often said those very words to me, in the old days.

"I promised to find someone to help out, and before he could object again, I added, 'I think I know just the person, if she is free. Efficient and dependable, and you will hardly realize she is here.'

"Then I waited.

"Finally, he said, 'But they can't both be away at the same time,' and I knew I had won.

"He was still suspicious, and he asked me if I intended to propose myself for the position. I assured him I did not. Because, Martha, I am not the one Will needs with him. It must be someone who does not remind him in the least about the past, and can challenge him to face the future. Someone who may be able to lead him back and save him. 'I'll try to arrange six weeks,' I said. 'Niko and Tita can each have two weeks away and before that all three of them can have a fortnight here together.' He smiled again, then just closed his eyes as if he was glad someone cared.

"And that, chère Marthe, is why I am here. I have left unsaid more than I have told you, but you know enough to make a decision. There is no one else."

Martha rose, walked to the window and looked into the silver night where a waning moon lighted spectral trees. She knew there were logical questions she should ask, and convincing reasons why she could not leave home so precipitately to accept a task which might be no more than a futile gesture and a painful experience if she failed. But she also knew that her friend had crossed the ocean solely to seek her help.

"Of course I'll go."

"Oh, my dear, I am so relieved." A tear of gratitude ran down Avril de Dinde's cheek. "We leave tomorrow night. I can't miss the birthday on Sunday."

"I suppose tomorrow is no more impossible than a week from tomorrow," sighed Martha, "if we can get seats on the plane." Then suddenly: "But of course, you already have them!" And they both laughed aloud.

Later that evening when Martha had retired to her room she again gazed out onto the moonlit trees and the sleeping town. Minty would miss her but Herbert would surely invite her to Christmas luncheon; and the children would enjoy the holidays on their own with their Robert in Gramercy Park. No one else really mattered. She closed her eyes, then suddenly opened them. Lord, she thought, what have I let myself in for this time...

They landed at Paris-Orly and parted there when Martha continued on to Switzerland. At Zurich she changed to the train and relaxed as it sped along the lakefront. When Chur was announced she transferred to the local and started up to the top of the world. The day was December grey, but when the train emerged from the long tunnel Martha was blinded by the brilliance of the sun reflected off snow-laden trees and great expanses of white beneath the blue sky — that recurring miracle of the Engadine.

Niko was waiting for her at the station. Small and smiling, he greeted Martha with a little bow.

"We are glad you are come," he said in her native tongue, his fifth language.

"Madame de Dinde sends her greetings," said Martha, "and thanks you for calling her."

She sat with him in the front seat of the vintage Mercedes as they climbed the hill and drove out the Pontresina road.

"What have you told Mr. Fenton?" she asked.

"Only what I know, Madame. That you are engaged in his behalf by Madame la duchesse."

They lapsed into silence as Martha marvelled at the winter landscape. Niko wanted to say something more but he was struggling to find the right words. Finally, he tried.

"Madame, be patient with a man who tries to forget many things."

"I understand. He has suffered a great loss."

Niko made no reply, and presently they turned off the road into a private drive which, swept clear of snow, led over a rise and down through dense woods until the chalet came into view. It crowned an open slope and faced an infinity of white and blue.

"The house is enormous," Martha exclaimed.

"Mr. Fenton built it for himself, and for his books."

The heavy door swung open as soon as they stopped and Tita came out to welcome them. She ventured a shy smile as she curtseyed. The urgency of her first words, however, alarmed Niko and worried Martha.

"Thank heaven you have come, but I propose, Madame, that you wait until evening, then Niko will tell Mr. Fenton you have arrived. That will be easier."

"Unless he has heard us," said Niko.

"We have prepared the small guest room because it has the best view."

Martha knew she was in good hands. They were in the hall when a bell jangled somewhere in the house.

"He has heard," said Niko. "He will want to see you now, Madame."

Martha managed a cheerful reply because she saw it was needed.

"Of course, with the greatest pleasure."

Moments later Niko knocked on an elaborately carved door, then opened it without waiting for a command, and made way for Martha to pass before him. She found herself in a large book-lined room. Facing her at the window, which framed a magnificent prospect of distant peaks, was a library table cluttered with papers. Behind it, in a swivel chair turned towards the mountains, sat a man, motionless.

Niko discreetly cleared his throat, then silently closed the door behind Martha. She waited patiently. At long last, without turning to greet her, John Julian Fenton spoke.

"If you are a doctor, detective, psychiatrist, spy, butcher, baker or candlestick maker, Niko will take you back to the station now."

He swung around wearily and faced her, the fine figure of a man, as her father would have described him, but infinitely sad, as if drained of all vital energy. He looked at her long and intently. When he spoke again his words were conciliatory.

"Thank you for coming. I am doing this for Niko and Tita. Let me see as little of you as possible."

But the dismissal implicit in these words was not reflected

in his eyes where apathy was replaced by a steady gaze, even curiosity.

"Madame de Dinde sends you her greetings," said Martha, and when he did not react, "I believe you are friends."

"Yes, she is a friend."

Then he jumped to another thought without any transition, a characteristic which Martha soon came to expect of him.

"Am I supposed to ask you questions? Niko will answer all of yours."

"I settle in quickly, Mr. Fenton. Niko and his wife have already made me feel at home."

"I wonder what they told you. Well, you wouldn't say. Don't wear a uniform, please, like matron in the ward. If that's a problem Niko will drive you into the town and you can buy some clothes. He will take care of the bill."

Then he gave the first hint that he might have a sense of humor.

"Nothing giddy, mind you."

"I do not have a uniform," Martha confessed, not meaning to boast; she had simply forgot that a nurse-companion might have been expected to wear white.

His mood changed abruptly, and he snapped, "I hope you're not an impoverished gentlewoman who wants to take her meals with the family. There is no family here."

"I am quite happy to take my meals in the kitchen," she replied, coolly. "I prefer it."

"Don't be touchy or you won't last."

"I will last, Mr. Fenton."

Minutes later in the kitchen, where Tita had made them coffee, Martha asked in wonderment, "How have you managed for almost a half a year?"

"He will be different tomorrow, Madame," Niko assured her.

"I hope so."

A good night's rest restored Martha's spirits and she soon fell in with the routine of the house. She discovered that insofar as Fenton was concerned it meant leaving him in peace, which made her real task more difficult. If she were to help him she had to find a way to him.

Fenton took his meals on a tray, at his desk on days when he was busy with paperwork, before the fire and staring into the flames at other times. On the most difficult days he would simply sit facing the window, just as she had come upon him the first afternoon. He never left the house.

Niko had been right: there were ups and downs. The day after her arrival Fenton made amends for his behavior of the previous afternoon.

"Is it Miss Prescott?" he inquired affably. "We couldn't tell from the wire."

Tita spoke up before Martha could reply. "Mrs. Prescott, Sir." She pronounced it Mizzuz.

"Ask Tita a hundred questions a day. She won't mind. And forget my opening barrage yesterday, please."

"Of course. I might have asked Niko to take me back to the station if you had not added the butcher, the baker and the candlestick maker to your list."

"Whimsy will out, Mizzuz Prescott, even in extremis."

As soon as they had closed the door behind them Tita smiled and said, "This is a good day."

Yes, thought Martha, but how many good days are there going to be when he realizes I have no intention of remaining discreetly out of sight and mind?

As time passed there developed between Martha Prescott and John Julian Fenton a series of exploratory skirmishes, unacknowledged but persisting. She was determined to draw him out of himself without seeming to do so, and he was equally determined not to allow her to succeed, unconsciously at first but in the end wittingly. She had one small advantage — he became increasingly curious about Martha, and his curiosity could not be satisfied if she stayed away. However, his own great advantage was that as the master of the house he could cut her off, in midsentence if he wished, and he did not hesitate to do so.

One evening soon after her arrival he asked suddenly, as if to throw her off guard, "Who was your last employer, Mrs. Prescott?"

Without hesitation she replied, "The Maître Durant-Perrichon in Normandy. I have the address if you would like to write for a reference."

"Too late," he said, defeated for the moment. "Were you with him very long?"

Not wanting to say 'For a weekend, by mistake,' Martha replied, "Long enough to succeed in the task I was given. It was not easy."

"No case histories, please."

Another day Fenton found Martha absorbed in a book

when he entered the library.

"Have you found something to read, Mrs. Prescott? I don't stock mysteries or romances."

She replaced the book on the shelf and said, dryly, "Perhaps you should."

He did not smile. "Did your Monsieur Perrichon-or-Whoever discharge you for impertinence?"

"No. I was engaged to take charge of a difficult child, and I succeeded."

This time Fenton permitted her to have the last word, but when she was gone he went to the shelf and pulled out the book she had dipped into. It was a volume of St. Simon's Memoirs. Later when Niko came in Fenton gave him half a dozen books, memoirs or biographies from the reign of Louis XIV or the Regency, as well as the St. Simon.

"Put them in Mrs. Prescott's room, Niko."

Thus a day which had begun badly ended well. But another day, the Tuesday of Christmas week, began promisingly and ended in disaster.

Encouraged by Fenton's thoughtfulness in selecting the books she did enjoy, Martha decided to test her luck. She chose what seemed a propitious moment, a sunny afternoon when he was busy at his desk.

"Yes?"

"Mr. Fenton, may I ask you a question and a favor?"

He looked up, surprised. "All in the same day?"

"All in the same breath."

He thought carefully before replying. "If I allow you a question I want the privilege of asking one in return."

"That is only fair. Mr. Fenton, why do you never go out for a walk on these beautiful days?"

"Like mad dogs and Englishmen?" he countered. "No, that was a facetious reply which you do not deserve. I simply have no heart for it."

"It would do you a world of good."

"Another reason why I never go out."

However, he smiled and she was encouraged.

"I don't know the property well enough to wander off on my own. If you would go with me one day I could go alone another time. That is the favor."

He closed the ledger he had been studying.

"I have no right to deprive you of a walk if it is going to be for your good and not for mine. Can you borrow boots from Tita?"

"She has already offered them."

"Then let's get on with it while the sun is high. Now, Mizzuz Prescott. Today."

He rose and, as he did so, slid a large file of papers into the wastebasket. Martha moved to retrieve them.

"No, that is where they belong. Tell me before we go, is this a plot?"

"Yes. A plot to get me some fresh air."

With Martha bundled in his own fur-lined greatcoat Fenton led her from the chalet into the sparkling world out-side. They started down a well-defined roadway which was covered with an inch of new snow and entered an evergreen forest where the sun's rays could no longer warm them.

"Can you believe there are summer days when these woods are my only refuge from the heat?" asked Fenton.

They were climbing gradually, and at length they emerged into the sunlight again, where the road snaked towards the summit of a rise. The going was increasingly difficult, and Fenton lent his arm to Martha. His grasp was firm, his foot steady and at one point he motioned her to follow him off the road into deep snow, laughing as they stumbled and floundered.

"You will have your reward," he promised when they stopped to catch their breath. "We're almost to the top. In the summer this slope is alive with gentian, edelweiss, all the Alpine wonders which have to grow and bloom and seed in a few short months before the snows return. You haven't said a word. You aren't impressed?"

"I am utterly content, and watching my step."

He gave her his hand and started again through the deep snow. Moments later they reached the top of the rise where they could appreciate the full splendor of the vista before them.

"Across the valley are the giants who guard my world — those mountain peaks. Down below are the meadows where icy water runs off in the spring and turns the lowlands green. Behind us over the tops of the trees you can see the chalet. Now you know why I bought this land and built my keep on it."

They both remained silent until Martha spoke up.

"And now it is your turn to ask a question."

"So it is. But I don't have one."

"Then why did you make the bargain?"

"Can't you guess?"

On thinking it over, she could.

"You should have known I was not going to pry, any more than you would have done. I just wanted to breathe this air."

"We will come again."

Martha felt for the first time she was talking with the Will Fenton whom Avril had described. More than ever she was determined to succeed in her appointed task, and to restore permanently the joie de vivre which had deserted this vigorous man.

"Tea," he said, "it's waiting at the house."

He started down the far side of the slope with Martha literally following in his footsteps through the deep drifts. At one point he shouted over his shoulder, "You're not what a Mizzuz Prescott is supposed to be."

"And what is that?"

"Oh, a metronome, sitting by my side all day, tick tock."

She scooped up a handful of snow and threw it.

"That was unprovoked aggression," he complained.

"Not entirely unprovoked."

"I was afraid you had been sent to spy." He said it suddenly and quietly.

Unguardedly she exclaimed, "But you knew I came from Avril —" Martha paused only an instant before correcting herself by completing the name: "— de Dinde," and hoped he had not noticed.

He started off again and she followed, her spirits still high. Because she could not see his eyes she did not realize that Fenton had noted her lapse.

When they came to the exact spot where he had often paused in happier times to watch the western sun strike the peak of the highest mountain, crowning it with red and gold, he turned to Martha with a sudden question.

"You are a friend of Avril, aren't you?"

"Yes," she replied, "she is my oldest and dearest friend."

His next words were sharp and accusatory.

"Then this week has been a game. A deception and a lie."

"Not at all. Avril realized you needed someone, she asked me to come. Because I love and trust her, I agreed. And today you have made me glad that I said Yes. That is the whole story."

"Is it? Do Niko and Tita know all this?"

"They only know I came from Avril. There is no harm in that."

"No, there's no harm in that."

They walked on in silence and Martha hoped Fenton had thrown off his morbid suspicions. But she did not yet understand how vulnerable, how deeply suspicious, he was, how close to paranoia. Seeking to comfort him she put her hand on his shoulder. He stopped, but he was tense.

"When my husband died, I thought I could not survive, and at first I did not want to," she said. "Then I realized that Robert would live in my memory as long as I kept him alive there. That gave me strength and later, hope. Finally, a kind of happiness."

With a convulsive movement he turned on her and his words tumbled out: "Yolande does not exist, in my memory or anywhere else. She is dead and I don't want consolation. Bring me food and drink if you will, so Niko and Tita can get away, then go back to your own world and forget you were here, but don't feel sorry for me."

Fenton strode off and left Martha uncomprehending and shocked. When she reached the chalet, she saw that Tita was aware something had gone wrong.

"Tita, which is he? The man who was happy standing at

the top of his world out there, or the most unfortunate of God's creatures, full of self-pity?"

"Drink your tea, Madame. He will be better tomorrow."

Martha was close to tears. "He doesn't want to be better."

"We have known that, Madame, since the day we found him unconscious. We were lucky, the doctor came quickly."

"Was that when Niko rang Madame de Dinde?"

"Yes, the next day. Did you speak to him, out there, of Madame Yolande?"

"Yes, indirectly."

Then Tita almost whispered. "It was not a good marriage. She was not what he thought. We knew, but he loved her and he would not admit it to himself. She was with someone else when the plane crashed."

For the first time Martha realized that Fenton was struggling to accept not loss, but the betrayal of love.

The next morning when Fenton's tray was ready Martha appealed to Niko and Tita. "May I take it in?"

It was easier than she had anticipated because Fenton took the initiative. "I owe you an apology. Will you accept it?" he asked.

"If you accept mine."

"Yours is not required. But you must be sorry you agreed to come here."

"Standing at the summit in the snow yesterday made it worthwhile."

"As I promised, we will go again, even if it does me good." And he smiled.

In Martha's judgment, a man whose sense of humor had

survived was not a lost cause, and with no more than that wisp of encouragement she started to contemplate a plan.

"Tita, I think we should have a festive luncheon on Christmas Day. We can ask Mr. Fenton to join us. He might find his spirits revived despite himself."

"You can ask him, Madame, but he will not accept."

The next day Fenton declined politely. "I have nothing to celebrate and I don't want to be a spectre at your feast."

However, the following afternoon, which was Christmas Eve, he again walked with her to the summit. He told her it would snow during the night and into the next day, according to the sky. But otherwise Fenton remained uncommunicative and was not the exuberant man she had shared that walk with the first time.

The next morning they were closed in, the mountains hidden behind a veil of gently drifting white flakes which settled into the corners of the windowpanes. "Perfect holiday weather," observed Martha, busy in the kitchen with the Christmas pudding, her contribution to the feast. Later, a tantalizing hint of the sizzling goose wafted through the room, and Martha, with malice aforethought, took a spartan tray to the library, taking care to leave the kitchen door open so the fragrance of the bird would follow her. Fenton murmured his thanks and hardly glanced up from the papers on the desk.

By mid afternoon Niko, Tita and Martha were ready to sit down to their feast. Niko carved expertly, separating the crisp skin from the flesh of the goose. Covered dishes held spaetzle, spiced red cabbage and rich, dark sauce. Martha had instructed Niko to bring a bottle of Haut Brion of distinguished vintage from St. Moritz, and she proposed that they begin their meal with a toast. They raised their glasses and drank to being together, each of them silently wishing for a miracle which might bring peace to Fenton.

"The goose," said Niko, "is Tita's specialty, but we are curious about your pudding."

Martha had seen Tita's eyes when she asked for carrots and potatoes as well as currants, sultanas, candied fruits, and spices.

"My grandmother's recipe," she said. "Devised to spare her family from the traditional Victorian pudding, which is black and soggy with suet."

Thereupon Martha cut into the delicate golden form which sent up a spiral of scented steam.

"Bravo!" exclaimed Niko while Tita clapped her hands.

"Bravissimo!" added Fenton whom they had not seen in the doorway. Niko and Tita started to rise, but he motioned them back to their seats.

"You had a very resourceful grandmother," he said to Martha. "No doubt you inherited the characteristic from her."

"Are you going to taste our pudding?"

"Of course. I had no appetite until you made certain I could smell the goose when you brought me my oats and whey. Open a bottle of champagne, Niko."

They drank with him, Niko and Tita immensely pleased, and Martha for the first time in days hopeful.

"Niko," asked Fenton after the pudding had met the fate it so richly deserved, "when do you leave?"

"On the first day of January, Sir."

"He will go to his mother in Santa Maria, and then to see our new grandson down in Bignasco," said Tita.

"Why don't you leave a few days early, and spend the New Year with your mother?"

"She would like that, Sir."

"Then, it's settled. The ladies can manage without you. I promise not to give Tita any trouble and only to harass Mrs. Prescott if she provokes me." Then he added genially to Martha, "What are your intentions?"

"Honorable," she replied. "More or less."

What Bernard Shaw Said...

*D*uring the week between the holidays the innkeepers of St. Moritz again had their way — sunny, crystalline days and a light blanket of fresh snow at night. On two afternoons Fenton and Martha explored the out of doors. Niko had already left for Santa Maria over the mountains, and when they returned to the house to warm themselves by the fire, Tita brought them their tea.

"Mizzuz Prescott, I'd like to tell you something about the ordeal of John Julian Fenton before we get to know each other any better."

"I don't want to pry."

"Shouldn't you, if you want to help me?" Then he added four sardonic words: "Isn't that the theory?" Again it was one of those swift changes of mood. "Does my attitude bother you?"

"No. My father always said one had to be patient with the rich and powerful."

"Ouch," he said and relaxed again. "You've struck with your rapier-like wit, which is quite a blunt instrument."

"Tell me about yourself," she said, sipping her tea contentedly.

"Well, I was born with a somewhat tarnished silver spoon in my mouth, because my father devoted his life to spending money. But my grandfather had foreseen this. 'Never mind,' he'd say, 'there'll be enough for you to build on and you'll enjoy that. Just remember, Will, that money exists for you and not vice versa.' He always called me Will and thought of me as his namesake. I loved him dearly.

"So, I'd been prepared to succeed, and with luck I did, starting with one small company we controlled, then adding others until FENTON INDUSTRIES was on the big board. If this was a fairy tale that would be the happy end, but there is more and I want you to hear it. Maybe because I have to tell someone and you, worse luck for you, are the one staring into the fire with me."

Martha said nothing.

"Part Two. Will Fenton in Love. I was living in Paris when I met Yolande. She was younger than me by quite a few years and the most beautiful creature I'd ever seen. At first she wasn't particularly interested in me and certainly not in the things that were important to me, but she was gay and sparkling and I decided right away I was going to marry her. Her own brother — they were Belgian and Laurent was an attorney I brought into the company — Laurent told me not to rush into anything, that she wouldn't go away. But a man in love doesn't listen to reason. A month later Yolande allowed herself to be swept off her feet and into the registry office in London. We returned to France man and wife to the astonishment of our friends and maybe ourselves as well. At least that's the way I interpreted it then.

"Yolande warned me she was an independent soul, but that made her even more desirable in my eyes. I wanted only to please her and in the beginning — I still think — I succeeded. We traveled together, we built houses together and we had our own lives as well. I had FENTON LTD and Yolande had her friends. As I look back now, I realize that first period of passion and, on my part, love, was not succeeded by the affection and friendship which are essential to a happy marriage. Hindsight is always crystal clear, but when you are drifting the view is clouded.

"Gradually I realized that Yolande had a deep sensual need which I did not share. I suppose I felt I had failed her and I tried to make up for it. It was my pleasure to deck her out in the jewelry she adored. I encouraged her to buy and to build — in Morocco, Sintra, Palm Beach. And I made over blocs of FENTON stock to her, gifts she accepted laughingly over the years as if they meant little or nothing to her. I knew she was pleased and that was enough.

"Did she have lovers? It crossed my mind because in the end we were apart more often than together. But we lived in a society which enjoys rumors, where somebody is always eager to drop a hint 'for your own good,' and I heard nothing. I suppose I became a complacent husband. I preferred my own life here at the chalet, where she never came. Then from one day to the next everything changed.

"Yolande was in Sintra. She rang me in London and asked me to come to her that afternoon. She wouldn't tell me why, only that it was important. I said I was flying to Paris to meet a Kuwaiti I'd been wanting to see for months. She insisted but she refused to give me any hint of why. I took it as a whim and said No. She rang off.

"Then a suspicion started to unravel in my mind. We are always being warned about kidnappers. Was she under duress to get me to Portugal? It was farfetched but I couldn't get the idea out of my head and finally I rang my pilot and told him to radio for permission to land in Lisbon that afternoon."

Fenton rose and leaned against the bookshelf, thinking as he had thought hard a thousand times during the past months, recreating in his mind the circumstances of that fateful day in June.

"When we landed I drove myself out to Sintra. It never occurred to me that it might be a foolish thing to do if she was really in danger. I remember how peaceful the village was that day, reassuring me that nothing was amiss. Then I turned into our drive. I braked in the outer courtyard — it is one of those Moorish houses — because I had startled a man walking across the gravel. I don't know which of us was the more surprised — me, or Yolande's brother. I jumped out of the car and asked if Yolande was all right. His first words were his first lie. 'Will,' he said, 'she phoned me in Paris this morning and asked me to come down. Yes, she's all right.'

"As I found out later he had been there a day and a night, but he was thinking fast to find a way to warn Yolande that I was going to be in the inner court and up the stairs in less than thirty seconds.

"He managed to slam the doors when we entered the

house, and made quite a racket. Almost at once Yolande came to the railing on the upper level, and called down. 'Laurent? Luis says I have to ring him again. But I know he won't come.' I looked up. She was barefoot, and wearing a negligee. Just as we caught sight of each other a man approached her from behind, put his arms around her, and kissed her on the nape of her neck. She pushed him away. In the instant before he understood why, I had a frontal nude view of a tall, muscular Latin. He disappeared and Yolande followed him. Yes, she locked the door and I pounded on it. Laurent tried to calm me with more lies. He had just found out about Luis and we'd better both try to understand, and please let him talk with her first. But Yolande spoiled that for him. She threw the door open and said much more than Laurent wanted me to hear. She was near hysteria, the way the guilty are when they are found out. Buried in the recriminations she poured on me for breaking in, spying and so forth, was what she wanted—her freedom to marry Luis. I said we would discuss that another time. Why had she called me in London? She didn't remember. Then she sputtered, 'Laurent knows. Tell him, Laurent.' Her brother shrugged his shoulders, too elaborately I now realize. 'I think she only wanted you to transfer a few more shares of FENTON into her name,' he said. 'Maybe for her security.' Even under the stress of that confrontation I knew she already had enough in shares and property for much more than security.

"'Or for Luis' security?' I asked. Then I think I shouted, 'Where is he? Hiding under your bed?' I took Yolande by the shoulders and shook her, partly to get a coherent reply and partly to release the tension inside me.

"She was in no condition to talk. I told Laurent I was leaving and that Yolande had better get rid of Luis. She heard that and tried to slap me, missed, and fell backwards into Laurent's arms. Just like an old Hollywood movie.

"Laurent stayed. He said he would see me in Paris the following day. At the door he stopped me. 'There have been others. Didn't you know?' I hadn't known, because Yolande did not play in the gardens of our friends, she obviously reached into another world, and kept the secret for herself—and Laurent.

"He came to see me that next afternoon in Paris, ready to pave the road towards a reconciliation of sorts. I exploded. 'What do we do with Luis? Make him a director of the company?'

"Laurent went right along with the prevailing wind. 'You're right, but she says she loves him. She wants to marry him.'

"'Will he marry her? The man's half her age, if that.'

"Again that shrug, and then Laurent asked if I would meet with Yolande, to talk, if she came to Paris. I said No, not until she had got rid of Luis.

"An hour alter Yolande rang to say she was going away with Luis. I told her they could go to hell and—"

Here Fenton paused and chose his word with great care.

"—and that is what they did. On the way to Marrakech the storm overtook them. The papers were full of it. All on board lost. One passenger and a crew of three: pilot, co-pilot and a cabin steward. Nobody ever inquired after the cabin steward. Luis was probably not even his name.

"Even before I had absorbed the shock I knew the crash

had been a blessing. Yolande would have had to live in a vacuum with her lover, on the edge of the world she belonged to.
They'd have grown to hate each other. And Yolande had a
capacity for hatred I had not even suspected. She mailed me a
letter from Lisbon before they flew south. After I read it I
couldn't even mourn my loss. But the biggest shock was still to
come. I called Laurent in to talk about Yolande's estate, as we
were each other's heirs. There wasn't much, he said. Some
property and jewelry, whatever was left after Luis and the others. I pointed out that her shares in FENTON alone made her
a very rich woman. Laurent wouldn't look me in the eye. He
said his sister was a very ambitious woman. I asked him point-
blank what he was getting at, and then he exploded the bomb.

"Yolande's stock, he said, was no longer in her estate. She
had transferred it to his name. He tried to tell me Yolande had
the crazy idea that the two of them should take over the company and that he had tried to humor her until he could
straighten her out. But I knew who was ambitious. Laurent
had always wanted power. If I had agreed to meet her in
Sintra she would have been alone, with Laurent and Luis safely out of sight. Yolande didn't know that Laurent already had
shares of his own in the company. They didn't need any more,
but he was greedy.

"I told him he was fired. He laughed and left before I
could throw him through the window. The transfers were
legal. And because of the accident he didn't have to share with
anybody. He controlled FENTON. Since then I have tried to
figure out how I could get the company back again. You've
seen my scribblings. But what would I get? Something that no
longer interests me. And FENTON won't hold together with

Laurent in charge. He is a follower, not a leader, even if he doesn't know it. It will be swallowed up by somebody smarter. Maybe my Kuwaiti. And that is the sordid story."

He stopped and looked at Martha with a rueful smile. Then, as if to throw off all thoughts of the past he spoke jauntily in a stream of words.

"What are you doing tomorrow? Nothing special? Good. I'll have the sleigh brought around and we'll drive down to the valley. We'll go in to St. Moritz for coffee at Handelmann — après see instead of après ski." He winced. "Oh, that was awful. And in the evening we'll see the old year out. Are you up to it, Martha Prescott, woman of mystery?"

"O.F.G.S!" she combusted spontaneously.

"Oh, what?"

"It's something Charles taught me. But you don't know who Charles is — yet. Yes, I am up to it, Will Fenton."

The next morning when Martha entered the library she found Fenton at a desk almost entirely clear of papers.

"They are all in the fire. Warming the room and clearing my mind. I have burned my bridges."

He had ordered the sleigh for eleven o'clock and two hours later Fenton and Martha set off drawn by a perfectly matched pair of bays. They glided along the snow-covered road silently except for the reassuring jingle of the bells and the outrider's encouragements to his team. The road wound down, at a gentle slope, into the valley floor.

"We follow the stream from here. It is frozen now, at least on the surface, but deep down the water is moving, swiftly and eternally towards the lowlands."

"Geology or philosophy?" asked Martha.

"You decide," he replied and he pointed to the frozen waterway and the spectral branches which extended over it, ice sticks with a coating of new snow on top.

"Somewhere here do we cross the stream on a covered bridge? All gingerbread?"

"How do you know that?" he exclaimed.

"I was hoping we did," she replied, evasively.

"Just before the bridge there is a road off to the right. It used to lead up to a gingerbread house which burned down before my time."

Martha kept her silence until their outrider stopped the horses before the covered bridge.

"He knows I come here in summer for grenouilles," Fenton explained. "Tita has a recipe for frogs' legs that she calls cuisses de nymphes à l'amour."

"Nymphs' thighs indeed, I'll thank you to keep a civil tongue in your head."

"Shall we drink a cup of hot tea to that?" he asked, taking out the thermos.

"Yes, and let's drink to tomorrow. By which I mean all our tomorrows."

"Heinrich," Fenton cried, "trinkt mit."

"Ja wohl, Herr."

Dimly comprehending — you never knew what the Herrenvolk really meant with all their talk — the outrider jumped down from his mount and took the proffered cup. Solemnly, then, all three drank their tea after which they clattered on through the bridge.

"Who is Charles?" asked Fenton.

"To tell you about Charles," she replied, "I will have to include Roberta, and to explain Roberta I have to start with Robert. Shall I?"

He nodded Yes. Thereupon Martha told him about those who were nearest and dearest to her.

"How lucky you were," he said when she was done, "and your example strengthens my own resolve."

Martha hoped he meant a resolve to cast off his depression. That was indeed what Fenton meant, but in a way Martha could not have anticipated.

Later in the day, in high spirits, they drove to St. Moritz. The town was filled with the crowds which traditionally gather in the Engadine to welcome the New Year. Fenton led his guest, as he had now come to think of her, directly to Handelmann. When they were seated he said:

"You have been here before." It was a statement, not a question.

"Yes," she replied, "years ago. Robert and I were in St. Moritz to visit our friend Nuri Bey. The gingerbread house in the valley was his summer retreat."

"Another surprise from the astounding Mizzuz Prescott."

"It was Nuri's last summer in Europe. He had enemies in Turkey, and he knew what might happen if he returned to Istanbul, but he went back because it was home. He died there mysteriously."

"If he was a wise man, perhaps he was glad to go."

Remembering Nuri, Martha thought not.

"Now if you have no other surprises, we can go about our errands, both clandestine. First we are going to buy a bottle of whisky and not tell Tita."

"She wouldn't approve?"

"During the past months, as I sank into my slough of despond, Tita and Niko, good souls, removed all spirits from the house. I suppose they thought I might get dead drunk one night and have to be carried to bed. Anyhow, they were taking no chances, and I can't blame them."

"I don't think Tita would feel that way now."

"We won't risk it, because tonight I want to toast the old year out and champagne is not my preferred drink."

"It is mine," said Martha, "so we will also acquire a bottle of Lanson Brut."

"Agreed. The other clandestinity is what Tita asked me not to tell you. But I will if you won't betray me, which would embarrass her. Tita wants me to collect her prescription from the pharmacy. I am to tell you if you ask that it is just aspirin. In fact — her diet pills. She has made a New Year's resolution. Twenty pounds must go."

"I wish I could put Tita under Mrs. Brimston's care. She would be the one with cuisses de nymphes."

"Watch your language, Madam."

That evening Fenton asked Tita to join them in toasting the coming year. It was just after nine when he opened the champagne and filled three fluted glasses.

"To the year ahead," he said. "The great adventure."

They drank their wine then Tita left them to await a call from Niko. Outside the sky was moonless, inky and filled with stars. In the library the fire sputtered and crackled lazily. For Martha it had been a happy but tiring day, and she was not disappointed when Fenton presently said, "I'm glad to bid the old year adieu, and I don't intend to honor it by keeping vigil until midnight."

"And I prefer to greet the new year as the sun comes up," she said. "I am a morning person."

"Then good night, morning person. And thank you." He stopped at the door. "Why don't you ask Tita to finish the champagne with you. I'll have a night cap of the other stuff in my room."

Alone, Martha filled her glass and gazed into the obsidian sky which came to life only where the milky way was scattered across it. In his room, Fenton also stood at a window, a tumbler of whisky in his hand. Martha sipped, Fenton drank, each concerned with the past and the immediate future.

"Tita," said Martha an hour later, "I dozed off in front of the fire. Did Niko call?"

"Yes, Madame, I told him we were happy. You and Mr. Fenton will not welcome the new year together?"

"We will welcome it in the morning. Mr. Fenton will have a nightcap in his room."

"Ah, yes, the champagne."

"No, the — " Martha remembered in time to stop. Tita, however, sensed what she might have been about to say.

"There are no spirits in the house, Madame. Not since the day we found him."

"Those days are behind us, Tita. And I can see no reason to be secretive. Mr. Fenton and I bought a bottle of whisky this afternoon. He prefers it to champagne."

Tita was immediately alert. "Did he buy anything else, Madame?"

"Nothing."

Tita persisted. "You are certain, Madame? You must tell me."

Martha suddenly knew how she could explain their errand at the pharmacy without embarrassing Tita. "Only your prescription. Mr. Fenton did not tell me what it was."

"Madame," said Tita gravely, "I ordered no prescription."

Instantly the two women were aware that Fenton had been playing a role, perhaps for the past several days, and that this might be a moment of extreme danger.

Tita took command of a situation she had faced once before. "Come quickly, Madame. If it is not true, he will answer when I knock at his door."

They went swiftly to Fenton's room. Tita knocked, quietly at first, then insistently and louder.

"Mr. Fenton? Sir?"

She pounded on the door. There was only silence. She turned the handle.

"It is locked. Go to my bathroom," she said to Martha. "In the cabinet is a small bottle marked 'Ipecac'. Bring it at once. I can get into his room from the balcony. Pray God he did not lower the jalousie."

Martha left her, and when she returned moments later with the bottle the bedroom door was ajar for her. Inside, Tita was leaning over Fenton, who sat slumped in a leather armchair. She was trying to slap him into consciousness. He responded, but weakly.

"He must stay awake. Give me the bottle, and a glass of water."

Somehow in the next minutes — Martha never knew

exactly how — they got Fenton to swallow the Ipecac, he was sick, then they walked him, and kept him conscious. He neither spoke nor tried to resist. He was groggy and apathetic.

At one point Tita said, "The balcony. Bring some snow and rub it on the back of his neck."

When Tita was satisfied that he had given up most of the pills he had swallowed they got him onto the bed. Tita wiped the cold sweat from his brow and listened to his breathing. At last she looked up.

"We were just in time," she said.

"And I helped him to do it." Martha murmured, distressed and perplexed.

"You could not have known, Madame. A desperate man is very clever. He will sleep now, but he will also wake again. I will stay with him. You must rest so you can relieve me in the morning. One of us must be with him at all times to see that the breathing is regular. Go now. Together we will bring him back. Please, Madame."

Martha's mind was full of contradictory thoughts as she retired to her room. Fenton had seemed genuinely happy. She could hardly believe that he had been planning for a second time to end his life. She was determined more than ever to learn the whole truth about this man of whom she had become fond despite the protective devices with which he sought to isolate himself. It was well after midnight before Martha fell asleep, and she woke the next morning with a start, thinking she had overslept. But the dawn was still grey. She drank a cup of tea, heated milk for Tita's coffee, then anxiously opened the door to Fenton's room.

Tita reassured her. "He is breathing normally."

Impulsively Martha kissed Tita on the brow.

"Your coffee is ready. Then you must rest."

Martha in her turn then began the vigil at Fenton's bedside. It was almost midday before he opened his eyes. Martha smiled faintly to encourage him. When he spoke it was in a hoarse whisper.

"I have been thinking..."

"Oh, Lord," Martha breathed.

"No, seriously —"

"Very seriously, I should think."

"Don't scold," he said, which made her feel guilty as she had not intended it to show. "You are talking to a man who did not want to wake up on this side of the sky."

"You are only here because of Tita."

At that moment Tita looked in, awake again after a short, deep sleep. She saw that Fenton's eyes were open.

"Forgive me, Tita."

"You wouldn't be here if it were not for Madame," Tita said.

"Then you will both have to share the guilt," he said lightly, after which he closed his eyes and sank back into a restful sleep.

When Fenton awakened that evening Martha was again at his side and he was no longer groggy. He sat up and rested his head against the pillows.

"I want to issue a bulletin," he announced. "The patient is glad the sky is still above him. That is to say, he prefers looking up to gazing down."

"That is good news."

"Yes. Tita can dispose of what's left of those pills. But

there is no need to waste the whisky, if she has not already poured it down the drain. Have you any questions, Dr. Miracle?"

"Only one."

"Shoot. I owe you an answer."

Intuition told Martha that an honest answer to the question she wanted to ask might reveal to her and to Fenton himself what had caused and sustained his depression, what had deprived him of the will to live.

"What did Yolande write to you in that last letter?"

For a long moment she was afraid he would not respond. Then he spoke, deliberately and with great effort.

"She said many things in a few words. That Luis was the only one she cared about. That there had been many before him, including Laurent. That she was leaving me. That she pitied me." Here he stopped, then made himself go on, "Because I was old and I disgusted her." He spoke the final words as if they were branded in his mind.

Immediately Martha sensed that she possessed the key to his problem and its resolution, but she waited, in silence, for a considerable time before she spoke. Then she said, "Will, it is so clear that Yolande was the one who was afraid of getting old. If there was disgust, it was for herself. She wanted to transfer her fear to you, and somehow she succeeded, because you loved her. But you of all people know that years have very little to do with age. And in the long run, others do not destroy our lives. Either we destroy ourselves, as Yolande was doing, or we manage to reach shore and survive. Now that you have survived you have a great deal to discover all over again...including love."

He was embarrassed that she had peered so deep into his mind and heart and he attempted a jest. "Watch your language," he said, "remember that at our age, to talk of love is considered obscene."

"Nonsense. If I thought life was going to be nothing but hobbies and good books from now on I wouldn't be very enthusiastic about the future. Love and affection don't belong exclusively to the young. In fact the young are often just the ones who do not know how to deal with either one. Please grow up and be Will Fenton again."

His eyes met hers resolutely.

"The patient is out of danger. Do you believe me when I say that?"

"Tita intends to ask Niko to return," she replied. "I am going to tell her it is not necessary."

"I take that as a vote of confidence."

Martha concluded in her best bedside manner: "You will be up and around in no time, but meanwhile I have you in my power, which I shall thoroughly enjoy."

She rose, confidently, to leave Fenton alone for the first time in almost twenty-four hours. At the door she paused. "Do you remember what Bernard Shaw said?"

"He said about thirty volumes worth. For example?"

"— that youth is wasted on the young."

Snow fell steadily the next day. Martha told Fenton they called it Currier and Ives snow at home.

"How are we going to enjoy life today?" he asked.

"No mountain climbing. Not yet."

"I'm glad. I respect my mountains and I've never wanted

to stand on top of them. Of course if there was a flight of steps to the top, I might take that as an invitation."

"If you are ever in Hangchow," Martha observed sagely, "ask about the Yellow Mountain. It is near the city and has steps all the way to the top."

"You've invented that, but I am flattered. It shows that the doctor will do anything to please the patient."

So began a sequence of days during which Martha was happier than she had been since Robert's time. After the storm, she and Fenton walked again in the snow, and ordered the sleigh to take them for long drives. They drank Fenton's whisky together at dusk, and Tita cooked them splendid dinners.

One morning Fenton said, "I have a bone of contentment to pick with you. There *is* a Yellow Mountain near Hangchow. I looked it up, and it does have steps to the top. Ten thousand of them."

"Didn't you believe me?"

"Did you expect me to?"

"Of course."

"Then you won't find it difficult to believe the letter we are going to post in St. Moritz this afternoon. It's addressed to my Kuwaiti in Paris confirming my offer to him of all my FENTON stock. One day he will control the company, and do you know, I don't even mind that Laurent will end up very rich. Of course I am human, so I'm not wishing him any special happiness. Now where would you like to go tomorrow? Over to Davos for lunch?"

Almost sooner than they realized it was time for Niko to

return, after which Tita left for the Ticino and her visit with their family. The household was relaxed and Niko managed cheerfully.

One day Martha said to Fenton, "I'm not earning my salary any more."

"You are earning much more. Points. A staggering number of points, so don't leave in a huff."

"Is that anything like a dudgeon?"

"It's more like a dither, not quite a snit."

"Or a pet or a stew?"

"What next?" laughed Fenton.

"Luncheon," said Niko, puzzled, in the doorway.

It was late the following afternoon, when Martha and Fenton came back from a walk through the woods, that Niko gave her the cable he had brought from St. Moritz.

"Forwarded from Madame la duchesse in Paris," he said.

"What wonderful news," Martha exclaimed a moment later and gave the wire to Fenton, who read it aloud.

"HERBERT AND I MARRYING JANUARY 29. DOUBLE CEREMONY. RING. EXPECT YOU. LOVE. MINTY."

Without comment he handed it back and waited for her to say what he wanted to hear.

"Of course, it's slightly garbled," she said instead. "Minty will have meant to say Double Ring Ceremony."

Fenton was not to be put off. "Is she going to be very disappointed when you can't be there?"

Martha replied, "Drinks here, in an hour?"

With foreboding Martha joined Fenton that evening, not certain he would understand her inevitable decision. Since New Year's Day they had become real friends, with none of the pressures that had made December difficult for Martha and catastrophic for Fenton. Now a circumstance beyond their control threatened to end, or at least to interrupt, an idyll which might still be too fragile to be revived. But Martha knew she had no choice and she wanted Fenton's support.

"Will," she began with calculated nonchalance, "do you suppose Minty had to propose to Herbert?"

"Martha," he said, pursuing his own plan, "You hardly know Spain and you've never been to Santiago de Compostela. Let's fly to Andalusia where the spring is early. Granada, Cordoba, Sevilla. After that we can drive through Huelva — it is beautiful and nobody goes there. On to Portugal and north by the back roads and into Asturias to Santiago, just like good pilgrims. After that we can follow the spring north to Paris.

Martha saw her strategy was not going to work, any more than his was with her.

"Will," she began —

"You can't go, Martha." He said it gravely.

"It isn't forever."

"How can I be sure?" Then he continued with eyes narrowed. "And it is too soon. I am better, but are you sure I am cured?"

"Yes, I am sure, and it is unfair of you to put my staying or going on that basis. Minty needs me. The cable was sent to Paris on the 19th, then forwarded. There is little more than a week before the wedding."

His response was sharp, as if the spoiled child in him had been brought to the fore by his disappointment. He snapped his words out testily, so that a kind thought sounded censorious. "Isn't it about time you stopped living other people's lives and started thinking of yourself?"

They were drifting into dangerous waters as mood begot mood and Martha responded curtly. "I know how my sister would feel if I wired her 'I'm enjoying life here, have a nice wedding.'"

Hitting out to save a situation he felt was going against him, Fenton managed to make it infinitely worse. "Martha, you haven't led your own life since your husband died. Make a life of your own while there is time to enjoy it."

"Stop, Will." His words hurt because of the grain of truth in them.

"No, you can't cut me off. I want you to live in the present instead of your precious past."

It was a plea, but it sounded petulant and that encouraged an answer in kind.

"If you weren't determined to have your own way you would understand," Martha said, but she was almost ready to capitulate until his next words precluded it.

"Understand why you prefer the past to the future? If your Robert was everything you say, he wouldn't want to hold on to you from the grave."

That was cruel and she replied coldly. "I will ask Niko to drive me to the station in the morning."

"The first train with a connection to Zurich is at nine," he replied.

They did not dine together. Niko brought a tray to Martha's room, where she had started to put her things together. The next morning, when Niko came for Martha's bag he was somber and withdrawn.

"You will manage for a few days on your own," Martha said. "I am sorry not to say good-bye to Tita."

"We will never forget you, Madame."

Niko said nothing about Fenton and she did not inquire. But when they reached the hall, where she had stood with Niko and Tita that day in December when the bell from Fenton's desk summoned her to him, Fenton appeared.

"Good morning," he said quietly. "Forgive me, although it is you who are breaking my heart. I know I protested too much."

Immediately the tension evaporated.

"Yesterday was difficult for both of us," Martha admitted. But she knew she had to leave as planned.

Fenton walked with her to the car.

"Will I hear from you?"

"I am a good correspondent," she replied, "and I always answer letters promptly."

Martha despatched two cables from the airport in Zurich. The first was to Avril in Paris, a message which would please her friend: WILL FENTON LIVELY AND WELL. The other went to Charles, asking him to send Mr. Barrett to collect her at the airport.

When Martha emerged from the customs barrier in Kennedy, she saw Berte and Charles waving. It was an unexpected and happy reunion. In the car en route to Gramercy Park where Mr. Barrett was to drop the children (as she thought of them) Charles asked, "Am I right in thinking you haven't spoken with Minty?"

"I knew I'd be seeing her today."

"Then you don't know anything," said Berte.

"Minty cabled about the double ring ceremony."

"Double ceremony," said Charles, correcting her. "It isn't usual, but then neither are the circumstances."

"What does that mean?" Martha asked, sensing complications. "Don't tell me Herbert didn't propose after all."

Martha saw Berte and Charles exchange glances and her worry escalated into alarm.

"Oh, yes, he must have proposed," said Berte.

"But not to Minty," Charles added. "Herbert is marrying Alexandra Kimberley-Faucitt."

"Lord have mercy on their souls." It was all Martha could manage; and then, "Poor Minty."

"Not poor Minty at all," Berte assured her. "She is radiantly happy."

"How could she be?" A horrible possibility crossed her mind. "Minty didn't dash out and snatch up a husband on the rebound, did she?"

"Not at all," Charles said, "Herbert is marrying Alexandra, and Minty is marrying Henry."

"Who?"

"You met him in England, Aunt Martha. And you liked him. Henry Kimbolton."

With a tremendous wave of relief and joy Martha realized that her sister was about to become Araminta, Countess of Harborough.

"Minty," Martha asked later that evening, "how did it ever come to pass?"

"Henry and I had been corresponding ever since the summer. You knew that."

"How could I have known? You never mentioned it."

"Didn't I? Soon after I came home from Monte Carlo he sent me a present of Sawtry butterflies under glass. That's how it all began. He is a gentle, wonderful man."

"And Herbert?"

"Herbert and I will always be friends. He and Alexandra have been very close ever since they went to New Hampshire together."

"I am sure she left no stone unturned," observed Martha.

"New Hampshire is not rocky," Minty replied. "That is Maine, I believe. Henry came to America in December and he proposed on New Year's Day, after lunch. That same week Herbert plighted *his* troth."

Martha could imagine who had done the plighting. "But why a double ceremony?"

"Because of Dr. Cutler. You know he has bats in his belfry."

"We don't speak about it, Minty."

Oblivious, her sister went on. "He has arranged to have them removed. The scaffolding goes up next week, so Alexandra suggested a double ceremony on the only Saturday available. Herbert is going to give me away, because he is my oldest friend, and Henry is going to give Alexandra away —"

"— because he is the only earl in town. Alexandra will be thrilled."

They heard a distant chime.

"That is Herbert, with Alexandra. I asked them to come tonight because I need your help. Henry and I want a small reception but Alexandra wants to hold it at the Dower House and invite the town."

"The reception should be elegant, not a circus. Moreover, it should be held on neutral territory. In this case, my house."

"I was hoping you would agree to that, Martha."

Minty's housekeeper opened the sitting room doors and Alexandra Kimberley-Faucitt swept in followed by Herbert Detweiler, who did not sweep.

"Dear Martha, how good of you to hurry home from Europe for our nuptials," said Alexandra expansively.

"Hello, Martha," added a somewhat sheepish Herbert.

"My congratulations to you both," Martha said, wondering the while how much mutual loving, honoring and obeying would be generated by their union. "And of course I am delighted for Minty and Henry Kimbolton. I've just told Minty that my present to you all will be the wedding reception."

"How kind," said Alexandra, a shadow falling across her face, "but there is so much more room at the Dower House."

"There is, indeed, and it would be wasted if we are only to be family and close friends. How many did you say, Minty?"

"Twenty, no more."

"Perfect. We will simply serve champagne and wedding cake. It is rather bad taste these days to bother with an elaborate sit-down meal. Don't you agree, Herbert?"

"I do," he said, not getting the signal from Alexandra.

"Well, I know Alexandra wouldn't think of contradicting you, so it is settled." Martha quickly changed the subject: "Minty, where is Henry taking you for your honeymoon?"

"We'll be at sea. That is, Henry has to get back to Buckden Court, so we are sailing on Monday."

"And you, Herbert? Have you decided where to take your bride?"

"No," he ejaculated, prematurely as it turned out.

"Oh, yes," exclaimed Alexandra, bound to celebrate at least one victory. "We are going to Egypt. I have connections there, you know. The dear princesses I went to school with in Switzerland."

"An excellent choice," Martha said. "February is the best month for Egypt. Fewer flies."

Minty beamed, Herbert smiled vaguely, and Alexandra scowled. Martha was pleased that no one in Sliepskill had changed — least of all herself.

The days which followed were filled with frantic activity on Elm Street. Minty was fitted into a lace gown adapted from their mother's wedding dress. Alexandra agreed to appear in pink when it was pointed out that only Minty was marrying for the first time, and when she was convinced how much more flattering its pale blush was to her complexion. Henry Kimbolton arrived from a lepidopterists' meeting in Philadelphia and turned out to be every bit as pleasant as Martha had remembered him. Sir Willoughby and Lady Irene were only briefly referred to; both were again in residence at Shivverly, just as Phillips had predicted.

Invitations to the reception were delivered by messenger and everyone accepted, including Florian and Lucille, although she was known not particularly to enjoy happy occasions. Arrangements were made to fill St. Anselm's with baby's breath and tuberoses, no one anticipating that Elmira Crisp would be overcome and faint dead away before the ceremony. Herbert and Henry had become fast friends, which was not surprising, as they had a great deal in common. The champagne was ordered and Mrs. Brimston baked the wedding cake herself. Elm Street buzzed with happy speculation and even the Lower Town was aware that something was going on.

Each night, when Martha sank exhausted onto her bed, she remembered the chalet, the mountains, the long walks with Fenton, and wished she could share the goings-on of these hectic days with him. She wondered when — or if — she would hear from him.

Finally, after a last-minute complication with the champagne ("No, Mr. Luchetti, it must be Lanson Brut and vintage!") the eve of the wedding was upon them.

Berte and Charles arrived to spend the night and to dine with Martha and Minty. Henry had stayed the week with Herbert and the two of them were devoting their last evening as bachelors to a somber game of chess. Up at the Dower House Alexandra was still frantically trying to get through to the princesses in Cairo, having forgotten that after the Egyptian revolution those hapless creatures must either have escaped with whatever they could carry, or were in no state to receive an old school friend and her new husband from the capitalist West.

After dinner, while Charles was walking Minty home, and when Berte had said good night, Mrs. Brimston came to Martha with an apology. "Mrs. Prescott, I didn't tell you about the telegram. I put it over on the sideboard and forgot all about it."

"Never mind," said Martha, "you've had a great deal to think about today."

It was a cable. Avril? Or...

Upstairs, as soon as she had closed the door, Martha sat down at her dressing table and tore open the envelope. She read:

WHOM THE GODS LOVE DIE YOUNG. SOMETIMES AT QUITE ADVANCED AGES. SPRING IN SANTIAGO POSTPONED TO ACCOMMODATE DELINQUENT PILGRIM. RENDEZVOUS GRANADA ST. VALENTINE'S DAY. PERIOD NOT QUESTION MARK. CHAPEL BOOKED. WILL.

Martha looked into the mirror and saw her reflection aglow with her best Gioconda smile. She took a pencil and started to write, on the back of the cable form, the response which would determine her future.

Post Script

*T*hat spring Minty's house in Sliepskill was sold for a fortune to a rock star (Did that signal the end of Elm Street?), Alexandra and Herbert were on safari in Kenya (the princesses now lived in Los Angeles), Joanna DeVine won the Pulitzer (for an American tragedy involving women's lib, equal rights and cancer), and I ran into Tom Swift at the Yale Club.

I took Tom home for a drink with Berte and me and learned that he and Sloane had broken up.

"Friendly farewells?" I asked.

"I thought so until the lawyers got busy," he replied. "But have I met a girl!" Then he changed the subject. "Roberta, what's your Aunt Martha up to?"

"She lives in Switzerland," I said before Berte could. "Martha finally met her match."

"This came today." Berte gave us a postcard on which we saw a blue sea, dramatic cliffs, and green mountains.

"They are traveling again," she said.

Tom had been there and he had the last word. "Small country, big problems. Your aunt might be just the one they need. Can you think of anyone else who can lead them down the road to peace, prosperity and progress before they know what has struck them?"